"**RavenShadow has the impact of a hurled war** ' . With the skill of the fine novelist that he i⸱ ̄ kes a modern Oglala Sioux radio i⸱ f his ancestors, including the ⸱e."
— *Dee Brown, author of Bu*

"Win Blevins has long since ⸱⸱ace among the West's very best. *RavenShadow* adds a new dimension to his reputation." — *Tony Hillerman*

"With the help of a medicine man, Blue's (our main character) spirit is transported to that bitter cold day in 1890 when the Seventh Cavalry fired on a village of starving Sioux, including some of Blue's own ancestors. His soul is redeemed by his difficult vision, with a journey both painful and beautiful for the reader." — *Publisher's Weekly*

"Blevins tells the story of Lakota Indian Joseph Blue Crow's unique midlife crisis, which leads to a journey–both geographical and spiritual–to save his soul. The narrative slips neatly back and forth between the 1990s and the 1890s without the least bit of confusion."

"Blue finds himself, but the reader finds even more in Blevins' tales of Lakota lore and his reexamination of one of the darkest episodes in American history. Blevins' prose is razor sharp, his characters are clearly defined, and his heart, like so many, is at Wounded Knee. An outstanding novel." — *Booklist*

"A strong, thoughtful story of minorities within the dominant white culture, and how the past lives inside the future, and how we move through it." — *Kirkus Reviews*

". . Win Blevins has written a searing tale of lost faith and crowning redemption that is destined to become an American classic." — *Roundup Magazine*

"The powerful story of one American Indian's spirit journey in an attempt to heal his past and claim his future. . . Win has written a most powerful and poetic book. At times, the story is troubling. It touches readers deeply, as we follow along with Joseph Blue Crow as he struggles to regain the long, lost Red Road." — *Tulsa World*

"Few books really get into the Native American mindset as well as *RavenShadow*. Instead of being steeped in mysticism, Blevins' story is centered on people—for it is there that the true connection can be made. You'll suffer and triumph along with Joseph as he makes his journey of self- discovery. I felt a part of the long march to redemption. I felt the cold, the loneliness, and the hurt, and ultimately the triumph." —*Comics Corner*

"No one can come away from this magnificent work without feeling humble and meditative about the artificial life he has created. It is a book that transcends man and reminds him of his close relationship to his creator. It is a book I wish I had written.

"Blevins beautifully and skillfully merges the past and the present into a "now," which in the hands of a lesser gifted author would result in nothing more than pompous medita- tion and sermonizing. Blevins, however, has higher aspira- tions. . . . Blue Crow's search for the peace and harmony that belong within his spiritual being is a rite of passage for all who read this novel." — *El Paso Times*

RAVENSHADOW

RavenShadow

By

Win Blevins

ISBN-13: 9780692203712
ISBN-10: 0692203710

This novel is dedicated to
Sitanka Wokiksuye,
the Big Foot Memorial Riders

Part One
Blue Is Lost

Blue Introduces Himself

Mitakuye oyasin—We are all related, we are all one. *Mitakuye oyasin*—those are the words we use to end all our prayers, we Lakota, the ones you call Sioux. I'm telling you this story to teach it to myself.

You can call me Blue.

My full name is Joseph Blue Crow. It is one of my names. I am the man of many names. I am the man of more than one voice, more than one language, more than one culture. I am the man you do not know, do not want to know, cannot permit yourself to know. To see me is to feel the cold beneath the shadow of the Raven's wing.

Look at me. Here I stand before you, a buffalo bull of a Lakota Indian, six and a half feet tall and up toward three hundred pounds. My skin is dark, my hair blue-black, and I wear it in one long braid. I look like I belong in another world, any other world, not yours.

Will you listen to my story? You must listen very carefully.

I set out on a journey to save my soul.

Maybe I will save it.

And maybe, as my witness, you can save yours.

HATING YOUR LIFE

How you find your way in this life is, you get lost, you figure out you're lost, and you hate it.

That's where I was last August, year nineteen and ninety. Hating it.

I still had a good job. I was a jock at KKAT, an AM station in Rapid City, strong in that market. My job was spinning those groovy tunes. Went off to college and learned radio, whoop-tee-doo, got the skills to do that upbeat patter, segue from the tunes to the news and from the other stuff into a feel-good day. Hey, any year-round job is a good job for an Indian here in South Dakota. The white part of the state is enemy territory for Indians. The rez is a black hole for jobs, and lives.

I was in an emotional black hole. The winter before, my marriage ended after five years invested. One day Marietta went to court, the judge granted our divorce, and everything was swept away, wife, children, family, all swept away, just like a gullywasher come down the coulee.

Let me be blunt about whose fault this no-fault divorce was. Demon rum. Marietta and I were both drinking big-time. We met when we were drunk as skunks and screwed. Whenever we saw each other in bars we'd get drunk as skunks and screw. So we got married and stayed drunk as skunks and screwed, until the booze got more interesting than the screwing. By the end it had been more interesting for a long time.

I don't want to tell you all the things we did while we were drinking. The worst was, we used to leave the kids in the car while we went into the bar. Go out and check on them every couple of hours. Beery conversations, basketball on behind-the-bar TV, life-long friends we'd never met before and would never see again, the world-weary talk of bartenders—all these were more interesting than our children. Who huddled in the car in wet diapers, hungry, crying, nothing to do. Cold too, in the winter. Wonder we didn't freeze them to death. Actually, we did freeze them to death, except not physically.

We did other things, which you might think even more rotten. Leaving them in the car by themselves is just the one that sticks in my craw the worst.

That's the way it was. After the divorce I boozed even worse (though I never used—being a traditional Indian, I go for firewater). I'd get drunk and drive down the rez roads at eighty, hundred miles an hour. Rolled my car, crushed the top. After that got a convertible—cut the top off with a blowtorch. High style on the rez, baby.

Actually, that car was a 1967 Lincoln Continental. Bought it for nothing, thinking I'd fix it up and have a classic, live in the proper style of a radio jock. Tore it up instead, but never mind. It had one feature came in very handy, cruise control. You could set that and not have to use the accelerator. This seemed sweet when I was drunk and felt like cruising. I'd stand up on the bench seat, steer with one foot, and weave down the highway like a running back dodging phantom tacklers. Oh crazy Jesus!

When I missed a curve one night, I personally went cartwheeling out through the sagebrush, while the car coolly coasted to a halt, engine idling. I *ka-thumped* across the dirt and came to a sudden stop. I regarded the stars until they slowed to cruising speed. I wiggled to see if my bones worked. I creaked myself up and fingered sticks, stones, and dirt out of my eyes, mouth, ears, collar, waist, shirt sleeves, and out of my other nooks and crannies, and chucked them into the darkness of the high plains. Then I jumped back in the car and tried for instant replay.

It is God's grace I am alive. (More about God's grace later.)

That August, the time I said I'd got all the way lost, I was still living in the house in Rockerville, the one I used to share with Marietta and the kids, who were gone back to her first husband, the kids' dad. She was white—Jewish, actually—and her ex made beaucoup bucks shooting TV commercials. Her promise was, You'll never see me or the kids again. When the Rockerville house sold, she would get half the money, and I would be on the street.

Lost, no one has ever been more lost. I didn't know diddly about anything, including myself. Took a crazy juke to let me figure out even one thing. I had to get even with Long John Silver.

AN OFFENSE

L ong John Silver wasn't his name, but that is what I called
him, after his mane of hair, thick, sleek, and silver. John
Karnopoulos also had a slender body, a fine Greek nose, an
easy smile, elegant manners, a tanning salon complexion,
and a radio actor's voice, soft and plush as a down comforter.
You never saw a guy look so good approaching seventy. You
never saw a guy with so much on his head and so little on
his mind.

He was the owner of my radio station, sort of. He was
married to the real owner, Patty Karnopoulos. He was handsome, she was homely. She had money, and he liked money.
In this way, and presumably in the sack, they made yin yang.

It was apparently true that he'd been an actor, some soap
opera in the sixties. I'm sure he hoped to become America's
heartthrob. Then he spent a couple of decades on the edges
of the scene in Hollywood, always the hail fellow, always the
perfect guest, the poised escort. Late in life he had graduated to radio station owner, which allowed him to imply that
where he once was hired help, he now was kingpin.

For sure he had power, and he behaved in the American
way—he abused it. There are a thousand and one tricks to
milk a radio station if you have no ethics, and Long John
used every one. He'd promise non-profits to match their
schedules, meaning give a free spot for every paid spot, and

never air the free spots. Or double-sell inventory if the client wasn't savvy enough to ask for an affidavit. Or dummy bills. Everyone in the office knew his tricks, except Patty, who thought the station was earning an honest profit.

So by various means Long John Silver lined his pockets. And somehow, at the same time, he seemed through affability to extend his influence, make people envy and fear and even admire him. All this he did amiably, happily, without a second thought. His notion was, This is what everybody with power does—else what's it for?

He abused his power with women too. I don't just mean he screwed them, because we all want to do that. I mean he bamboozled them with bullshit and entranced them with coke and took his pleasure and left them empty-handed and empty-hearted. He dangled the promise of a raise, a better station job, better air time. (He even dangled the prospect of my spot, six A.M. to ten A.M., the best air time a station has.) If these were not enough lure, Long John brought up the possibility of a mention on the air. Once he got them out, usually to a dinner at an advertising restaurant, so he could get a freebie, he romanced them with stories of his leading ladies, until it sounded like by laying down they would actually be rising into honored company. When he was done with them, he dropped them cold, and let others know with a wink and a shrug that he'd had his fun but ...

His latest playmate was Amy the receptionist, who had been warned but was too thick to grasp the fate of her predecessors. Since Amy had the build of a tank and the spirit of a drill sergeant, no one much cared. We did joke about Long John getting lost between her twin turret guns.

All the hired help but Amy the Tank hated John—the jocks especially did. He never caught onto one simple thing. You don't walk into a studio and berate a jock during a

8

show. Yes, he's playing music, or she is, and your complaints won't go out over the air. But think about the jock. He has to slip into an oldie smoothly (say, the Righteous Brothers), listen to you cuss him for three minutes, hold up a finger to indicate he's going back on the air, and prance in lightly with something like, "Wow oh wow, doesn't that bring back the memories? Bright and sunny sixty degrees in Rapid City this fine autumn morning, how could life get better?" And he has to sound like he believes it.

I guess, though, Long John did what a station head really has to do. He was sociable. He made himself an affable member of every group, from Rotary to the Elk's, where potential advertisers saw him. He was affable with the United Way chairman, the head of Special Olympics. He was smooth as single-malt scotch at the country club. He was flashy and gleaming and silver, like the hood ornament on my old Lincoln.

None of this seemed ultra-personal to me until one transgression made me want to smash his head with the hood ornament on my Lincoln.

Sybil, the woman who manages our traffic, said as I wheeled out of the studio, "Take me to lunch." Something in her tone made me say yes. Sybil was a friend.

We went to the Firehouse because the margaritas are good. I knocked back the first one, made small talk, and enjoyed Sybil's bird-titter laugh. Somehow her laugh always sounded like a flock of birds chirping. Today there was an odd note in it.

"What's the matter?"

"I'm pregnant."

Sybil was Long John's playmate before Amy the Tank. When he dropped Sybil a couple of months ago, I took her out for drinks to cheer her up. I congratulated her. I sang the "Michigan Fight Song" to her. Hell, in twenty minutes she was rejoicing in her good luck.

No rejoicing now. I knew she hadn't dated anyone else for a long time. "What did he say?"

"That I can't prove it's his child. That he won't pay for an abortion. And would I not tell Amy."

What do you do at a time like that? I couldn't think of anything but to look grim.

"Then, after he thought about it for a day, he fired me. I'm gone a week from tomorrow."

Bile lurched up my gut. At the same time Sybil started sobbing, long and hard, sobs that had real sorrow in them, and real regret, and real self-dislike.

I held her. (Sorry to say, with the other hand I used the second margarita to douse the bile.)

I held her and held her and finally said, "Maybe I should talk to him."

That did it. She hooted, not chirping birds now but honking geese. That free and real laugh was my favorite thing about Sybil.

Suddenly, violently, while every instrument in her orchestra was laughing or crying at full volume, I wanted to kill Long John for what he did to her.

Finally she pulled out of my arm and slugged down some of her own margarita.

I started with, "They don't put you in jail for being an asshole, do they?"

"When I'm first woman president of the United States, they will."

My emotional pots and pans wouldn't stop clanging. I ordered another margarita to silence them.

"What are you going to do?"

"Go home. That's first. Right to my parents." I knew she came from Chicago. "Then I'll decide whether to have the baby."

Anger sloshed around inside me. "You can get severance pay. You can get unemployment. You can sue him for wrongful termination."

She looked at me sadly. "That's the last thing on my mind." She sipped her drink. "Believe me, *the* last."

We drank in silence.

"So he gets away with it."

One corner of her mouth curled up. "What else is new?"

I pondered.

"For once in my life I'd like to *do* something."

We drank across another silence.

"Maybe," said Sybil finally, "you could do something to embarrass him on the air."

A dim light went on in my brain. "Yeah."

Her eyes got big. "He'll fire you."

"Or if he *thinks* it's on the air," I said. The light got brighter.

I blinked, trying not to think what I was thinking. *If he thinks it's on the air.*

I called for the check. We left without even one more drink. On the sidewalk I gave Sybil a squeeze on the shoulders. Our walk had a little bounce. My brain was teeming, and my teeth were smiling.

Get-Back Time

I passed the coming week in a tizzy. I was so nervous I screwed up the simplest things. Soon I realized that I might as well go ahead. Sybil had lost her job—she was already gone—I was gonna lose mine.

Oh yeah, I have cause a-plenty, but I'm gonna get canned. Better yet, canned the Friday before Labor Day, the big foofuraw in honor of the hired help of America.

And then where was I going to get a job? Going back to the rez did not feel like an option. There Indians with jobs are an endangered species, and unemployment runs eighty, ninety percent. Indians with forty-grand-a-year jobs like mine are scarce as manure in a shopping mall. We got radio stations, but the pay is zilch.

The problem was even bigger than that. Indian people who make it off the rez, who go to college, who find a niche in the white-world economy, these Indians do not go back, for a lot of reasons. Not if you're lucky enough to get out.

No radio station would hire me after Long John passed the word about what I did to him, not in the Black Hills region. So what the hell was I gonna do for a job?

All I knew was, I meant to get Long John Silver.

Fortunately, my idea took hold right away and knocked my mind off being scared. I was looking at a news release from the United Way when my plan began to form. The local chapter was honoring our station for a wonderful job helping raise money. These sorts of verbal bouquets came along week in week out, payback for giving the charities free air time. At Long John's request (read Long John's order) I slipped such honors into our community news spots.

Now, my program is a little bit of everything: national news, local news, music, commercials, announcements, promos, and interviews. The trick is, some of it is canned and some live— national news on tape, local news read by me, music on CD, announcements live, commercials tape, and so on etcetabravo. Wonderfully, in the studio I have complete control over all this. On one side of me are CD and cassette players, so I can get cuts ready and play them when the time comes. On the other side is a commercial cart. In it go stacks of tapes recorded earlier. They look like eight-tracks, and they're numbered. I check the paper log, push a button, and lo and behold, the cart hypes the right product.

This next bit will become important. I wear a headset and hear everything that's on the air. Anyone else in the studio is without headset. If they go on the air, they use a standing mike. In summary: When I'm doing live, anyone else in the studio hears what we're broadcasting. When a cart is playing, there's silence, to everyone's ears but mine.

With the United Way news release in hand, I sat and puzzled it out. It would work. Maybe. Yeah, it was bingo on the button. The method wasn't so tricky—I was surprised no one, as far I as knew, had done it before. The result would be simple and delectable. And with luck it wouldn't cost me my severance pay, or my unemployment checks. Which was only right. He'd got out of paying Sybil, but he wasn't going to get out of paying me, who had paid unemployment taxes to the state of South Dakota for eleven years. I'd put up with Long John Silver for a very long time, and I wanted something for it.

The next-to-last week before Labor Day (taking my time, enjoying my last paychecks!) I got started seriously on the setup. Found an old release on letterhead stationery from Oglala Lakota College out on the rez, Office of the President, Dr. Frank Brown Bull. Typed out a letter from Prez to Long John and printed it on some plain paper. Cut the logo off the letterhead and taped that onto the new letter. Ran the taped-up letter through the fax-copier machine. Presto, a fax from the President of OLC to Long John, asking to give Long John and the station a plaque recognizing their many services to OLC. (This really meant announcing dates and times of powwows, graduations, and such like.) AND ... Dr. Brown Bull would be in Rapid City this Friday and wanted to present the plaque in person and ON THE AIR. The president was available from nine-thirty to ten, which coincidentally was the last hour of my show, and the way I was planning things, the last hour of my tenure at KKAT.

I read it over about five times looking for errors. Not until the last time did I notice I'd put into the president's mouth the greeting, "Dear Long John." I felt an ice-cold drop weave all the way down my spine. The next time I got it right.

After my show the next morning, a Monday, I walked into Long John's office, gave him the letter, and watched him read it slowly. (Contrary to rumor, his lips didn't actually move.) I asked casually if 9:50 on Friday, would work for him. I listened to my insides scrape in fear. He gave a smile that kept widening for a full minute. I thought he'd seen through me.

"Kind of neat," says I.

He handed the letter back to me. "Guess I can make it," he said, and wrote it down in his daytimer.

Hot damn! Labor Day I'll be celebrating unemployment!

I continued with the setup. Tuesday, Wednesday, and Thursday I promoed the award, emphasizing LIVE and repeating the time, so there would be no backing out. I also prepared the next fax on the letterhead of the Prez, a long one. Dr. Brown Bull was obliged at the last minute to make an unexpected trip to Pierre, the state capital, it said, to testify before a legislative committee. Regrets were expressed. Since a Lakota was the disc jockey for the chosen time, however, would Mr. Blue Crow stand in for the president? The president's speech was enclosed. Would Mr. Blue Crow please read it on the air?

Now just one step left. I had to make sure it got faxed to the station, marked URGENT and to my attention, while I was on the air that morning.

I drove the seven miles from the house in Rockerville, once my happy home, to Keystone to see my best friend, Emile Gray Feather. "I'll fax it," he said. Collectors from all over the world buy Emile's work. He has a fancy fax machine and copier right in his studio.

"It's important," says I. "See, I'm gonna con Long John ..."

"Yes, yes, I'll send it." He lifted his brush hand from the shield he was painting, waved me away, and concentrated on the black he was laying on the shield.

"Near nine o'clock," I said again.

"Yes, yes." Emile is very slight, kind of feminine in his figure, and very elegant. It was a crow he was creating. I wasn't sure I had his attention.

"Real close to nine o'clock."

He flicked his eyes up at me and back down. With a half smile showing his childlike teeth, he said, "Never fear, I will help you spread your chaos."

Emile talks like that. He's strange. He likes boys instead of girls. He's been my best friend for over twenty years.

I took a last look at the emerging crow and left. Crows give me the shivers, though my own name is Crow. There's a lot to say about why. For now, let me point out that to us Lakota crow and raven are the same bird. Our word for them, *kangi*, doesn't mean crow or raven, just big, black bird, which covers both. So my name, Blue Crow, could as well be translated into English as Blue Raven. The stories native people tell about Raven are also stories about Crow, and vice versa. When I speak of one, I am as well speaking of the other. I feel close to ravens and crows, close and queasy both. The story I'm telling you is called ravenShadow.

I didn't sleep that night. Around eleven o'clock I killed a six pack watching MTV, but I still couldn't sleep. I laid there until twenty to five, turned out before the alarm went off, shuffled into my clothes, and headed to KKAT for the last time.

TGIF and humming along—hummm, baby, hmmm. Each week I came up with an idea for thanking God it's Friday. This morning I was playing the *bad* boys, the Rolling Stones, Jim Morrison, the Dead, and Kiss, sending out dark energy and an unstated dark message to the folks. The station's hottest times were 7:50 A.M. and 8:50 A.M.—most folks on their way to work, revving up on caffeine and the sound of my show. At 9:05 Amy the Tank marched in with the fax from Emile. *Hot damn, he's right on the dot.* I read it trying not to smile. "Amy, would you tell Long John to come in here a minute?"

Appearance! Long John Silver, sacrificial lamb, unknowing but not innocent. He walked in while I was doing the local news, never yet having learned to observe the ON AIR light when it's on. I held one finger up to him, asking for silence. This was perfect for my purposes, no discussion. I handed him the fax from the Prez. He read it, and I saw the lines on either side of his mouth deepen. I pointed to the script and shook my fist like it was the ultimate accolade. Sounding out the last of the news, I scribbled him a note. "Great stuff! 9:50 sharp!"

He nodded, gaining confidence.

I did a rat-a-tat-rolling segue into community announcements, rolled my eyes at him, grinned, and started hyping local events. He left with enough courage to give me thumbs up.

The bait was swallowed whole.

Long John actually put on his suit coat and snugged up his tie to look good on the radio.

I stood and shook his hand. "Congratulations," I said, with just the right air, trying to imply that an honor from OLC— well, to me, Joseph Blue Crow, that was something really special. I motioned to the chair on the far side of the counter from me and moved a mike into position for him. "You may want to say a few words when I've read the president's script."

I sat back in my chair with my jock, in-charge, up-energy attitude on. I cocked my head like I was listening to the music, and pretended to hit buttons on the CD player to fade the tune. Actually, I was doing absolutely nothing, since I'd set three cuts to play back to back. Having no headset, though, Long John had no idea what was or wasn't going out over the air. I set my coffee cup in front of the on-air switch, so he wouldn't be able to see whether it was on or off, not that Long John had ever learned how a studio works. He was gonna think we were on.

I took one very deep breath, gave myself a big inward grin, and launched into …

That was the question, wasn't it? What was I launching myself into, really?

"Dr. Frank Brown Bull," I began, "President of Oglala Lakota College in Kyle, planned to be here today to recognize KKAT and its president, John Karnopoulos, for their contributions. The recognition is a handsome plaque—can you see it on the radio? Anyone will be able to see it starting this afternoon because it will be displayed proudly in our reception area."

I held my hands out and pantomimed displaying the plaque to a crowd. Long John may have experienced his first doubts right about now, because instead of a plaque I was holding up a poof of empty air.

I barged on.

"However, Dr. Brown Bull had to go to Pierre today, legislative business. In his stead I will read the letter of commendation."

I set down the imaginary plaque and picked up the phony fax.

"Know one, know all by these contents, it is proclaimed by the board of directors of Oglala Lakota College: We appreciate deeply the contributions of radio KKAT and especially of its president, John Karnopoulos, to the College and to the Lakota people. Among many deeds worthy of remembrance and gratitude, we cite the following:

"One. John promised to be a media sponsor of our White Feather powwow, getting us to put the station logo on all our stationery, T-shirts, and other promotional materials, and then without telling us replaced the announcements of the powwow with paid commercials. No station could have snookered us slicker, and attendance at the powwow went D-O-w-w-w-n."

The look on John's face was simply blank. I've never seen a rock that blank.

"Two. He seduced a veritable treasure trove of KKAT female employees over the years, using promises or implications of promotions or raises as a lure. This was a deed worthy of the tradition of American small business owners. He has enough women's underwear in his office closet to start catalog sales!"

John's face was beginning to mobilize, and his mouth. "Liar! Fake! This is bullshit!"

He'd forgotten to speak to the mike, not that it mattered.

"We want also to tell some special people secrets about John's exemplary deeds they may not know: Patty, Mrs. Karnopoulos, the employee your husband John is screwing now is Amy the receptionist. They party at the Alex Johnson Hotel every Thursday evening, when he's supposed to be at his AA meeting. Amy's predecessor, Sybil, was dropped when she committed the indiscretion of getting pregnant."

John picked up the mike and started shouting into it. May God forgive what he would have done to our listeners' eardrums if we'd been live.

"You bastard, you Injun, you red nigger, you're fired!" And more on that order, spewed out loud but not creative.

"Amy likes John because he's a bottomless well of the lady cocaine. For anyone who might be interested, he keeps his stash in a ZipLock bag taped to the back of the mini refrigerator in the wet bar. In fact, I now have it right here!"

I held up the ZipLock bag I had snitched. John ought to have known that if every woman in the office knows where your stash is, it won't stay a secret.

Long John abandoned rhetoric for violence. He swung at me, but the counter was wide, I dodged backward, and he missed.

He crawled onto the counter. Then THE look came over him. It meant he had just remembered that he is a skinny fellow, along in years, and I am one very big Indian.

I rose into his face.

He launched himself at me.

I grabbed his forearms, both of them, forced him to his knees on the counter, and held him fast.

"John," I said to him levelly, "we're not live!"

He head-butted me.

I hurled him backward. He went *ker-splat* on the floor.

I rubbed my forehead. "John, we're not live! We're not on the air! We're not broadcasting."

He flew around the counter and threw himself at me again. I grabbed his shoulders, lifted him off the ground, and shoved him toward the wall. He collapsed in a heap.

"John, we're not live! None of this has gone out over the air!"

A light came dimly into his face. He stood up. Rage made him move jerkily, like a puppet. He staggered sideways. "Not live?"

"Look at the on-air switch!" I moved the coffee cup so he could see it. "None of that was broadcast!"

His eyes focused weirdly on me, and his mouth took a cunning shape. "You bastard! You did this on purpose. You set me up. You're fired!"

He opened the studio door and called down the hall. "Amy!"

Just as I heard Miss Turret Gun's metal track click-clacking on the linoleum floor, the third cut ended and we were back to me, live.

Live! I gotta do something.

"That was the Righteous Brothers, and my personal favorite recording of one of a great songs of all time, 'Unchained Melody.' "

Amy rumbled into the doorway. Pointing at me, John bellowed, "This red nigger is fired!"

Christ, this WAS going out over the air.

My training took over, and I tried to keep it smooth. "We seem to be having some technical difficulties here folks, we'll get them fixed as soon as—"

"You bastard! You bastard! You dirty Injun! I'll have your red ass …"

Amy took position in the middle of the room and rotated her turret guns in my direction.

I continued smoothly, "The ten o'clock national news is up next, followed by local news, and be sure to stay tuned ten to two for the latest, gr-r-reatest hits brought to you by …"—I couldn't even remember the name!—"whoever the next disc jockey is!"

On that high note I punched the button, the cart took over with a commercial, and I had closed out my time at KKAT. Rapid City would not hear the likes of my final minute again for a long, long time.

Long John shifted to controlled hostility now. "Amy, Joseph Blue Crow is fired, effective immediately. Escort him out of the building. Get his keys. Clean out his desk and send him whatever's in it. Tell him to forget his severance pay."

Did he think I would surrender to her guns? I held his eye. I walked over to the cassette player, popped out a cassette, put it in my pocket. Then I walked straight at Long John, staring at him like a worm. I reached out and grabbed his shirt front. I shook him. Fabric tore.

Amy tracked to my direction and started to move. I turned and shoved Long John into her. They dominoed onto the floor, John between her legs but facing me.

"Now hear the rest. I have a list of all the double selling you did on my show the last two and half years. That's fraud. I know who all your sweeties have been. Patty will see that as cause for divorce. And every employee you got knows where you stash your coke in that ZipLock bag—the sheriff will love that."

He got up, but I pushed him back into the wall. "The best of all is what you just gave me. You called me racial epithets on the air. Live. I've got a tape. The station has tapes. If need

be, the FCC and the Civil Rights Commission will have tapes."
I thumped him against the plasterboard. "They can take your
license away! They *will* take you license away!" I was bellowing
so loud it hurt my throat.

"So here's a tip. If my severance pay comes through real
smooth, and there's no trouble about my unemployment,
I'll keep my mouth shut. If not, I'll scalp your scrotum! I'm
on the goddamn warpath!"

I slammed him against the wall and dropped him. I
reached to the counter, seized the ZipLock bag of coke,
unZipped the Lock, and dumped a thousand bucks worth
of the white lady right on Long John, from the part in his
hair to his eyebrows and nose to his necktie to his lap.

He sputtered, mewled, and howled all at once.

I strode down the hall and straight out of the building.

It scared me, how violent I felt, how angry I was. I was
shaking.

I sat in the Lincoln for a few minutes to calm down. I
breathed deep in, deep out, deep in, deep out.

The sun was glaring off the hood of the Lincoln, and it
shone in my eyes. I felt something odd, like I was sleepy, but
I was too agitated to be sleepy. The sun slashed at my eyes
and made them want to close. It shone on the hood of the
car until it became a mirage light, hallucinatory.

And I saw ... broken pictures. Magpies. Flowers. American flags
upside down. Half-moons. Flowers. Pictures like that, all in frag-
ments, and they were all moving, swaying, swooping up and down,
like flotsam swelling upward and dropping downward on pitching
seas. They were all in a swirl that made no sense....

Behind the pictures quavered a song in the old style and in the
Lakota language. It was different from the songs I heard as a young-
ster, not a single male voice, nor a group of men around a drum, but
the voices of hundreds of people, men, women, and children together.

No drum. Or if there was a drum, it was the sound of moccasined feet on the Earth. The people sang. From the style, I half recognized one phrase, a kind of chorus, but I could not catch the words.

There in the car, but not in the car, I strained my ears to hear the words of the song that came from ...

A-a-w-wk! A-a-w-wk!

This was Raven, perched on the hood ornament, black and menacing, huge and apocalyptic in the blinding glare.

A-a-w-wk! A-a-w-wk!

I jerked with fear, and moved somehow toward ordinary consciousness. Raven still perched on the hood.

Some people know the sound of their own death. Mine is, *A-a-w-wk! A-a-w-wk!*

Raven always comes to me, or at me, black, shiny, and mocking. If he was a character in a carnival, maybe a fortune-teller, he would laugh at you and put his hand on your shoulder and lick your inmost ear with his tongue and whisper, "Death, death, death." His tongue would be the coldest thing that ever touched you. Not being human, though, he gleams the message at you with the shininess of his feathers and the cold brightness of his eyes. When he flaps his wings and the black feathers catch the sun, somehow they are wild, mocking laughter. It speaks poetic of the body dead and moldering. *I am a-wing, and you are arotting.*

Raven makes me shudder.

This time Raven gave a great flurry of wings on the hood and opened and closed his big beak without a sound. He cocked his head sideways, peered at me through the windshield. He flapped his wings but didn't lift off. He was so big and ominous that for a moment I thought he was an ordinary raven, instead of Raven.

Then suddenly he was sitting on the steering wheel, beak in my face.

I flung an arm at him, and he backed off. Morphed backward through the windshield and sat on the hood.

Raven was a comfort in a way. Instead of pretending to be afraid of unemployment, poverty, and degradation, I could just go for the big one and be afraid of death.

AND HOW DO YOU LIKE YOUR BLUE-EYED BOY NOW, MR. DEATH?

That afternoon I drank. *If you're gonna see things, you might as well be drunk.* And I played a game. How do you drink just enough to keep you going? Going from bar to bar, as you drive south through the Black Hills from Rapid to Hot Springs? Going from drink to drink instead of drink to jail? How do you stay sober enough to drive but drunk enough to forget Raven?

This is a white-man game, this management of inebriation. White folks are good at it—teeter but don't dodder.

I'm not that kind of drinker, and not many Indians are. We don't want to play around the edges. Maybe this is because of our traditions—we make a place for altered states of mind, whether reached by trance, Father Peyote, firewater, or even seizure. Anyhow, we are binge drinkers. I am a binge drinker. When I tipple, I don't want to get a pleasant little buzz. I want to get barbarically drunk.

So I had a problem. I was determined to drink until the sun went down and then meet Sallee Walks Straight in Hot Springs, at the south end of the Hills. I had been pursuing Sallee for a month, no luck. Had a hot date tonight to celebrate something special, I told her. Didn't tell her I hoped to get lucky in a meadow, pass out with a blanket wrapped around us, and wake up a free man—no white-man job! Free in the center of Black Hills, Paha Sapa, our sacred lands.

You white people don't understand how special the Black Hills are to us. Since before the memories of the grandfathers of the oldest men, my people have sought their visions in Paha Sapa. Our ancestors, since before the memories of the grandfathers of the oldest men, have been buried there. The Hills give us all things good—poles for our tipis, meat, berries, grass for the ponies, clean water. Most important, and seldom told, is that the Hills mirror the stars, and by traveling in a sacred spirit through the Hills on a certain route, we align ourselves with the heavens themselves. The Hills mirror what we call the Racetrack Constellation, which you call Capella, Pleiades, Rigel, Sirius, Procyon, Castor, and Pollux.

A hundred years ago Yellow Hair, George Armstrong Custer, came along and hollered in print, "Them thar Hills are full of gold." Prospectors flooded in, followed by miners, followed by bartenders, whores and gamblers, followed by preachers, teachers, and the whole gamut of your so-called civilization, which has about killed us. The final insult was for you to name a town after Custer in our Hills.

But my date with Sallee was for about dark, Indian time, which means any time in the evening. I had all day to tipple and not pass out.

I remember puttering along south through the Hills. I had a few in Rockerville and went over to Keystone to find Emile and thank him for the help, but he wasn't at home. I checked out the taste of beer in Hill City, and in Custer, where I stood in the parking lot, pretended a handicapped parking sign was Custer's grave, and pissed up at it. I think I remember taking a nap—you might call it an involuntary nap—in the state park named after the bastard along the way. The whole time I watched for Raven in the corner of my vision, but I never saw him. He was there, but I never saw him.

At twilight, one way or another, I was whooping it up in Hot Springs with Sallee, who unfortunately was flanked, or chaperoned, or something like that, by her cousin Rosaphine.

Sallee never drank, in fact maybe wasn't old enough to drink. She didn't say why and I didn't ask, knowing that any young, eligible red woman with good sense would rather find a red man who's both sober and straight, which is near impossible. Nobody loves a drunken Indian, and I wondered whether that might be why I hadn't gotten lucky with Sallee, but I didn't care. Getting laid was dicey, getting drunk a sure thing.

Trouble was, she had me a little entranced. She was tall, slender, willowy, quiet, mysterious. From the first look she seemed to me somehow mythic, bearing a spirit larger than life. Later I realized what she reminded me of. Emile did a painting, back when he was doing canvases and not just hides, of White Buffalo Woman. She is, well, you would call her one of our great mythological heroes. She first appeared to two young men, walking in a sacred manner. One of them lusted after her. She held her arms out, he embraced her, and a cloud enveloped them. When the cloud disappeared, the lustful young man had turned into a pile of bones. To the other young man she said, "Take me to your village." He did, and the gift she bore proved to be the greatest of all boons to the Lakota people, the sacred Pipe.

In painting her, Emile was once more performing the sacred deed, taking White Buffalo Woman to the people. The figure was slender, pure-looking, sheathed in a beautifully quilled buckskin dress, walking in a modest way but bearing invisibly the gift of the sacred.

Sallee reminded me of Emile's White Buffalo Woman. Later I found out why—she'd been the model. Her face wasn't shown, but it was her carriage I responded to, and her aura of being special.

Like the ill-advised young man, I lusted after her. I told myself I wanted to ... get lucky with her.

I knew Sallee wanted much more from life. She wasn't likely to find it in a bar in Hot Springs, but if you live with your uncle near the hamlet of Oglala on the Pine Ridge rez, a bar in Hot Springs is only five bucks of gas round trip, and a date with an alcoholic red man with a forty-grand-a-year job, hey, that's a step up.

"*Hoka hey!*" says I, and lifted my glass. Sallee gave me her special smile and slid onto the bar stool. Rosaphine the bulldog barked "*Hoka hey!*" and slid right onto my lap. Her talk always sounded like barking, and she had a jutting lower jaw, which is what reminded me of the dog. Rosaphine wasn't pretty, but she was a party girl, and sexy. This time the play in her eyes said she'd knocked back a six-pack on the drive over, which was par for the course with Rosaphine. Just like me.

I slid from underneath Rosaphine and stationed myself between them, touching on both sides. I needed the stability of touching, and the illusion it lent. I motioned to the bartender to give them whatever they wanted. "A Virgin Mary," says Sallee. It was all she ever drank, and she acted interested mostly in the celery. "Bud Light!" roars Rosaphine, like it was the answer to a quiz-show question. She waggled her ass like she just won a case of Reese's Peanut Butter Cups—it wasn't in Rosaphine's fantasy world to win the sixty-four thousand dollars. The waggle made me want to lean against her more. Yeah, she was started toward blimpdom, which Lakota women seem to achieve early, but she was warm and pliant.

"You get it done?" I says to Sallee.

She scrunched her shoulders up and shook her head no. "Frustrating. I'm ruining my third piece of the silk."

Sallee was working on a big fabric painting—that was what she wanted to do, paint on cloth. I met her at Emile's one day. She was showing him a big piece, a horseback warrior on a periwinkle blue banner shaped like a guidon.

"Good idea," he said. "Indian warrior, U.S. Army symbol, I like that."

You can hear what people are not saying, too.

She raised her arms and eyebrows like, That's all?

He finally grabbed a big sketch pad and re-drew the horseman three or four times on different pages, really fast. The last sketch—it's hard to find words for this—had a sort of flow in the lines that made the paper almost pulse, like it had electrical energy.

"Mine just lays there," she said, looking back and forth.

Emile nodded.

She looked like she wanted to cry.

I got her to have coffee with me before she drove home.

Now she was working on a truly big piece, the size of a banner like you hang in front of a store to make a statement. For it she needed white silk, and had no bucks to buy it.

One day at the Sioux Nations Shopping Center, where she clerked for minimum wage, she took me out in the parking lot and showed me what looked like a backpack. "My Eureka," she said.

She started unstuffing some white cloth out of the pack. Silk. "My uncle's World War II parachute." *Silk.*

"Wonderful idea," I said. I also thought, Typical Indian artist, broke, and creative as hell.

"Donan says he'll hang it from a pole in front of the gallery for the fall show. If I can get it finished." Donan was a Hill City gallery owner.

The barman brought the Virgin Mary and the beers.

I said, "You know, I'm celebrating. Here's my Freed from Labor Day promise. If you ruin all of it, I'll buy you another parachute."

She grinned, but her eyes showed this hurt. "If I ruin it all," she said, "I'll get another Eureka."

Sallee had the affliction of artists—they're unhappy unless they do the one thing that turns them on. I'd learned that real good from Emile.

"What you celebrating?" says Rosaphine.

"My freedom," says I.

I looked around the bar. I reached down into the lungs of the biggest chest in the room, found my biggest radio voice, and hollered, "Ten—n-n-n HUT!"

The white drinkers, a mix of fifteen or twenty tourists and Hills folks, looked over at the drunken Indian. (One more time, lads and lasses: Nobody loves a drunken Indian.) I laid the words out like thunder. "Today I took my freedom. I told that white employer, that boss, that overseer, I sang in my best Johnny Paycheck imitation, 'TAKE THIS JOB AND AND SHOVE IT!' "

One of the rednecks softly seconded, "Right on!"

"So, LET'S CELEBRATE! Bartender, this round's on me. SET 'EM UP!"

I lifted my glass, listening for the roar of approval. Instead there were a lot of funny looks, and from the back came a comment in a redneck accent, "Once in a lifetime! An Injun's buying!"

The bartender set to work.

I looked happily into Sallee's eyes and saw hurt. I didn't get that. Then I thought, Generosity means more when it isn't boozy. I felt ashamed. I said, "I did quit my job."

She nodded and noshed on her celery. I found it sexy. She was looking White Buffalo Woman-like again.

The bartender filled our glasses, including more veggie juice and celery for Sallee. I gave him some twenties. Rosaphine and I drained our beers.

Rosaphine slipped an arm around my waist. "So tell us."

I did, the whole story—Long John Silver's corruption, his grave offense via Sybil, my setup, the beauty of my deception off the air, and the crowning glory of Long John shouting RIGHT ON THE AIR vileness I never dreamed to get out of him.

Rosaphine haw-hawed, slapped her thigh, slapped my thigh, squeezed my thigh, and haw-hawed a lot more. Sallee looked worried.

Suddenly I thought, I could tell her more of the truth. I could say, "Sallee, I wasted a huge piece of my life working at a job that paid the rent but did nothing else for a soul, either red or white." I could say, "I got stale spinning the top forty fads of the month, many of which I never bothered to listen to. I became the master of razzmatazz phrases that said nothing," and similar truths. But all that seemed ... I was too drunk, and probably too cowardly.

"Don't worry!" I cried. "I've got money! I could buy rounds from here to Christmas!" I started on about the bucks I would get from the sale of the house, the severance pay, the unemployment checks, but then I saw I'd lost Sallee's attention.

"Let's dance!" I said to her, holding out my hand.

She looked at me appraisingly, took the hand, and we walked to the juke box. "Into the Mystic," she punched, Van Morrison, and off we juked. The dance floor was the size of a bathroom stall.

Rosaphine put some quarters in the juke box. Up comes Bonnie Raitt all fast and funky. Rosaphine hands me another beer, chugalugs her own, and joins us. Sallee is an elegant dancer, using the whole body without emphasizing sex, almost in a virginal way, but very sexy to me. Rosaphine looks like she'd have done well in burlesque—make them tits spin, grind that bottom, bump your partner's ass, and with a sultry look bump your pelvis.

I am just drunk, only half dancing, half lurching, on the edge of stumbling.

Rosaphine bumps toward me with a provocative look on her face. She spins and backs up to me, her big bottom jutting out. I bump her butt with mine, we sidle around each other, and bump two or three more times.

I whirl away and look at Sallee's face. She's dancing, but her eyes look strained. Oh, what the hell, nothing wrong with a little fun. I spin back toward Rosaphine, and she goes into her shimmy.

A shimmy on a roly-poly, five-foot body is hard to describe. Her head tilted slowly from side to side, her smile stayed fixed like a beacon, her eyes gleamed wild, and her tits begun to move. I mean shake. I mean wiggle and wobble. Flip and flop. Dive and soar. At the same time her belly began to quiver, just quiver. Her hips began to rock. And roll. Sometimes one went up and the other down. Sometimes one went back and the other front. Sometimes both of them humped back and then BANGED front. And all at the same time her big thighs quivered. It was somethin'. I mean, it was SOMETHIN'. I guess my eyes about jiggle-jangled out of their sockets beholding Rosaphine's shimmy. Maybe the room was dark, but I was seeing fireworks.

I glimpsed Sallee watching us from the bar. Well, that was good. I wanted to give my own show, the Blue Crow Crawl, or the Blue Crow Sound and Light Show. I prayed, *O God of Booze, flow in me!*

Rosaphine was sailing, and I sailed my six-and-a-half-foot body into its performance. I couldn't rightly say what my body did. I strutted. I pranced. I spun. I did freeze-frame. I stilted. I pretended there were strobe lights and jerked from posture to posture. I did a dizzy, drunken, dizzied, drunken, dizzying, drunken dance.

Near the end I caught Rosaphine's eyes. We segued into the grand finale. We bopped, we banged butts, we flopped, we flipped, and wrapped it up in an orgy of boozy woozing.

At the end I fell flat on my back. Thinking to save the moment, I raised one leg straight up, and then let it slowly, slowly droop down, like a wilting cock.

From the back came three claps of mocking applause.

Rosaphine helped me up, snuggled against me and held my hand. I said, "Where's Sallee?"

She wasn't on the bar stool. Up close we saw her purse was gone. Her glass was empty. She'd even taken her celery.

The car was gone from the parking lot.

Rosaphine turned into me, put her arms around my neck, and kissed me full, with plenty of tongue. She pulled back, grinned, said, "Looks like I'm stuck for a place to sleep," and kissed me again.

Not only did I kiss her back, giving as good as I got, but pushed hard against her down below, so she could feel what was up.

Since my divorce in January I had spent a lot of evenings in bars and ended a lot of them in the back seat of the Lincoln. I preferred the moans of orgasm to the cries of *a-a-w-w-k! a-a-w-wk!*

On this day of my triumph over Long John, and celebrating my subsequent independence, however, a large gesture was required. And I had a really juicy idea, one I'd been saving. It was inspired by Grandpa and Unchee, my grandma. They told a story about driving the C&NW tracks up to

Rapid City one winter in the sixties. Highway 79 was drifted over, but my sister Angelee was bad sick, and they had to get her to the hospital. Trains traveled when cars couldn't, so the tracks were clear. Drove those railroad tracks all the way to Rapid, and made it. What they'd have done if a train came … they didn't have a clue.

Unfortunately, my juicy idea was not based on honoring that memory. I wanted to add some kick to a quickie in the back seat, in fact a lollapalooza of a kick. Imagine me cruising the C&NW tracks, topping Rosaphine in the back seat, head down, my mind on hurling myself into her hole, and maybe hurling us into the black maw of death.

C&NW freight trains don't run on any schedule.

Doesn't that make it delicious?

You never know when.

"Come on," I said, pulling her by one hand to the Lincoln. "I got an idea you ain't never seen the like."

She didn't catch on right at first, it was too crazy. I lined the tires up square on the tracks. I let some air out, so the tires would stay, the way Grandpa said he did it. Rosaphine was looking bamboozled. I pulled her to me and fondled one breast. She ground against my leg. "We'll ride them tracks right into Rapid City, exit at the first street we see, and find a bar will serve a red man a drink." Pause for kiss and fondle. "We'll ride in the back seat."

Her eyes got queen-sized.

I positioned the car right, engine running, in neutral. Turned the lights out—wanted to run in the beautiful darkness. Set the cruise control, hopped into the back seat with Rosaphine, who wore no underwear under her bluejean skirt. I got my Wranglers down, reached forward and popped the gear lever into drive, and started to turn and pop me into Rosaphine when … I got beguiled by the sound and feel of the car on the tracks, like a silk stocking easing up a leg.

34

It was an utterly delicious, smooth ride, rubber to rail, seamless, eerily quiet, a world as undisturbed ...

Raven, fold me in your wings.

My face up in the air, my eyes on the velvet darkness ahead, Rosaphine behind me, I slowly took my clothes all the way off. I turned my face down and regarded my risen cock with relish. And I rolled on top of Rosaphine.

Then I saw, or maybe felt. She'd passed out. *Lay down, pass out. Well, hell, I've done it myself.*

I stood up, found my balance on the spongy seat between Rosaphine's sleeping legs, bared my chest to the warm wind, lifted my face to the sky, and looked at the moon. It was a half-moon—yin-yang moon going toward new moon. I said a traditional prayer—Grandmother Moon waning, take from me the things I do not need!

Not far ahead I saw a curiosity. A trestle was coming up. Enough booze, you don't see the problems. I figured if we met a train, I would wrench the steering wheel and we'd plunge off into the sagebrush, bouncing and laughing. Plunging head first through the air into a ravine, though ... *Raven, bear me up into the night sky.*

Did you know everything sounds different going over a ravine? Real spacy, kind of echoey. Downright eerie.

Back onto solid earth, more or less. Something woke Rosaphine. She sat up and looked up at her fool date, erect in two different ways.

Curve. Another trestle. Deeper ravine. Cooler air. I fell silent. My ears crawled all around the edges of the swishing sound of the tires, listening for the approach of my own death.

Rosaphine passed out again. She laid there fully clothed but her legs up and knees spread, dark shadow between, a mockery of sexual invitation.

Doesn't Raven feel seductive?

O Raven, you have been doing your dance before my eyes for years, waiting for me!

No, it is me who's been waiting, bride of one true suitor, a lover cooing and inviting and subtle and knowing, knowing, knowing.

Solid ground again.

I took thought. That country between the Badlands on the east and the Black Hills on the west is ravine-ravaged. Hadn't considered this. The ride to Rapid City would be dipsy-doodle, with a lot of time suspended high in the death-defying air. *Where you invited me, Raven.*

Now my past prowled out of the corners of my mind and yowled at me, sang into my ears like an angry, moaning wind. I knew well what I was supposed to be, the way I was supposed to live. *Supposed, supposed, supposed,* that word like a gavel thudding down on the judge's bench and declaring, Guilty, guilty, guilty. I'd been picked out by my family and by Spirit for things far higher than boozing, far higher than broadcasting. Every day the black-robed judge in the back of my mind reminded me what I was supposed to do, supposed to be, supposed to do, supposed to be. Every day I plugged my ears and tried not to hear, neither the judge's words nor the sentencing gavel. The sentencing bang was all I really could hear, of course. I spoke it to myself so constantly it became my flesh, my hair, my belly. *I have lost the world of Spirit I was born to. I have gotten lost in the profane world, the world-not-mine. And I am weary of myself, weary unto death.*

The wind whipped around my head, fierce, and its little eddies wandered into my ears and made echoey sounds, despair, defeat, despair, defeat … *a-a-w-wk!*

I waited for the train to come. I sailed over trestle after trestle, dark ravine after dark ravine. I looked and listened for death, but the bastard wouldn't come. I watched for Raven, but the black bird hid in the black night, waiting.

After a while I saw ahead the crossing of the dirt road east of Buffalo Gap. The road cut a white, moonlit slash through the sagebrush.

Escape! *I can get off!*

I looked down the tracks, silver lines running into a dark hole. I wanted no escape. I wanted to roll on into the embrace of Raven. I wanted to dive off a trestle. Or smash into the skull of an engine. I imagined it. The engineer saw me, even with my lights out. He hit the air brakes. The whistle shrilled. The steel wheels screeched on the steel rails. The will of the engineer said stop, but the momentum of a hundred freight cars said, Crush.

CRUSH!

Suicidal anger? Suicidal depression? Who cares? Gavel, guilty, rapping, guilty. I want out, out, out.

Rosaphine? *I don't want to hurt you.*

A pair of ghostly lights rolled up to the tracks and slowed, a pickup truck with a wooden house on the back. It hesitated, jumped forward, hesitated, stopped, lights bobbing. Evidently the driver could see our dark shadow. The headlights blinked up and down, like a beacon, an offer of refuge. *No thank you, no refuge for me.*

We sailed past the crossing serene as a cloud sails in front of the moon.

As we cruised past, I lifted a hand and waved goodbye, a shadow bidding farewell to light and rushing into shadow. Goodbye, whoever you are. I screwed up. Screwed up, goodbye.

Then I looked back and thought, Wasn't the shape of that rig familiar? But I was leaving all that was familiar, *except for you, Raven.*

I looked ahead into the night, and smiled. If I could describe that smile to you, every twist of emotion that was in it, you would understand everything about that night.

I do not much recall the next twenty miles. Rosaphine zonked. I stood on the back seat, facing into the wind and smiling. Smiling, yes, smiling big. The smile of the man who has come to know himself, and despises himself.

I opened my mouth, summoned the full power of the radio voice of a six-foot-six man, and as loud as humanly possible roared the cry myself—"A-a-w-wk! A-a-w-wk!"

I was dimly aware also of my spirit surging around inside of me, moving in great tides, quiet as ocean, eloquent as wind, saying something else. Something very else. But I wasn't listening. *I look for you, Raven.*

Finally, after twenty-something miles of cruising, Raven darkness? No, light ...

Most people imagine death as a great darkness. Some who've crossed over and come back say it is a white light and that you pass into it with a feeling of vast benevolence. Mine was to be a bright white light, and Raven's malevolence.

I felt relieved. Sad, disappointed, but relieved. That's the main feeling I remember. *Come, sweet light.*

Except that it was two lights.

I tossed my head and rejected that. Optical illusion. Imagination playing tricks on me. One white light would be enough, wouldn't it? You can't die twice, even if twice is deserved.

Two lights. I shook my head, waggled my eyelids.

Two lights, with some kind of glow behind them.

"Hey!" I shook Rosaphine with my foot. "Hey, wake up!" I jabbed her hard.

"Hunh?" She jerked and sat up. "What the hell?"

"What do you see?" I shook her with my foot. "What do you see ahead?"

Oh, sweet Raven. I will ride your wings into the blackness.

"A car on the tracks!"

"What?"

"A car on the fucking tracks! Stop this thing!"

"What!?"

She dove for the cruise control and slammed it with the heel of her hand. The Lincoln began to coast.

She vaulted into the driver's seat and jammed on the brake.

From my standing start in the back seat, I took flight.

I groped for the lift of Raven's wing but found nothing. I zinged through the darkness toward the double light. I reached up for Spirit but plummeted toward earth. I held my arms out and arranged my fingers like Raven's wing tips. Somehow I rotated face up. Upside-down I tried to croak like Raven but ...

A steel rail clobbered my shoulder ...

A fat tie cracked my head ...

Cinders peeled my back and butt ...

I rolled like a log spinning downhill across some very nasty ground. I came to rest. I waited for the world to stop whirling.

Footsteps fast on the cinders. A voice growling over and over, "What the hell ...?" I knew that voice. It was not Raven. It was not even Wakantanka. It was, it was ... My mind surfed through clouds of confusion.

Emile!

I giggled. This was funny. Here I was, naked as nothing, drunk as a skunk, looking for a way to throw my life on the ground—BUT IT IS NOT A GOOD DAY TO DIE. Not really. And Emile pops up like magic to save me. Again.

Now I understood. That was Emile's rig at Buffalo Gap; I should have recognized it. He saw us cruise through the crossing, saw me in my naked, backseat bowsprit pose, and caught on. *Oh, yes, Emile, you know the despair of being Indian, you know the despair of the bottle.*

"Emile, you saved my life."

"Both our lives." Rosaphine was suddenly sober too. She stood there as dressed as I was naked, as serious as I was silly.

"You saved my life." I was surprised at the gratitude in my own voice, and in my heart.

He felt of my shoulder.

I hollered.

"You're going to the emergency room."

Another drunken Indian in the ER. Nobody loves a drunken Indian.

"Blue Crow, you have gone nuts." Rosaphine's voice. She was getting it. "JESUS!" She got it now. *Yes, yes, I did try to kill us.*

"I'm taking him to the ER. Help me."

They prodded me to my feet and trundled me into the front seat of Emile's pickup.

Rosaphine said loudly, "I got to get out of here. FUCK!"

"Drive his car to my studio." He told her where. "Sleep on the couch. I'll be along."

Nothing more from Rosaphine. The sound of the Lincoln starting. A screech of tires. I didn't hear from that girl again for a long time.

"Brother," said Emile, "when you get out the hospital, you got to go on the mountain."

Those words took away my silliness. Each one of them hit me like a ten-pound sledge.

I'd been waiting for the call, what I thought would be the voice of the Raven. Here was the call. It was the voice of my other life, my real life. It was the call to live again in the world of Spirit.

Some dim part of me recognized it.

I slurred out the words, "I got to go on the mountain."

PART TWO
WHERE BLUE CAME FROM

THE VOICES IN BLUE

I knew what Emile meant—"You got to go on the mountain." He and I had been raised in that same old world, where Spirit reigns, the world I told you about, with magic, visions, and the poetry and song of the unseen. We even grew up together part of the time, a hard part, our white-man schooling. We had an awareness of Spirit that would stay with us. It would help Emile, because he was true to it. Because I wasn't, it would haunt me.

Emile is a special man, and to understand how special, you got to be willing to expand your white-man mind some.

When Emile was five, living with his grandparents, an elder told his grandfather that Emile was a *winkte*. This is a word we Lakota have, means man-woman, or something like that. Man who wants to be a woman. Man who lives as a woman.

Hanh, I know what you're thinking. Means queer. Or whatever insulting word you want to use.

This is where you got to expand your mind. The old-time *winktes*, yes, they had men's plumbing and they did their sex with men, this much is true. But if you think queer or fairy and imagine bathhouses and a gay lifestyle, you got it all wrong, for sure.

The old-time *winktes* were picked out by Spirit to live as a kind of third gender, neither man nor woman. They

43

adopted women's way of living completely. They wore women's clothes, took on women's responsibilities, married men, even spoke like women, for in our language words take one form for men, another for women. They were female in every way, and were addressed and treated always as women.

They were good at this switch, too. Old-timers tell a story about a Catholic priest whose church was near the house of an especially good old woman. The priest and the elderly lady were friends for thirty years. When she died, the priest laid her out for burial, and was shocked to discover that she had a penis. That's how completely she lived as a woman, so that the people called her she, and even today I call her she.

Men-women lived in this way because it was revealed to them that they should. Sometimes, I guess rarely, a Spirit told them to change back and live as men, and they did that too.

They were important in our old-time way, these men-women. Certain ceremonies require them—you cannot start a Sun Dance without a *winkte*. They also made the best flutes, which were used in courting, and were the strongest in elk medicine, the power of romance. If a young man wanted a strong love song, he got it from a *winkte*. And I think generally they did exceptional beadwork and other arts.

Emile was picked out to be a *winkte*, but you can't really do it the old way anymore. Lots of our people, even, don't understand the tradition and don't accept it. Emile wears men's clothes and is called *he*, like any other guy. He's what the modern world calls gay. But it's a misunderstanding, and he's never quite going to get over it.

When Emile was a kid, though, his grandparents kept him out of school, just like me. That elder who was also a *winkte*, that elder came and taught him how to live right. I don't think it's an accident that Emile makes his living as an artist. At his studio on the highway near Keystone he creates his work and sells it—paints hides, drums, parfleches, robes, and such, and sells them to tourists, collectors, and museums.

I was held out of school to learn some old ways, but different ones from Emile. I was chosen even before I was born. My grandmother, my father's mother, said she saw signs during my mother's pregnancy. No one told me what she saw, or heard, or in any way how it came to her—she didn't communicate much with me. What it came down to, I was picked out.

Selected for what? To be raised to carry the old ways. To be raised by my grandparents, not my parents. To live away from town, away from white people, even away from Lakota who were white in their ways. I spoke Lakota, no English. Instead of learning the ways of the grocery store and the refrigerator, I learned the ways of the hunter of animals and gatherer of plants. Instead of learning the ways of television and the automobile, I learned the ways of the sweat lodge, the vision quest, the Sun Dance, and the *yuwipi*.

We grandparents' children, that's what they call us, we are held apart exactly to be carriers of the old ways. White people call us back-to-the-blanket Indians, backward people, people to be left behind by time. In fact we are the keepers of our people's spirits.

It was a hard way to grow up, serious and dedicated to a great mission, without the normal time for play and other childish things.

What was even harder was to learn that way of living, then to learn the ordinary rez way—you gotta be one of your own people—then to learn the white way, which is the way of the world.

That's how I come to have four voices.

You've heard my jock voice, a hepped-up personality I put on for my radio show. Then there's my college-educated, white-man voice, a different mask I wear in restaurants, at the grocery store, and to write this book. Then there's my rez voice, Indi'n patter. The last voice is the one I was raised with, the voice of the traditional Lakota in touch with the old ways. Some days I can own it. Here's how I would tell you about Emile and me in that voice.

Hanh, of those held away,
The grandparents' children, we are two.
Of those who live close to Earth,
And who remember the old ways of our people,
The way of the Pipe,
And the seven sacred rites of the Lakota,
We are two.
For as long as these ways are known to some,
And kept by some,
The people live.
When the Pipe is forgotten,
And no man cries for a vision,
The sacred hoop will be broken forever,
And the flowering tree will wither and die.

To get by, I've needed all my voices. One for my show. College-educated white-man talk for most of the world, because it gets respect from you white folks. Rez talk to be a regular guy, someone my buddies can hang with. It means saying "he don't" and "them cows," and even more speaking in a kind of soft slur that's hard to describe. I use my traditional voice for …

Well, the truth is, I need it for my sanity, but I haven't used it much in a long time. More than twenty years.

I need to find it, and you need to hear it. The traditional voice is for speaking of sacred things. In truth, I can speak of these only in my own language. English does not serve. But since you understand no Lakota, I will make something like it in English, as I did above, and I will speak to you sometimes in that.

I don't claim Lakota is only a poetic language, or only a sacred language, like the Latin of the Catholic liturgy. It is an everyday way to talk, usable for everything human beings do—you can call a dog, curse your wife, or gamble away your life savings in it. But it is also the language of the knowledge of the *wakan*, the mysterious. It is the knowledge my people are perishing without, and your people are perishing without, and the world will perish without.

If in English it has the cast of an older and higher wisdom, that is what I intend.

Does it confuse you that I am a man of many voices?

Then think how it confuses me.

Not only many languages of the tongue but languages of the body. When I am in the white world, I hold my body one way, in the rez world another. A Lakota speaking to a group of Indians does not take the posture or the tone of, say, a white professor addressing a class, or a white politician addressing a crowd.

One example: We traditional Lakota do not look our elders in the eye. To us that is disrespectful. We see them, of course, but we do not make eye contact with them. Old-time Lakota men could never, ever, ever look their mothers-in-law in the eye, or women their fathers-in-law.

Among white people, though, if your boss speaks to you, or your sergeant, or your teacher, you better look him in the eye. Otherwise it's, "Look at me when I talk to you, boy." And if you don't, they think you're evasive or shifty. When you're only trying to be respectful.

Learning to speak white body language has been harder for me than learning English, by far. Sometimes even today I get confused and act inappropriate. Sometimes I have to make a choice, with both red and white folks in front of me. It's hard.

I don't claim, though, that all four of these voices aren't me. For better and for worse, they are. The traditional voice is the one I was raised to. The rez voice is the first one I picked up, the everyday way of my people. The educated white talk is one I wanted badly to master. It was my key to college, a career, and a good-paying job. The radio voice was my last acquisition. Got it and my show-biz name from the radio station, out there in Seattle. My first real job— I'll tell you about it later. My PERSONALITY, on the AIR. Cause I was GOOD, baby. Do it to it, Blue!

Natcherly, this hipster voice isn't me. This white-man life isn't....

Until they began to be me. Until Crow's voice sounded like me, even to me. I forgot the old voice. Hey, pretend long enough and you become what you're pretending to be.

So that's where I was the night Emile rescued me. A traditional Lakota who'd become a hipster, big-city boy, divorcee, and drunk.

And Emile spoke to me of going on the mountain? *On the mountain? Back to the old ways? What am I, a museum?*

So what was my new life? Jive and booze. Can jive and booze be your whole life? Yep, booze alone can be your whole life, and your death, too.

The way out? To go back to my beginnings and rediscover the good red road—that's what Emile was telling me.

Here's what my beginnings were.

CROW'S RAISING

Grandpa, Unchee (my grandmother), and I lived near the mouth of Medicine Root Creek, in a back corner of the Badlands. The Badlands are beautiful, but they are a hoodoo place. The ancient peoples were strong here, Stone People, Rooted People, and Animal People, before human beings, and their bones are here yet. The paleontologists have found thousands of fossils of the original peoples. Sometimes even a kid can find a dinosaur bone imbedded in the Earth. In a way the Badlands were even badder a hundred years ago when the Ghost Dancers retreated there to dance their visionary dance, away from white people and from Indian unbelievers. And they were bad when I was a kid—only scattered, remote homes, two-tracks for roads, wagons and horses more common than cars.

My grandparents had a *cabin*, you could call it, except the word cabin calls up the wrong picture. Basically it was a freight car. Where Senior (that's my dad) got it, or how he hauled it to my grandparents' little piece of land, I'll never know. The rest of the house was (and still is) catch-as-catch-can. Tree trunks support the roof. Tarpaper, newspaper, scraps of two-by-four, odd remnants of plywood, pieces of two-by-twelves. We even had our version of the great housing fashion of the 1950s, a picture window. It was a two-piece windshield filched from a wreck and carefully framed by Senior into the kitchen wall. In the summer we could have another picture window, a giant one, plus air-conditioning—we just slid the big freight-car door open.

Grandpa and Senior built a privy and a squaw cooler too. This was a brush shelter, pine boughs on poles. In the summer Unchee cooked on a wood-burner in its shade, we ate there, and it was our hangout place away from the heat of the house. I remember her squaw bread fondly, and the black coffee with molasses, and the dried corn with berries. That was a good time.

When I was a kid, during the 1950s, Senior was over at our place all the time, building this and that onto the cabin for Grandpa and Unchee. Since he was my dad, it didn't seem strange. Not until I moved to town did I realize, really, that the shack my parents lived in was much poorer. My dad spent his time, energy, and dollars fixing up his parents' house and short-changed his own family. I have not decided whether that was love for Grandpa, Unchee, and me, or the out-of-kilter behavior of an alcoholic, or something else.

My dad was a natural builder. Give him the magic implements of his trade—as little as two kinds of hammers, a rip saw and a crosscut saw, a plane, and a sack of nails—and he could make your dream come true. He learned his craft in the Army Corps of Engineers, and he had that can-do attitude—can do anything with any materials under any handicaps in any amount of time, just point me in the right direction. He got his chops building bridges for American armies on the move up the Italian peninsula, and he was proud of it, to the extent he had any pride at all.

You should remember some stuff about him. He built a good house for his parents and lived in a hovel himself. Most of the time he didn't have any tools because he'd pawned them for drinking money. He beat my sisters. I don't even know where he is now. One day he's gonna freeze to death in a snow bank with a bottle in his hand.

Maybe I loved my father those days, but for sure I hated him. Here's one reason I'm walking the red road now. If I have any children, I don't want them to say the same about me.

Want to know how confused my childhood was? Think of all the names my own family called me. To Grandpa and Unchee, when I was a little kid, I was Dreamer. To my sisters, Angelee and Mayana, I was Bud. They wanted an English name to use for me—they didn't speak much Lakota. So they came up with Bud, of all things. Well, Grandpa liked it because it seemed like a common, ordinary, white-man name, but also meant a beginning a leaf or flower, a little miracle—so he thought it was a perfect disguise for an Indian. Mom and Dad called me Junior. (After I got permanently mad at him and refused to call him Dad, I called him Senior.) White people and my schoolmates (after I started going to school) called me Joseph.

Also, our family name was Good Road, but I was given the name Blue Crow.

Altogether I didn't know who I was.

I just said something about going to school. That was the earthquake in my life, brought by none other than Oliver Walks Far.

THE EARTHQUAKE

The year 1967 was a big one in the white world too. When
I got into music and became a jock, I learned all about
what it meant to my white friends. The summer of love in San
Francisco, hippies, the Monterey Pop Festival, the beginning
of flower power, Bob Dylan, Joan Baez, the Beatles, the flowing together of rock and folk and protest songs into the new
music—a new era, the dawning of the Age of Aquarius.

Which just went to show how far their life was from mine.
I was a fourteen-year-old kid on the Pine Ridge rez, living far
from electricity. My color TV was the Badlands, my music was
the sacred song and the drumming, and my new era would
start when I went on the mountain and got a vision to live by.

Oliver Walks Far ended all that. He was a life-long
acquaintance of my grandfather, I do not say friend. Oliver
was a strange, solitary blanket Indian even to us blanket
Indians. He had once been a *yuwipi* man, but no more. He
liked to live way out by himself and see nobody.

Oliver lived further back in the Badlands than we did,
because (in my opinion) he was an ornery old bastard who
couldn't get along with people. I didn't see why Grandpa and
Unchee acted so respectful around him. They went even further. They said, "That fellow, he knows things." This is a quiet
compliment among our people, not given to just anyone. It
means, 'That person is wise, pay attention to what he says.'

That summer Oliver Walks Far got sick and came to see Grandpa a lot, because Grandpa was a *pezuta wicasa*, the sort of medicine man who cures people, not with drumming and singing but with herbs. Old man Walks Far came a lot for treatment of whatever was wrong with his lungs, and by way of payment he stayed to help Grandpa around the place.

Part of Grandpa's living came from the horses and cows. We ran them on Grandpa's land and wherever they felt like going in the Badlands. Grandpa broke the horses, and he had a reputation for making gentle saddle mounts.

"I do it the old way," he told me. "I hand-raise them. Just let them hang around the house like dogs, like pets." Grandpa also handled them all the time, and told us to do the same. They nosed around the kitchen door a lot, looking for treats.

"Comes time to get up on a horse," he said, "no trouble. That horse, he's learned I'm always good to him, I never hurt him—he trusts me completely. Doesn't sound like a secret, but those white ranchers, they never figured it out yet. What they do, they treat horses like somebody separate. They fear their horses and their horses fear them."

Maybe what else Grandpa did was a secret. When they were born, he put his head close and mingled his breath with theirs, and his spirit.

Later he got a good price for those saddle horses, though he never had much use for the ranchers. They leased Indian property for grazing, and ended up being our bosses on our own land.

The rest of his living came from what people now call migrant labor. Plus Unchee made a little money by doing beadwork and selling it at the trading post.

Though we never had much, we had enough to eat. Once a month we would go for the issue, the commodities the government gave us, staples like lard, unroasted coffee beans, rice, white flour, beans, and sugar. This lousy food is what has made my people fat—it's given lots of us com bod, the lard body you get from commodities that are all fat and sugar.

Also, Grandpa and I would hunt. There were hardly any deer or antelope left in the Badlands in the sixties (for sure no buffalo), and we didn't have a gun, so we would smoke rabbits out of their holes and club them. Or we would catch mud turtles and sand turtles. Grandpa was very fond of mud turtles.

The hard part was, I was like an only child—just me, Grandpa, and Unchee. I was kept away from Indians who were white in their ways. Which left only a few back-country folk like us to talk to or play with, and we seldom saw them. So my main playmates were buffalo and ponies carved from cow bones, stones I used as marbles, and slingshots Grandpa and I made from inner tubes.

When we did see other people was at family get-togethers or issues or ceremonies. Ceremony was a big part of our lives not only spiritually but socially. Grandpa kept track of the days with a moon-counting stick, notches for days on one side, months on the other side, and a new stick every spring. When the time came, we'd take the wagon for miles and miles, didn't matter how far. Ceremonies were serious, though, and not as much fun as issues (where they issued commodities). At issues I first played the bear game (throwing sharp grass stems at each other), pit slinging, shinny ball, and grab-them-by-the-hair-and-kick-them. Mostly, though, I was one lonesome kid.

Back to that summer. Oliver helped us repair corrals and put up a little of the wild hay, when he was up to it. He would also rest a lot, and when I had time, I would listen to his stories. Lonely as I was, I'd have listened to anybody's stories.

I liked the stories. It was from him I first heard the tale of the Mysterious Lake, the story of Lame Rabbit, and the story of Stone Boy—these seemed like magic to me. But I didn't

like Oliver Walks Far. I liked him even less when he said what
he did to Grandpa and Unchee.

We were at the squaw cooler of an evening in late summer. The grown-ups were talking and I was stretched out
under a cottonwood, dreaming. Daydreaming, you white
folks call it. It's that and more.

The day had been hot, the evening was only beginning
to cool off. I'd look up into the canopy of the tree and hunt
for shapes. My favorites were the thunderbirds, not because
we needed the rain, though we did, but because the thought
of thunderbirds excited me—O powers of the west wind! Or,
moving only my head, I'd look at the shadows on the Badlands.
During the hot mid-summer days, when the sun was straight
overhead, the Badlands seemed fried, the grass dry, the ground
scorched, and earth and sky alike one big glare. In the evening,
though, the sun slanted shadows across the land. The strange
shapes of the bluffs and chimneys and other outcroppings
threw even stranger shadows across the jumbled ground, purple shapes on the yellow-brown earth. I liked to imagine that
I was a shadow, creeping across the land, insinuating myself
through a gully, slinking along a dry wash, easing up a cutbank
and wrapping myself around the spiky sagebrushes on the far
side, or pooling deep under the leafy roof of a cottonwood. I
liked that feeling of crawling along the ground, curling myself
around plants and stones, making deep darkness on the back
sides of boulders, fingering my way into things.

Anyway, I was doing my version of dreaming.

"Dreamer," called Grandpa softly. He was respectful of
my day-dreaming—said it was keeping one eye on the other
world, the one seen with the heart, which was my task in life.
Unchee often said my name in a different way, the tone white
people use impatiently for people who pay no attention.
Mostly Unchee didn't talk to anybody, lived kind of sullen

in her own world. When she spoke up, it was like as not to accuse me of being a daydreamer.

"This man has something to say to you," said Grandpa.

I knew right off away it was something I wouldn't like.

Oliver Walks Far sat on the only chair at Unchee's table—actually, he propped himself like a log, stiff and almost straight, on the old ladderback. He was a big man, head like a watermelon with his black hair pulled back hard, belly like a boulder, and he moved no more than need be. I noticed, though, that his eyes moved, following me as I approached the table and sat at the place Unchee was patting, on the automobile bench seat beside her. With Unchee acting real sympathetic, I knew it was something bad. Grandpa sagged against one tree like he was wore out.

"I been thinking about you," said Oliver Walks Far. "I think you are taking an easy path, not going to school. Nothing good comes from an easy path." This is a strong principle among us.

I glanced across at Grandpa. He wouldn't look at me—he knew what was coming, and he wasn't going to help.

The old man repeated it softly and gently. "Nothing good comes from an easy path."

I squirmed. I could guess what this meant, and I felt prickly about Oliver Walks Far meddling in my life. What fourteen-year-old wouldn't?

What I really was, was scared. Scared to go to town, scared to go to school.

When Lakota children are little, the grown-ups say, "Go to bed right now, or the *ciciye* will get you." When that monster ceased to be enough, they said the *siyoko* would get you. But when the kid was old enough to understand, they said, "*Wasicu anigni kte*"—the white man will come and take you away. That was enough to do the job.

A fourteen-year-old boy, however, does not speak either his fear or his anger to his elders, especially not to a man who "knows things." You simply thank older people for their wisdom. Since I didn't have the heart for that, Grandpa did it for me.

"What you say," Grandpa went on, "we will consider it carefully."

Oliver Walks Far rose heavily, eyeing me. Without another word he lumbered off toward the hay shed, where he slept. I could hear his feet heavy on the earth, thumping like drumbeaters.

The next morning the man who knew things was gone, two-footing home on those thick legs of his, and never mind the weak lungs. I never saw him again, and soon heard his relatives had put him on a scaffold. But he had rolled a boulder into the creek of my life, and the creek had divided, and now would flow sundered, split into two courses, red and white.

We did not in fact consider what he said carefully. We just did it.

After breakfast the next day Unchee helped me pack my belongings into a cardboard box, my clothes underneath my ceremonial things. I helped Grandpa hitch the team, and we had nothing to say. Unchee was almost as silent as she packed two gallon jugs of water, and some lunch. When she brought her parfleche of little beaded things, key rings, barrettes, and the like, each worth a couple of bucks, she said, "I want to stop by the trader." (If hippies were beginning to sport Injun stuff, the effect hadn't reached the rez yet. It never did.) I hoisted my skinny body and my heavy heart onto the plank seat, Grandpa clucked, and we were off. Uprooting my life from the only place I knew, casting it into the wind, like tumbleweed.

Kyle—I'd never lived in town. My family—I hadn't lived with them since I was a suckling. Their tarpaper shack—I was used to Grandpa's cabin. My sisters—I only half knew them. Mom—she hid behind Dad, I hardly knew her. Dad—he hid behind booze, I hardly knew him.

I was flat-out scared.

But I was going.

Had I been a couple of years older, it might have been different. I might have already gone on the mountain for the first time and brought back a vision, some medicine of my own as a guide. I could have claimed that I knew my way for myself, and meant to follow my vision. But a youth who lacks his own medicine, among our people, is a blind man, and must be guided by others.

BIRD WITHOUT A NEST

The three of us came around the corner, face to face with my family's place.

Have you ever been shocked, truly? Beyond a so-to-speak use of that word? Or is your white world too well protected for that?

Our house was burned to the ground.

Nothing was left but pieces of tarpaper, rows of char where walls once were, and little bits of studs sticking up like broken bones.

Where am I going to live?

For a moment, I swear, I smelled burning flesh. In my mind's eye I saw the blackened bodies of my two sisters, my mother, and Senior, smoldering.

I started to heave—the bile actually started to churn—when a kid's voice saved me. Mayana's voice, girlish and sweet! "Bud! Bud!"

She was waving from behind the hood of the half-stripped, rusted-out auto body that resided in Senior's yard. All four of them were there, kind of shuffling to their feet. I noticed Senior slip a pint-shaped brown bag into one pocket of his baggy pants. When we got close with the wagon, we saw they were eating supper right off the ground, without even a blanket. They looked ashamed and slinky, like dogs that have been kicked.

"*Washtay*," says Grandpa, meaning good, like in good to see you. What was good about it nobody knew.

"*Washtay*," everybody mumbled, including me. My tongue felt like a rock in my mouth.

We piled out of the wagon. Grandpa spoke up. "*He, he, he,* troubles." *He* meaning regret.

Mom came toward me, drew me to her. I was taller than she was now, so she couldn't fold me into her breast, but she did her best. "*Washtay, washtay,*" she said.

I couldn't get any answer out.

Unchee set aside her ill spirits for a while and pitched in. "Time to eat," she said in Lakota. Although my parents spoke Lakota fluently, and my sisters spoke it well enough, they didn't like to use it. Our family get-togethers were kind of funny for language. Grandpa and I didn't speak English more than a few words. Unchee, Senior, and Mom spoke both languages fine, though Unchee sounded like English was a bitter taste in her mouth. My sisters understood Lakota but didn't speak it much, or didn't like to. Old-timey stuff, they said impatiently. So my sisters and I communicated kind of hopscotch. I'd speak in Lakota and they'd understand, but they'd answer with gestures, or a few words of English and Lakota mixed. They didn't take any stock in back-to-the-blanket.

A glance told Unchee that the family's food was gone, and there was hardly any to begin with. We'd counted on supper with them. Unchee always packed plenty for lunch, though, so she set out the leftovers, jerk meat and dried corn with berries. We polished them off right quick, and I was still hungry. It was as sad a supper as I ever ate.

I didn't hear much of the conversation. My mind was raging—*Where am I going to live?* However, I pieced together bit by bit what happened to their home.

"Five days ago," I heard Senior mumble. That was when the house burned down. "In the middle of the night," said Angelee, like that was the worst thing about it. "We don't know why or how," said Senior. From Mom's look I knew she did know, and pretty quick I got a clear mental picture—Senior passed out in bed with a cigarette in his hand.

Grandpa gave me a warning look and spoke up himself. "Who has it in for you?"

"I'm sure gonna get whoever done it," said Senior. He futzed around and scratched at the ground while he said it. It was the performance of a man ashamed.

Nothing was ever admitted nor proven, against Senior or anyone else. I didn't need any proof.

What kept hurting my eyes was that auto carcass. The four of them were living in that thing. What few of their belongings they'd saved were stashed in the lidless trunk, and they slept inside, or underneath, or nearby, maybe on top, whatever worked. No tipi-dwelling Indian was ever as poor as my family. As Senior explained things to us, his tone was craven and his smile was fawning.

I cast my eyes down and tried to keep my stomach calm. The car said everything. It was the first car anyone in my family ever owned. Had no tires, wheels, fenders, windshield, windows, trunk lid, headlights, taillights, or license, but it was a car. Was once.

I walked off into the evening a bit and hunkered down. Then I walked back, looked Senior in the eye, reached in his shirt pocket, slipped out the pack of Marlboros and took one, and his matches. My first cigarette. I walked away and squatted down again and put my anger into the hard scratch of the match head and the first pull into my lungs. I held the match at arm's length and watched it burn. The flame died just before it touched my fingers.

I'd been carrying the embers of anger inside me for a while. At Sun Dance earlier that summer, Angelee was sporting a bruise like a pint-size eggplant around her left eye. "Where did you get that?" I said.

She snuffled and hid her face.

"Tell me Senior didn't put it there," I demanded.

She flung a wild look at me and hurried away, sobbing.

I didn't need to ask if he was sober at the time.

That's when I started calling him Senior instead of Dad.

I stubbed out the cigarette on the hard, dry ground. I stared at the dry hills all around me. My anger could have set them on fire.

One good thing about anger, it keeps you from knowing how scared you are.

When I walked back to the family, Mom pulled me down beside her, and my heart sank.

"I'm taking Angelee and Mayana to Wambli," Mom said to me softly.

Her words leapt at my throat.

Wambli was where her family came from, over east toward Rosebud.

"I'm going to Martin to look for work," said Senior.

I raised my eyes into his, not caring about respect, not feeling any, and wanting him to know it.

"Tomorrow," said Senior. "We're all leaving tomorrow."

Which meant they'd planned to leave without letting us know.

I stood up, unsteady. "Grandpa, I want to go home," I squeezed out.

He looked at me and his eyes were hard as rocks. Though he was a kind man, he could be hard. "The school will board you," he said.

Watch out, be good, or the white man will come and take you away!

So that's how it went. Grandpa and I spent the night under the wagon in case it rained, the last time I would see him for the longest month of my life. Unchee, Angelee, and Mayana got the wagon bed, Senior and Mom the front and back seat. In the middle of the night I woke up. Probably, until then, I'd never wakened in the middle of the night in my short life. I felt odd, out of sorts, itchy. Little sparks ran up and down my arms, like flicks of electricity. I looked up at the black bottom of the wagon, and suddenly couldn't stand being penned in.

I rolled out. The sky was brightened by a half-moon, the this-or-that-way moon. The hills around caught the moonlight and held it. The grasses glowed softly, and even the parched earth of August looked gentle, inviting, and beckoning. My legs felt jumpy. I could take off. I knew that. I could take off. There would be spot work on the ranches— it was haying season, and beet harvest time. Maybe I could hook up with someone and do the Indian rodeo circuit, which attracted me. Maybe I could improve my hoop dancing and do the competitions on the powwow circuit. People did make a living that way. My legs were jumping, saying "Go, go, go!"

I turned and looked at the wagon. The women were out of sight behind the sides, and Grandpa was invisible underneath. I looked at the car. Somehow a glance of moonlight hit part of the front seat just so, the driver's side. My father's head, upper chest, and arm were caught in the light. The arm was crooked against the steering wheel in a way that looked uncomfortable, and the head propped against the door at an awkward angle. It looked to me like his neck was broken. My lungs and belly felt a breath of fire.

I stood there in the moonlight a long time. Finally I crawled back under the wagon. *Nowhere else to go.*

In the morning, without breakfast, they caught a ride to Wambli. Senior went along, intending to thumb to Martin from there. Martin is a white-man town between the reservations. I told myself that this time he would really look for ranch work, that he wouldn't just booze everything away, that he would put together some money, go get my mother and sisters, and make them a family again.

But I knew the real story, past, present, and future. The story of booze doesn't change.

I didn't have much time to think about it. "I have something to give you," Unchee said. She looked at me, and it seemed like she was there with us, not off in her own world. I felt ... hopeful.

From underneath the wagon seat she took a long, hide-wrapped something. Grandpa stood to the side and looked on.

Had I not been in a funk, I would have been thrilled. I knew what it was.

Unchee set the package on the seat and unfolded the deer hide. There lay a Pipe bag, elaborately beaded. "Open it," she said.

Reverently, I took out the Pipe within. The bowl was an L shape of pipestone, which you call catlinite, with four parallel rings carved in the upright part, representing the four directions, and lead inlaid in the rings. The stem was of water birch, decorated with brass tacks, and near the mouth part, tight beadwork with tiny beads. Tied to it with red ribbon was sage. Though the Pipe had the look of something a hundred years old or more, the sage was fresh. I looked at Unchee and thought, You have been changing the sage regularly all these years. Her face was unreadable.

This was the long stem of an important man. If you were going to carry such a Pipe, you need to be working for the people. Correction, if I was going to carry this Pipe, I needed to work for the people.

I touched both stem and bowl gently. The bowl of a Pipe is of stone, and it represents Earth. The stem is wooden, and represents all that grows upon Earth. The Pipe is the center of the Lakota way, and has been since White Buffalo Woman brought it to us long before the memories of the grandfathers of the oldest men.

Grandpa looked uneasily at Unchee, back at me, back at Unchee. Finally he said, "This Pipe belonged to Unchee's father. She wants you to have it. When the time comes for you to carry a Pipe, you may carry this one. In the meantime, take care of it."

No, I was not a Pipe carrier—not old enough. I wanted to be. And I wanted to go on the mountain and get a vision that would guide my life.

I put the bowl and stem in the Pipe bag and wrapped them both in the deer hide. *O yes I will take care of it.* I looked around at the dusty, nowhere town. I made a point of not tearing up. *It is my connection to you, and to being Indian.*

"I have something else to give you," said Unchee.

I waited respectfully.

"You will not understand yet, but it's important. From this day take a new last name—Blue Crow."

I felt conked on the head.

Unchee waited.

"I take the last name Blue Crow," I said respectfully, but I felt confused.

"So today we enroll you in school as Joseph Blue Crow."

Right away they took me to the boarding school. It was a Saturday, but we walked through the half-dark corridors, hoping to find someone. A white man with white hair and a sweet face, kind of like that guy Dave in the Wendy's commercials on TV, he was working in the main office, said he was the principal, Mr. King. (These days employees of the Bureau of Indian Affairs are mostly Indians, but not in 1967.) He asked some questions about who my family was, where I'd been living, and what my schooling was. Unchee had to answer, on account of she had the only English. Mr. King did a double-take when she said I hadn't been to school, and a triple-take when she said I didn't speak any English. She treated him the way she treated all white people, like he was a worm. I didn't know what it was she had extra special against the whites, not yet I didn't.

Nevertheless, Mr. King enrolled me, said I could go home for Christmas. *Christmas!* my mind screamed. I couldn't go that long with seeing Grandpa and Unchee—it was months away. Besides, it wasn't any holiday of ours. "I'll come to see you at the half-moon," said Grandpa to me softly. Mr. King scowled at hearing words in Lakota, though he didn't know what they meant.

"This is a BIA school," said Mr. King. "That means it's free, devoted to helping Indian children make better lives for themselves." (When Unchee translated that word "children," she put a little stress on it, underlining the implication.) "We're not like Red Cloud Indian School," which was near Pine Ridge, "or St. Francis," southwest of Rosebud, both run by Jesuits. "Kyle is a U.S. government school and promotes no religion." He emphasized the last phrase with a smile.

"No religion?" Grandpa asked through Unchee. His tone was surprised.

Unchee and Mr. King back and forthed a little. "No *particular* brand of the Christian religion," she summarized to Grandpa. She added her opinion. "It's better to get an education without the white-man religion."

Grandpa eyed her and said, "Both religious and secular are basically an attempt to nub the red out, so it doesn't make much difference."

Silently, I agreed with Grandpa.

Mr. King stood, came around his desk, and stood next to me, sort of like saying we'd talked among ourselves enough. "Everything is going to be fine," he said. That was the first of a thousand lies. "You've made the best decision."

He put his hand on my shoulder, and I knew I was trapped. A schoolboy for the first time in my life. Not a student for the first time—my whole life was learning—but a schoolboy. My skin jumped under his touch.

Because Mr. King looked like Dave Thomas, to this day I can't go into a Wendy's.

Grandpa and Unchee got an early start home. They'd shared the last of their food with the family, had no money, and would go hungry until they got back to the place on Medicine Root Creek.

We walked outside, the four of us. Kyle didn't look like much those days, no handsome Little Wound School, no college, not even a Wild Horse Cafe. Kyle was just a few houses, a place to get gas, and two general stores. Except for the school it wouldn't have been a town at all. The school was a red brick affair, unimportant-looking.

I don't remember ever being so scared as when I watched Grandpa flick the lines at the horse, and the wagon pulled the two of them away, their backs toward me.

"Everything is going to be fine," said Mr. King beside me, patting my shoulder to reinforce the lie.

School Days

I am going to take no truck from you about what Indian schools are like. BIA schools, church schools, it makes no difference. The lie is that they're charitable institutions, established to help Lo, the poor Indian. The fact is that of all the white man's gifts, they are the most insidious.

First, let's get clear about the purpose. Someone said, You can't Christianize an Indian until you civilize him. (That's absolutely true, and I am doing my best to avoid both.) So what they do at boarding schools is try to beat the red out of us, and the white in.

For more than a century Indian children of every tribe have been shipped to the Carlisle School in Pennsylvania and other boarding schools, on and off the reservations. When the children left home, they and their families wept openly at the train stations. Indian families aren't used to being separated. We don't send children to schoolrooms or daycare centers. They go everywhere with their parents and do everything. This is considered a vital part of their growing up.

So when Indian kids were taken away to boarding schools in the old days, they were acutely lonely. Often they didn't go home at all during the school year, not even at Christmas. Sometimes they didn't see their parents for years. This isolation was the worst thing boarding schools imposed on Indian children. Many of them committed suicide.

At boarding school they learned English, they learned to be white. They got punished for speaking their own language. They got punished for singing the songs they grew up with, even the lullabies. They got punished for being Indian.

On the Lakota Sioux reservations in my day you went to school or else. If you tried to stay away, a cop would come and take you—a truant officer or a BIA policeman, and either one might be Indian, for all that meant. We thought school was worse than any of the white man's inventions, even jail, because it was inflicted on children, and pretended to be kindly.

The Kyle School was run on military lines. Roll call at start and end of day. Stand at attention. March in step. If you disobeyed, corporal punishment. Simple as that, just like Catholic schools. One advantage I will admit to a BIA school. Since we didn't have priests, we didn't have pederasts.

The first day of class was the most humiliating day of my life. I was fourteen years old, already over six feet tall, yet I was in first grade. A kid half my age showed me the way to the boys' room. I was looking to go outside, because I didn't know what the sign on that door meant in English. He showed me how to use the toilet, and the sink.

The teacher, Mr. Banks, didn't speak Lakota, so he taught us English by pointing at pictures and saying the words. Picture of bovine with bag. "Cow." Picture of bovine with tool box. "Bull." Picture of prairie. "Grass." If I'd known more English, at least I could have added that up to "bullshit."

I was punished twice that first year for speaking Lakota. The first time I was forced to kneel on two-by-fours for hours, and that hurts. The second time I was hung up by my thumbs from water pipes. The only way I could relieve the pressure on my thumbs was to stand on my high tiptoes, and you can't last long at that. My body ached terrible when they let me down—I can't remember it aching like that, ever. Mr. King said it would teach me. It did. Taught me not to speak Lakota where adults could hear me, not even Indian adults, because they would sometimes turn you in.

I had my hands whacked by yardsticks. Once Emile was whacked by a yardstick with brass studs. (He was lucky they never found out he liked other boys—they'd have thought up a really nasty punishment for that.) I was made to stand in the corner nose and knees touching the walls. They deloused me by force. They cut my hair by force, and it had never been touched.

None of that was the worst. What I hated was losing my freedom. At home I would roam around every day. If I wanted, I would ride, or work with one of the horses, teaching it to stand ground-tied, or back up. Or I would straighten and fletch arrows—I loved to shoot. Or hunt. Or roam and gather sage, cedar, willow bark, or bearberry. Whatever I wanted.

At school I had to do what Mr. Banks said. Sit in a hard chair at a desk for hours. Ask permission to go to the bathroom. Eat on schedule. Work on schedule (it was our job to keep the school clean). Go to bed at lights out, get up when ordered, do roll call, stand in line for oatmeal, and so on and so on.

Among my people a hint from an elder was word enough. These white people just bossed you around directly and loudly, told you exactly what to do, and if you refused, dished out the punishment.

I hated it. *Who are these people,* I said to myself, *to tell me what to do with my life?*

So what did I do?

I ran away. After I got the hang of it, I ran away every day. Figured out how to disappear between first roll call and last, didn't go to class. At first they didn't catch on—Indian children are always coming and going for various reasons.

But the third or fourth time Mr. Banks saw me at meals, he got suspicious why he wasn't seeing me in class. Must have gone upstairs, because Mr. King gave me a sharp talking to.

I kept disappearing.

Then they assigned an older boy to keep tabs on me. This was Emile, though we didn't know each other yet. The first day he policed me real good, and I had to stay in class. That night we had supper together and then stayed up late in his room talking in the dark. He was from Big Hollow Creek, even deeper into the Badlands than me, and was related to me on Grandpa's side. Not close related. What you whites call cousins, we Indians call brothers and sisters. Emile was a cousin in our way.

The next day Emile ran away with me.

Those were great times. For a week Emile and I went out to the lake every day. We swam, we fished, we walked, we roamed, we caught crawfish below the outlet, and we made friends. He told me he was called to be a *winkte*, and what that meant. I told him how I was picked out to carry the old ways, but now I was also picked out to learn the white world, and I hated it. I even told him I feared it. In short, we became friends enough that twenty years later, when Emile saved my life on the C&NW tracks, it wasn't the first time either of us saved each other's lives.

The next summer at a powwow Emile and I did the ceremony that made us *hunka*, brothers by choice. That lasts for life. Emile Gray Feather was the best thing I got out of Kyle Boarding and Day School.

They caught on, of course. Whacked us with yardsticks and assigned other older boys to keep tabs on each of us.

That worked on Emile, who dreaded being beaten and wanted only to be left alone with his colored pencils and paper.

But when they beat me, I turned defiant. I kept running away. I dared them. As long as my days were free, I didn't give a damn about the beatings.

It was fun. I only needed a couple of minutes' head start. I could get it when I went to the bathroom. Or when my guard went to the bathroom. Or I could come up with something so much fun that the guard would run off with me. Thomas Red Creek guarded me seriously for several days, but on Friday he hitchhiked all the way to Mount Rushmore with me. Though we didn't have any money to get in, we figured the place was really ours—the whole Black Hills are really ours—and we slipped in through the woods. Then we climbed to the top of those big, funny heads and looked down George Washington's nose at the tourists, just the way he looked down his nose at Indians.

It got to be a good game. Every day I would slip away, and every day they would let the truant officer know. Sometimes he would come after me, sometimes not—he didn't like me getting the best of him. Folks in town would give him leads about where I went (or sometimes misdirect him). He knew pretty well that I liked to hang out at the pond north of town, which they called a lake, or a couple of places down Medicine Root Creek. I developed skills to hide from him. Learned to build a brush shelter that looked natural, like part of the landscape, and sit inside while he went by. Learned to sit so still among the rocks he wouldn't see me. Once in November I built a snow cave and slipped inside. It was a good game.

I hardly ever played with the other boys. Sometimes I did stand by the schoolyard and watch them play basketball. But they thought I was strange—a bush boy—and I thought they were snobs.

One place I never ran off to was home to Grandpa and Unchee. Every half-moon Grandpa came to me.

The half-moon around the white-people holiday Thanksgiving he came, and like always he took me down to the store for a dreamsicle—I loved those babies. He got a pop. When we sat down outside, he looked at me and said, "I hear you been running away."

I nodded yes.

"You haven't been in class learning."

"I have learned some," I said. I started to follow with the English words I'd gotten good at, *Goddamn, holy shit,* and such, but thought better of it. I hadn't turned white enough to act disrespectful to Grandpa. "I haven't been in their classes much," I admitted.

He looked at me for a long time. Finally he said in a certain way, not harsh, but unmistakable, "You won't run away any more."

I didn't. I wasn't worried about Mr. Banks, or Mr. King, or the truant officer. I was worried about Grandpa.

JUMPING JU

I went through one month of hell, from Thanksgiving to Christmas vacation. I didn't run away even once, and it was the hardest thing I've ever done. I sat and listened to Mr. Banks and pretended to memorize his English words. I tried to memorize his numbers, and get the idea of how to figure with them, addition and subtraction. I learned to repeat back whatever he said to me, like a dummy. Every sentence I learned was like swallowing a thistle. I hated it. I wanted to puke it back up. But I had made up my mind to do what Grandpa said, and I was going to do it or die.

The day before Christmas break, Gordon True Bull came and found me in my room. His three sons, who all went to Kyle School, stood behind him in the hall, looking embarrassed. This family lived down the Medicine Root Creek road, less than halfway to Grandpa and Unchee's place. We'd never had much to do with them, because they were the sort of Indians I was supposed to steer clear of. They lived a lot further into the twentieth century than we did. Had a truck. Used propane instead of a wood stove. Even had a TV on an antenna. Gordon drove that truck to Kyle every day and worked on people's cars. He had magic hands, they said, could fix any kind of car or truck or any machinery at all and make it run. His sons rode in and out with him, every day.

Gordon says to me in Lakota, "Your grandpa asked us to give you a ride home tomorrow afternoon. You come over to the station right after school, bring your stuff."

I looked at the True Bulls and my heart sank. Gordon was a big man with a big belly, and his older two sons were taller than he was. They looked intimidating, standing there. Besides, though the sons were schoolmates, they were just the sort I didn't hang out with. They didn't board at the school. They did real good in class, spoke good English, and were proud of it. And the older two were on the basketball team. In another year there would be three True Bulls on the team. Over all, I plain felt stupid around them. I was the tallest—I'd grown that autumn, and the school nurse measured me at six foot two. But they were in the junior high and high school grades, and I was in first grade.

Keeping my eyes down respectfully, I nodded and murmured "*Washtay*" to Gordon True Bull.

I walked away with my heart down. Grandpa and Unchee weren't gonna come and take me home. I understood it—the trip took all day in the wagon, and more if the weather turned. But I wanted them to come. Emile's parents were driving over from Porcupine, he didn't have to ride with strangers. I wanted to be with him, my only friend in the world. I felt abandoned.

I sat on my bed and futzed. I didn't think things over, 'cause there was nothing left to think over. I didn't want to come back to school, but Grandpa would have no truck with that. There wasn't any rodeo circuit or powwow circuit or farm or ranch work in the winter, so I couldn't run off and make a living. Senior was with my mother and sisters up at Wambli, no job but plenty of booze—I'd be damned if I'd go there. I was at the end of my rope.

Mr. Banks had read us a story with the English phrase "end of my rope" in it. I asked what it meant. I was speaking enough English now to understand stories, and they were the only part of school I liked. Mr. Banks said it meant, like, when he was looking for fossils in the Badlands and saw a spot maybe fifty feet down that looked likely, a place he couldn't get his Jeep to. So he tied a rope to the bumper and lowered himself hand over hand. Turned out, though, the spot was more than fifty feet down, and the rope didn't reach. Mr. Banks was fifty feet down and twenty feet of nothing below. That was being at the end of your rope. If you weren't strong enough to climb up, you'd be shit out of luck, another phrase I liked.

I didn't feel strong enough to climb out of the hole I was in, and didn't have the desire.

I got my coat on and went out into the road. I wanted to go to the store and get a pop or a fudgesicle, but I didn't have any money. So I walked the east-west road a ways out and back, then walked the Allen highway out and back, and the Medicine Root Creek road. I stood around and shivered. Mr. Banks had told us tomorrow was the shortest day of the year. Clouds covered the southwestern horizon like dirty gray blankets, though, and I couldn't even tell if the sun was all the way down.

I stomped my feet to warm them up. I rubbed my ears. *At the end of my rope.* Slowly, I walked each way again, east, south, west, north, automatically taking the directions sunwise.

At the furthest northern point, where I was turning back, I noticed some dark shapes moving out in the field. They were hopping around, and sometimes lifting off the ground head-high, and going back to the same spot.

Ravens. Something's dead.

I walked over there. The snow was blown off, except a ring left around the bottom of each sagebrush root. I wondered what the carcass was. Road kill, maybe, something that had got hit and run off to die.

The ravens squawked at me as I got close. Most days I would have been scared, but today I didn't give a damn about anything. The birds skittered away, then jumped and flapped around and awked. After a minute they got quiet, but they stayed close, mostly on the ground within a few steps. They didn't mean to give me long.

It was a deer, a doe. She hadn't been dead long, just today or last night, probably hit by a car. Probably a drunk.

I looked at her close as I could but didn't touch. She had no eyes anymore. Big rips opened her skin, and great chunks of flesh were missing. Maybe some dogs or coyotes had been at her first, and got their fill. Now the ravens were getting theirs. Bugs would finish the job.

Suddenly a raven flapped into the air and flew straight toward me. It hovered over the deer, and I felt like it was looking me in the eye, and its eye was ...

Raven's eyes bugged out. They stood in air at the sides of his head, impossibly, turned straight toward me. They gleamed at me. Then they turned red hot and glowed, and I fell topsy-turvy into them.

Hitting the hard, cold ground snapped me out of it. Panicky, I scrambled to my knees, then to my feet. *Will the ravens eat me?*

Then I saw. Six or eight birds, perhaps following the boldest, pecked at the carcass. I wondered which one was Raven, who had entered my mind. None of the birds paid me any heed.

I ran back to the road, and to the school.

Raven stayed with me through supper, at the edges of my consciousness.

I was last. Emile was already gone. I ate alone, in a corner. I still had the shakes from Raven jumping at my mind.

Somehow it kept striking me that everything I was eating had been alive and was dead. Green beans. Potatoes. Spam. Alive once, now dead, about to cycle dead through me. Earth was a place of death. Things got born, and I'd seen that sometimes, but I saw death every day. Death was big, death just kept eating, and eating, and eating.

After supper I made a quick trip to my room, looked under the socks in my one drawer, got my turtle pouch, and hung it around my neck. Then I walked down the road to the west, pretending to myself. Didn't want to admit what I was thinking. As I walked, I stuck my hand between my coat buttons and fingered the pouch beneath my shirt.

You must understand, this was the first time Raven came to me, my first knowledge of him.

Less than a mile out and off the road was the shack of a man I knew a little bit, Plebus, had seen him on the roads and nodded. Plebus was the local shine man, had a still somewhere, made his living on shine. Though it was illegal to sell booze on the rez, it probably was the best living. At maybe fifty Plebus drove a decent truck and was a big-belly.

I knocked softly on his door and stood well back till he came.

"Come in, come in, siddown, siddown. You want some coffee?"

We both knew what I really wanted, but he made the offer and I accepted. Politeness.

"Some weather," says he, "freezing one day, damn near hot the next. Hnnn. Damn!"

A little profanity, show that we are men talking together, old enough to drink like men.

The coffee had lots of sugar in, the way his mother or grandmother probably served it. I wondered if he spoke Lakota.

"You gettin' an education. I see you, up at that school. Gettin' an education, you real lucky. Wished I had one, wished I did."

He went on considerably about the weather, the benefits of an education, and how lucky I was. The message was, You are now a man, cause a big-belly is treating you like a man, talking to you like a grown-up and not a kid. It was the forthcoming whiskey that made me a man. Plebus was not only a shine man but a salesman.

I knew what he was doing but felt neither angry or embarrassed. I just sipped my coffee, said nothing, and stared at his nose. It was big, bulbous, and pocked deep with holes. I didn't see thousands of bottles of shine putting those pockmarks there, though that's what did it. Instead I got pictures of Raven pecking holes in his nose.

Raven pecks all the holes of death in this world.

At last he fell silent, worn out by keeping his end up. I said softly, "Whiskey," and my voice sounded to me like a croak.

He disappeared behind the kitchen and came forth with a bottle, a fifth. The label was Jim Beam, but that wasn't the product. I wondered where he'd found the bottle, whether he haunted the trash barrels behind the taverns in the white-man towns or maybe paid kids like me to bring 'em.

"Ten dollars," he said with a smile, like we were old comrades.

"I don't have any money," I said, bare, naked truth.

His smile got bigger, and he winked, but I could see a red flash of irritation in his eyes.

I reached into my shirt, got out the turtle, and put it on the table. "I wanna trade," says I.

His eyes shifted from red to the green of greed. *Frogskins,* I could hear him thinking.

The turtle was worth something. It was the fully beaded pouch Unchee made for me when I was born. In the old days every Lakota kid had one, and wore it to the age of five or six. Inside was my umbilical cord. Though I'd never worn my pouch, it was real traditional stuff, our way of recognizing our connection to our mothers. The custom was mostly gone by the 1960s.

This wasn't a pouch made up for tourists, this was the real thing. "Lemme see," says he. I handed it to him, and he felt through the skin for the cord inside.

He glanced up at me, not letting himself smirk. For a moment I didn't get what was going on with him. I thought it would just be the lust for frogskins. He could sell this piece to a serious trader for good money, twenty-five dollars at least. But that wasn't all of it, I could see; not even most of it. He held the pouch in both hands, kind of bent over it. Suddenly he looked at me, full in the eyes. Before I could cast my eyes down, I saw it. He was corrupting me, and he liked that. He was the one delivering the inevitable blow. I was giving up my old world for a new world that was seductive. The bottle. The modern world. Living the white way.

He jumped down behind the kitchen again, taking the bottle with him. In a snap he came back with another bottle, no label this time, a pint. He extended it to me with one hand, and put the turtle in his pocket with the other hand.

I took the bottle and left without a word.

I hardly even felt bad, hardly felt I'd surrendered or betrayed anything. Because I wasn't, as Plebus thought, giving up my heritage for a drink. I didn't need my people's past any more. I wasn't going to drink this bottle tonight, or become an alcoholic and waste my life. I was going to wait until I said goodbye to Grandpa and Unchee, without them knowing. Then I was going to walk into the Badlands late one afternoon, to the river and then deeper into the Badlands, until I was too exhausted to take another step. Then I was going to find a comfortable place to lay down, contemplate the Star People, leisurely drink the entire bottle, and pass out. The cold would get me. I'd heard it was a good way to go, an easy way.

After the cold got me, it would be the ravens' turn.

Remember, this was my first time under the sway of Raven. I didn't know his ways, or know how to keep his *awk* from becoming my song—not yet, not yet.

It was the True Bulls that saved me. Seems funny, but it's true.

That first evening home I just moped around the house, wondering if I should go soon or wait until after Christmas before doing my bottle trick. I was feeling contrary. Grandpa asked me after supper how my spirits were. I answered in English, "My spirit feels white." He didn't understand, of course, and looked miffed. When Unchee translated, softly, he looked more miffed. After that the two of them didn't have much to say to me, and I had nothing to say to them.

Bed time, as I was on the way to lay down, Grandpa said, "I been helping Gordon True Bull on the weekends. Why don't you come?"

I felt my back stiffen, and I wanted to give him a look, or say I was done taking orders from him, but I wasn't white enough to be rude to my grandfather, not yet. I nodded.

In bed I thought, well, what the hell, it would give me a last horseback ride, and that would feel good. I wondered if Grandpa would let me take the zebra dun, my favorite. An hour's ride up to the True Bulls, an hour back ... That horse had a beautiful lope.

Didn't matter what we did in between.

You will guess that I was in the shadow of Raven's wing sometimes, and sometimes not. As are we all, all our lives. But mostly I was living under it, and that is a choice.

The next morning it was fine. December is a variable month in the Badlands. In fact, at school Mr. Banks told us the story of Wounded Knee, how Big Foot's people came from Cheyenne River and down the wall of the Badlands and all the way to Porcupine Butte, trying to get to Pine Ridge, and had a whole year's weather on the way. Some days were warm and balmy. Some days it blew so hard Waziya must be angry with us, and worse than angry. Then balmy again. Then, right after all the killing, it snowed. That's what he said.

Made me think I ought to ask Unchee about that story. She was Mniconjou, from Big Foot's band. I wondered if any of her ancestors were in that fight. Unchee was born right around that time. But Unchee was forbidding, and if she didn't bring it up, a kid didn't dare ask.

After breakfast I grinned at Grandpa and set the dun to the lope that suited her and eased along. We didn't need any saddles, and sure didn't have any.

At True Bulls' it turned out we had a hard job, but a perfect day for it. They were making a paved driveway and parking area. I had to bite my tongue, 'cause nothing is rarer on the rez. Today we had to finish getting the forms ready and pour the parking area. As I drove stakes and held plywood and leveled it, I kept wondering why in hell the True Bulls would waste money on such a thing, considering Gordon's tires had long since made a lane and a bare spot to park. I also kept giving myself the only answer that came to me. Pretension, pretension, pretension. The three boys seemed awful excited, and I thought less of them for it.

The work was a little tricky. Jamie, Evin, and Lee, the three brothers eldest to youngest, spoke little Lakota beyond the words you use at ceremonies and in prayers. Grandpa spoke no English, and I only half spoke it. So Gordon had

to pass messages back and forth. "Hand me that hammer."
"You bet!" But we made good progress, and I learned to use
"You bet!"

We ate a big dinner in the house, lots of fried Spam
sandwiches, and then did the actual pour, which was time-
consuming and back-breaking work. Then, before the
screeding was done, Jamie, the oldest boy, eighteen, he does
a little jig and says, "Hot diggety damn."

Well, I was disgusted. If that wasn't the whitest way to act
on a day of white foolishness....

"It's time!" he went on, and his happiness included even
me. "Come on, you ball players. You too, Joseph." I walked
along behind the brothers, my limbs feeling stiff and foolish.

Behind the house stood a pair of tall, black-painted basketball standards. Plus a backboard, plus a hoop, and even a
net, all of it brand new. "Let's do it, *kolas*." I flinched a little
at the way he put an *s* on *kola* to make it mean more than
one. When does ignorance become disrespect?

Quickly Evin and Lee began to pour into a small hole
I hadn't seen at the edge of the big pour, and I pitched in.

Now I got it. Gordon True Bull wasn't building just a
parking area—he was making a basketball court for his
boys. That made a little more sense. They were big players
at school, and now they could practice at home. *Washtay!* I
felt kind of excited.

We mounted the standards in the holes and staked and
strung them with rope. We took care with the level work.
Hey, a basketball court, kind of snazzy!

Over supper I talked some with Jamie and his brothers,
Evin and Lee, and even felt some comradeship with them.
They'd ignored me at school—I was a blanket Indian, and
too far behind them in grades anyway—but now we were
starting to be friends.

"When'll it be set, Dad?" That was Jamie asking Gordon.

"We'll put the backboard up tomorrow after dinner."

"Come for dinner and we'll play," Jamie said to me. He had big buck teeth that made him look funny, but he was simple and sincere.

I couldn't help myself. "Washtay!"

The wild part of it was, I could jump, I could really jump, and it was fun.

First Jamie wanted to play horse, and I lost every game. Except for a little fooling around alone on the schoolyard at Kyle, I'd never touched a basketball. I was poor at shooting and terrible at dribbling. Jamie, Evin, and Lee were terrific, natural athletes playing their sport.

So I wanted to try something different, anything different. I'd watched kids play defense on the schoolyard, and thought I'd do better at that. I said to Jamie, "You shoot, I'll defend."

His face lit up. "For money?"

I scowled and took position. "For the honor of the True Bull family," I said, mock-growling.

Jamie bounced the ball lightly a few times, holding my eyes, deciding. Then he made a crossover step, went around me like I was a snubbing post, and flashed in for the lay-up.

Swat! He couldn't have been more surprised when I whacked the ball against the backboard. I was shocked myself.

I'd got beat on the first couple of steps, but I came hard behind him, and when he laid it against the backboard, I leapt over him and knocked it away.

"Illegal!" snapped Jamie, glaring at me.

"Pretty damn neat, though," said Evin. "Let me try you."

He faked toward the basket, made a quick step back, and shot from the foul line.

I took the fake, got caught too far under, lunged back out, and blocked it clean.

"Hot diggety damn," says Jamie. He liked that expression.

Lee tried me, Jamie tried again, they all tried. Short jumpers, driving lay-ups, hooks, finger-rolls, everything. I got a hand on about half the shots. Hey! Though I was bulky, then, now, and forever, I was tall and I could jump.

Couldn't dribble. Couldn't shoot. Couldn't pass worth a damn. Couldn't drive. But I had quick feet to stay in front of a ball handler, I could jump, and I had a natural timing for blocking shots.

I was loving it.

We played three against one, long shots forbidden. They had to come under the basket to shoot. Point for them if they scored, point for me if I blocked it.

They did some nifty passing. First game, they'd fake, get me in the air, pass it to another guy, and he'd score. I got whipped something like 20–3.

Lee showed me how to read the fake, wait for the jump. Next I got whipped 20–10.

Third game I actually won.

We played until suppertime, and I rode the dun home in the dark.

I went back every day the whole Christmas break. Jamie, Evin, and Lee gave me real tutelage at basketball, and I loved it. At the end of the two weeks I had three pretty good skills. I could block shots, I could rebound, and I could make lay-ups.

On the last day, when I was ready to ride home, the three of them kind of lined up and spoke their piece. "We want you to come out for the team." That was Jamie.

"Yeah," said Lee.

"You can do it," chipped in Evin.

I shook my head. I shuffled my feet. I mumbled something.

"Forget it, Bud," said Jamie, "we're not taking no for an answer. You can do it, and you're gonna do it."

"Team can use a big defender," added Evin.

I rode home slowly, my head in the clouds.

That night, packing my stuff, I found the bottle I'd bought from Plebus. Held it. Turned it around and around in my hands. Looked at my face distorted wide on its round surface.

I didn't see the young man who'd wanted to do away with himself.

That young man seemed like another person.

I felt all jiminy-jeepers about that.

Hadn't learned yet that the blackness is never another person—it's you, in the shadow of the raven's wing. You seldom get out from under, not for long, anyway, Not if you're an Indian. But for the moment, I was out.

Jamie took me to Coach Ragsdale the first day back. He took a look at what I could do, and what I couldn't, and said quiet-like, "Be at practice this afternoon. Monty will check you out some gear."

Hoka hey, Indian teams don't operate like others.

What you gotta understand is, basketball is king on the rez. Anymore these days, young men have no other way to win honors. In the 1990s you gonna steal ponies or scalp enemies? The hunting is damn near zero. You can't hardly get a decent job, can't much provide for your family. The Pine Ridge rez, where I come from, is the poorest county in the U.S.A.—highest unemployment, lowest income per capita. How do you think that makes us men feel?

In the old days a man got his rep by striking coups, and then counting those coups in front of all the people. That's how he got respect, got a woman, earned his place in the tribe.

Nowadays there aren't any coups. So we go for the closest substitute—points, assists, rebounds, and blocks, and a big crowd to cheer us on.

We go for the closest thing to war, games against other high schools, Indian and white.

The women do their old-time trilling for a good play.

Instead of the scalps on a coup stick getting you laid, it's that uniform.

So when Coach said, "Be at practice this afternoon," that fired me up. I got stoked. I was somebody.

That first season I didn't get to suit up for a game— Coach was waiting until I learned the ropes and saving my eligibility. But I started to do good in class. I wanted to speak English beyond "fast break" and "dunk." Soon as I got interested, they put me up a couple of grades.

My second season, first game, Coach subbed me in to guard a big center. Blocked his first shot, and one more after that. Also got two rebounds, turned the ball over twice, and missed the rim twice from two feet, a line score of twos. After that Coach put me in the rotation, and I got some minutes.

The next three seasons at Kyle I started at center. By then I was my full height, six-six, I could jump like an antelope. I didn't have much bulk, but I was quick and agile and such a good leaper I felt like I could defend any center in South Dakota. Most of all, I had a big wing span, bigger than a crow, more like a raven.

Pretty quick I learned enough English to flirt after the game with any white girl at any Dairy Queen in the state.

Coach Ragsdale taught me several things I have never forgotten, aside from basketball. He'd do a thing with his hips and shoulders and say, "You wanna be tough, you gotta swagger." I am still pretty good at swagger. He'd lean into my face (actually up at my face) and glower and command, "You wanna play big defense, you can't back down, not ever." And he taught that the family (in that case the team) is more important than the individual. "Here's where the individual really, truly gets his highest and best by throwing himself into the family, the team. Feel that energy moving you as one creature, feel where you need to be, what you need to do to be a perfect part of that. This is one of the meanings of *mitakuye oyasin*."

Thanks, Coach.

I wish I had learned as much in my classes as I did from Coach Ragsdale, but the classroom still wasn't my thing. I wasn't a scholar at anything. I did graduate, though, and I did start playing guitar. The used guitar, of indifferent quality, was a gift from Emile one birthday. First music was folk, I think because the songs were little stories, not newspaper stories but something more universal, little ways of telling how this romance felt, and that lost love, people expressing the goodness and the sadness of their lives. Anyway, what time I didn't spend practicing or playing I spent picking that guitar, and I got pretty good.

Need I say that my music led to many adventures, plenty of wonders, and all sorts of trouble?

JUTO THE WHITE WORLD

My music and Coach Ragsdale opened a door that
changed my life. You be the judge whether good or
bad.

Coach got me a basketball scholarship to Mary College
up in Devil's Lake, North Dakota, and reading taught me
the ropes enough to take it.

Mary was one of those places you never heard of, an
NAIA school that took a fair number of Indian students and
a few Indian ballplayers. At big schools, known schools, schol-
arships for Indian players were never-never. Just didn't happen. Think about it. There's a pipeline from the ghettos to
college ball. How many Indian players you ever see on TV?
In high school we're the best players in the whole mountains
and plains region. We're shut out of college, except for the
places you never heard of.

We're not gonna talk reasons, least I get mad.

Coach Ragsdale finagled this athletic scholarship, and
the tribe came up with a stipend. I was leery of it at first.
Can't tell you what it's like to come off the rez and live
among white people, and going to college was definitely
doing that. To us they are pushy, impolite, indecorous,
and generally out of line. We don't understand them,
they don't understand us. You white folks who've gone to

Mexico and been irritated by Mexican slowness will know what I mean.

And Coach came up with the one thing more I needed—like a roommate, only better, someone who would put me up, listen to me, help me out, steer me. No one needed one more, and my guide was named Bradley Dornan.

I was skeptical, living with some old teammate of Coach. Bradley was a grizzled, pipe-smoking black bachelor with degrees in communications, as the college called it. He ran the radio station. He broadcast the basketball games. He was a guy of wry humor and a skewed sense of life who never fit anywhere but was amused wherever he went. He let me have the basement apartment in his old Victorian. He fed me. He gave me advice about life and basketball. He listened to me when times were hard. He turned out to be my best friend.

Wouldn't this piss parents off? You get the important part of your college education from three people, your roommate, the one professor you hit it off with, and one professor you can't stand. My roommate was Bradley. He introduced me to the traditional college vices, getting loaded and getting high. He played guitar duets with me. And he showed me the way around the best of all your music, the blues. Bradley had an incredible collection of old-time blues musicians on 78s, the music that came up the rivers to Memphis, St. Louis, and Chicago—Blind Lemon Jefferson, Mississippi John Hurt, Henry Johnson, Huddie Ledbetter, Muddy Waters. Unfortunately, I also contracted from Bradley one of the intellectual diseases of our age. You call it agnosticism. I call it being a Great White Doubter.

Before I get to that, I'll tell the other parts of my college career. The basketball went fine. Played all four years, did good, starter the last two years. Never considered trying to go pro—not big enough, neither high nor wide. I had a lot of fun. My teammates called me Wings (another one of my gajillion names, inspired by Crow)—it was for my long arms to block shots, and the fans picked up on it. It was fun.

I learned that white college girls think of athletes as, well, stallions standing at stud. I got irritated about that sometimes. Other times I took advantage of it.

I did okay in my studies. My freshman English teacher was the one prof I couldn't stand, the blonde, fair Mrs. Standish, who looked like she'd just graduated from Young Republicans. She was always on my ass about one thing or another. Mainly, it was what she called my attitude. One day Mrs. Standish put it to me hard; she asked me, "Why are you all angry at white people? Isn't that visiting the sins of the fathers upon the sons? Is that fair?"

I said I'd tell her in one of those papers we had to turn in every Friday. Here it is. I forgot about it, but Emile saved it all those years.

Your ancestors did the stomp dance on my ancestors, yes, and that's a pisser.

You say, that was then, this is now. We're not doing the stomp dance anymore. Not fair to visit the sins of the fathers on the sons.

Yeah, it's not fair. So let's talk about your own sins, right now.

It's impossible for traditional Indians to live the way we want to today. We accept most of the compromises with good hearts. We start our cedar burning with cigarette lighters, and we drive to Sun Dance. But our old hunting life is gone. Our old religion is in tatters (your government consciously worked to destroy it). The ways that made us a people, that gave us a good life—they're gone. You made the world we live in, we didn't. In this world money and material things, that's what counts. In our world nature counted for more, spiritual things counted for more. Your poet Housman wrote, "A stranger and afraid in a world I never made." Though we're past being afraid, we feel like strangers in your world.

We're poor, very poor. Meanwhile, you're prospering on the lands you took from us with smooth words and bullets. How about a good example that happened to my people? The Homestake is the richest gold mine in world history. It sits in the middle of the Black Hills, which you signed over to us for as long as the grass grows and water runs downhill. When you found out there was gold in the Hills, you land-grabbed them. Your own Supreme Court says that's in violation of the treaty.

And how is that today? The mine is still producing gold. Every day now, every year for a century, it has minted money that made you rich and us poor. When my nieces have to hitchhike, the thought of the Homestake makes me mad.

More. You're doing the Great White Father crap. You control tribal governments through your Bureau of Indian Affairs. You give us the housing you think we need, the job training programs you think we need. You try to tell us how to use the minerals on our lands—our own sovereign lands—or not use them.

[I wrote this paper in 1974. Today I'd add that you want to tell us whether we can have gambling on our lands.]

I am warming to the subject. You assume we are lazy, dumb, shiftless, drunken, etc. (The black folks have told you about that.) Whether you want to help us because of it, or look down on us because of it, the assumption is in your faces—lazy, etc.

Which reminds me. You treat us like a conquered people. Some of you are proud of that, some ashamed of it. Either way, equally, you regard us as a conquered people. And you teach us to think of ourselves that way.

Think about that. What does it do to people, thinking of themselves as conquered, subjugated, defeated?

Last thing. Some of you believe we are noble savages, some believe we are dirty savages. Notice what those labels have in common—the word *savage*. Some of you idealize us, most of you despise us. Either way, we're not people to you, regular folks to hang out with. You don't see us. You see Crazy Horse and Sitting Bull way clearer than you see me and my relatives today. Five hundred years after you got here, we are ever more the invisible people. And that pisses me off.

What did Mrs. Standish say about my paper? Well, she made notes about spelling, comma splices, and vulgar language. She commended me for quoting Housman. About the content of the paper she said not one word. She gave me a B.

Afterward, I looked up comma splice. It means running sentences together without a period. Ever since, I have written all of those I want.

Generally, I made good grades. Thought I'd major in Indian Studies, which was hot in those days. My first teacher was a Chicago Jew named Ron Sternberg. He was the one professor I hit it off with, the person who changed my life. He was the sort of teacher common in the seventies who's probably on the outs now, was a hippie, a child of the sixties, with a Jewish Afro, jean jackets, and Birkenstocks. He was wild about his subject, anthropology, and completely devoted to his students. He hung out in the student union with us, drank beer with us (he wouldn't smoke dope because it would get him fired), drank endless cups of coffee with us, and talked about books, movies, philosophy, anthropology, and life. To spend an evening with Bradley and Ron was to go roaming through the whole world of ideas and the life of the mind. (Remember, what the white man sees as the life of the mind is not the life of the spirit.) The first personal thing Ron ever said to me was that I should major in Anthro and not Indian Studies, which for me would be a free ride. That's how I became an anthropology major in college.

It was Bradley and Ron who, without any particular intention, set me to thinking like a white man big-time. One night right before fall practice started we went to see *Straw Dogs*, a Sam Peckinpah movie that Bradley and I loved and Ron hated. We stayed up half the night drinking beer and talking about the movie, and the other half playing blues and talking about life. That night we added considerably to the decor—Bradley and I were ornamenting my apartment with the world's largest collections of beer cans, stacked floor to ceiling in the living room, all Budweiser for looks. Eventually it got so I had just a corridor to the sofa, TV, and coffee table—the rest was red, white, and blue aluminum.

Peckinpah's movie was said to be based on some books by Robert Ardrey, *African Genesis* and *Territorial Imperative*, which in turn were based on the work of anthropologist Raymond Dart. We went up and down and across, conversationally, about what they meant, these anthropologists' discoveries about the origin of mankind—Dart's evidence that human beings millions of years ago were meat eaters. The discoveries of the Leakeys at the Olduvai Gorge and Koobi Fora that proved humankind is much older than previously thought, and the implications of that for our notions of our human ancestry. We debated the Peckinpah-Ardrey notion of violence as a fundamental of human nature against the position that human beings were ancestrally vegetarians and cooperative, rather than competitive.

O, ye intellectuals, divining the nature of man! While denying the divine, of course.

It was exhilarating—the world of intellectual speculation was new to me, and I could hardly sleep for excitement after Ron left close to dawn.

The very next week, Intro to Anthropology class, we talked about the creation stories of indigenous peoples. Ron explained the basic kinds of creation in the U.S., Stacked World stories and Earth Diver stories, and he told a couple—how Earth was all water and Duck dove down to the bottom and brought up the first earth, and the world was made out of that, a classic Earth Diver story.

After class I went and talked to him, and we switched from "Professor Sternberg" and "Mr. Blue Crow" to "Ron" and "Blue."

"Ron, I don't see much in talking *about* creation stories, analyzing and classifying them in this way. I mean, the magic and mystery is taken out of them, the meaning is taken out of them."

Ron grinned. "I agree. So why don't you tell us a story, not analyze, and give us the poetry of it."

I'd trapped myself.

Nervously, I said I'd be ready at the next meeting. Hell, I remembered a lot of old stories, but I was no expert, and I didn't know what you would call a comprehensive Creation Story like a Stacked World or Earth Diver story.

That night I found a big book on Lakota mythology in the library and got a story out of it. It involved creation, but really it was the story of how Evil came into the world. And it was a hodgepodge—even the author admitted the stories were never told in this way. Still, it was made out of old, traditional materials, and I decided to go for it.

When the class was settled in, Ron nodded at me. "Ready, Mr. Blue Crow?"

"Come to the front or stay here?"

"As you like."

I took a deep breath, walked to the front of the room, carrying my sheets of paper. I turned and faced the white people. These were the people I'd been envying all my life. They had money, relative to me, who grew up without electricity. They had the power of knowledge—they'd made everything that ran their world, right down to the fancy building we went to class in. They had privilege—an employer would assume any one of them was smart and on the ball, and was likely to assume I was shiftless and lazy. You bet I was envious of these people. And now I wanted their approval. I started with a comment. "I'm going to use the word *god* here. It's not right—*mythic hero* would be close. But *god* is your word for these guys. Here goes."

I read the story out loud, the way I'd typed it up.

"The four first gods, Sun, Earth, Sky, and Stone, were lonely and longed for companions. Sky gathered them together and granted to each the opportunity to create a companion. Sky himself made Wind. Sun made Female Sun, or Moon. Stone made Thundercloud. And Earth made Passion, a beautiful woman.

"Passion was so beautiful that Earth became jealous of her. They quarreled, and Earth cast Passion into the waters. Then Earth was without a companion, and once again lonely."

I forced myself to make eye contact, especially with Rhonda, an attractive, blonde, pre-med student I'd been flirting with. I hoped she wouldn't think this story was anti–woman or anti–beautiful woman.

"Passion was angry, and appealed to Sky. 'Pity me, for Earth hates me, and I am an outcast.'

"Out of pity Sky gave her the waters as her domain, and ruled that she could associate with the gods.

"Soon Passion was bemoaning her outcast state to Stone. So entranced was Stone by her beauty that he forgot his companion Thundercloud and took Passion unto himself. And soon a son was born to them."

Jeez, my words sounded like Bible stuff. I looked nervously at the class fundamentalist, a farm boy, and the class atheist, a former fundamentalist with a chip on his shoulder.

"This son had an evil disposition, so Sky named him Evil One. Because of his rages, he is also known as Wind Storm."

My fear said, *Two names for the same god, Evil One and Wind Storm—that's gonna confuse them.* I shushed the fear.

"Evil One grew into a giant who loved rages and reasonless destruction. Passion sent him to torment Earth. Evil One also set out himself against the gods Beauty and Wisdom. But Beauty calmed him with her greater powers. Wisdom said to Evil One, 'We are sons of the same father, Stone. As the older brother, I require you to obey me.' So it is that when Wisdom and Evil dispute, Wisdom prevails."

I could just hear them muttering, The hell it does.

"Now Passion became infatuated by her own son, Evil One, and she bore him a son. For this infidelity Stone set aside Passion forever."

Is that why rock is so hard?

"The offspring of the incestuous act of Passion and Evil One was Demon. He was beautiful, alluring, cunning, and deceitful.

"Demon and Passion schemed to get him permission to live on Earth. Demon finally charmed Earth into admitting him to her abode. Now Passion had her revenge against Earth for making her an outcast—Demon would cause Earth trouble forever."

This was probably the first scheme, mother and son against the goddess Earth.

"On Earth, Demon's way has been to incite his father Evil One to greater mischief. Cunningly, he usually escapes blame. His special pleasure is tricking men and gods into ridiculous or shameful deeds, and then laughing at them. He even delights in tormenting his mother, Passion, his father, Evil One, and his grandfather, Stone."

Ungrateful child, an old theme. Other old themes were coming—rejection, resentment, and revenge. The dramatic part was coming up, too.

"Thundercloud looked angrily on the love between his creator and one-time companion, Stone, and Passion. Therefore he declared himself the enemy of the beautiful Passion and her child, Evil One. He sent his storms against them everywhere in the world.

"Passion asked Sky for help, so Sky decreed that Thunderstorm could not enter the realm of Passion, which is the waters.

"Evil One, whose other name is Wind Storm, defiantly went against Thunderstorm. Their battle was awesome and terrible. Thunderstorm cast his awful glance at the Evil One again and again, but Evil One is the son of a god and cannot be destroyed."

The thundercloud fighting wildly with the wind storm— I liked this part.

"Evil One struck over and over at Thunderstorm but could not hit him. The clouds boiled, lightning flashed, thunder boomed. Evil One (Wind Storm) roared back. Growing things were torn up by their roots. Forests were smashed. The strife between Thunderstorm and Wind Storm goes on to this day.

"So came evil onto our Earth. So walks evil here now."

I fidgeted, wondering what they thought. In a pretend offhand voice, I added a comment. "Your culture also has its story of how evil came into the world. Satan fell from the grace of God. Eve partook of the apple. So the whites also recognize the play of the large forces of evil in this world. Our account of the origin of Evil is different from yours." I ran my eyes around the room to see how my version of their culture suited, but I couldn't tell anything.

"Beautiful, beautiful," Ron said.

I took a seat.

"Beautiful, beautiful," Ron said again. A couple of the students echoed his sentiments—thanked me for doing it. But finally Ron himself broached a hard question. "We've heard a lot of these stories now, myths from all cultures." He stopped and looked imploringly at me. He wanted me to know what he was saying wasn't against me personally. "I wonder how we should understand these stories. I have a kind of theory. We seem to treat these stories like children's playthings, beautiful baubles of the imagination. I don't think that's how they're meant.

"Mr. Blue Crow, when you heard this story. Who told it?"

"My grandfather." I squirmed under my own answer, and under Ron's scrutiny. "Also, a lot of it from a book."

"When you learned this story from your grandfather, how did he expect you to understand it?"

I was too embarrassed to play this game. I just shrugged.

"I mean, everyone here is dazzled and charmed by this story. But when we leave here, we'll all rush back to trying to understand the implications of the theory of evolution for mankind. We'll talk about nature raw in tooth and claw. We'll look for missing links. We'll beat the bushes of New Guinea and search the dry canyons of East Africa for bones that fill in the picture. And we won't, any of us, give thought to the idea that your story, or other Lakota stories we call myths, may have light to shed on anything.

"Am I right?"

He looked around the class, but no one was ready to jump in fast, probably from social sensitivity.

"Well, I don't think that's the spirit in which your grandfather taught you the story. Is it? I mean, I think he was offering the story as a truth to stand on, a place to begin to understand the world. Wasn't he?"

Ron waited, and finally I said, "Yeah."

"Well, I want to put this question to all of us. We're all well-intentioned here. We all enjoy these stories. My question is, Do they have some real truth to offer? Or should we just listen, be charmed, and rush back to our scientific explanations? To Darwinism and its successors in the theory of evolution?"

Long pause. Finally Ron added, "This is very important. I open it up to the class."

Immediately the farm kid piped up and said his creation story was not any theory of evolution, it was the story as the Bible tells it. God created the world and mankind, and the Bible tells how it was done. He said this in a kind of belligerent way.

Ron nodded and thanked him.

Rhonda, the girl I wanted to go out with, spoke up next. "I'm pre-med. I don't see how this is debatable, really. This method, the scientific method, it's gotten us everything we have. Automobiles, airplanes, the landing on the moon. I mean, buildings, heating and air conditioning, penicillin, treatments for cholera, smallpox, tuberculosis, polio." She shrugged. "I mean, how can we ask whether to rely on science or on myth when we know what science has done for us?"

Ron said, "Some people say there's no conflict between the religious and scientific way of seeing things."

"Oh come on," said the class atheist, who was the best student besides Rhonda. He was a black-haired kid, intense, skinny as a willow limb, wanted to be a writer. "The Bible says we were created at a certain time and in a certain way. You can count the generations back and practically name the date. Science shows that the world is four billion years old—we have the geological evidence. Mankind is three million years old—we have the bones.

"I don't get this stuff." He sounded as impatient as he looked. "I was raised a fundamentalist, and I'm here to tell you, we don't need to go back to those superstitious ways of seeing things."

Silence. Rhonda broke it, looking at me regretfully, but speaking strong. "I think the world has passed the religious way by. Science tells us the truth about the world. Scientific medicine tells us how to heal people. All this old stuff is … It's in the way. It's holding us back. To heal people I don't need myths. I need statistical studies. And medicines. And medical technology."

She looked at me again and said in a kindly way. "I'm sorry, Blue."

"Mr. Blue Crow, you got things you want to say?"

I shook my head and said truthfully, "I don't know what I think about this."

Someone else did have something to say, and other discussion followed. I didn't hear it, really. I was in a carried-off state. The discussion wasn't meant to get anywhere anyway, ideas were just getting tossed around, like balls being juggled. Ron recommended that everyone think about the issues and let us go.

He turned to me immediately. "Thanks for the story. This is what our class should be."

And he walked off, leaving me holding the bag. I tried to catch up with Rhonda but missed her. I remember wanting to make a gesture of togetherness. And I remember thinking, without any reason I could explain, that I was making a choice, a fateful choice.

I never did get to go out with Rhonda.

A couple of hours later I took Bradley to the airport in his Saab. He was flying home to Chicago to go hear Josh White and spend time with a woman. My weekend was the season's first basketball practice Saturday at midnight. The college always started basketball practice on the first legal minute, and the fans turned out big for the midnight session. There's not a lot else to cheer about in North Dakota.

After Bradley said goodbye at the gate, I stood at the cyclone fence, fingers clawed in the wire diamonds, and watched the plane take off. It struck me how that big machine represented the path we'd been talking about very well. Magic travel, journeying that in the old stories would have been made into a miracle. Yet explainable, modern air travel, if you knew the science to grasp it. Talk about lift and pounds per square inch. No need to call down a magical eagle to bear you up.

On the way back from the airport, I carried my mind carefully, in a state of suspended animation, like it was infinitely delicate and about to break.

Unaccountably, old stories rose in my mind. How Inyan, Stone, the first being, alone in the world, took from himself and created Earth, and let his own blue blood flow and they became the blue waters of Earth, and the spirit of the water separated itself from the waters and stood upon the edge of Earth, and became Skan, Sky, which is not material but spirit. And so Stone created the first two other great gods, Earth and Sky.

I simply let this story, and others, play in my head, like music. Sometimes as I drove I looked in my heart and I saw, with clarity, two most strange feelings there. One was exhilaration, excitement at my new discoveries. The other was anger, not at whites this time. Anger at my people, anger at my family, anger at Grandpa, anger at my ancestors.

For some reason I couldn't go to my apartment. I felt restless. I drove around aimlessly for a while and finally went to the gym.

Here at least I belonged. I had a locker, sweat clothes, shoes and shorts, and a basketball. I dribbled on the cement of the locker room floor. *Bang-bang-bang-bang! Pound it into your head, Blue Crow, the old ways don't work.* I dribbled awkwardly around the benches, out the door, and down the hall. I never was much of a dribbler. When I got into the gym, I took on my athletic personality, Wings.

My mind two-tracked now, thinking philosophy and playing ball. I looked up at the lights and knew without words that science gave us the big banks of bulbs that light up whole gymnasiums. I took the ball hard to the basket, went up, and absolutely without frills, nothing but force, made a power dunk. I'd never become a shooter (no touch) but I could dunk and make some moves under the basket.

The ball whacked the floor, bounced right up through the net, and fell soft as a feather back through. I'd never seen that happen, and took it as a sign that things were super-cool.

Stand back to the basket, think. The sweat lodge—I sla-a-a-mm DUNKED it!

Free-throw line, eye the basket, rim made of metal—metallurgy is a science. The ball is the Sun Dance—one big step and jump to the bucket—THROW it down! THROW it away!

I felt savage. I laughed out loud. I was throwing away savagery, I was embracing civilization, and *I feel savage!*

Back to the basket, look back up at the glass, which science teaches us to make out of the silicon in sand. The ball is the Yuwipi ceremony—jump, turn in the air, and JAM it to the floor!

I hadn't missed a dunk. I wasn't going to miss a dunk. I was rockin' and rollin', I was in a groove, I was playing unconscious.

Right side of the basket, in close. The ball is, is ... the painted skull of the buffalo. Fake left, go baseline under the basket, JAM behind my head.

I was sweating way more than I should. I was breathing way too hard for a few minutes' workout. I was excited. I was avid. I was rambling and raging.

Same spot, other side, same move, harder for me from this side. The ball is the staff draped with eagle feathers. One dribble, drive beneath the basket, THROW it down, and it's GOOD!

For the next twenty minutes, alone, I played maybe the best basketball of my life. From every angle I attacked the basket. I pretended the ball was the *hanblechia* ceremony, the *hunkapi*, the *tapa wanka yap*, all our ceremonies, and I dunked every one, I threw them away and never missed a shot.

Switch shots—I was going to shoot hooks, harder for me. Back to the basket: The ball was the sacred hoop, it was the eagle-wing fan, the eagle-bone whistle—everyone of these emblems became a hook shot, and every hook shot fell. I couldn't miss—I'd never been so hot.

Everything I could think of that stands for medicine, our spiritual way of looking at things, which that day I was calling superstitious, I hooked it down or dunked it down.

When I could think of nothing more, I dribbled around the court, sweating, panting, wagging my head from side to side, working my mind. What have I not thrown away? When I'd thrown away everything, I was going to go to the other end, stand at the free-throw line, and shoot a three-quarter court set shot, which I was sure *would go in!*

Then I thought of it.

I hadn't thrown away the Sacred Pipe. Neither my own Pipe, the one I inherited from my great-grandfather, nor the father of all Pipes, the one brought by White Buffalo Woman and held by the nation's Pipe Keeper.

Desire rose in me like a hot geyser. I wanted to throw away the Pipe, all Pipes, and I would do it with jump shots. Normally, I was a lousy jump-shooter, but today I would make anything I let fly.

I picked my best spot, fifteen feet right of the basket on the baseline and threw the Pipe at the basket.

It hit the front rim and bounced back to me.

I shot it again. Hit the front rim and bounced back.

I shot it once more, harder. Hit the front rim and bounced back.

I shot it a fourth time, way too hard. Hit the back rim and bounced back.

I dribbled around. *Four times is enough. This doesn't feel right. Something …*

I went for a sure and easy shot, ten feet straight in front of the basket. This time I would throw away the White Buffalo Woman Pipe, the most sacred of all Lakota relics.

Dribble—I am a doubter! Dribble—I am a destroyer! Dribble—I am rampaging.

Leap and shoot.

It bounced back—I couldn't see which rim.

Leap and shoot—bounced back—couldn't see front or back rim.

Leap and shoot—looks perfect—the hoop sent it back.

It was like the old phrase says, there was a lid on the basket.

I tried a fourth shot. It was right in but I knew it had no chance. I reached out and palmed the rebound.

Couldn't throw the Pipe away. Well, hell. *I'll keep my Pipe as a sign of … a great past. Hell, I want to keep it anyway.*

Funny, it was like medicine made all those shots go in, and medicine kept the last one out. Funny, 'cause I was throwing away medicine. I gave a twisted grin and headed for the locker room.

I stood in the shower a long time. It takes a long time to wash away the past. *Go!* I said in my head. *Down the drain! Tradition, gone. Medicine, gone. Wash it away with the soap of science! Cleanlinness is next to white-man-ness.* I looked down at my bare, red body, and watched the white soap float down all over my skin, and took pleasure in my whiteness.

I felt my eyes well up, but with the shower water hitting my head, I couldn't tell if tears flowed.

It doesn't matter. It hurts to throw away a past, even a burdensome past. Tears are okay.

I am an agnostic. I am a skeptic. I am an agnostic. I am a skeptic.

I didn't yet have the term Great White Doubter.

I am a white man.

I dressed slowly, hoping no one else would come in. I walked out of the gym alone. It was twilight, the early evening of autumn in the north country. I looked around at the dark clouds, their edges lined with weak sunlight. I ran my eyes around everywhere, and suddenly I realized I was looking for Raven.

Raven? Why now?

Then I grinned and walked on. *White people aren't haunted by Raven.*

I checked out how I felt. Certain bounce to my step there. Wild, loose feeling in my joints. *Hey, I feel liberated. Yeah, liberated.*

I waggled my ass.

And maybe I feel queasy, too.

I hesitated, then kept going.

Now I can do stuff. Now I can go forth and succeed.

I waggled my ass with almost complete conviction.

It's okay. It's hard to become something new.

I'm liberated!

From that day I threw myself into college life in a new way. No more did I go home for visits, not to Grandpa and Unchee at Medicine Root Creek, not to Mom and my sisters at Wambli, not to Senior, wherever he might be. It was partly that I had an awful dilemma. I couldn't tell any of them, especially not Grandpa and Unchee, that I had thrown their ways on the ground, that I was walking not the red road, not the black road, but the white road.

To them agnostic, skeptic, and Great White Doubter would be just other words for white man. The killing at Wounded Knee was not an ultimate defeat. The loss of their offspring to the white man—that was defeat. I could not bring myself to deliver that blow.

Yet I was not like my ancestors, I was not like my family. I was setting down the old, dying ways, and taking up the new, the way of the future. I was setting down superstition, ignorance, poverty, and misery and taking up the path of science, technology, knowledge, productivity. I was setting down the ways that had lost, and taking up those that had won.

I was a Great White Doubting apple, red on the outside, white on the inside.

I was a turncoat.

I sought consolation immediately. When I picked up Bradley at the airport, I told him about my crisis of spirit, and my new stance—"I am an agnostic."

"Yes, I know." These quiet words felt like solid footing, a new beginning.

The next day I found Ron in his office and told him, "I am an agnostic." (You're with white people, you talk the way they talk.)

"That's the way it works," Ron said.

I can hardly describe to you, during that long North Dakota winter, how alone I felt. I stopped seeing my Native friends, simply stopped—I was not like them. I could not go home. I made new white friends—Bradley's crowd at the radio station—but they didn't become my friends exactly, they adopted a Native as a friend—it isn't the same. For the first time in my life I was truly alone, more alone than I had been in the early days at Kyle boarding school.

I was determined, though, absolutely determined, to live my new way, wherever it took me. And I had one great consolation. Though my family and my people would be disappointed in me, they were few. All the wide world of white people would support me. And they held the keys to the doors of success. If only I could outlast the hurt in my heart.

Luckily, Bradley came up with a good idea. He said I was the best interview on the team, and got me on the air after every game. Finally one day when we were sitting around his office at the station, he suggested, "Why don't you do an interview show with college athletes?" he asked. "You have a good voice, you have ideas, the athletes see you as one of them, it'll be good."

I did it and it came off well, a five-minute gig once a week. I liked being on the radio and began to work on my voice.

"Why don't you do an hour show on the blues?" he asked.

I thought about how much I liked the music, gave the show a shot, and loved doing it. I think Bradley was tickled by a red guy pumping the blues to a white audience.

Whatever, it worked out kick-ass. Bradley had tapes and records enough to fill a U-Haul. I was hot—knowledgeable, enthusiastic—and getting hotter by the day. My senior year was basically broadcasting Muddy Waters and John Lee Hooker, throwing myself into it. I picked the tunes, I intro'd them, I commented on them. It was fun. The Blue Crow, my show was called.

And it was looking like a door. I mean, I was a red kid, an outsider, thrown into the turbulent waters of a world that wasn't mine. How would people accept me? How the devil was I gonna get a job? You don't exactly see help wanted classifieds saying, anthropologist wanted. And I sure wasn't going to go to university for five or six more years and get any Ph.D. Oh, hell no.

I knew what would happen when the companies came recruiting. Who would get the jobs, the big fellowships, the government appointments? Wasn't the old-boy-white-boy network gonna take over? Wasn't the red nigger headed back to the rez the day the white boys and girls got their real start? Wasn't the red boy's first career move gonna be unemployment?

With Bradley and Ron's encouragement, I began to think, Hey, I am good at this stuff of spinning platters, even at punching out the news. I could make a living at this. It's a damn silly job, but it's a start. And maybe …

I had no faith at all. *Hokahey*, faith was a big part of what I threw away. You don't believe in spirits, you gotta make your own way off the rez.

In the end radio and my new white-man road did come through for me. For good and evil, they brought me Delphine.

PART THREE
RED ROAD, BLACK ROAD, WHITE ROAD

DELPHINE

"Mr. Blue Crow," said this voice on the phone, pearly but very professional. "My name is Delphine Ryan. I'm with the National Lawyers Guild Task Force on Racism and Jury Selection. I'd like to talk to you."

I mumbled something.

"Do you have time to meet with me? Perhaps tomorrow morning at the International House of Pancakes? I'll buy your breakfast."

I mumbled something she took for agreement.

She named a time and finished off with, "See you then."

She showed up with Santa Fe Red, a guy I knew from down at Cannon Ball on the Standing Rock Reservation. Red introduced us awkwardly, because our eyes were already making like magnets, couldn't let go of each other. She and Red sat across from me. I couldn't believe what I was seeing. To me the name Ryan meant Irish. Picture an exquisite, catlike creature, with small, high breasts, a sleek body, perfect—like she was turned on a lathe and given a high polish. She couldn't have been Irish because of two details: the kinkiness of her red-brown hair and the color of her skin. The skin was the color of coffee with a lot of cream, I mean a lot of cream. I thought she was the most beautiful thing I ever saw. Especially the most beautiful black woman I ever saw.

She was dressed in a dark red silk suit and cream-colored silk blouse with matching Gucci purse and shoes, saddle-colored. Gold stud earrings. I learned later that Delphine never wore jeans or other casual clothes. She always looked fit to be photographed for *Town and Country*. Even the long, slender, brown Sherman cigarettes she smoked looked elegant.

First off she launches into her spiel, forming her words and sentence with that same elegance. "I am a law student. I haven't taken the bar yet. At Standing Rock I'm doing some research. The National Lawyers Guild Task Force on Racism and Jury Selection sent me to Pine Ridge, actually, to find out why Native Americans never get on juries. We think a red man deserves a jury of his peers. The Task Force intends to help formulate some new rules, or procedures, or whatever is needed."

She paused for breath and I jumped in with a tease. "So folks like me can be hanged by people of our own skin color."

"Something like that." Her eyes smile for the first time. She rushes on with those words. "I have just arrived at Standing Rock, with the same questions I asked at Pine Ridge. Do you have anything to say? As a Sioux you must be concerned, and as a member of the media perhaps you'd like to speak out. I would be glad to quote you."

She took all this very serious, and I guess I do too. But right then I was feeling like Billie Holiday had walked into the House of Pancakes in Nowheresville and was lighting it up. I wanted her to sing "God Bless the Child That's Got His Own."

I mumbled, I stumbled, I moved my mouth and said nothing. Finally, I supposed I guessed I didn't know anything about it. They brought me pancakes, and I buttered and syruped. Ever after, Delphine would be linked in my mind with hot butter and sweet syrup.

Out she came with a whole bunch of questions. "Do you know that juries are selected from lists of registered voters?"

"No."

"Do you know that Shannon County, down at Pine Ridge, is a jillion percent Lakota but only a small percentage of the registered voters are Indian?" (She quoted the numbers, but I don't remember them.)

"I didn't know that."

"What do you have to say about why Indians don't register to vote? Or vote?"

I just shrugged. But I was glad she was asking me. She had me mesmerized. I kept mumbling things like, I suppose I guess I don't know.

"You're an important person in the college community," she said. "You have a radio program, you're a star on the basketball team. You ought to inform yourself about issues that concern your people."

Feeling real BMOC for the moment, I said, "I'd like you to teach me." I reached out on the table and covered her hand with mine. She left her hand there.

"About time," said Red. "You two gonna do it right here or you gonna go home to bed?"

Delphine and I laughed, and turned a corner into our future.

Delphine Ryan spent the weekend in bed with me, gentle and sweet and loving and altogether terrific if you didn't mind listening to her theories. Monday morning she pointed her Datsun 240 Z, which fit in the Dakotas about like banana trees, toward Pine Ridge, bound to do her job. She drove back every weekend until school ended, and we experimented with blending sex and politics. I got an education in what white folks think should be done for red folks. (Funny that she was always the leader in this department—she wasn't the redskin.) She tried to teach me about modern jazz, which I hated (and still do). She told me about her ambitions. She was going to represent her home district in Congress. The first woman, she said, never said a word about being the first black woman, from the somethingth district in Seattle, which I presumed was a black area. She talked politics, she talked philosophy, she talked social change.

I listened, after we'd made love. I didn't care what we talked about. I loved the color of her skin, and its softness, like the skin of a peach. I loved her perfect body and her elegant way of moving. I loved her Nefertiti head. I loved the way she used her eyes, her hands, and the language of her body in place of words. I loved how loving she got, and how loving she made me. I loved Delphine.

In bed in our motel room one night (she always got us a motel), I woke up without knowing why. We were a mismatch in one way. Not long after the sun went down, those days, I got sleepy and went to bed. Maybe it was the basketball workouts. Anyhow, ten o'clock was near my limit. So she'd come to bed with me, make love, and get back up. Stay up through the dark hours, she would, sometimes write, write, write in her journal. Seemed she never slept.

This time she was sitting on the edge of the bed looking at me, looking at me serious and deep. As usual, she had that way about her. Dressed in nothing but a big T-shirt, Delphine could look like she was fitted out in cocktail party dress, high heels, and a single strand of real pearls.

I looked back at her. I could never read her eyes when they got dark like that.

She says, "I want to talk about the future."

I sat up on some pillows. I didn't want to talk, really. What future? I was about to finish (not graduate) and go back to the rez. She was slumming between Stanford and the House of Representatives. *'S been good to know you, kiddo,* I thought, but I didn't say the words.

"Come with me," she says. "Live with me." And then she gives her quirky smile and says,

Come live with me, and be my love,
And we will all the pleasures prove.

She was like that, quoting things. It felt like ... wearing drop-dead earrings or a really fetching silk blouse of a color so exquisite it hurt your eyes. It made life seem ... special. Elegant and formal. But formal with queen-sized play of emotions just under the skin. Even that theoretical stuff she was always going on about, it animated her face and eyes and made her skin glow and you could see her passion. If you turned the discussion real personal, she'd clam up or steer it back to politics. But you could see the passion. "I have a great apartment in Seattle. I'm going to spend months studying for the bar. Come live with me."

Oh, Delphine, I loved you.

So my heart said, Go for it. I confess it also said, Meal ticket.

I reached out and took her ever so gently by the ear lobes and pulled her to me, kissed her seductively, and said, "Sure."

She nuzzled me, and let me hold her a long time before she got up again. When I turned over at two or three in the morning, she was standing by the window, taking turns between writing in her journal and smoking a Sherman, staring into the dark glass. For the first time I wondered, *How dark is the shadow for you, the shadow of your Raven's wing?*

I didn't even go see Grandpa and Unchee, just wrote them a note that I was going to Seattle and I'd send my new address—that's how far I'd gotten from the way I was raised.

Delphine had an apartment overlooking Lake Washington, west of the university, handy for her law school years. It was handsomely furnished, and I noticed she had enough money that she didn't even sublet it while she was gone. I was just beginning to get the plenty-of-money picture, and I wondered how a young black person gets affluent. But I waited for her to tell me, all in her time.

Right away she drove me downtown—in that 240 Z—and got me fitted up with a couple of good-looking suits, not old-fashioned three-piece outfits like from Brooks Brothers but slick threads for a swingin' dude. I was still waiting.

Hoka hey, I was also feeling pretty good. Good digs, good threads, good entree to the world I'd been shut out of, good woman. Woman shadowed here and there, maybe, but good materials, the best. And I was feeling queasy all at the same time. I mean, Delphine had confidence, but me, why should I? Man with red skin out in the white world, nothing he can go back home to. Good woman but no job. No lead on a job. And maybe no white people want me to have a job. How long can a red man keep a woman if he doesn't have a job? What happens if the meal ticket gets canceled?

The second week Delphine took me home. The family pretty much spent summers on the island, she said, like I knew what "the island" meant. Turned out we drove up to Anacortes, rode the ferry to Friday Harbor, and Delphine's dad picked us up there in a Land Rover.

"Welcome, Blue," he said to me, holding my one hand in both of his. First surprise—Michael Ryan was white as the Michelin Tire man. She'd said he was a lawyer, a partner in a powerful downtown firm. I expected him to look more like Ed Bradley than Morley Safer.

He steered the Land Rover up high to a house that had a splendid view of the harbor and the Sound. Matter of fact,

Puget Sound spread out in every direction, looking like gold leaf in the sunset. You might have thought, How beautiful. I thought, From a place like this, even the ocean looks like money.

"The ladies are late," Mike said as we entered the house from the garage. "Sailing—it's racing season. I leave that to the younger generation now," he said with a self-deprecating smile. "Poe is a judge."

"Poe is my mother's name," said Delphine. From what she'd said, she thought her mother was a waste.

Mike steered us to a big living room with a spectacular view of the Sound. My mind was straying. Since this man was utterly white, Poe must look like Cleopatra, right? It would take a Cleopatra of a black woman to win a man as upscale as Michael Ryan.

At that moment three of the best-looking women you'll ever see in your life strode up the stairs and greeted me. Delphine's sisters, Meg and Bess, led the way with sisterly hugs. Poe gave me a bigger hug, and murmured, "Welcome, welcome, Blue. We've heard so much about you, all of it wonderful." Delphine hung in the background, half-smiling, watching my face.

I hardly heard what was said. I kept looking at the color of Poe's skin. It was radiantly pink. Her eyes were green. Her hair was blonde.

I checked out the sisters. Fair as could be, one auburn-haired, the other blonde. Any of them could have auditioned for the lead role in the life of Grace Kelly. Poe showed me photos of Meg and Bess racing on a variety of small craft, each representing more bucks than Grandpa would make in a lifetime. They were so keen, even now they were using their vacations to race together. Their talk of Cal 20s, spinnakers, steering downwind, and hitting marks was Greek to me. I thought, Well, Lakota would be Greek to them. It didn't occur to me, not yet, that they wouldn't care.

Mike told a Greek story, as a matter of fact. "In the glorious summer of 1954, twenty-four years ago," and here he gave Delphine an affectionate smile, "Poe and I went to Europe for the first time. To Greece. It was our first real vacation."

"A month! I always had a thing about Greece," said Poe. "You look at those statues and you think, they're the best-looking men in the world." Poe looked tickled.

"We went to Delphi," he pronounced it del-PHEE, "where the oracle is. There's an amphitheater in Delphi, thousands of years old."

"A natural amphitheater," put in Poe, "where they do Greek drama."

"But not that night," said Mike. "Your mother and I went up to the amphitheater late. There was the thinnest of new moons, and we wanted to see it."

"I wanted to see it," said Poe. "Your father was never that romantic."

Now Mike smiled a smile of deep delight in the past and affection for the present. "We sang a Greek song in that amphitheater that night, your mother and I. Nine months later this one was born." He put an arm around his youngest daughter's shoulders. "So we named her Delphine."

The sisters' eyes seemed to express ... I couldn't tell what.

Poe went to the kitchen to check on dinner, and a moment later Mike made an excuse and followed.

The three sisters were eyeing each other strangely.

I saw Mike put his arms around Poe and kiss her in the hall, a passionate-looking kiss.

Finally, Delphine said, "Blue, you should know we've heard other versions of that story at other times."

Meg said quietly, "Delphine"—a warning.

"We don't know which of the stories ..."

Beth coughed as a caution. Mike and Poe strode back into the room, beaming.

So what is it, a question of infidelity?

O Delphine, do you wonder whether there's a nigger in the wood-pile?

At that moment my heart leapt the distance between my lover and me, and I understood her completely, and loved her utterly. *The shadow.*

Soon Poe led the way into the dining room, where a Vietnamese woman in a uniform served a dinner that was too refined for my taste. I just nodded when they exclaimed about the wine. I was sitting between Meg and Bess, trying not to look too much at Delphine. My mind was going, Why didn't you tell me? How come they're white and you're black?

Had she ever said even, "My family, they're lighter than I am"? Not that I could remember. She had a soft, whispery, come-hither voice. Feeling the way I did about her, I didn't always listen to the words.

She sure didn't say, "My family is white as pastry dough, and they live all the way white. My father makes money like a pasture grows grass. My mother heads up charities that give money to people like you. We're into sailing, where even the clothes are white. One of my sisters is on track to become a federal judge, the other wants to start her own publishing company. They'll probably make it. And then there's little old me, with the touch of the tar brush, ain't it cute?"

I spent dinner smiling and nodding and agreeing and wondering what every damn one of them must have wondered, and probably still wondered. Who, where, when, how? Who slipped it in, where? Grandparent, great grandparent?

What were the circumstances? Was it passion, carrying the lovers to mad heights? Was it a one-night impulse? A rape? An episode between patriarch and servant? A liaison between woman of the house and gardener? Who was the man standing in the shadows of Delphine's past?

Did Mike and Poe sometimes think they made one child too many? What did they say to each other when Delphine got to be a toddler and her skin color was no longer an infant aberration? And when her hair didn't soften as she grew, but coarsened? And Delphine just generally looked like, looked like, well, she looked ... Negroid!

Did the sisters sometimes want to disown her? Did they ignore her on the playground of the Montessori school? Did they want her with them when they tried on clothes at boutiques? Did the parents want to send her to Pine Ridge to get her out of the way? Just sometimes, to their embarrassment, under the cloaks of their smiles, behind the wash of their embraces, did these lovely, gracious people wish their daughter and sister didn't exist?

And, *oh yes, and, Delphine, why didn't you ever talk about this?* I kept looking across the table at her, but she wouldn't meet my eyes. She was in her Egyptian empress mode, poised, polite, and impenetrable.

How deep is the shadow of the Raven's wing for you?

Before we left, Mike called me to one side. "I understand you like broadcasting," he said.

"Yes."

"You want to continue in that." It was a statement—clearly Delphine had prepared him.

My throat felt half clogged. "Yes."

He two-fingered a sheet from a message pad from his shirt pocket. "This is the name of the general manager at KSOL, Kay-Soul, they call it. And the phone number.

Delphine thinks this is your sort of station. Give Ed a call. I think he'll help you out."

Delphine wanted to risk only a quick overnight at the island house, not a whole weekend. In the morning we got up late. Fruit, cereal, and milk were set out, but everyone was gone to the yacht club. On the way to Anacortes Delphine and I stood at the back rail of the ferry. We were each lost in thought, and the ferry was lost in a gray, low-clouded day.

I'd just had my first experience of the old-boy network. Me, Joseph Blue Crow, a kid from the Badlands who never spoke English or went to school till he was fourteen—me, plugged into the old white-boy network, and maybe even using that damn thing to get a job in radio, in the media. Ain't it a hoot?

Ain't it something else too?

But I wasn't quite sure what something else. My feelings about it were squiggly, and I couldn't quite get hold of them.

But it's good, ain't it, getting on the inside? Where we've always felt excluded, we who ain't white? This is what I've always wanted, isn't it?

When you throw yourself into a new world, when you have nothing to go back to, you hold on to whatever bit of flotsam you can.

I touched the message slip in my breast pocket, took it out. The wind made it flutter, but I held on.

I turned to face Delphine. She was looking down, into the ship's wake, a churning white in a sea of gray. It was beginning to mist, or rain lightly, and I felt chill, summer day or not. I tucked the slip back in my pocket and put my arm around her waist.

"What kind of job at Kay-Soul?"

"Ask Ed. But apparently you start cueing records and reading commercials and learn the electronics stuff, then work your way into a jock spot."

"Jock." I'd never got used to having that word mean disc jockey, not a real jock like me.

She turned to me. "The deal is, you start as a caddy to a jock. When you're ready, they try you when they don't have many listeners—midnight to six A.M. on a weekend, maybe." She took both my hands in hers. "It's a good shot. Call the guy." In the mist her eyes looked bright, the one glow in a gray day.

I squeezed her hands a little. "Thanks. Thanks a lot." I meant it and didn't mean it. Glad to have a shot, a shot at anything, but unsure about ... *Well, hell, it's the way of the world, isn't it?*

I squeezed her hands hard. She gave me her eyes this time. "How come? How come you didn't tell me?"

A wry smile.

"Who are you, dark lady?"

This she decided to answer. "I'm the same as you, one of the dispossessed." Her lips were all quirky, but her eyes were sober. She spoke no more. She turned and looked down into the wake of the ferry.

"But you're dispossessed in the midst of it," I said to her shoulder. "Right in all that good stuff, wealth, position, power, influence. You're in it but not of it. It's them, it isn't you. Huh?"

She turned her head sideways and looked at me. Droplets were forming in her hair. Finally she said, "We have a chance, you and I. Let's not throw it away."

That was the strangest of all, for Delphine did not say it in her own voice. She said it in Raven's voice.

I waited, stunned. *How?*

She turned her face back to the waters.

"Delphine." She looked at me in a spirit of challenge, offering the angle of her Egyptian head and the light in her Ethiopian eyes. Those were her only answers.

So I took her shoulders and pulled her to me and kissed her. Her nose was wet and cold, but her lips and tongue were warm. Cool words, hot mouth. I held her close and wouldn't stop kissing her. I wanted to pull her inside me. I felt … strange.

Finally she lowered her head, held herself against me for a moment, and turned back. I saw her eyes go to some island, behind us, whatever island, a fleck of granite and evergreen between a dark gray sea and a light gray sky. Then she looked at the horizon—just gray, stretching forever, sea and sky the same, maybe the same all the way across the North Pacific. Finally she looked down, at the wake of the ferry, a great froth of whiteness spuming behind us. She watched it, with no expression I could see.

I watched it. I felt its draw. I felt how it would suck you down, into the depths.

VENTURING FORTH

At Kay-Soul I was no more a water boy than the other jock caddies. I bided my time, paid my dues. I worked on my voice. (I am deep-piped, a bass clarinet. Not a reedy bassoon or a brassy tuba—a velvety, silky bass clarinet.) I showed them I could cut a mean commercial. I listened to the pros and worked on my patter. (You don't stick astrophysics between cuts of bubble-gum rock.) I learned pop and folk and rock, to go with blues. Where a decade before I didn't know who the Beatles were, I now became a walking encyclopedia. I was good. Took me only six weeks to get trial spots in the middle of the night on weekends, and management told me I was in line for a regular spot. I was a young man on the rise.

Delphine did her bar studying. She dropped me off at the station in the Z car and picked me up after work. In between she crammed. When she entered the bar, her dad had promised her a place in the firm. The firm would be privileged, he said, to have a graduate of Stanford and University of Washington Law. She said she hadn't told him her actual ambition, to get elected. She studied with a determination I didn't quite understand. I mean, the grades were only pass-fail, right?

She told me regularly how proud of me she was. She told me I was going to make it. She told me I'd already achieved far more than most people ever did, just getting off the rez and through college and into a good job. After I got my own spot, what did I have in mind? Did I want to develop a show devoted to the blues? Did I want to develop an Indian music program? Public radio might do either one of those, she said, and it could go syndicated.

I listened and I tried to believe her and believe in a bright bauble of a future and I never stopped being afraid.

I learned not to talk about my past. Never told her much about Grandpa and Unchee. Never told her at all about being called to bear the traditional ways of my people. I'd gotten ashamed of all that. It was something I'd overcome. Talking about it would be carrying a burden into the future.

I didn't think about it either, refused to think about it. I started putting away beer so I wouldn't have to think about it. I anticipated the day when I could forget it with Wild Turkey instead of Oly. Like the jocks did, like the lawyers at the chi-chi downtown lunch spots did, like the real-estate agents and stockbrokers and all the on-the-rise people did. Wild Turkey obliterated more than Oly did, and faster.

I was rising. I was becoming white bread.

Indians who are red on the outside and white on the inside, on the rez they call these people apples. I prefer to call them white bread. Red-brown on the outside, white on the inside, all the good stuff bleached out, and puffed up.

I never wrote Grandpa and Unchee that first year, not once. Just didn't. Couldn't bring myself to do it. Slammed my grandparents into a bottom drawer of my mind, put others in there, too, like Emile. Never opened that drawer. Spent a lot of time, mentally, not even looking in that direction.

Delphine and I made new friends. With her making friends seemed a kind of program. Seattle was multi-racial and not necessarily a bad place to have a face of a different color. Unless you are dealing with cops or rednecks, naturally. Could even be an advantage, sometimes, if you needed something from just the right people, the hip, the with-it. After all, it was a brand-spanking new 1978, and things were different. Now everybody of every color had an equal opportunity to become white bread.

Our best new friends were Dennis and Li Ming Oh, a Chinese-American couple our age. Dennis was doing a Ph.D. in economics at UW. Li Ming worked in an art gallery downtown and was a painter—huge canvases, completely abstract, but with a wild vitality, made you feel like they were full of action. Good people. And people of color who were moving into the mainstream, like us. Li Ming had been born and raised here. Dennis came from Taiwan.

We went for pizza, we went to the movies, we did a few rock concerts, we talked through the night at coffeehouses. When we wanted to splurge (or Delphine wanted to treat), we went to a Sonics game, especially against the Trailblazers. I'd still loved basketball, and these guys were the best in the world. Altogether we were friends. Our biggest deal, really, was the Monopoly games we had. You cannot imagine. Every Saturday we went out or played Monopoly, and those games were a blast.

Good times. We talked about the music we loved, hot new movie stars, going to Mexico for spring break, how the Supersonics were doing, and our hopes and dreams. It occurs to me only now that we never talked about our families, the worlds we came from, our roots, the religious ways we were raised in. (For one thing, our ways now were purely secular, based on science, aimed at success, which meant money.) We didn't even talk about the present. Our thoughts were on the future. Maybe that was because we were young.

We didn't learn about where each other came from. Li Ming's parents were immigrants, Confucians or Taoists or Buddhists, I guess, but we never spoke of it. Dennis's parents were ... I think their religion was the Hong Kong stock market. Delphine was raised a Catholic, but it never came up. Nobody even asked me about my religious ways, which were supposed to be interesting those days, and I never brought it up. None of us wanted to be that uncool.

I remember a curious event about the way our pasts hovered near us, but we ignored them. I kept the family Pipe on the headboard above our bed. Our bed was king-size, with one of those fancy bedspreads that folds back over the pillows. Delphine and I kept the house immaculate (her insistence), and we displayed the Pipe handsomely, like you would put out a good piece of African art or something.

Mind you, I wasn't a Pipe carrier and had never smoked that Pipe. Carrying a Pipe is a solemn responsibility, its sacredness honored by a ceremony. I left that road before I was old enough to carry a Pipe.

Dennis saw it through the open door, my handsome pipe bag, fully beaded, displayed on a folded, white-tanned doeskin.

"What's that?" he said. He walked into the bedroom and looked at it close.

"Beautiful," said Li Ming. She was right behind him. Dennis wore little wire-rimmed glasses that made him look like a jeweler oculating something small. Li Ming wore the biggest glasses you ever saw, like coasters in front of her eyes. Right now their eyes were soaking up my pipe bag.

Sitting at the dinner table, counting out money for the Monopoly game, I didn't think anything about their words.

"Blue, what is it?"

I got a bad feeling and jumped up.

They weren't touching it, though, just standing by the side of the bed and looking.

I went straight to it and picked it up.

"My great-grandfather's Pipe," I said. "My grandmother gave it to me to keep."

Delphine appeared in the doorway.

"There's a pipe in there?" chirped Li Ming.

"White Buffalo Woman brought the Pipe to my people," I said. "Centuries ago. A Lakota carries a Pipe because it brings him power."

"Oh!" she squealed, like she'd heard a fairy tale that charmed.

"Can we see the pipe?" asked Dennis.

I looked at them. I knew what their feeling was. They were really keen to see it. Like they would have been keen to see an ankh, a scarab, a Zulu mask, or a staff made from the dried penis of a walrus. They were curious. They were titillated. They wanted a glimpse back into an exotic and romantic world.

I regard what I did next as a personal low. I undid the thongs that held the Pipe bag, reached in, drew out the stem and the bowl, and displayed them to my friends.

I take a little comfort in the fact that I didn't put the Pipe together, making it into a living vessel of power. Very little comfort.

And I didn't let them touch it. They wouldn't have asked, any more than they would have asked to touch a Picasso etching.

I noticed that Delphine had come close. She was looking hard at my face, not the Pipe.

Li Ming and Dennis oohed and aahed. They asked about the circles carved in the upright part of the bowl, and I explained that these represented the four winds. Dennis asked what the bowl was made of, and I said catlinite, and told how it came from a quarry in Minnesota. They asked about the stem (water birch), the brass tacks, the paint, the feathers. I told them something about each bit, all of it factual, none of it true.

I say not true because I omitted the truths that were crucial. This was not a quaint object to me. It was not old-fashioned. It was not an example of old-time, primitive beliefs. It was not a relic of an enchanting past.

It was my great-grandfather's Pipe. It was power, handed down through the generations, now residing in my hands. Even if I believed its power was past, not present, it was part of my family's story.

So I was encouraging my friends to look at my family as something quaint. At the very least.

Tadpoles swam up and down my spine.

I put the Pipe away and we went back to our game and laughed and cut up and competed like robber barons and had a good old time. For me every smile was fake, every laugh was hollow.

For once, late that night, Delphine played the aggressor in bed. She came at me, she played, she had fun, she rioted. A lot of the time she really did have fun. Some of the time she watched to see how I was reacting. And she tried to fuck me back into her world.

It didn't work. I tried, oh, I tried, but it didn't work.

And the next morning I felt perfectly empty.

I saw a woman in a TV commercial pantomime saying, "Oh." She formed her lovely lips into this impeccable circle and said, "Oh." Except no sound came out. She spoke, and nothing came out.

I felt like her little "Oh."

Oh, the Monopoly games. Very intense, at least for Dennis and Li Ming. I am a hoot and holler player of almost anything. I chant when I roll the dice. I squeal when someone lands on my property, and moan when I land on theirs. I like little pranks, like shorting people a buck or slipping them a buck too much. During our Saturday games I mostly made popcorn, told jokes, and was the first player to go bankrupt.

My cavalier style frustrated Delphine, who was my partner, but, hey, I considered it *playing*.

Delphine went at Monopoly like a dynamo, wheeling and dealing for property and wealth. She had a definite idea what she wanted, which was not so much money as power. And the way to power was to build alliances. Early in every game Delphine would make deals with other players—"Give you free rent on Indiana for free rent on St. James." With these deals a tangled web she would weave, though she did not practice to deceive. They would become elaborate, and sometimes would not work to her advantage—Indiana might have a house and St. James none. But Delphine honored whatever deals she had made, believing that the honor of the player was crucial, and firm alliances were more important than quick payback. She would maneuver shrewdly, turn down a deal that looked good, do something that helped a partner a lot. On the other hand, if you were going down, Delphine would let you go fast. "First rule of politics," she would say, "don't keep your money on a horse that's out of the race."

Sometimes when Delphine made a trade of properties, she would ask for something extra in the deal that was political—"Pacific for Ventnor and your support for the ERA." (O times gone by! Twenty years ago ERA didn't mean baseball as often as it meant the Equal Rights Amendment, one of her most avidly championed causes.) Or she would say, "Let's show 'em cooperation is better than competition."

I got into that spirit too.

Delphine usually allied with me or Li Ming, not Dennis. "Family is the first loyalty," she would say, "women the second. Dennis, you're a natural-born Republican." This would get a laugh. "You're in love with money." Sometimes, when only she and her ally were left, she'd suggest quitting and both celebrating victory.

Delphine won a lot, but Dennis won the most. (I never won, but I had the best time.)

Dennis *was* a natural-born Republican, or at least moneymaker. While the rest of us just played, he calculated cost and benefit ratios, or whatever you call it that means figuring your risk against the probable return, and he calculated them naturally and almost automatically. To Dennis it was not a game of chance.

Li Ming played from a different place yet. She played cheerfully, politely, wisely, and with a sort of supreme confidence that she was entitled to come out on top. (I think maybe the Chinese *do* feel that way.) When she had an advantage, sometimes she would team up with Dennis and sweep around the board majestically, conquering all. I said once she charged like a Mongol horde. She frowned slightly and answered, "I advance like an Empress making an imperial survey."

The frown was probably because of the reference to race. Our way was to be racially equal by acting like race didn't exist. I never once heard Dennis or Li Ming speak of discrimination against them. On the contrary, they acted like members of a privileged class, with a right to whatever their hearts desired.

Another part of the code was that Delphine could talk about Native Americans to a fare-thee-well, and Hispanics, and blacks, but never could she say she was black. Never mentioned a slight she got because of her color. Never said a word about how she felt about being black. Around these folks I worked at being color-blind too.

Publicly, Delphine was always optimistic. I wondered what she felt inside, and what she confided to her journal.

I learned that the way I was raised and taught about money was different from everyone else's there. Delphine was born to money and had no desire to accumulate hoards of it. Money was a tool that got you what you really wanted, alliances and power. Dennis and Li Ming, though raised in different countries, had a common attitude about money. It was fascinating, went something like this—*Money is worth having in itself. Safety and power in the world mean getting lots of it and putting it away.* These two were in their midtwenties, living poor, but already each of them had an IRA.

The way I grew up, and most Indian people—hey, way different. When you wanted something, like a good mule, you went to work and made money until you had enough. Then you quit the job, bought the mule, and enjoyed your life. When you wanted something else, maybe a truck, you worked until you got it and quit. This stuff of having a job all the time, making money and THEN deciding what to spend it on, *hoka hey*, to us that was white-man foolishness. Life was the point, not money.

So, one way and another, I didn't feel the same about the Monopoly game. I mean, I didn't feel like money was green blood.

One night when Li Ming partnered with Delphine instead of Dennis, something odd happened.

First came the usual. Webs of relationships, bands of power, shifts of wealth from one monopolist to another. (Never to a janitor or groundskeeper, of course.) Dennis played superbly, I played badly, he tried not to show his impatience. Finally my incompetence landed me on Marvin Gardens when I couldn't hack the rent. "Think I'm done," says I.

"You can pay me if you mortgage everything," says Li Ming.

I shrugged. "Let's not kid ourselves. Myself." I looked at Dennis. "Make an offer."

"I offer what you owe Li Ming."

134

"Hey! The bank would give you more than that," puts in Delphine.

So I said to Dennis, "I'll sell you all my lands for what I owe Li Ming and a promise that the Black Hills will be mine as long as the grass shall grow and waters flow."

"Deal!" said Dennis with a big grin.

The women gave us dirty looks but protested no more.

I headed to the kitchen to make popcorn. "I'll do a play-by-play of the rest of the game," I called.

"Noo-o-o!" the three of them chorused.

Sounds of dice clattering, small victories and defeats. I dumped the popcorn on the hot oil. Loud popping. Finally I took the pan off the heat.

Low from Li Ming's voice, "I'm reneging on our deal."

"What?" Delphine couldn't believe her ears either.

I went to the doorway to hear better.

"I'm reneging on our deal," Li Ming said simply.

"What? You can't do that!"

Delphine not only sounded mad, she sounded like she'd never dreamed of such treachery.

"You know I can. This is business. Partners change." Li Ming was calm.

I was tickled.

"You're my sister in business."

"He's Chinese."

Delphine jumped up and charged down the hall to the bathroom. I had the impression she was about to bawl or brawl. She reappeared in a minute, perfectly composed.

I made a mental note that Delphine didn't really fight hard. When things went against her, she accepted her fate, as though she expected to be a victim.

Now Li Ming looked across at Dennis. "Want to make a deal?"

"Sure."

Delphine gave them the fish eye.

"No rent either way."

"Right."

It was a good deal. Delphine owned the railroads and the purple properties just past the jail. Li Ming and Dennis owned everything else.

Of course, had Li Ming kept Delphine as her partner, their monopoly would have been almost as powerful. The end would only have come a little slower.

Delphine studied the board and fought off the feelings that competed for her face. Her cheeks got darker in spots.

I served the popcorn.

"I don't think …"

Delphine fell silent.

"I don't think I have a chance any more."

Silence.

"I quit."

"Dah-DAHM!" sang Li Ming. She stepped over to Dennis, held a hand high. He took it, and they did a little parade around the table, their arms making a tent. Dennis lah-lahed "Pomp and Circumstance" for the procession of the king and queen.

I ate popcorn. Delphine stepped across the living room.

I heard the hiss of an LP, and Creedence Clearwater Revival came on the stereo. Delphine was trying to recoup her poise.

"That wasn't really fair," said Li Ming. Her tone said, *But it was fun.*

I could guess how much Delphine wanted to say, "Damn straight." But she held her tongue.

Chairs scraped, and I saw that they were all sitting back down.

Hands dived into the popcorn.

Delphine's color was still mottled. Amazing how seriously white folks take a game, if it involves money.

We chatted another half hour, but Li Ming and Dennis left early. The conviviality never did come back that night.

For the most part, though, I thought Delphine and I were happy. More or less happy, sort of happy. We didn't quarrel. We were affectionate. We enjoyed ourselves in bed. (I was gentle and persuasive, she was either avid or slightly indifferent. For some reason we never let our wolves howl in the sack.) We had enough money (hers was from a trust fund) to do what we wanted. A good life. Since we were each up and coming in different ways, we were headed for THE Good Life. We kidded ourselves you can have a good life in the shadow of Raven's wing.

Those good times were coming on quick. I got more and more chances to babysit listeners through the dark hours, and compliments on my performance. It was fun, spinning the grooves that keep people connected to the radio through the black hours, connected to the music, connected to life. It's not a finger-snapping, strike-up-the-band kind of time. It's mellow, soft, deep, with edges of darkness. A bass clarinet like me goes well in those hours. I quickly learned the tone to hit, the cuts to play, the way to help people stay tuned. Soon I was a Saturday night regular, and I liked the job.

Since we were all music all night, I especially liked taping the show Friday afternoon and walking out into the winter sunset. Delphine would pick me up at the curb and we'd go down to a place on Elliott Bay and have a drink and watch the sun set. On clear winter afternoons Seattle is gorgeous. And I liked getting a window seat in that bar that time of day. The light came in off the water and turned Delphine's skin a creamy gold. She knew I liked to look at her that way.

We'd talk about my job, politics at the station, how I could build my listenership, how I could appeal to sponsors. She'd mention getting her father to ask the marketing director of the chain wholesaler of audio equipment to listen to the show some Saturday night. The idea was to get me lined up for a permanent slot of my own, daytime or evening, a spot I was identified with as the host. Hey, you have to shoulder to the front of the line.

I never thought until later how I felt about a lot of things. Did I really want a career in radio? (*I don't know, radio's a good thing, uh … It's a door that is willing to open, and I'm walking through, dammit!*) Did I really want Delphine? (*Delphine's a good person, and we're friends, and we both understand how it feels to be on the outside, and …*) Did I really want Seattle? (*It's beautiful here, and they accept me, mostly, and …*) Did I want to be white? (*Dammit, Indian people can do everything white people can do, and do it better! If you don't know that, I'll prove it!*) Did I mind being dependent on Delphine? Was it okay that the wind in my sails was hers?

I never asked myself if I missed my grandparents. Never asked myself if I missed my mother and father and my sisters. If I missed the Badlands. If I missed my people. When you give up the road of the Pipe, you give up all the rest. I would have to walk forward and find a new family, a new tribe.

How did that feel?

Screw you, Buster, I can do it.

But what about the parts of myself I lost? The desires? My love for my family? My people? Our sacred ways? Our land? What about things that nourished my heart, my imagination, my spirit?

I pretended they didn't exist. I pretended I didn't have any feelings about that.

I was a man standing on one foot, standing very erect and with excellent balance, and feeling slam-bang about how erect I was. But standing on one foot.

Delphine and I got into a Friday night habit. We'd have that drink and then walk in a little park on the north end of Elliott Bay. It was a small park, flat, with grass and some trees, a place for strollers or runners or Rollerbladers. I remember it was the first day of spring, or at least the first Friday, and we were holding hands. I felt good toward her, good enough to ask what had been on my mind. "What do you want with me?"

She rotated that Nefertiti head slowly toward me, one eyebrow raised. For Delphine that was a big gesture.

"I mean, I don't know what you see in me."

She cupped my face in her hands and kissed me lightly on the lips. "You mean, aside from a gorgeous hunk who's talented and brilliant?" She kissed me more sensually. "You foolish boy," she murmured, and looked at me with that eyebrow cocked.

I felt like I still didn't know, not really. We walked on.

I will say this. Delphine acted good to me. I never was around anyone who was so consistently good. We hardly ever quarreled. Everything she did showed she'd thought of me. Sometimes I felt like the niceness was her training, not her response to me. Sometimes her answers didn't seem real, like when I asked what she saw in me. She seemed withdrawn, silent. She was living in dark spaces where no one else was allowed to go, or she wouldn't invite anyone else, not even me. She never invited me to read her journal.

I wondered what she wrote there. I supposed it was about color. Being black is damned hard in America. But black in a white family, the black sheep. *Not to know if your father is your father.*

I checked out the situation on turning up black in white families. It happens. Yes, even when the father is known for sure. It can happen several generations down the line—*the dark outshines the light.* Mike could have been her father. Or maybe she was picked by fate to carry the blackness in the family past. I was betting on an act of infidelity, and I bet that's what Delphine suspected in her heart. Suspected that the man she loved wasn't her father. Tried to get closer to him. Always yearning for …

Now I wonder why I didn't speak up, ask her what was going on, what kept her up writing late at night and put her in the dumps. What shadow fell on her life. How it felt. Whether I could help her find the light.

I should have asked. I was her mate, the one person who's supposed to share everything with her, and hear her speak her heart.

I never did. The reason is simple—I was afraid of rocking the boat. I felt like I had to move gingerly, always, around Delphine, be careful of her. So I let her flounder without help.

O Delphine, you were living in the shadow.

I was living in hers and mine both.

The whole Ryan family went to the island for a week for Christmas. The invitation came with caution words from Delphine's mother, "Come every bit of you—don't bring any work. Let's just be together for this time." Delphine and I knew the words were ritual and really meant for Meg and Bess. Her sisters were young women on the make. Bess would bring manuscripts to read (she worked for a publisher of self-help psychology books in Los Angeles). Meg would bring files on the cases she was prosecuting. It worked. Mom and Dad sent plane tickets to L.A. and D.C., respectively, and the sisters arrived without briefcases.

The only extra baggage was me, in fact, as Delphine's sisters came without male friends. I arrived late, halfway through the week, on Christmas Eve, a Wednesday. Mike made me feel hugely comfortable. That was a great part of his charm. No matter how often I told myself he'd done the same for other boyfriends of his daughters in years past, I was taken in by his warmth, and the warmth of the whole Ryan clan.

Mike even talked me into sending a telegram to Grandpa and Unchee, wishing them a merry Christmas. It was a preposterous idea, really. Our family sure didn't celebrate any holidays of Christians, and I never even heard anyone say "Merry Christmas" until I was a teenager and at Kyle school. But I got a kick out of the idea of them getting one of those yellow-on-yellow ticker-tape-looking messages from Western Union. So I sent one to Mom, my sisters, and Senior too (on the chance that he was hanging out with the family those days). "Merry Christmas," I wrote, not being able to think of anything else to say. I wondered if they would think I'd become a white man. "Wish we were together. Maybe next year."

The sentiment was sort of genuine, even if the wording was off. Later I was disappointed to find out Western Union didn't go for the ticker-tape-like messages anymore, they just sent telegrams that looked just like ordinary letters.

Christmas was a big day. As though on command, the sea brought in a heavy snow, which they said almost never happened on the island. Marooned by impassable roads, we were tickled pink. There were wagonloads of presents (in bed that night Delphine called it "the Neiman-Marcus catalog parade"). Fortunately, she had shopped extravagantly for everyone and signed all the cards with both our names.

I don't remember what all I got, except for a Chinese dressing gown (they didn't call it a "robe") so gleaming

I loved to put it on but nearly refused to be seen in it. Delphine gave me a set of tapes of live performances of old-time blues, completely illegal and absolutely unique. There was an involved story about their origin. This friend's father recorded them secretly in Chicago clubs over forty years before, the friend inherited them but didn't much care for blues, etc. I had to promise to treat them like they belonged in the Smithsonian, which they did.

An embryonic yuppie, before the word existed.

One of Mike and Poe's gifts to Delphine was really special. It was a group of a dozen matched frames and mats, and in the frames were ... blueprints? Mike and Poe were grinning huge as they arranged them artfully on the dining table. I didn't get it. Meg and Bess were watching Delphine closely.

"Oh!" Delphine squeezed out a half-smothered cry. I couldn't quite read her face—conflicting feelings, looked like, behind the regal eyes.

"Delphine's first ambition," Mike explained for my sake, "I mean, after kissing a frog until it became a handsome prince, was to be a marine architect. These are some of her drawings."

"Oh, thank you!" Delphine managed. She put an arm around her dad's waist, squeezed, and laid her head against his shoulder. She was always far more affectionate with him than with Poe.

The blueprints showed various views of boats: side, top, bottom, sectioned, like that. They were schematic—diagrams, not art.

"We think she showed real talent."

"I copied them out of textbooks," Delphine said in a pooh-poohing tone. "I learned to draw them, not engineer them."

"Still," said Mike.

Delphine reached for one at the end of the display. Then I saw that the first eight or ten showed sailboats, the last three work boats.

"These are my favorites," said Delphine, pointing to the last three.

"When Delphine developed social consciousness," said Poe in a fastidious tone, "she stopped drawing pleasure craft and started on work boats."

"We're proud of the social consciousness of all our daughters," said Mike.

"This is a fishing boat." Delphine held it so I could see it, then displayed another. "Tug."

I reached for the last one. "What's this?" It was the only one that made no sense to me.

"The bottom of a ferry," said Delphine. "The workings."

"Delphine was always interested in inner workings," said Poe.

There was a dark lining in this comment, but I didn't know why.

Mike's words seemed to boom. I heard his fondness more than the content. "We thought she'd make a boat designer," he said.

Delphine looked up at him and held his eyes. Her eyes spoke giving in, or resignation, or some such. "The world needs me to work for change," she said.

Mike snapped his fingers and sang the Burt Bacharach tune, ["What the world (beat) needs now (beat) is love (beat) sweet love ..."]

That evening we played charades, a family Christmas tradition. I couldn't believe these rich people would act so silly, and have so much fun. I got to charade Ichabod Crane, and that was a hoot.

The other two days felt perfect. Delphine and I slept late and found our own breakfast at nearly noon. In the afternoons we went for long walks on the island's dirt roads, sat on boulders and looked at the sea. We understood each other completely enough not to need to talk, or so I thought.

As a family we ate huge, wonderful dinners. One evening we watched the home movies Mike had made over the years, proud papa, and the other we played parcheesi. Each night Delphine and I made love in the bed she'd slept in as a child and teenage virgin. We slept to the sound of the surf, woke in the early light and made love again, and dozed away the mornings. I felt really damn good, in a white-bread sort of way. This was fun, and after a while I would really enjoy it.

Except that I didn't. Not for another dozen years, until now, did I begin to see why—the why on my side. Not all of me was there. Hell, there were parts even I had forgotten about. Except you can't forget, you can only pretend.

Of course, there was a worm in Delphine's rose, too.

I didn't see it yet.

HOW DELPHINE WAS
SEEING THINGS

I am going to tell this next chapter the way I think Delphine saw things. Yes, I'm taking a liberty, but she told me a world, and finally I got to read her journal and get her private thoughts on things. This is honest. Here we go.

After dinner on Friday Delphine took a martini in each hand, power drinks, and shepherded Mike into his study. She touched his shoulder in the way that always meant daughter to father. "We haven't had a chance to talk, Mike." Strange to do daughter-father—*I will never know if you are my father*. Yet her mother, her definite biological parent, her mother she never felt close to.

He nodded and let her steer him. "Just you and me," she said, closing the door behind them.

He sat in his favorite chair, an overstuffed affair of Moroccan leather. She used the ottoman. She felt a pang. *Should I put myself at the feet of a man I want something from, and my head lower than his? Bad policy.* But this was her daddy. And it was odd. She had stopped calling her parents Mommy and Daddy when she was a young teenager, when she first began to figure out the channels power used in the world. She called them Mike and Poe, on principle. She was comfortable calling her mother Poe, always had been, always would be. But this man was singular. Mover and shaker in the Democratic party. Major donor. Privileged to a first-name basis with congressmen, senators, federal judges. She never addressed her father as Mike without quailing a little, without wanting to say in a child's voice, "Daddy?"

He was waiting for her to begin. He knew her. His eyes looked sparkly and kind.

"Mike, I need help." She heard that her voice was firm, decisive. Good. A beggar can't afford to sound like he's begging. "I've decided on my course."

She watched his brown eyes carefully. They darkened for a moment, then grew very bright. *Good. I have managed to surprise the great Michael Ryan, maybe even shock him.*

He took his time before saying gently, "Aren't you coming into the firm?"

"No," said Delphine evenly. "I want the center of the action." She watched his eyes. *Are you thinking, Too conspicuous, not tucked away enough, a potential embarrassment? Are you thinking, a give-away of the family secret?* She couldn't tell. She could never tell. Her mother sometimes had thoughts like that. Sometimes her sisters did. She couldn't tell about her father, never had. Did he think, *You, my darkie daughter?* Or *You, some other man's daughter?* She'd never known. Long ago she had decided she didn't care. She had trouble making the decision stick.

She watched him take in what she'd said and wonder what was next. "What do you want?"

She pitched in. "I want to make a difference. I want to finish the revolution women and minorities started in the last decade. Congress is the right forum for me." She was speaking her heart. And it didn't hurt to let him hear the campaign rhetoric straight from her, let him see that side of his daughter.

Then she saw swirls behind his eyes. She guessed what he was thinking. Attractive. Well-spoken. Nicely turned out.

Smart. Passionate. Knows the political ropes, grew up with them. Skin color and Negroid features ... perhaps an advantage these days. Native American husband, an advantage. Home and rearing an advantage. Has made every step right so far, including this one. Yes, she's right for it, it's right for her. That's what she hoped he was thinking.

"What are you asking for?"

Now Delphine rose to her opportunity, the invitation to claim the boon she sought. Her father would understand her as he would any bright, young, politically ambitious lawyer. "I want a spot as aide to Anderson."

She rehearsed the rest in her mind, ready to lay it out. Maybe four years as a legislative aide to a liberal representative, working up positions and legislation, making contacts in the party and public to ensure re-election, finally getting to manage a campaign, getting to know every important Democrat in the state. When the congressman stands for the Senate, run for his seat.

Mike spoke slowly and gently. "I promised Meg I'd speak for her on that."

"What?"

He didn't repeat the words, just held his sympathetic eyes on her.

"But Meg wants the federal bench."

"She changed her mind. She used almost the same words you did, 'the center of the action.' I promised her. The day she got here."

Delphine had heard falcons dive at two hundred miles an hour. Her heart dived faster than that.

"I can speak to DeLacey for you."

Andy DeLacey, Representative from Spokane, a good fellow and friend of her father, but strictly middle-of-the-road, not an agent of social change.

Heart plummeting, mind reeling, Delphine considered this offer. She didn't want to work for a middle-of-the-roader, she wanted to work on the edge of change. Besides, it wouldn't work at all. Two young Ryan daughters laying the groundwork to run for Congress, two Ryans standing for election, even two Ryans in the House. No way. Sisters competing—ridiculous. *All because she spoke up a few days sooner.*

Now she could raise her eyes, but not her heart. Mike had that look of vast kindness pasted on his face. *But you know it wouldn't work. Your offer is phony. It's a sop.*

Mike Ryan rose. It was hard to say if he took in the meaning of her look, but he was ending the interview. "I'll talk to Andy. When I'm back in the office."

All because Meg spoke up a little sooner.

Delphine took a deep breath and let it out. She preceded her father to the door. *So I will have to call you before January 1, say I've considered your kind offer, but I pass. Ohshit ohshit ohshit.*

He touched her shoulder and she turned to him. He took both her hands in his big ones. It felt like a nuzzle. She wondered if Meg got a hug.

"I'm proud of you, Delphine. Proud of all three of my daughters."

He opened the study door and they headed for the family room.

Everyone was reading, each in his own world. Meg and Beth had decided to spend the vacation rereading Tolkien in tandem. Delphine looked at Meg with what she knew was hatred. Suddenly, as though drawn by a force, Meg looked up from her book. Their eyes met, and knowledge passed back and forth.

"Parcheesi!" cried Poe. The board was already set up on the table. Poe and Bess dived straight for it.

Said Meg, "You know why games are fun in this family?"

Said Delphine, "Yeah, everyone brings the spirit of a junkyard dog."

Blue rambled toward the table, grinning at Delphine. *You never realize how magnificent you look,* thought Delphine.

Poe said, "Six for parcheesi. Well, let the couples play as one."

Delphine pushed up chairs for her and Blue. *Career crushed. What the hell will I do?*

Meg and Beth started arguing over who got the green piece.

I could move to California and start fresh. Unconnected. Some start.

She scooted her chair close to Blue's and looked into his eyes and tried to find some comfort there. He was smiling at her. He didn't know.

When will they announce Meg's new job? wondered Delphine. *Probably when it's* fait accompli. *And what am I, who am I? The hanged man.*

GULLS

Saturday afternoon, our last full day on the island, we took a long walk along the shore. Clambered over boulders, watched the surf pound the rocks and spray high into the air. It has an effect on me, landscape. It feels like walking in a different sort of time. The watery sea and the waves of sagebrush hills, the murmur of surf and the lift of bluffs, they all take me to awareness of the long, long pull, they make me feel Earth's rhythm, time after time after time.

Delphine spoke looking out to sea. "I had my talk with Dad." I'd noticed how she came out of the study with her father looking serious, but I didn't ask. With Delphine, you waited until she wanted to tell you.

She ran the whole thing down for me, how she asked for a spot with Representative Anderson, how her ambition might be fulfilled. She gave words to her idealism and her ambition. She told the whole story right up to the climax. She looked up at me and whispered, "He turned me down. Not in so many words, but he turned me down."

I walked on for a few numb steps. Before I could speak, she went on.

"He gave it to my sister. Meg." Then she recounted the story of the offer of DeLacey, and explained why that wouldn't work.

It sounded rough. I knew Delphine had been angling toward this a long time, probably since she was old enough to think about politics. *The way you sound, it's worse than rough. Your Raven ...*

We walked some more. I put my arm around her, but on the uneven ground it felt like her body was jostling against mine. I looked at her. *You're in your own world. Your grief. Me out, everyone out.*

I dropped my arm and walked along ... feeling vague, the way I was spending a lot of my life feeling. *So you wanted us to move to Washington, D.C., and you weren't going to say anything until it was arranged.* I looked sideways at her. Her head was hanging, her eyes cast down. *I wonder if you were going to have Mike pull strings at NPR, get me a job, something for the hubby to do.*

I fell a step behind her. *I wonder if I would have objected. Or just gone along.* I stumbled but caught myself. *Just gone along, I think.*

STOP IT!

Sometimes I need to just stop my head. Otherwise it spins like a motor not connected to transmission, wheels, and ground. When I need to do that, I look around at the hills and the sky, which were here before us and will be here after. Today I had the sea to add in. I looked first at the sweep of sea and sky, the vastness, and then at the point where they met, and there was a kind of glow, and you couldn't see which was which. I listened to the surf muttering and then booming. After a while of this I stopped and turned my eyes to Delphine.

She looked stricken. Her cheeks glistened with tears.

What am I going to do-o-o-o?

I heard it sharp as anything, but her lips did not move—Delphine didn't say it. Her soul said it, her spirit wailed it.

And I heard it.

I reached for her, but she pulled back and turned away. After a moment she started walking again. I followed.

Before long we saw a crowd of gulls fussing over something. We looked at each other, and saw the same pull in the other's eyes, something strange and something we had in common. Delphine ran up to the edge and looked down into the clump of rocks first.

"Sand shark," she said. I couldn't identify sea creatures without a menu. Whatever it was once, now it was just a bunch of frazzled flesh, bones, and innards. Soon just bones.

We watched. They pecked and fluttered and pecked, the way carrion eaters do. And I blinked.

Suddenly, as in a click, the scene reversed colors like a photo negative. The white gulls were black. Black-black.

I blinked a couple more times. Still black.

I reeled. I felt like I might fall down there, among the dead flesh and the feeding ... ravens.

The doe. That day before Christmas. I saw it again like eleven years ago. As in a dream or a vision, the ravens fluttered around the deer carcass. Only now it was like they were dancing. They flew slowly, ceremoniously in circles. Right on the beat some of them landed, on the beat they launched once more. They flapped their wings like wizards' cloaks. They flew slowly in circles, like a constellation of black stars rounding a dead sun. They wheeled about by a prearranged and divine or satanic plan. From time to time the dark shapes coalesced into symbols, arcane representations of ... I didn't know what.

Their leader came forth toward me, beak gaping, wings spread wide, claws down and open, grasping. In a formal way he approached, this ambassador of darkness. I wondered, *What is your message?* In front of my eyes, he puffed himself up, wings spread. He squawked in my face, he yawped. He cocked his head and leered at me. Then, suddenly, he hurled himself straight into my eyes.

"No!" I shouted. I fell down, covered my eyes with my hands. "No!"

Time passed.

I felt Delphine's hands touch my face gently, her fingers loosen my hands from my eyes.

Where was I? How long was I there? Raven went through me, or into me. I am not hurt. Yet.

She held me and murmured comforting sounds. *You're back.*

I let my head clear. Arms, not wings. Delphine, not Raven.

I cast my eyes around. I could see again. I stood up rockily. Getting back my balance, I stepped to the edge of the rock and looked down queasily. There were the gulls, white, strutting, content. They peered back at me. They were white, they had never been black.

Mind, were you playing tricks on me? Or were you telling me the truth? Not the facts, but the truth?

I stood, shakily.

"Blue?" She put an arm around my waist.

"I'm okay," says I.

She squeezed me. "We don't need to look at that."

She pulled. I resisted for a moment, taking in the white gulls. Then we walked on. I shook my head. I was feeling clear. I turned to Delphine, put my arms around her, snuggled her close. *You're back.*

She kept her head down, against my coat. When she leaned away, I got a good look at her face, and I saw something.

"Did you see the ravens too?"

She cocked her head to the side, birdlike, and gave me a peculiar look.

I persisted. "Did the gulls look black to you for a moment?'

"Oh, Blue," she said, "we're just alike."

"Sometimes I live in the shadow of the Raven's wing," I said. "Do you?"

"That," said Delphine, "is our soul connection."

Sunday was ferry day for Delphine and me—ferry, rental car, and airplane for Meg and Bess, all the way to D.C. and Los Angeles. Mike and Poe were staying on the island a few extra days. I had the impression it was a romantic time for them, but maybe that was wishful thinking.

On the ferry Delphine right away brought it up to Meg. "Congratulations on your aide spot."

"I don't have it yet," Meg demurred.

"Chickens, hatching," said Beth.

Delphine and I looked at each other with the same thought. Meg had shared the news with Beth but not with Delphine.

We were all fidgeting with Styrofoam cups of bad coffee with powder for cream. The ferry saloon was cold. I couldn't tell what Meg and Bess knew about Delphine's ambition, or her request to Mike. Seemed to me there were a lot of eyes avoiding each other at that table.

"Ambitious lot, aren't we?" Meg finally said.

"You take Congress," Bess said to Meg, "I'll take the media, Delphine will take whatever she wants, and Ryan girls will run the country."

"Hear, hear!" said Meg, making a teasing toast with her Styrofoam cup.

"Won't work," snapped Delphine, much too loud. "You're white, I'm black." She stood up and glared at her sisters. Then she stalked off, her low heels pounding the deck.

I got up to follow. "Let her be," said Bess.

"She's always like this," said Meg.

"She likes making herself a loner," said Bess.

I eased back into my chair. Half I was curious what else the sisters had to say, half I knew Delphine did want to be alone.

"Do you find her difficult, Blue?" This was Meg, with a raised eyebrow and lips that wanted to smile but were held straight.

It was an invitation. I didn't like it.

"I find Delphine a miracle," I said. I held Meg's eyes. Then I got up and headed after her.

She was standing at the very front of the ferry, next to the ramp that lowers to let the cars off. I stood a little back and watched her. Since she stood like a bowsprit, the wind whipped her thick auburn hair hard, like a rug being shaken. Her hands held the rail knuckle-white, like she might be blown backward. Her delicate jaw line was set, and the muscles worked.

I eased close, and her eyes were fixed down, on the maw beneath the raised unloading platform. The water charged under the boat like stallions galloping into hell. Nowhere else could you get a sense of how hard the boat was going.

I put an arm around her. "I didn't know," I said softly.

"Oh," she said dully, like it was the farthest thing from her mind. "They don't matter."

"Have they always been like that?"

She curled a half smile at me. "They don't matter," she repeated. "They never mattered. Not Meg, not Bess, not Poe."

I pondered that, not knowing what to say to the woman I lived with and mostly loved.

She cast her eyes back to the water. The stallions still plunged into the darkness.

I squeezed her. "They *don't* matter," I echoed. I doubted she believed that.

She nodded her head, and nodded it, and looked at the rushing waters.

Suddenly she turned and buried her head in the crook of my neck. After a long while she drew back and looked into my eyes so hard it felt like dashing water into my face. "I say, 'Fuck 'em all.' "

DELPHINE

One more time I'm going to tell a chapter from Delphine's point of view. I base it on what she told me, what she wrote in her journal, and what others saw.

Delphine gave a disgusted shake of her shoulders and slipped out of bed. She zombied into the dining area, picked up the bottle of cabernet, advanced to the front window, held the bottle against the street light. Dead soldier—not the smallest angle of liquid. She looked down at the dark street. Then she cranked open the tall, sideways-opening window, and leaned out. There was no one to see her in her Dead Head T-shirt and underwear, no one on the street at three A.M.

I am a sweet rich li'l nigger girl in her silky La Perla panties. Don't you wanna take a gander?

She resisted throwing the dead soldier down onto the sidewalk. Like a good girl she retreated to the kitchen and *klunked* it into the waste basket. Then she got a hard pack of Shermans, fingernailed one out, and lit it with the Ronson lighter. She plopped onto the sofa and stretched out. Another bout of darkness in the darkness.

Since before Thanksgiving, she had been waking up like this. She would stay up late, drink half a bottle of wine to kick her head toward sleep, lie down and doze an hour or so, and sit up wide awake. She didn't know why. She spent the hours filling her journal. Or she spent them brooding in the darkness.

She stubbed the Sherman out half-smoked. She smoked little except during these brooding sessions. She lay back on the couch and flung her arms and legs wide. Scrunching against the thready texture of the sofa, she pictured her own crotch, a dark shadow encased in smooth, pearly cloth. She half wished the couch threads were nails so they would hurt.

Abruptly, she flung her feet to the floor and sat up. She levered another Sherman out of the box, lit it, sucked the tarry smoke into her lungs, and settled back. *A long winter's night, while visions of sugarplums rot in my head.*

It wasn't that she was worried about anything in particular, she told herself. *I mean, only a fool wouldn't worry, given that life is a train wreck anyway.* She worried constantly about social justice, poverty caused by racism, unemployment, lousy education for the poor, the destruction of minority cultures, the drinking and drugging caused by despair— what was not to worry about? *But I don't worry about myself.*

She fanned some copies of *Cosmo* on the glass-topped coffee table and stared at the covers. One model wore a tight dress, leaned into the camera, and squeezed her shoulders together to create far more cleavage than seemed possible for a size-five body. Stories were teased in short headlines:

The Frankest Discussion of Intimacy We've Ever Published
Why Sex Was More Fun When It Was Considered Wicked
How Holding Back (a Little) Can Restore the Big Bang
8 Color Pages of Girls in Their Clingy, Sensuous Nightgowns
24 Questions *Crucial* to Your Love Life
The New Chastity–Why More and More (Desirable) Women are Dropping Out of the Sexual Rat Race

I'm not important enough to worry about. I do have an image to keep up: young, bright mulatto bearing the banner of success into the world of the New World. I need to look like a success. Unfortunately, I can't spend my days in a shooting gallery.

Delphine had never touched hard drugs—she knew that if she did, she would dive in and never come out. *I long for oblivion.* And would swim into it, except that it would make her useless for the forces of change. *I mean, who gives a shit about me? I certainly don't.*

At first she'd thought she was an insomniac because she was afraid to ask her father for the big favor. She'd dreamt over and over about the moment of asking. Always she was ushered by a secretary into her father's office, not his office downtown, or his study at home or on the island, but a silly parody of an office. Her father dismissed the secretary with the words, "That will be all, Delphine."

Then Delphine—the real Delphine—would walk across acres of deep grass-carpet, up to her chest, toward his desk. The grass-carpet was marshy, and she had to watch out not to get mired down, to sink forever into the swamp.

In front of the desk she clambered with difficulty up onto some rocks, stood up tall, and looked toward her father. Her eyes were at the level of the desktop, and her vision obscured by his nameplate—MICHAEL RYAN. Somehow the letters were made from statues of great presidents and founding fathers—*M* was Washington and Lincoln shaking hands, *I* was Jefferson, *C* was a roly-poly Ben Franklin, and so on. She commanded herself to rise taller, and she did, though not up to the level of her father's eyes.

She drew a deep breath and began. "Great White Father..." She spoke at length, but in the dream she never heard her own words—she only saw her face, composed in a brittle way against fear, and her father's face, noble as a statue, smiling eternally, omnipotent and benevolent. When she finished asking to enter the hallowed halls of government with her paternal aid, he smiled even more broadly, lovingly, indifferently, and enunciated these words in the voice of the Burning Bush: "The touch of the tarbrush."

That was all he said.

When she knew that would be all, the marsh opened and sucked her through a wet hole. Abruptly she found herself in space, falling. Slowly turning head over heels, she fell through infinite reaches of space, and she was as an angel, a dark angel cast out of heaven, deprived forever of light, and the sight of the face of God.

Now she had a reason to be an insomniac. "I promised it to your white, red-haired, capped-teeth, yacht-club-elegant sister."

I sure as hell can't sleep.

I am a strong person. She wouldn't ask for help, not with this sort of thing. She wouldn't go to Blue, and least of all to her parents. *I have to handle this. And I will.*

In the last couple of weeks she'd drunk so much wine after Blue went to bed that she'd considered giving up booze. *But I don't have to. Not yet. Probably not at all. That's not the problem.*

She thought of Blue in the bedroom, stretched out like a giant and gorgeous sea lion on the bed, clutching the pillow to his chest like a shell with delicious meat inside. He was *so* big and silky, he never realized, and she liked to sleep next to him, curling in a ferret space beside his long bulk. That part she had liked. *Innocent Blue.*

Anger spasmed through her. She sat up. *Why am I angry?* She couldn't think. *Innocent? What does that mean?*

She was alert now, wired. She hated that. *No sleep tonight, and feel like shit tomorrow.* Her hands would fidget, her feet would fidget, her mind would fidget.

She lit a Sherman. She went to the front window and gazed down at the street. *Empty, empty.* She gazed at the shadows. *Empty, empty.* Shadows were supposed to be places where creatures lurked, perhaps rapists, perhaps adbuctors, at the very least black cats doing the bidding of their mistresses. These shadows were empty.

A bolt again—anger.

She felt riven by shots of anger bolting into her body. The anger gathered in her, ran strong as an electric current, forcing action. She hurled the cigarette down on the polished wood floor and stubbed it out with her bare heel. She didn't even notice the pain. She marched into the bedroom, not bothering to be quiet. Innocent would never notice. She got out her creamy beige dress with the short skirt, a true fuck-me dress.

Insane to wear this at three A.M.

O, I love the dark-side boys. Jim Morrison, Mick Jagger. I will be one of the grateful dead.

She put on her matching Gucci belt and high heels, got her small evening bag, clicked into the bathroom, pinned her hair high on her head, her ultrasophisticated look, at least ultra for this time of night. She went to the hall closet and got the knee-length sheepskin coat Mike and Poe had given her when she went to South Dakota. The coat showed fur at the collar and cuffs, and had pewter clasps shaped like feathers. Coat and dress were an outrageous combo, but *I am outrageous.*

She stored the car keys deep in the pocket of the sheepskin coat and locked the door behind her.

She'd been thinking of this for weeks. Samuel Johnson. Dr. Johnson, she called him, and he didn't get it. That was worth a chuckle. He didn't get it.

She clickety-clacked across the concrete floor of the underground parking lot without even a glance around. She scooted into the 240 Z, slammed the door, varoomed the engine, and gunned the car up the ramp and onto the street. *Well, Dr. Johnson, you are going to get something you like, oh, ain't you now?*

She rolled down the windows of the car and flashed through the empty city streets at sixty miles an hour. The cold felt delicious.

She had met Samuel Johnson at a party her last year of high school. She'd gone with Pamela, a black girl from the same girl's finishing school Delphine went to—maybe they were the school's gesture at racial balance in the senior class. "It's my cousin's birthday," Pamela said, "over in central district." It was the mention of the central district that intrigued her. That was probably in the black slums, where Delphine had never been, except to drive through—they were a foreign country to her, an enticing foreign country.

Samuel Johnson was a tagalong. She never did figure out exactly why he was there, a dude in his thirties at a birthday party of college kids. She also didn't know why she was attracted to him. Later she admitted to herself that she thought maybe she would meet a fantasy black guy with a big 'fro, or dreadlocks, a guitar genius, Jimi Hendrix come back from the dead. She would have been fascinated. But Samuel Johnson was just a guy who spent his day working on cars and hoped to inherit the garage from his dad one day. Though he was big in every direction, his three hundred pounds were mostly fat. His fingernails had dirt that would never come out. He had no prospects. What he had on his mind was nothing.

She started by sitting on the arm of the big stuffed chair where he was planted and popping Olys. "You want another beer, Dr. Johnson?" she purled out. He snorted. "Am a grease monkey, ain't no goddam doctor. I do like a beer." She cursed herself for thinking he had heard of Dr. Samuel Johnson, the literary man, and brought the mechanic a beer.

She talked to him for a long time, though it was mainly her talking and him grimacing or giving one-syllable answers. Samuel Johnson, it turned out, was one angry man. He was getting divorced. His wife was giving his kids a new father, and she told him, "Don't bring your sorry ass around here, no matter." Samuel Johnson didn't have time or space for Delphine or anybody—he was busy being pissed off.

She found his anger exciting, and knew that was trouble. She sat on the chair arm and popped Olys with him all evening. When everyone was leaving, he said roughly, "You wanna come up to my pad?" He didn't even offer an excuse like a nightcap. She understood, and said casually, "Why not?"

In the years since, at odd intervals, she had gone back. It took a certain mood, it took a certain blackness. But Samuel Johnson was not a nice man, and he would honest-to-God, honest-to-the-Devil, fuck her.

She pulled into the Starlight motel parking lot, took the ticket, and went down ramps to the bottom. She always parked here, two blocks from Samuel's place, because her car would be left alone.

She watched the street as she walked. Three A.M.—this was the one risky part. Then she clicked up a half dozen steps to the entrance of the apartment building. When the elevator delivered her to Samuel's floor, she clicked smartly to his door and rapped confidently four times. The way he answered he must have been awake. The TV glowed phony color in the background. The way he looked at her made her self-conscious about her legs descending from the cream-colored skirt that barely hung below her bottom. "You look good," he said. "Damn good." He put a big paw around her waist and drew her to him.

"I don't want nobody here when I ain't here," Samuel Johnson growled. Delphine reflected that was the longest sentence he'd spoken in her hours there. He stood in the bathroom with the door open, pissing. So she slipped out of bed, flung on her fuck-me outfit, and scurried out of his apartment ahead of him. She clutched her evening bag in one hand and car keys in the other, rode the elevator alone, and emerged into the bright daylight of New Year's Eve day, 1978. The miniskirt made her feel self-conscious before eight o'clock in the morning, among people who were going to work.

She walked two blocks back to the motel and paid. She redid her makeup in the rear view mirror. *I look impeccable.* Studying her face, she felt grateful to Samuel. In his unpleasant way he was perfect, and he had never known that.

She gave a twisted smile at the mirror. *I'm impeccable. Unmarked. Perfect.*

Beyond the little go-up-and-down gate she left rubber and slid left onto the one-way street. It felt damn good.

Blue, I'm sorry to worry you. He would have been awake an hour or two by now, alone in the house, wondering. *Soon you will understand.*

She knew now. *It's good to know.* She pushed the accelerator with her knowledge. She felt a weird exhilaration.

On the way to the ferry she stopped at a drug store and bought a legal pad. While she waited in the car in line for the Bremerton Ferry, she wrote a note to Blue. She wished she had some of her own stationery, but there was no way. She folded the yellow sheet in half, wrote Blue's name on the blank side, and put it on the passenger seat, carefully squared to the sewn lines in the fabric.

She looked at the next blank page on the pad. After a few minutes she was able to write, "Daddy and Poe." But she couldn't go on.

In a few minutes the lines of cars advanced on to the ferry. Delphine ended up toward the front, which pleased her.

She stayed in the car until the ferry had been underway for ten or fifteen minutes. She kept looking at that blank sheet. She couldn't think of any words she wanted to put on the page.

After a long while she signed her name to the blankness, folded the sheet, addressed it, and tucked it under the sheet for Blue. Then, briskly, she stepped out of the car, wrapped herself tight in the sheepskin coat, and walked to the front of the ferry.

Once there she set out on one deliberate circle of the boat, counter-clockwise. She didn't look at any of the people, not the ones at the rail looking out at the seascape or back at the cityscape, not the ones inside drinking coffee out of Styrofoam cups and reading the newspaper. She didn't cast a glance at the city behind or the town ahead, at the sky above or the ocean beneath her feet.

The gulls were scattered behind the boat, like torn bits of paper in a whirling wind. She stared at them, white in the bright morning sunlight. Then, deliberately, she blinked her eyes hard, twice.

Yes!

The gulls turned black, black as ravens. *Thank you, Blue.*

Resolutely, she completed her circle. She held the coat tight around her—*I don't want to be cold.* As she walked, like an efficient executive, she thought once more through the details, so the job would be done right. Fortunately, she knew the engineering of the bottom of a ferry. She knew that the propellers blasted objects away from the stern, so it made no sense to go in there. She knew that the bow made a compression wave, but she also knew how to avoid it. She knew how the water coming under the bow made its vicious venturi, how the V shape of the hull funneled sea water straight into the propellers, to give them more bite. She knew exactly what would happen to a stick dropped into that venturi, or a sheepskin coat, or a human being. *Simple, so elegantly simple.*

She stopped at the car and left her small purse. She put the billfold with driver's license on top of the legal pad and squared them, corner to corner. She noticed the stubby receipt from the parking garage on the floor on the passenger side and started to reach for it, then changed her mind. She rotated out, legs together, stood, shut the door, left it unlocked, and without a glance backward marched to the forward loading ramp. It was raised now, and the sea roared into the gap it left.

She put her hands on the rail that guarded the passengers from the sea, and felt its cold metal. The wind was cold, slapping her face, whipping her hair like a flag. *The water will be shockingly cold, but only for an instant. It will happen very, very fast.*

She looked around a last time. She saw no people except for a couple of shadows behind the drivers' sides of windshields, mere glassy reflections, far, far from her.

She clambered over the rail awkwardly. The coat was in her way, but she refused to take it off. *I have just a miniskirt underneath.*

She held onto the rail behind her with both hands. She looked down into the seawater rushing beneath and made herself see what was going to happen. A falling body. Seized by vicious currents, jerked into the funnel with incredible force. Two propellers, each eight feet across, each grinding tens of thousands revolutions per minute. A collision ...

Beyond? Nothing.

Her mind drifted up a dream picture. A propeller squirted a darkness out behind....

She put a slight, quirky smile on her face. She listened to her mind sloshing into darkness.

Delphine Ryan took one step forward and pitched herself into the sea.

AN ENDING

White people do death dazed. Everything is muffled and hushed. Muffled makes numb. The Ryans walked around numb. You didn't want to raise your voice. You didn't want to ask a question or state an opinion. You wanted to act like, well … Out of sympathy you acted a little bit dead.

The news got to us quickly. A driver jiving to the radio in one of the cars saw her go. Another driver reading a newspaper remembered which car was hers. Billfold with picture ID, credit cards. Since her driver's license still gave her parents' North Capitol Hill address, the cops went there first.

They got to our apartment about noon, a suit calling himself Detective Macy and a uniform. Though I was supposed to be at Kay-Soul, I was fretting about where Delphine was. The cops wouldn't tell me a damn thing except they were supposed to take me back to the Ryan house. And, "Bring Delphine's Rolodex."

"What's happened to Delphine? Why are we going over there?"

In the back seat with no door handle and a wire screen in front of me, feeling like a red man in the control of cops, I got pissed off. I said a couple of things, they said a couple back. When I added a little sting, the suit called Macy turned around and glared at me with malicious triumph.

"Look, chief," he said, "your girlfriend threw herself into the drink. On the Bremerton Ferry. Right into the propellers. *Right* in." He snickered. "There won't be any remains to identify."

I cannot tell you how I felt, I cannot tell you. I was like a person deafened by a great explosion, head reeling, surprised by how odd the world suddenly seems, reduced to the perceptions of a toddler, dizzy....

When I got to the Ryans', I stumbled inside, no idea what to do. Suddenly I knew. I turned around and confronted Macy, who was just inside the front door making nice to everybody, delicate and wheedling as an undertaker—it didn't suit him. I stood close, too damn close, towered over him, and rudely threw anger at him with my eyes. "Tell me what happened. How do you know she's dead?"

Macy took me into a bedroom and closed the door. "You stupid bastard," he began. He lost me right there. He explained what the bottom of a ferry looks like, where the propellers are situated, and how water is funneled into them. Water, sticks, candy wrappers, seaweed, fish, and any human beings who happen to be floating by.

Maybe my anger at Macy numbed me against the truth he told.

"We need you to come clean," he said, looking at me sharp. "What was she doing in a cocktail party dress?"

I glared at him.

"You said you two stayed home last night. Why the dress? Why was she carrying an evening bag? Why are you lying to me?"

"I don't have a goddamn thing to say to you."

He practically jumped into my face. "You want to do this downtown? You arrogant enough to give me trouble? Why ain't you cooperating?"

I hit him with my biggest radio voice. "Because I don't know anything, you asshole!"

When I said that, the damnedest thing happened. Tears sprang to my eyes. I couldn't hold them back. They snaked down my cheeks.

He laughed in my face. Laughed big, so close my cheeks felt the breath chuff out of him. He seemed delighted by my tears. Maybe he thought it was a show of weakness.

I felt humiliated.

He backed away a little. "When did she leave the apartment?"

"I don't know, I was asleep."

"Was she gone all night?"

"I think I saw her when I got up to pee at twelve or one o'clock."

"Where did she go?"

"No idea."

"You ever hear of the Starlight Motel?"

"No."

He showed me a stub from the parking garage of a motel with that name. "Why was this in her car?"

"No idea."

"Don't you know nothing about your own woman?"

I just looked at him.

He glared back. He wanted me to think he could get it out of me, he could show he was the tougher guy. I was supposed to forget I was a foot taller and thirty years younger and more fit.

Suddenly I could stand it no longer. I walked past him. I barged out of that room and through the house and out the front door, acknowledging no one. I sat on the lawn for a long time. Human beings came and went and tried not to look at the crazy man on the grass with his head between his legs. Finally, a woman with a helmet of hair came out and got me.

This time Poe met me at the front door, said a shushed hello. Some people are diminished in the presence of death. Poe actually looked enlarged, like a bird that fluffs itself up to look bigger in the face of trouble. "Michael is in bed. They gave him a shot." She didn't have anything else to say.

Helmet Hair stashed me in the living room. "Meg and Bess are coming as quickly as they can. Coffee?"

She turned out to be the wife of one of Michael's law partners, and she took charge of everything, ordering food and drink, looking after callers, saying the right words, seeing to it that everyone was fed and watered, handling the funeral arrangements, talking to the newspaper. She took the Rolodex and set a secretary to making the sad chain of phone calls, telling all of Delphine's friends, acquaintances, and relatives that she had left us. "I'll take care of everything," she murmured. "You just ..."

The hush alone was enough to kill.

I sat there for a couple of hours or a couple of days, how would I know? Helmet Hair brought me coffee, introduced me to a few people. Finally Poe sat down next to me, didn't look into my eyes, and handed me two folded yellow sheets of paper. She looked perfect in a midnight-blue dress, matching waist-length jacket, and black pearl stud earrings. It was as though she was perpetually ready to look right to mourn the death of a daughter. Her hair was slick as if she'd just come from the beauty salon, her makeup impeccable, her dignity and grace at flood stage.

I wanted to grab her and shake her. *Don't you understand? She's dead! Chopped up. She turned herself into pieces too small to bait a hook.*

Can't you see? None of us meant anything to her.

169

Oh, sister Poe, you're her mother. Cut your hair off, slash your arms with a butcher knife, and scream out your grief, the way our old-time mothers did.

Or maybe it was me that wanted to hack my hair short and ugly and scarify myself. Maybe that would keep me from replaying in my mind, over and over, the sight of Delphine being sucked into those propellers as a human being and coming out as … something else.

"Blue, you need to read these."

I set my attention more or less on the yellow sheets. The first one started TO BLUE in block letters and continued with some legal rigmarole ("Being of sound mind and body," etc.). Then it willed to me the cash in her checking account (a few hundred bucks), our household goods and furnishings, the Z car, and her journals. She specifically mentioned the journals. Then, "I'm sorry. Delphine."

I vomited right on Poe's midnight-blue knees.

She jumped up and fled, hoohooing.

Helmet Hair directed me toward a bathroom and called for someone to clean up.

IknewIwasbeing—what'sthefakeword?—inappropriate.

When I got sorted out, Poe came back at me with the yellow sheets. I set the first sheet aside, not reading one word again, and looked at the other one. It was addressed, "Daddy and Poe." The rest of the sheet was blank. At the bottom was her signature, a pretty, ornamental affair with lots of flourishes. I snorted a little. Addressed to Daddy and Poe, signed at the bottom, blankness in between. Not even "Love, Delphine." Nothing. Blankness. Blackness.

"Blue, what does it mean? A blank sheet? Do you have any idea?" Her eyes violated her composure, they were pleading.

I shook my head. My mind was going into zombie.

"A blank sheet, Blue. Why? Did she have nothing to say to us?"

My mind clicked up by rote the words, *Nothing or too much*. But I just shook my head. *I don't know.*

"Blue, say something. She's our daughter."

It was like the words kicked me in my butt—I was on my feet. "I don't know, Poe," I said brutally. "I don't fucking know."

I stomped out of the house. The Z car was sitting in the driveway, and I had a key, but I wasn't going to touch it. I started walking. In a few minutes I was out of the neighborhood, one of those areas where a man of color can get stopped by cops just for walking the streets, and onto a main road. I flagged a cab, told the driver, "Pioneer Square." It's a downtown area where Indians hang out and get drunk on cheap wine. I mean get drunk, not pansy-ass a few drinks and look sober. The area is yuppified, and the yuppies resent us—nobody loves a drunken Indian. But the Indians are not going anywhere. We need a place to get crazy, and Pioneer Square is it.

I am not gonna spell this out for you. I got blotto. We drank Thunderbird. We made friends, and by sundown I knew these were the best friends I'd ever had. Soulmates, good red soulmates. I don't remember where I slept that night, and I hate to think. At one point two of us went to a place that advertised cashing paychecks. I had one (good thing there weren't ATM cards in 1979), and it kept us in drinking money for a another go-round. I stayed drunk. I was giving new meaning to the words, "feeling no pain." I never forgot, however, what pain I was not feeling, and I told my buddies the story of Delphine, and the story of being forced to go to school, and all the other sad stories that were my life, and sometimes the good stories too.

I might still be on that bender if Dennis hadn't showed up the second evening. There he was, in the tweedy suit jacket that was his graduate student uniform. He was just standing in front of me, avoiding my long legs, looking down.

"Morning, white boy," says I.

"It's late afternoon," says Dennis. "Blue, you're needed at the house."

"Needed!" I cried. "The hell I am. They killed her and they can mourn her and bury her all by their white-man, tight-assed selves."

"Blue," said Dennis, "there's been a development."

"What is this shit? Who are you, the Chinese Lieutenant Columbo?"

"You're needed, Blue." He reached down a hand and pulled on mine, trying to hoist me to my feet. He wasn't near big enough, and I was stubborn.

"Blue, they found out where Delphine was that last night. They need to ask you some questions." He waited. I didn't say anything. "And if you want to understand your own life, you want to know."

In his car I says, "How'd you find me?"

He says, "In Seattle everybody knows where to find a drunk Indian."

I took it quiet because I deserved it.

He took me to the apartment first. I went in the bedroom to change clothes. I stretched out to take a short nap. When I woke up, the sun was coming in the window. Dennis whipped up bacon, eggs, and coffee. I ate, and now I was getting half grateful that he'd rescued me. I changed clothes and showered (sanitized myself for the white folks). As we headed out the door, I saw the light on the answering machine flashing red at me, but I didn't give a damn what it wanted. He drove us to the Ryan house. On the way my thought bubbled up and out. "Did someone kill her? Have they found out she was murdered?" Wild stuff was going through my mind—mind control, hypnosis, Svengali.

Helmet Hair met us at the door and said, "The funeral is tomorrow. Blue, Poe needs to see you."

Inside Li Ming came up and gave me a big hug without words. "Thank you," I said to her, and then to Dennis, really meaning it, "Thank you."

Poe, Meg, Bess, and Lieutenant Detective Macy were needing to see me, it turned out. "Father is under sedation," Meg began. "In bed." Still. "Blue, the family has questions, and the police have questions. Reports must be completed. Perhaps it will be easier if the Detective and I do this together. You won't have to do it twice." Meg the lawyer.

"I hear you've found something out," I said. "Where was she?"

"You answer our questions, then we'll answer yours," said Macy.

I nodded, and kept my eyes down where he couldn't see what was in them. I wanted to catch Macy in a dark alley one night. But he's the sort of guy who would always have one up on you—a gun, for instance.

"Blue, was she depressed?" This was Meg.

I guess two days helps. Your mind works, even if you're trying to stay hammered. I muttered out a truth that was new to me. "Yeah. She always struggled with demons. Lately it was worse. She couldn't sleep. She drank a lot. Really a lot."

Poe cried, "Why? She had everything, *everything*..."

I glared and spread my arms theatrically. I felt like an ass-hole. In a white world, though, you use white body language.

She turned her head into her shoulder, the oddest gesture, like a bird tucking its head under its wing. And she stopped talking.

"Why was she depressed?" Meg, pushing on.

I shrugged. "Her demons."

"Were the two of you getting along?"

"Real good, I thought."

"Did you fight the night before?"

"Nope. I went to sleep, she stayed up, like always. In the morning she was gone."

"Had she had any bad news?"

I said it bluntly. "She lost the job she wanted, aide to Congressman Anderson."

Meg didn't even blink.

"But that wasn't it," I added truthfully.

"What was it, Blue?"

I just looked at her. She knew the reason. They all did.

"For God's sake, tell us," Bess put in.

"Was she seeing anyone else?" This was Macy in his grating, insulting voice. His eyes had that look that meant, You look dirty to me. But he probably always had that look, even to his kids.

"I don't think so."

"Why?" moaned Poe. It was a sax wail, starting high and sliding down.

I kept my eyes lowered.

Meg knew when to wait for the witness. They all waited.

I didn't know what to tell them. I could try saying that when the going got tough, Delphine had no resources of the spirit. She was raised in a world without God, without gods, without the presence of ancestors, without the awareness that there's more to the world than what's physical and visible. A world where there's nothing but yourself, your desires, your strengths, your weaknesses—no spirit to call on for help. And when she got into trouble, that wasn't enough, not near enough. It never is.

But these white folks wouldn't understand that. They sat at the same table as Delphine, and didn't know they were starving.

"There's nothing I can say," I told them. It was true, far as it went. But there were things I knew. "Nothing I can say."

"Come with me," said Macy.

We sat on a bed in an unused bedroom, me not wanting to know if it was Delphine's or a guest room or what. Macy had a tape player and something for me to hear.

"Pay attention, Chief."

I hurled anger at him with my eyes. He should have been offended, but only smirked.

"This is an interview with one Samuel Johnson. He's a black man big as you are, plus a hundred pounds of fat. You ain't gwine enjoy it."

The want to hit him flashed into my arm like a jolt of electricity. I suppressed it hard. *Ain't gwine? Who do you think you're talking to, Little Black Sambo?*

He gave his flat, hard cop look. "Samuel Johnson is the last person Delphine spent any time with. He's where she was from 2:49 A.M. till 8:12 A.M." He smiled at my puzzled look. "The parking stub. And some solid police work."

He was right, I wasn't going to like it.

The tape began with identification of interviewer and interviewee, Macy and Samuel Johnson. When these formalities ended, Macy paused the tape. "Don't be thinking Johnson killed her. He's in the clear, he checks out all the way. This is about something else." He hit PLAY again.

MACY: *What was your relationship with Delphine Ryan?*

Long pause on the tape, and the sound of asthmatic breathing; must have been Johnson's.

JOHNSON: *She was one of my fucks.*

MACY: *What?*

JOHNSON: *A real interesting one.*

[Pause.]

MACY: *Why don't you begin at the beginning? How did you meet her?*

JOHNSON: *At a party. The rich bitch's cousin or something. Don't even remember how I got there. She came on to me. Think she wanted to get next to a real nigger, know what it was like. I mean, she was half tan. I'm black black. Turned out she wanted to get right next. Maybe she got more than she was looking for. But, whatever, she liked it.*

MACY: *When was this?*

JOHNSON: *Don't remember what year. She was still in high school, junior, senior.*

MACY: *You dated her?*

JOHNSON: *No, I only fucked her. Don't think anyone on her side of the tracks knew about it.*

MACY: *When did your sexual relationship start?*

JOHNSON: *First night, after the party. I said, "Let's go up to my place." Didn't make no secret of what I wanted. She plenty willing.*

I was feeling mean that night. Wife left me about a month before and ... well, a lot of shit. I was pissed in general. Didn't feel like no come-on with Delphine. She walks in, there's a couch, back to the front door, facing the TV. I come up behind her, reach around, put both my hands on her little tits, rub 'em, rub myself against her butt. She responds good, tries to kiss me, but I ain't gonna do that shit. Funny thing, I never did kiss Delphine, wouldn't let that happen, no time. Anyway, right then, I just pushed her forward against the back of the couch, bent her over, lifted her little skirt about the two inches that was needed, and fucked her from behind.

She was a virgin. Bled all over me and the couch.

Then I pulled her rough by the hand to the bedroom. I laid down on the bed, all my clothes on but my cock out. Told her to straighten her clothes back up, make herself nice. She did. Then I told her to take it off, one piece at a time, sexy as she could every step, regular dance of seduction—give it all you got, baby. She done it. All the time looked at my big black cock. When she was jaybird naked, I saw how her body was a girl's, not a woman, and that turned me on even more. I told her to suck my cock, and she done it and done it. Rest of the night she done everything I told her. There ain't nothing you can think of I didn't tell her to do, no place I didn't give it to her, the ass included.

When I was done, kind of in the spirit of the thing, I told her to get out and go home, I didn't want her around. Middle of the fucking night. She done that too.

About a week later she was back. Same story.

Ever since, she shows up time to time, same story. Girl like it rough. Not physically rough, no, but rough talk and rough treatment, like she was a bitch. Which she was. A rich bitch.

MACY: *Without enjoying yourself over the details so much, how often did this happen over the last ... what is it ... eight or nine years?*

JOHNSON: *Coupla times a year. Never called ahead. Once she showed up when I had another bitch in bed. Told Delphine to strip and get her ass in bed and get fucked. She done it. Funny, I wasn't that crazy about talking rough, but she wanted it, and with her it was fun. Delphine probably thought I was like that with every woman, but I saved it special for her.*

MACY: *How often?*

JOHNSON: *Maybe while she was down in San Francisco going to them colleges she missed a year, I don't remember. Sometimes she came twice over Christmas vacation. I do recall once I asked her how them college boys liked it, what I'd taught her. She said she never let one of them touch her. And she looked at me like, weird, seemed halfway like telling me I was the only one. Stone fox, stone crazy.*

MACY: *She came to you on the night of December 30, morning of December 31?*

JOHNSON: *Early morning before New Year's Eve? Yeah, she came.*

MACY: *What happened?*

JOHNSON: *Same as ever, maybe better.*

MACY: *She say anything to indicate she was depressed, feeling down?*

JOHNSON: *What she said with her mouth wasn't words.*

MACY: *Suicidal? Thinking of killing herself?*

JOHNSON: *Far as she said, far as I could tell, she didn't have anything on her mind but getting laid. Which she got in fine fashion.*

MACY: *She say anything to you about having another relationship, a man she was living with?*

JOHNSON: *She hadn't been around in a while. Quite a while. Whatever else she had, though, seem like it wasn't enough to satisfy. Don't it?*

When he shut it off, he looked at me with triumph naked in his eyes. *Congratulations, Detective Lieutenant. Put the lippy redskin in his place?*

I calmed myself by breathing slow and easy. "The Ryans hear this?"

"They know the contents. Nobody has heard it but you."

"I'm going for a walk," I said mildly.

Whatever he'd figured on, that wasn't it—his eyes and mouth were all surprise.

I took myself outside and thought about Delphine. Walking clears my mind, my feelings, my spirit. Walking helps me be me.

I pondered Delphine and the darknesses she held inside. Delphine and the darkness she played with outside. Delphine and the darkness she jumped into at the end.

I wondered what would be in those journals.

I knew that Delphine lived deeper in the shadow of Raven's wing, even, than I did.

I tried to think of the stories my people have about darkness. We have lots. They're different from white people's stories in some ways. In the white stories darkness seems very alien, the other, the enemy. In ours it's more a part of things. Though I couldn't think it out, I knew this made a difference.

After maybe twenty minutes I turned back toward the Ryan house. Something had changed in me. I had a feeling for Delphine that seemed new, several feelings about Delphine that seemed new. One was compassion.

And when I felt compassion, a knowledge came to me.

I told Helmet Hair I had something to say to Meg, Beth, and Poe. She asked me to wait in the library. They arrived with Detective Lieutenant Macy. I told him to wait outside. He started to rebel, but Meg and Beth told him the same.

I sat on a plush sofa and took a moment to sort things out. For I had another feeling. It was anger, and I was willing for it to be with me, but I didn't want it to run me.

I raised my eyes to theirs, trying to use white-man eye contact. Felt the anger and the compassion and the knowing and all the rest of it come right to the front. "Yeah," I said softly. "I have an idea what happened to Delphine." I hesitated, but I needed to come out with it. "I … It was simple. She … She felt like a nigger."

I lowered my eyes. I didn't want to see the faces. Neither did I want to feel the emotions blasting at me—offense at the word, shock at the thought, and then raging denial. But the women hurled the feelings at my head and shoulders, and I felt them.

I raised my eyes to theirs and got battered by all those energies. I waited, giving them time. I hoped they would see something good in my eyes, understanding. Then I repeated, "She felt like a nigger."

I didn't add, Like me.

WILD, STRANGE WINDS

When I got back to the apartment that evening, the light on the answering machine was still blinking. The next morning when I came bleary out of the bedroom it was still blinking. Irritably, I crossed to the little table by the sofa and I hit the PLAY button.

First one was a hang-up. Also the second and the third. I was getting irritated, and I almost whacked the REWIND button. The fourth one had a voice.

"*Washtay*," it said. From that moment I knew it was Grandpa and what the message was. Far as I knew, he'd never talked on a phone in his life. He must have gone to the True Bulls' up the road.

His gravelly voice picked its way forward in the Lakota language, "Your grandmother has finished her journey." His breath was audible on the line, and his hesitation audible. "Funeral is Friday afternoon at Wounded Knee."

Click—he just hung up.

I fell, literally fell forward, onto the sofa, face down.

Whoosh! Collapse. The air farted out of the balloon. The wind was out of my sails. Now my ship was shlip-shlopping, lurching about, rocking crazily at the mercy of the waves.

In a little while I realized it was stuffy to breathe. I turned my head sideways and woke up to the fact that I'd been lying with my face in the sofa cushion.

I became aware of tears on my face, and I didn't know I'd been crying.

Why am I crying?—this thought razor-slashed me.

It wasn't that I was so fond of Unchee. True, she'd raised me, and done the thousand things a mother does for a child. But she'd done them grouchily, and I'd never felt glad to receive her attentions.

It wasn't that I would miss her. Since I decided I was a Great White Doubter, I hadn't gone home once to see Grandpa and Unchee. I had put my grandparents behind me.

With these thoughts I broke into a wail—an old-time, heart-piercing, soul-wrenching moan, sob, and cry in one. It shook the apartment. It shook the windows. It shook me.

I had no idea why I was wailing. Unchee, Delphine, my years as a white man—hell, all sorts of things frothed into my mind as reasons to be miserable, even the latest Sonics loss to the Lakers. I threw them out and went back to wailing. I wailed my heart out, and then did it again, and yet again.

O world of sorrows!

I cannot say it in words. I could play you some music. I could play you some blues. Or I could sing for you one of the songs of my people, a song that knows the great sorrows, a song in which sorrow flows eternally, as water flows in a fountain.

I was adrift, my sails slack, and a raging sea of emotion battered my ship.

I didn't know where these storms of feeling came from, or why. I could feel that they would wreck me, if I did not take action.

The next two days were the strangest days of my life—Delphine's funeral in Seattle on Thursday, Unchee's at Wounded Knee on Friday.

Delphine's funeral was at St. Joseph's, the parish church where she'd been baptized and confirmed. Delphine hadn't been there in eight or ten years, and the priest didn't even know her. He knew the Ryan family, though, and did it up proper. The mass the Catholics say for the dead has a formal beauty that seems to come from time immemorial, and it is memorable.

A lot of important people in the city, particularly in the Democratic party, showed up and paid their respects. Poe and her daughters showed they still knew how to work a reception line. Michael Ryan stood like a zombie, and he was still drugged up.

White folks are restrained at funerals. Can't think of a word that suits the case better. There's emotion, but dignity is all. If the tears aren't all small and quiet, people are embarrassed. Even at the graveside pathos is framed in decorum.

I felt like I was barely there. The Ryans were full of nice words—"Blue, stay in touch, we don't want to lose track of you." But I breathed in a new awareness in their company, like acrid smoke that fills the air. I didn't belong there. Even the nice words were a dismissal. I didn't belong there.

From the cemetery I went straight to Sea-Tac, used the cash in Delphine's checking account, and took my first-ever airplane flight—Seattle, Denver, Rapid City. Emile met me, put me up overnight in his apartment in Rapid, and drove me out to Wounded Knee the next day.

The white Indian returns.

O strange, O agony. I saw Grandpa, and Senior, and Mom, and Angelee and Mayana for the first time after several years. I quivered with fear of harsh words. Grandpa shook my hand warmly. So did Senior. Mom and my sisters gave me big hugs. I cannot speak more about that yet.

O strange, O fearsome. Why are we at Wounded Knee? I knew Unchee's mother had died near the battle time, but knew nothing more. Sure didn't know that Unchee or Grandpa felt any attachment to the place, or why one of them wanted her service there. What I knew was, I didn't want to be there. As a kid I'd never wanted to go there, read the big sign about the so-called battle, look at the mass grave, think about my people who died there, or those who survived, any of that stuff. The one time the family stopped for a few minutes, I sat in the car and waited. Now, as a Great White Doubter, this was what I'd left behind. It felt to me like I couldn't breathe here.

But it wasn't a time to ask Grandpa anything, and truth is, I didn't want to know why we were at Wounded Knee. I was still being driven before strange, wild winds, and I was lost.

O strange, O baffling. The little church on the hill, by the mass grave, was Catholic. Most Indian families, even traditional families, have a Christian church to fall back on for occasions like this. But neither Grandpa nor Unchee had any truck with Catholics, or any Christians. *Why have we come here?*

I didn't ask.

O strange, O torment! How did I feel about Unchee, and how did I feel about Delphine? I didn't know. That was the truth, I didn't know. My lover died Sunday, and her funeral was yesterday. My grandma died Tuesday, and her funeral is today. I meant to march through these funerals and be on my feet at the end, erect as a tin soldier. That was all I knew. Feeling like a tin soldier, too.

I decided not to tell the family about Delphine. Coming in from the airport, I told Emile. My small friend didn't say much, as is his way, but I could feel his concern, and his support.

As we walked up to the little church, on the hill above where the massacre took place, I said to him, "Not a word about Delphine."

He nodded, already knowing.

An overwhelming sense rose up in me, a picture. I saw myself speaking words, and the words came from the pit of my stomach, which was all bile. Whatever words came from there would be false—utterly, perniciously false. I must not say anything of consequence, for whatever I say will be a lie.

"I need to talk about nothing to no one."

Emile nodded.

I felt a knee start to go, and he grabbed my elbow. I smiled at how a very small artist can help a very big athlete, and thanked him with my eyes. I got my balance and took a deep breath.

A lot of people, more than I realized Unchee even knew, came to pay their respects. Before the mass several men and women I didn't know shook my hand and said they were from the Survivors' Association. At the time that didn't mean a thing to me. A couple of them murmured, "She was one of the last." I didn't understand that either. I just shook their hands and moved on. *Accept, nod, say nothing, get on with it.*

As we went into the church, Albert Four Horses, a medicine man Grandpa had known all his life, smudged us with cedar smoke. I hadn't been smudged in several years, and I felt a pang.

Inside I slid into the row with the family, and Emile followed me. He touched my forearm, and I nodded—*I'm okay. I'm going to make myself okay.* I was not going to say anything about Delphine or Unchee. *I won't let the goddamn bile come up.*

I straightened myself up emotionally by thinking about how Indian funerals were like and different from white people's funerals. Delphine's was the requiem mass, formal, ancient, honorable, all elegy and dignity. Unchee's was also the requiem mass, but we turned it coyote. Our people, by God we showed our feelings. We held hands, we cried out, we sobbed loudly, we moaned. Some people went up and threw themselves on the casket and wailed.

When I say we, I mean they. Not me. I was holding the bile down. If I so much as moaned, the whole foulness would come out. I would mourn for and Delphine and myself, alone, somehow, sometime. But for now I held myself aloof.

The priest conducted things just like he would in front of white people—no mention of the four directions, of Mother Earth or Father Sky, of Tunkashila. No smudging. "Fucking white service," I whispered to Emile. White priest, white church, red people, red corpse.

At the end of the service, I went carefully forward with Grandpa and the pallbearers. Grandpa covered Unchee's face with a scarf, and closed the casket on her forever.

As we carried the casket out to the truck, my people turned into a mass of wild pagans. Passing the priest, I checked his face for shock, but he'd seen it all before. People clutched at the casket, raked their hands along it like they were trying to hold Unchee back. The women set to wailing—especially the old women. Every step I took, carrying that casket, was walking through the deep water of despair. The women wailed, they found all the grief in the world and gathered it in, all the grief that has ever been, the griefs of our ancestors every one, and the griefs of all human beings and all beings that walk the earth, or fly, crawl, or stand from roots. They let this grief run, like the greatest flash flood of a river ever was, they let it pour through their bodies and through their voices and into the air until the world vibrated with it.

I didn't wail. I kept my face even and my step even. Inside my heart was pounding, and on every beat it pounded out a name, Delphine, Unchee, Delphine, Unchee.

Emile walked next to me with a worried look.

When we slid the casket into the truck, everyone weeping, weeping, weeping, tears coming with abandon, and the songs of sadness pouring from their throats, then I permitted myself one gesture—I touched my head to the foot of the casket and said, "Goodbye." That word felt true.

I hear tell that in the old days our women sang out their grief even bigger. They cut off their hair, too, and took butcher knives and cut their arms so they'd bleed, all to say their grief.

I needed that, all of it. I needed to reach for the belt knife I didn't have and cut my arms and let my blood flow with my tears. I would have done it, here, now—I cared nothing for what people thought. But I had no way, couldn't find those feelings, couldn't get there from here.

Somehow I squeezed into a car with Grandpa, Senior, Mom, Angelee, and Mayana, and we all got moving in a big line of vehicles to the cemetery near Red Cloud School, where Unchee would be put in the ground.

At the cemetery I kept my equilibrium by thinking about how things were being done. All was in the Indian way. Albert Four Horses said some prayers, a lot of prayers. Then he smudged us all with cedar smoke, smudged even the bottoms of our feet, so nothing bad would cling to us. On top of the casket we set a bag of Unchee's belongings, things she loved and things she might need for the journey she now had to take, beyond the pines. Then we didn't do like white people do, walk away and leave the grave diggers to put her in the ground. We lowered her ourselves, and we, her relatives, took turns shoveling the dirt on top of the casket. Then we escorted Grandpa back to the car, and Unchee was gone.

It was done. I put Grandpa in one car and walked back and slid into Emile's truck. I looked into his eyes, and we exchanged something. *I survived.*

Everyone went to Angelee's house to feed. On the ride I was thinking about the tears we shed, the wails we uttered. My thought was, *I am Indian.* I had funny feelings about it.

My older sister lived in one of those HUD houses at Pine Ridge. They're depressing, being all the same. I guess they're better than trailers, but I'll be damned if I don't prefer the sort of house I grew up in, patched together from a railroad car and other found stuff, a odd house, but real.

We all fell in together somehow around the house, the grown-ups seated and the kids running in and out and letting the cold in. Angelee and Mayana made pot after pot of coffee and served what my mother called "funeral chicken," Kentucky Fried. (She would never eat Kentucky Fried—it was so common at funerals it had come to mean death to her.) From time to time someone would let some tears flow, but now things were changed. After a while Grandpa looked out the window and said, "It's almost sundown." Or Mom reminded people of the same. In our belief you're not supposed to cry after sundown—it's asking for more death. By sundown you wipe your tears away.

I kept my silence. These people who didn't know about Delphine, who didn't know that the woman I lived with died—no, she killed herself—hey, they didn't know me.

And my belly is full of foulness.

I am an outsider here, therefore only an observer. So I looked around and looked around. (*O, yes, from a distance the Great White Doubter observes the people who believe in spirits.*)

My family. *Tiyospaye*, we call it, which has a lot bigger meaning—extended family. My family and my ways, the ones I was born to. (*Now an outsider.*)

They talked jobs, those they had, and mainly those they wanted and wouldn't get. (Shannon County, which means the Pine Ridge rez, according to government statistics, is the poorest county in the United States—lowest income per capita, high unemployment, etc.) They talked relatives who weren't there. They talked relatives who weren't with us anymore (not using their names—we don't say the names of the dead.) They talked times past, better times, it felt like.

I stayed out of the conversations. Maybe needed to talk to Grandpa, Senior, and Mom, or my sisters, but wasn't ready and might never be. Just peered around im-peer-ially. So I was irritated when Aunt Adeline plopped herself down next to me.

She was Grandpa's oldest daughter, from Unchee's first marriage to a man named James Horn. I'd never liked her—to me she was just crabby all the time. I noticed at the church and the cemetery, though, she was hanging close to Grandpa, almost crowding in on him. Now she acted determined to get her say, which is not usually our way.

"Bud, I'm gonna watch after your Grandpa," she said.

"Call me Blue," I said. *I'm not a kid anymore.*

She went on like I hadn't spoken. "He's getting on, you know." Grandpa was eighty—Unchee had just turned eighty-nine—Aunt Adeline herself was sixty-nine. She spoke English, as she'd done around me all her life. Her Lakota was probably pretty rusty, but I guessed she could talk to Grandpa okay—you don't forget the tongue you grew up with.

"He needs caring for, Bud, and I'm the only one." For all she was born into a traditional family, Aunt Adeline was white-man pushy. She'd worked most of her life in a cafeteria at the VA hospital in Denver, and was married to a white man, maybe that's why.

I just nodded and said politely I thought Grandpa would appreciate it. I wondered what was really on her mind. Maybe she was thinking that combining her Social Security with Grandpa's, paying no rent 'cause Grandpa owned his place outright, she'd make out better than on her own in Pine Ridge. Maybe she wanted Grandpa's place. That made no difference to me—I didn't want anything to do with the rez—but it was irritating.

"Sure you wanna live out there in the Badlands, few neighbors and no electricity?"

She looked at me sharp and kind of mean. "How come you never want to know nothing about your own grandmother? Your own family?" Then she chugged off, apparently having accomplished her purpose, acting prickly.

I looked around at my extended family, my *tiyospaye*, which Adeline said I didn't know anything about. These people, in the old way, would have been my center, and we would have lived our lives in the same meadows. What was my extended family a hundred years ago? No, a hundred and fifty? Because one century ago we were already on the reservation, and the *tiyospaye* was weakening.

Way back, we were a kind of small council fire within the bigger council fire of the band—one group within Big Foot's people. Big Foot's band was one circle within the bigger circle of the Mniconjou tribe, and the Mniconjou were one of the seven council fires of the Lakota people.

As one small council fire, in those days we stuck together—we were the one unit that could not be broken down smaller. Occasionally we traveled and camped by ourselves, separately. Or when we didn't want to do what the band was doing, like when Big Foot decided to lead everyone to Pine Ridge, we might have gone to visit relatives in another band. Most of the time, though, we were part of the Big Foot people. We did the big buffalo hunt as one people, made winter camp as one people, traveled as one people.

Sometimes we came together with all the Mniconjou—for the Sun Dance, for instance, and other great occasions.

Once in a great while, for a truly big issue, all seven council fires of the Lakota came together for one big talk.

As a whole family now, a hundred fifty years later, how was our *tiyospaye*, what was the state of the union?

Lousy. We were spread to hell and gone, me in Seattle, a bunch of my male cousins in L.A. Mom and Senior split up, only Grandpa on the family place on Medicine Root Creek. Both my paternal uncles were dead, one in World War II, the other in a one-car accident (that's code talk for the drunken Injun flip). Most of those left on the rez weren't really there, preferring the kingdom of booze. Hell, Senior himself would probably have missed his own mother's funeral if he'd been on a bender.

The women of my generation were doing about half bad. My two sisters had husbands, children; they were making homes. Of my cousins on my dad's side, one woman lived at Manderson alone, raising her kids. Another married a white man and lived in Pensacola, Florida, lost to the family.

(The cousins on my mom's side, naturally, were over at Wambli.)

Of the men of my generation, I was the only one left. My cousin Rob died in Vietnam. Left Hand was in prison in Minneapolis. Rodney was making a living on the powwow circuit and managing to stay drunk. And I was not, in fact, left. I'd been gone for years, and now lived in Seattle.

Suddenly I had a pang, a feeling of real loss, loss of all the things the world takes away. In a flash I saw Unchee's ancient face up close to my ear, and she was laughing about something, whether a good-hearted or mean-hearted laugh I couldn't tell. All at once I felt what a big part of my life Unchee had been, and how I missed her.

The tear that didn't come at the funeral came now, one tear, all I could manage. *More than I used to.*

Mom plopped down on the arm of my chair. I looked up at her face, feeling grateful. "How's my big boy?"

I blinked tearily at this woman who had worked so hard to hold the family together, and failed. I'd seen something I admired today. She walked around Senior neither paying attention to him nor ignoring him. He was just another member of the family. And I remembered that now over at Wambli she was volunteering to help battered women and children. "I love you, Mom."

"Music to a mother's ears." She grinned lop-sided. "Someone wants to talk to you." She nodded at him.

"Grandpa?"

"He's embarrassed to start."

"Mo-om," whined Angelee. "Can you give me a hand?"

"I'm here," Mom said merrily to me, and jumped up and ran off to change the baby or make coffee or whatever.

I looked across at Grandpa—he was smiling at me. *What could it be? If Mom prompted me, it must be important.*

He was halfway back in the recliner that probably came from the Salvation Army and facing the TV. Grandpa didn't have a TV (or even electricity) and didn't care for it, but people always put him in the biggest, most comfortable chair, which was always square in front of the set. I pushed a kitchen chair alongside him and said, "We haven't talked in a long time."

He didn't tread soft around it. He spoke right up in a firm voice, in our people's language. "That Pipe you got, the one Unchee saved for you? Her father's?"

I nodded. *Why bring up that Pipe now?*

"Unchee saved it for the right person."

Oh, shit.

"She never gave it to any of her own children. They weren't right for it. When you were in your mother's womb, Unchee knew you were the one."

GodDAMN it.

"You always wondered how you were picked out? Unchee did it. She knew what you would be, who you would be. That Pipe, it was all she had of her father's. She saved it for you."

He closed his eyes, and for a moment I thought he was going to doze off. When he spoke, his voice was clear and strong.

"That's why you were kept away from white people and white things. Unchee did it. She saw into your heart."

He was silent for a long moment. I didn't know what to say.

"Things change. You're different. Maybe you think so different the Pipe has nothing for you." He opened his eyes unnaturally wide at me, and they seemed to grow bright. "It has gifts. Count on it. That Pipe has very special gifts for you. From your great-grandfather straight to you."

I hesitated, then decided to go along. "Well, what?"

He shook his head. "Only you can find that out."

"How?"

"Pray with that Pipe. It's up to you, whole thing's up to you." He looked down, and I wondered what he was thinking. "The road is red, yes. That doesn't mean it's easy."

"It's been plenty hard, Grandpa."

"Things will be better for you soon."

I thought. *You don't know. I ventured forth, I failed out there, and I have nothing to come back to.*

My stomach lurched. *Delphine is dead, my life is lost.*

I shook my head. *How can I forget, even for a moment?*

"Hey, we need more pop, let's go get some pop."

Senior's voice. He was looking at me.

"Okay. More pop."

I followed Senior toward the front door. "Emile, may I use your car?" My friend came across the room in his fluid way and put the keys in my hand. It wouldn't be his style to toss anything.

Senior and I drove in silence down to Big Bat's, the filling station and everything store. He waited while I bought a couple giant bottles of Pepsi and came back out. I wondered whether he'd stayed in the car to sneak a drink. I could see he had a bottle in his inside jacket pocket. I knew he liked his whiskey in Pepsi.

I wheeled out of the parking lot but didn't head for the house. He didn't say anything. I found myself on the highway headed east, for no reason.

Shit, it's a day for talks.

I didn't know how to begin. I didn't want to call him Senior, which always had an edge on it, and I couldn't call him Dad. I didn't want to speak angrily, but anger kept sticking its head up.

Finally, I said, "I hear you got a new woman."

He jerked his head sideways. "Is that what you want to talk about, Bud?"

No, it wasn't. *What do I want to say? What do I need to say?*

I drove on in silence. When I came to the road that ran north toward Wounded Knee, I automatically turned. Then I realized what I was doing. *Hell, no.*

I stopped the truck under the big sign on the right side of the road, the one that tells all about Crazy Horse.

I didn't know where to start.

"I hope things are going well for you."

Though he kept staring straight out the windshield, I could see the softening in his eyes. "Things are okay," he said. So he didn't want to talk about who he was living with, what his life was like.

"For me too. I guess." I breathed in and out. "Not really. Things are not okay, haven't been okay."

The silence sat between us, years of silence.

"I wrote you about a woman I went to Seattle with."

193

He nodded. Actually I didn't write him, I wrote Mom, but I knew she told him, or passed the letter on.

I turned and looked at him. "She died. Her funeral was yesterday. I've gone to two funerals in two days, Dad."

I stopped myself. That word. "Dad," I'd said. Now it was out and I couldn't take it back.

I looked at him to see if it had caused any catastrophes. None I could see. But I felt different inside. Maybe I liked that, and maybe I didn't.

"We were living together. We were doing good." Three beats went by. "She killed herself."

I could feel his eyes, though they didn't turn toward me. I could feel all of his senses rolling around me like fog, touching me, checking me out, adding up what he found, trying to know my feelings.

I hated it.

I liked it and I hated it.

"She killed herself. I don't know why. No one knows why. We all thought she was doing good." Pause. "I thought we were doing good."

I'd left the journals behind—wasn't ready to read them yet.

He reached into a shirt pocket, got out his pack, offered me one. I shook my head. He lit his own.

Tell him about Delphine. Tell him ... I slammed the dashboard with my hand. It felt so good I did it again. You could feel the vibrations for long seconds.

Then, like an eruption I slung Delphine out for him to see, for me to see. I hurled pathetic words about my woman in front of us, the evidence of my guilt. Delphine, what she was like. Her blackness, and her family's whiteness. My comrade in the shadow of Raven's wing. How I identified with her. How good she felt to me, her body, how much I loved it. Her political ambitions. Her family's prominence. How odd I felt around her, like I never fit, but I wanted to fit among the white people. I wanted another world, Christ, I wanted another world, Christ, I couldn't stand the rez, the cramped life.... I wanted to be ...

"O God," I wailed, "why'd she do it? Why'd she do it?"

I began to cry then, big tears, big sobs. I let it come for maybe a minute and by God I cut it off hard, just cut it off. It was too much, I couldn't let it take me over. We sat for a while, neither saying anything. Finally he lit up again, and when he flicked the cover back on the lighter, he said, "I'm here for you, Bud, you need me."

That felt good, but it wasn't enough, not half enough. "Dad, I'm a traitor. I took our ways and tossed them out the window. I thought they were dead and gone and I threw them away. The white people were winning so I ... went over to their side. I became a white man." I looked at his face in the midwinter darkness. "I'm not ... one of us anymore."

He did the oddest thing. He reached out with a hand and cupped it against my cheek. After a moment, maybe uncomfortable, he drew it back. He said gently, "I'm your father, Bud. I always will be."

Those words felt good, very good. *Hell, you're my dad.*

I started up the car and drove back in silence. We went up to the house in silence. At the front door I looked at him and said, "Thanks."

He nodded his acceptance, and that felt like something, something real.

I sidled over to Emile and let it out, breathing the words, "I want to move back."

He looked up at me with his sympathetic eyes. "Good for you."

"Can we share for a while?"

No thoughts ran through his eyes first, like, *How will you pay the rent without a job?* "Sure." That's what brother-friends say.

I brought it up. "How am I gonna live here and have a career?"

He smiled lightly. "Welcome to the club."

I said the rest to myself. *How can I be anywhere else and have a life?*

I went to Grandpa first, squatted by his big chair again. "Grandpa, I've decided to move back."

He nodded three or four times. "That's good," he said. "When you're around your family, things will get better. You'll see."

"I don't know what I'm going to do for a job."

"A person never knows. You put your feet on the red road and good things come. You can't see them before you start walking."

I squeezed his arm and went to Mom. "Mom, I'm coming back. I'm moving in with Emile."

"Oh, Bud," she cried, and gave me a big hug.

"We'll still be spread out," I said. "Rapid, Wambli, Pine Ridge, Rosebud."

"Lot closer than Seattle," she said.

Angelee and Mayana were cleaning up the kitchen. I told them, and felt surprised to see real gladness in their eyes, pleasure to have their brother back. That made me think what I'd been missing.

"Will you stay with us?" said Angelee.

"Or us?" said Mayana.

Neither one of them had a nickel's worth of room, and I'd be living in the margins of someone else's life. "Emile," I said. Their faces registered what that meant, Rapid City, sort of close but not really. "I have to find a job," I said.

Suddenly I remembered. I would have some money, whatever I could sell Delphine's Z car for. Money meant time. I would have a little time to find my place here, my place to live, my place in the family, my place among the people.

"We'd be glad to have you," said Angelee, kind of sing-song. And they would. With Indians there is always room for family. But I couldn't do that, not anymore.

Senior—Dad—was last. His eyes were on the evening news. I wondered how often he followed the national and international soap operas as presented by Dan Rather. "I'm moving back," I said.

I waited, and after a moment his eyes focused on me. "Good," he said. "Good."

"I'll stay with Emile at first."

"You can stay with us." *You and the woman you never mention, who you didn't bring to the funeral.*

"With Emile," I said again, and squeezed his arm. "Good."

So we men bunked together in the living room, Emile and I on the floor, Senior on the couch, Grandpa right in the recliner. My dreams that night were different—easier, and full of dance music. I woke up early. The room was half dark—first light was afoot outside, the late, weak first light of the Moon of Popping Trees. I looked around at the huddled forms in the living room. Emile, my oldest friend. Grandpa, who'd been a father to me. Senior, my dad, who I'd begun to make friends with last night. It felt good. I needed these men in my life. A life without them ...

Then I noticed that there were blankets on the sofa, but nothing giving them shape. Senior was already up. I listened, and heard nothing. Quietly, I got up and looked out the front window. He was sitting on the front steps, elbows on knees, hands dropped between. He had no coat—wasn't he cold? I also was an early riser, had always been, even as a white man, I liked to say hello to the sun in a respectful way, early in the morning. I wondered if this was what Senior was doing. I wondered if I should go out and sit on the steps and do it with him, and take us both coats. I watched, held for no reason I knew.

Senior stood up, with some difficulty. Was he getting old and stiff? He was fifty-six. He made motions of fumbling at his pants, and then stood still, doing what I had done at dawn so many mornings. He did it copiously. I grinned. He took a step backward, turned, staggered, and fell into his own piss. His bottle skittered across the frozen ground.

I stared at him. *Pick your own damn self up,* said my heart.

I turned away from the window.

Welcome home, Blue.

Part Four
Going to the Mountain

FALLING BETWEEN
TWO BAR STOOLS

Click your heels three times," says Glinda, the good witch of the North, "and say, 'There's no place like home.' "

In the ancient stories, there's always a place called home. Maybe a man ventures out away from his village, has his adventure, accomplishes some important mission, and comes back home. The grand conclusion, in my people's stories, may be that he's able to help the people in some big way, and he now has a stronger place in the *tiyospaye*, his extended family, and in the tribe. In your stories the grand outcome is that he's able to make a woman his own and start a family. Or sometimes that he becomes king, or that he gets rich.

In the best stories, you see that it's coming back to the people you belong to, and being there in a good way, that matters. The people you belong with, where they live, where you grew up, that's your home, your center.

What I thought I was doing, after Delphine's death, was coming home. Turned out I wasn't. I lived without a complete circle of self, family, people. An arc is a fragment. A circle is something whole.

It's hard for me to think back on it now, and hard for me to tell you. Here it is, in the short version.

After Unchee's funeral I went back to Seattle and sat in the apartment and thought. I read Delphine's journals. I am not going to talk about those, except to say that they painted vividly a picture of a person tormented by what she did not talk about, her blackness. I gave the journals to the Ryan family. Poe called back to say they destroyed the journals, so the record is lost.

For four or five days I pondered what she wrote and our life together. I wrote my own journal about my realizations. I wrote that Delphine and I were soul-connected, as she said. We were drawn to each other because we both lived in dark shadows, and perversely tended the darkness, and kept the light out.

Do not ask me why I did not ask whether I might take my own life one day.

Do not ask me why I did not ask whether my people were dancing with death.

Remembering Grandpa's injunction to pray with my great-grandfather's Pipe, I tried it. I speculated dimly that it might lift the Raven's wing and dispel my interior darkness. I told myself I didn't expect any miracles. Therefore I did not receive any. Instead I felt self-conscious, and quit. Promised myself I'd do it back home, where it would feel more natural. Sorry to tell you, I didn't follow through.

So, stuck with myself, I settled things up in a determined way. I quit my job at the station, sold the furniture, and sold the Z car. Called the Ryans to say goodbye—Michael seemed regretful, and Poe brushed me off. Courtesy of Continental Trail-ways I went back to the rez. Note that I said back to the rez, not back to the blanket.

I had a good chunk of cash. Do you know what happens to money on the rez? You owe your relatives, they're like yourself. If they need something and you have some money, you help them. You pay for your niece's new dance outfit. After all, she needs to look good. And a dance outfit can cost a thousand bucks—all that expensive brain-tanned deer hide, those feathers and bells, the ermine skin she wraps her hair in. And you got a dozen nieces and nephews. Some brothers, sisters, two parents, three or four grandparents, maybe four or five great-grandparents, and more cousins than you can count. Remember, this is big stuff. The people you call cousins, we think of as brothers and sisters. So with us a very, very big family is tight.

You know why most rez people don't have a phone? 'Cause you let your relatives use it when they need to, long-distance included. You say "Fine," and you don't ask for anything in return. Pretty soon you can't pay the bill and it's disconnected. A year or two later you start wanting a phone again, you put it in, and go through the same stuff all over again. But, hey, your relatives are more important than a phone.

Emile and I got off to a good start. He was working at that big trading post in Rapid City, Prairie Edge, selling Indian arts and crafts. Emile was an asset there because of his gentleness and his beauty (which is funny, 'cause he's not interested in women). He doesn't talk much—Emile walks on eggshells around words, all words. But his looks and his knowledge of Indian arts made him a hit at Prairie Edge.

Right off, with my bucks, we looked for a good place to live. Emile wanted a studio, and a place where he eventually could have a gallery. That's how we came to the house in Keystone where he still lives and sells. With the first and last months' rent and cleaning deposit, plus buying a used Pinto (the Ford car, not the horse), I put a good dent in my money.

Right off also I went home to see Grandpa and Aunt Adeline, and to Mom over at Wambli. Took a couple of big boxes of groceries to each place, knowing that would help them out a lot. We had some good talks, but the truth was, I was a different person from the boy who left twelve years before. They sent me to learn to be a white man, and I did. Same with Angelee and Mayana, living in Pine Ridge. I didn't try to see Senior. He wasn't in Mission but was wandering around somewhere, drunk, which is a place unto itself.

It was with Angelee and Mayana that I got a glimpse of it. Nothing much to talk about. Angelee's husband was working at Big Bat's, and Mayana's was gone to L.A., presumably to get work and send money home, but she hadn't heard from him. Their talk was of unemployment checks, AFDC, food stamps, and their friends' pregnancies. Already, at twenty and twenty-two, they were getting fat the way so many Indian women do. It was depressing.

I skiddooed back to Rapid. Hey, I'd realized my family was important, but that didn't change my lifestyle. I didn't intend to be down and out. I meant to be a different kind of Indian, to make good, to show an Indian can be a success.

So I had a lot to prove, and damn, it started out easy. Long John Silver hired me right off—why shouldn't he? I was a good jock, I was young and willing to work cheap, and with me Long John could show he was doing affirmative action. I got my own afternoon spot, and things were hunky dory. I was gonna be an Indian that proved red folks can do it.

I cannot tell you what a weird life it was. Have you ever been walking a trail and suddenly there's water running down the middle? So you walk one foot on each side? If the water's wide, there's nothing awkwarder than that. It's about the way I felt, and it went on for a dozen years.

Nine to five working for Long John Silver. Nights dating white girls, nobody steady at first, quite a few women. Weekends dating or going to see my family. Medicine Root Creek, or Pine Ridge, or Wambli. Got a honey over at Pine

Ridge, went there pretty much every weekend, stayed with her. Monday morning back at work. Weekday evenings out dancing or in the bars.

I did see quite a bit of my family, I did spend a lot of time around Indian people. But I wasn't walking that path. I didn't go to Sun Dance, didn't go into the sweat lodge, didn't involve myself in tribal matters. The Pipe Unchee gave me was just a piece of decoration. I was just a well-meaning visitor to the rez, not part of the people.

Lots of reasons—I had a white-man job, I lived in the white-man town. Most of all, I *thought* white-man, I was a Great White Doubter. I thought the white way was *the* way, and the red way should get left behind.

After half a dozen years I got a steady white girlfriend. Marietta came to Rapid with a film crew, two little kids, and a husband back in L.A. We found ourselves eager to have a good time, which meant drinking. We took up country dancing, which kept us high in the bars. We took up studying wines, which kept us high in the kitchen. We took up every kind of drinking there was. I drank with her every night from quitting time until I passed out at her place or mine, or sometimes another woman's. Didn't see much of my roommate, though sometimes he found me where I'd collapsed. My drinking got so impressive it scared Emile. During the years I was gone, he'd gone to AA and quit drinking. But I wouldn't touch AA. I was having too good a time. I had a high, handsome piece of the good life.

Emile tried, I give him credit for that. He told me two or three times to go to AA or find another place to live—I was putting his sobriety at hazard, he said. Finally, when he was beginning to sell his paintings and had quit Prairie Edge, he handed me my share of the deposit and last month's rent and told me to find my own place to live.

I got mad as a grizzly bear, and I'm sorry to say I spoke harsh words. But he was firm. No drinking or drunkenness in the house—I could come back when I was sober.

Hah! I said. I'll show you. I went and married Marietta. How that story came out, you already know.

I never went back to Emile's house until he picked me up from those railroad tracks, all those years later.

Oh, please, do not ask me why I was drinking. Don't ask me why I loved booze more than my best friend, more than my wife, more than my life. You have been paying attention, haven't you?

So that's the story—I spent from '79 until last September spinning tunes, making a good living, marrying Marietta and taking care of her two little kids, staying sotted, and being a white man. And dabbling at being a red man on weekends, occasionally. When Long John needed to brag about having a minority working at the station.

In truth, though, I didn't have two skins, or two minds, or two hearts. I couldn't split my heart between red and white, couldn't split my mind. So I put all of me in the bottle, and pickled my soul.

I got to where Emile found me laying on the C&NW tracks, drunk, battered, and most of the way to hell. That's when he said, "You got to go on the mountain."

Blue Crow Stumbles Toward the Mountain

At the end of my first day in Emile's bed, he brought me some herbal tea. I opened one gummed-up eyelid and took it. I half wanted to hug him, but nothing on my body would move.

"I can't do it," I said.

"Can't do what?"

"Go on the mountain."

"And you can't stop drinking. And you can't keep trying to kill yourself. And you can't keep living the way you are."

That was a lot of words in a row for Emile.

"I am the Great White Doubter," I moaned. Making the effort to talk hurt, but I needed to talk, O I needed to talk.

So I told him about those long-ago college days, about Bradley Dornan and Ron Sternberg and the thoughts that led to my Great White Doubts. I even told him about the day I slam-dunked all the old ways into the trash can.

Emile shrugged without shrugging. He nodded without nodding. Finally he said, "What this got you is nothing."

I looked sharp at him. Maybe I was looking for a philosophical argument that would prove my Great White Doubts wrong, or whatever. Instead Emile had given me an observation about me, not the doubts.

"I can't go on the mountain. I can't."

Emile just looked at me. He said, "Because of your doubts."

"Because of my doubts, because I've shit all over myself and my people, because I threw our ways in the road and ran over them with a truck, because I'm a drunk, because I hate myself, because, BECAUSE."

Emile sat and thought a long time. Then he said, "Why do you love your doubts and your becauses and clasp them to your bosom? Look where they got you."

And he left.

At supper time he brought us cheeseburgers and a big mess of french fries.

"It's crazy," I launched in. "The mountain is crazy. Hanging tobacco ties from trees and fasting and going without water and hoping a bird will bring you a message—it's all wacko."

Emile said, "What's sane, repeating what you've been doing over and over? How many times you want to go flying through the air above the railroad tracks? How many times you want to try to kill yourself?"

And he went back to painting.

I wasn't up to thinking that evening. Besides, thinking didn't make sense. For more than twenty years I'd been spinning that left brain and it hadn't done a thing for me.

A worthwhile thought came, something from my insides percolating up on its own. *The problem is the Great White Doubts.*

I found the remote and clicked on the bedroom TV. Couldn't go down the route of thinking about that. Emile came in with a whole cheesecake, which we split. How can a guy a little over five feet and just over a hundred pounds eat as much as me?

"I have too many doubts," I said.

Emile turned his simple and sincere eyes to mine. You could always see Emile's heart, and it wasn't his way to speak other than simply and directly.

"You want an idea?"

I took a deep breath. "Yeah."

"Here it is. You committed yourself to reasoning things out. That made you the Great White Doubter. Now you hate your life.

"Try something completely different. Do this as an act of faith," he said. "Pure faith. Decide it's BETTER that going on the mountain seems crazy. Then do it."

Finally I had to look away from his face.

"What have you got to lose? Your life? Hey, it's gone. All your experience says your way isn't working. So as an act of faith, try the way of the grandfathers."

This time he touched me on the arm and smiled when he headed into his studio.

He called me to the table for bacon, eggs, fried potatoes, and toast the next morning. He asked me nothing, I volunteered nothing. We ate. He smiled at me with his childlike teeth. I hadn't been eating too good, but now I chowed down. Emile was making me this gift again. I looked around the house. This was where I'd lived with hardly a day sober. This was where I launched myself into the life of booze. I kicked one foot up and down, and that hurt. I thought, *Things couldn't possibly get any worse....* But I said nothing.

When Emile went to work, I laid in bed and replayed my life. A twenty-three-year detour through the white world. The last ten years on the teeter-totter. Going up—I'm feeling good with a couple in me. Going down, drunk enough to feel no pain. Going up—sober enough to work. Going down, drunk enough to feel no pain. "I'm feeling no pain" meant for me, *I'm as good as a white man, got a good job, job is stinking useless and I hate my life, but …*

I tried not to think. I tried not to feel. Feeling hurt like hell.

A voice inside me said clearly, "Go on the mountain."

I don't have a spirit to take on the mountain. Or none I'm acquainted with.

Inner voice: "Stop fussing and feuding. Go on the mountain."

I rested. I grabbed the remote and used the TV to quiet the voices arguing inside me. I slept and dreamt voices quarreling, getting nowhere. All day I did that, all night I did that.

The next morning I walked with firm steps into the studio. Emile stopped his brush in midair. He was painting a big featherburst on an elk robe. It was going to be beautiful.

"Thanks for what you're doing for me."

"You're welcome. You're my *hunka*." He turned back to his elk robe and made a couple of green strokes. Green is the color of Mother Earth.

"My inner voice is telling me to go on the mountain," I said, half proud and half sheepish.

"If you can hear your inner voice, that's a good start."

I shuffled into the kitchen and forced myself to stay on my feet long enough to make pancakes for both of us. Emile came when I called. "What do I do?"

"We'll go see Pete Standing this afternoon," he said. Emile had been on the mountain lots of times. The Great White Doubter would need a lot of help, we both knew that. And my doubts might yet get the better of me.

Taking me to see Pete was a way of vouching for me. My credit wasn't good with a lot of people around the rez, not my dollar credit but the reliability of my word, the trueness of my spirit.

"I'm going to the grocery store."

He cocked an eye up at me. "We'll go see Pete if you're sober," he said.

I made the short drive in the Lincoln and came back sober with groceries for the household and tobacco to offer to the medicine man.

INTO THE SWEAT LODGE

In the late afternoon we packed sandwiches and put coffee in a thermos and headed around the long road to Pete's place near Chimney Butte.

Pete Standing was fixing his woven-wire fence. He wore an old-fashioned white shirt, tiny, rimless glasses, and a belly big enough to honor a man of maybe sixty. He is a good medicine man—I know Grandpa respects him. Pete waited for what we had to say.

Not being a Pipe carrier, I couldn't ask formally in the proper way, offering my Pipe four times. I gave him the tobacco. "Will you put me on the mountain?"

"You don't sound sure."

"I'm not sure of much of anything." I tried to think how not to say it, but couldn't. "I've drunk myself into a dead end."

"You got a row to hoe, then." Pete looked at me bluntly. "I don't put no one on the mountain is drinking." He waited. "You bottomed out?"

"Yeah."

"Okay, here's what you hold in your mind. You've tried running things your way. It didn't work. Tomorrow, we sweat, you ask Spirit how to run things, and you listen." His eyes were no-nonsense. "We go in maybe six tomorrow." In other words, be here.

We showed up two hours before six, to help out. Build the fire, get thirty-six rocks hot—there's a whole list of jobs and it takes time.

You don't need to know much about the sweat lodge, *inipi*, we call it. It is one of the seven sacred rituals of our people. Heat rocks (preferably lava rocks) in a big fire and put them in a low, dark hut. Go in naked, pour water on the rocks, get it hot-hot, pray, sing, beat the drum. Take a break and cool off. Repeat three more times.

I'd done it plenty as a kid, and assisted Grandpa when he poured, which means when he ran the ceremony. After twenty-three years, just the thought gave me the heebie-jeebies. The sweat was the old, *old* way.

To calm myself down, to bolster myself my resolve, I went to the car and got out the blanket, tobacco, red cloth, and sack of groceries I'd brought. I handed them to Pete formally. These were the traditional gifts when you ask someone to put you on the mountain.

O, am I really going on the mountain? I was afraid. I was afraid of the hunger and thirst for four days. I was afraid of not being able to bear it and walking off the mountain early. I was afraid I would stand there and lie there all that time and all I would see was hills, trees, and the empty air. I was afraid of being a fool.

I murmured the watchwords Emile had given me. *Act of faith.*

My people use the sweat lodge to purify themselves, to pray and bring themselves closer to Spirit. There's power in a sweat, when the person pouring it knows how to bring it in. Grandpa used to tell me he'd seen amazing sights in a sweat lodge. Sometimes blue lights would flash around in the pitch dark. Sometimes pebbles flew around and hit people—this was one of the Stone People coming to you.

Grandpa got hit by a pebble once, and still wore it by a thong around his neck. At my last sweat, I was still a kid, and never had any such power.

First we got the fire started. The three of us formed a tripod over the fire pit with cottonwood limbs and stacked on others until we had a tipi. Pete offered tobacco to the four directions, and especially to Salamander, the Fire Spirit, and threw it on the rocks. Then he got the fire going with kindling.

Then we got the lodge ready. It was a low framework of willows tied together with red cloth, looked like a bowl turned upside down. We covered it with visqueen, Salvation Army blankets, scraps of rug, and pieces of canvas. The idea was to get it completely dark inside. When we got it covered, and the edges held down with rocks and dirt, the lodge became a living entity, representing the womb of Mother Earth.

While the rocks were heating, Pete prepared the lodge ceremonially. I didn't know exactly what he did in there, but he entered alone, and took a while. I smelled the cedar and sweetgrass he burned, purifying the lodge and inviting the spirits to enter. I heard him blow the whistle made from an eagle wing bone, and sing a song invoking the presence and power of the four directions.

I will not go over all that he did to prepare his Pipe to be smoked, and place it on the altar in front of the lodge. When the Pipe was ready, the road from the fire pit to the lodge was a living entity, and no one was allowed to walk between it and the lodge.

We were almost ready. "Emile, will you bring in the rocks?" asked Pete.

While Emile pitchforked rocks into the lodge, Pete and I stripped and took towels. We walked once around the outside of the lodge, sunwise, what you call clockwise. Then Pete led the way into the lodge, circled sunwise, and sat by the door. I sat in the back, Emile would sit by the entrance opposite Pete.

Some of the rocks actually glowed red. Pete used deer antlers to arrange them in the pit. Emile brought in the bucket of water and dipper, and Pete said some things.

I said silent thanks to the rocks. They absorb the energy of the fire and came to the pit to give this spirit up for us. When the water hits the rocks, they transform it magically into steam, which is the breath of Mother Earth, and our breath, our prayers, and our spirits, all of them rising to Father Sky.

Sweats are simple. We would sweat for four rounds, Pete pouring water on those rocks keeping it hot. In each round one of us would pray, and Pete might sing a song. Between rounds we open would the door and take a break. We would drink water out of the dipper, crying "*mitakuye oyasin*" as we did. We would smoke Pete's Pipe.

"Close the door."

Emile did.

It was dark-dark. I couldn't see anything—it was dark as my mother's womb must have been.

O-o-o-h! I got goose-bumply. The willies ran up and down me, like mice. *O, what am I doing here?*

"How you doing, Blue?" Pete's heavy voice.

"I'm nervous."

"You got anything will help him, Emile?"

Out of the dark came Emile's soft, firm voice. "That's why we call it an act of faith."

Silence. Then Pete welcomed us there, asked forgiveness from the spirits if we didn't do anything the right way, said we were just human beings come looking for help. "Emile, you wanna pray first?"

I am not going to tell you exactly the words that were spoken and sung in the lodge that day.

Prayers were said for our children, including unborn children. For our women. For our elders. For the Sun Dancers. For the keepers of Pipes and Bundles. For our spiritual leaders. For all our people.

Prayers were said for our families, especially for the sick.

Prayers were said particularly for me, that I might find the strength to stop drinking. That I get something on the mountain that would help me and the people.

The spirits were called upon in the songs Pete sang, the Four Directions, Mother Earth, Father Sky, and the Mystery. Eagle and other animal spirits were called upon.

As he raised his voice in song in our Lakota language, Pete poured the water upon the rocks. The heat slapped me in the face. I wanted to put my head down, on the cool earth, beneath the blistering steam. But I refused. *I am willing to suffer and offer the spirits my suffering.* I slapped my back with the sage switch, I prayed fiercely, anything to push my mind beyond the heat, to put my consciousness and my spirit into Pete's words, to experience this sweat fully and get whatever was there for me today.

Before the last round started, I declared my intention to go on the mountain and asked for Pete's help. Now I made my request formally, ceremonially, in a manner that honored my strength and his. I felt like I was stammering.

When we finished the fourth round, Pete asked Emile to bring the Pipe in. Holding it, he gave me a talking to. "You want to go on the mountain, no drinking, no using for at least thirty days. Let me know when you're ready."

I blinked, uncertain.

"You ever promised to quit drinking?"

"Sure."

"You ever prayed for the strength to do it?"

"No."

"You ever asked for the strength in an AA meeting?"

"No." I glanced guiltily at Emile.

"You go to an AA meeting every day, thirty days."

I fidgeted.

"You willing to do that?"

I fidgeted.

"Your feet aren't on the path, you don't do that."

I grimaced. "Okay."

"You ever asked the Pipe to help you quit drinking?"

"No."

Pete's eyes felt like they were jabbing at me. "You smoke this Pipe today. You smoke a Pipe every day thirty days. You ask it to help you quit drinking. You ask it for help. Maybe YOU can't quit. The Pipe, it got strength you don't."

He lit the Pipe in the normal ceremonial way and passed it to me.

"Pipe and AA, every day thirty days."

My college-trained mind said NO, but I took the Pipe and puffed. They call it an ACT of faith.

I Am Powerless over
Alcohol

Pete didn't waste any words or cut me any slack, did he?"
Emile's eyes danced over at me merrily, then back at the
road. The drive home from Pete's, circling a big roadless
area of the Badlands, is long and dreary. "You were hoping
for SOME drinking?"

I held my tongue. Part of me was complaining, *This is too
hard. I can't do it.* Abstinence was a requirement. If I didn't
bring it, Pete wouldn't put me on. If I drank and lied to him,
a payback might come from Spirit, and I wouldn't like that.

Emile says, "Talk to me about it."

I blurted, "I don't think I can."

Right then I realized—*That's what I truly believe.* Saying
"okay" to Pete, that was purely a shuck. I *knew* I couldn't do
it. I stared into the darkness beyond the windshield. *Hopeless.*

"The Keystone meeting is tomorrow night at seven
o'clock. To go every day, you must go around to different
meetings, different places." He looked at me with … what
can I call it?…. brotherly love. That's the truth. "I will go
with you," he said. "It will be good for me."

Well, toodlely winks. I didn't want to go to no meeting.
AA, that's white people's stuff. So I'd been telling Emile for
years. White people's stuff means, It works for them but it

doesn't work for us. Like hospitals and Christianity, good for them, bad for us.

He's willing to go with me every day. "Well, shit."

Emile looked sideways at me. "Do you have any power over drink? Can you stop?"

I shook my head no, feeling bitter about it, and nasty.

"Then it's time to make a first step. 'I admit I am powerless over alcohol, and my life is unmanageable.' "

I made a snorting sound. "AA isn't going to save me."

Compassion was in his eyes. "Try just one notion. 'I admit I am powerless over alcohol, and my life is unmanageable.' "

I stared out at the night. *I am hopeless, I am pathetic.* I couldn't keep a tear or two from dribbling down. *He's willing to go with me every day.* I was deeply ashamed. I said, "Two tears in a bucket, motherfuck it. Okay, I'll do it."

Emile said quietly, "How much longer you do you have in the Rockerville house?"

"Closes in a month."

"Move out now. Stay with me. Every day for a month we go to a meeting. You give Pete the thirty days of sobriety."

"Aw …"

"Every day for one month. You don't have a job, you don't have anything you have to do. Give yourself a chance. Every day for one month. I, your *hunka*, I am asking you."

"Okay." I didn't know how in the HELL I felt.

The next day I took one big step. I filled the Lincoln with my stuff and drove to Emile's. He gave me the bedroom, said he slept on the studio sofa most of the time anyway.

We went to meetings every day for a month. Hated the meetings for a week, began to like some, finally settled on a noon meeting in Rapid I liked. I never took along anything but what Emile said, "I admit I am powerless over alcohol, and my life is unmanageable." Nothing I said in meetings, really, was anything but that, how I'd been living and how powerless it showed I was. What I like most about the meetings was that I hadn't taken a drink yet. What I liked least about them was that they were nothing but white people.

I spent a lot of that month blaming white people. For bringing firewater to Indian people. For fixing things so brothers killed brothers and fathers raped daughters. For going on and on trading booze when they knew what it was doing to us, going on even when their own traders hollered that it was morally wrong. And for all the crimes that didn't relate to booze. I ain't gonna list them, you can do that near as good as me.

I was so mad and sad and outraged and vengeful it's a wonder I didn't get drunk. Long John Silver is DAMN lucky we didn't run into each other that month.

You may gather that something hadn't yet occurred to me. No matter how we got here, no matter how I got here, I had to get myself out.

I also spent that month, well, fighting with the station and with the government about my unemployment and severance pay. And repairing relationships. I told Mom, Angelee, and Mayana how sorry I was. They said I had nothing to make amends for. I think they were just glad to see me sober enough to know I'd messed up. Couldn't find Dad in Mission, word was he'd gone to California. Sure wasn't keeping in touch with us anymore. Tried to make amends to Sallee, but she wouldn't get together with me. Went to Rosaphine's but she wouldn't even open the door. Saved going to Grandpa's for last, because it would be hardest.

Grandpa acted very glad to see me. (Aunt Adeline fussed around us both, and acted like I was taxing Grandpa too much—he's ninety now.) I told Grandpa I was sorry, sorry

I'd gone away from the people, sorry I'd been drunk, sorry I'd wasted my life, sorry I hadn't walked the special road they held me apart for.

Grandpa waved it away with a wavery hand. "Maybe you needed to do that. Maybe you learned from it. Maybe you have something extra to give. Bud," he says, "maybe you just done took a long time to bloom." And he giggled at his pun.

He paused. He leaned forward and put his elbows on his knees—it seemed like the gesture of a man twenty-five years younger. He smiled sweetly, almost flirtatiously. "Dreamer," he said, "what are your dreams?"

I didn't answer—couldn't think of any answer.

After a bit he nodded to himself and said, "Bud, you ever smoke that Pipe, the one Unchee gave you from her father?"

"I been smoking Emile's Pipe with him. I am not a Pipe carrier." Should have been these last twenty years, but ...

"Emile's Pipe, that's good, good start. Now you go home, smoke your great-grandfather's Pipe. You ask to see things."

I hesitated. Then I thought, *This is the story of my life, hesitation.* Then I thought, *Even thinking that is a hesitation.*

Grandpa repeated himself. "You smoke that Pipe tonight. You don't need no ceremony, that Pipe, get started."

"Yes."

"*Washtay.*"

He sat back, looking fatigued from the effort.

"Grandpa, I'm going on the mountain."

He brightened at that. "*Washtay! Washtay!* You go on that mountain, have a big dream. Then you follow that dream. Also, smoke the Pipe. Start tonight. That Pipe, it has things for you."

"Yes."

"What else you want from an old man today?"

"I want to learn the old stories, the really old stories." I'd been thinking about Ron Sternberg and what he said about creation stories and that book I'd cribbed from, the one of Lakota myths, written by a white man.

Grandpa was good with that, he gave me names. "This man over at Porcupine, Thomas Tall Elk, he knows about Wakinyan, you ask him. A man works at Little Wound, Robert Kills Enemy, he knows about the trickster, Iktomi, you talk to him about that." A couple more names, too, and advice—"Those old people, they can tell you who else knows something."

I'd thought it out. Talk to the old people who know the ancient ways of the Lakota, and how these ways began, and the reasons for them. Sit and hear the stories. That's a better way than any books.

I couldn't finish without telling Grandpa the rest of it. "I'd like to get the stories on tape."

His eyes flashed up at me and then down and it was like he withdrew, visited some place within. Our people have rules about sacred things—no photos, no video tape, no audio, nothing. After a good while he came back. "Maybe that's the right way. Maybe we don't get 'em down, lose 'em." He paused again. "You ask that Pipe, you ask the Pipe, tell you about that."

That night I smoked the Pipe Unchee gave me. Every evening after that Emile and I went to a meeting and smoked Unchee's father's Pipe together. This was the true beginning of my life as a Lakota man.

Baloney, you're thinking. *Didn't your old doubts come back? Didn't you feel foolish? Didn't you take a drink?*

Yes, yes, and no.

The doubts came back a lot. Sometimes they felt like mice nibbling me to death. I felt foolish a lot. Sometimes I'd look around to make sure none of my sophisticated white friends could see me.

My faith was a step forward and a step backward.

But I clung to two thoughts. *I've given the white way a lot of years, and it hasn't worked.*

And, *I'm not drinking.*

I had as a guide also one feeling. My heart told me this was right.

Here was a classic division. We Lakota distinguish between the two eyes of the head and what we call the *chante ishta*, the single of the heart. The two eyes analyze and think. The single eye sees whole, entire, and being the eye of the heart, knows. Now the two eyes of the head told me the Pipe had no power. The eye of my heart told me it did.

I'm not drinking.

By following my head, I had nothing to lose but my life.

This is a story, so I have said enough about AA. But I have never stopped going to meetings. Nor will I. "I admit I am powerless over alcohol."

Here's the kicker. I didn't believe in a higher power. My well-educated mind knew better.

For a dozen years I drank more and more. I asked a higher power for help—I asked the Pipe—and I stopped.

Don't let your well-educated minds tell you different.

CHUP TAILS

Something else happened that first busy, unemployed month—I met Chup Tails. Saw him first time at a meeting in Hot Springs. It was a First Step meeting, which means you tell how and why you got started in AA. I liked those meetings—I was still working on that First Step—"I admit I am powerless over alcohol, and my life has become unmanageable." Hearing how other people tell how they bottomed out and washed somehow into an AA meeting felt real good to me.

"I'm Chup," he began, "and I'm an alcoholic and an addict." He was small and mild-looking. His face looked like he'd spent his life in bar fights. A thick scar ripped from one nostril almost to the ear. He was twenty years older than me and ten times as beat up–looking. I felt right at home with him and wanted to hear his story. Hell, in the room there was me, Emile, Chup, and about twenty people looked like insurance-selling Republicans. One curious thing. While he talked, he rolled a cigarette with one hand alone, a trick of old-time cowboys. He kept his eyes on the cigarette while he talked.

"I gonna tell my story full. I need to do this sometimes.

"I started drinking in high school. Dropped out, joined the army, went to Korea. Got my Purple Heart, came home to the VA Hospital in Denver. There I got really strung out, morphine, weed, beer, wine, you name it.

"Got out in six months, came back home to Oglala. Been raised in a traditional way, the old way, the red road. Now, though, no job, nothing to do but get drunk and stoned. Drove up to the Twin Cities with some buddies, all of us drinking all the way, good-timing along. In a bar in the St. Paul we got into big a fight. I hit a biker with the big end of a pool cue. Killed him. Freaky, I guess, fractured his skull, killed him."

Chup was real simple, the way he told it.

Now there was a new kind of silence in the room. A lot of people who'd been looking Chup in the eye lowered their gaze. Usually, confessions in meetings, they don't go to killing other human beings.

"They sent me up for manslaughter. What saved my life was some AIM guys came to the prison."

Not a lot of times a traditional Lakota gonna tell you AIM guys changed his life. To us they were city Indians.

"They told us we had a right to our religion, suggested we start sweating. We built a lodge, we done it. I started carrying the Pipe."

His voice was steady, but his eyes showed hurt. "When I got out, I started coming to meetings, Pine Ridge and here. Did an honest first step—'I acknowledge that I am powerless over dope and booze and my life is unmanageable.' Made myself learn the one-day-at-a-time lesson."

He looked around the room, using white-man eye contact. "Twenty-nine years, I'm still doing one day at a time. I've fallen off the wagon. I've got back on, quick and scared." He looked down at his knees and seemed to consider. "You know," he went on, "I've thought on what it means, this 'one day at a time.' To me it means, We must begin, and hope that after each step, we find enough light to take the next step. No more than that, but it's everything.

"I'm powerless over alcohol. Without the Pipe and these meetings, my life would be unmanageable. Without the Pipe and these meetings, I'd be dead. Thanks."

"Thanks, Chup," we chorused. That was the conventional group response, but I meant it. I respected that man. Laying his stuff out for a bunch of white people, I wouldn't have done it. I felt drawn to him.

After the meeting I shook his hand and spoke hesitantly. "Every meeting I find some one thing, at least, I need to take away with me. Tonight it was what you said, enough light to take the next step. Thanks."

"It's good to see Indians at this meeting," he said so quiet I hardly heard him. "Usually I'm the only one."

I asked for his phone number, and he gave me a card. "Chup Tails, R.E.," it said. R.E. meant Recognized Expert. It is the initials faculty people at our colleges get instead of Ph.D. if they don't have graduate degrees. "Indian Studies Department, Oglala Lakota College." He took the card back and wrote his home phone on it. In Oglala, I noticed, the closest rez town to Hot Springs, and where Sallee lived.

Ordinarily, way I am, I'd have a let a week or a month go by without calling Chup Tails, knowing I needed to and feeling quirky about it. Since I was working on my recovery full time, I called him the next day and made an appointment to have coffee with him in Hot Springs after the next AA meeting.

Chup didn't deck himself out like any professor. He wore a baseball cap with a fully beaded bill, and where some insignia might be, a beaded thunderbird. I wondered if the combination was a sort of witty way to bring tradition into the present. He was quiet and unassuming. I had the impression that if I didn't speak, he wouldn't.

I soon saw coffee to him meant one cup that he never touched. Instead he rolled those cigarettes with one hand, smoked them, and rolled another.

Emile waited patiently in a nearby booth and sketched. Emile was doing a world to help my recovery.

We fiddled for a few minutes, how are ya, who are ya. His who-are-ya was teacher of Lakota Studies at the college. I couldn't get up my nerve, so I shilly-shallied. "I don't know why I'm here, really."

He said simply, "Tell me your story."

I took a deep breath. *Is this what I came here for?* What I did then felt like jumping off a cliff. "I'm a grandparents' child. I had … ways I was supposed to walk. Instead I've been drunk my whole life." I breathed in and out to steady my feelings.

Chup just sat quiet, watching that hand roll that cigarette.

"I spent twenty-three years drinking, the last half drinking big-time. Twenty-two days ago I tried to kill myself. When I got out of the hospital, my friend took me to a meeting and to a sweat. I have twenty-two days of sobriety."

He nodded and smiled. "You ain't the Lone Ranger, Tonto."

He waited. I noodled in my head. *I sure do feel drawn to you.* I knew it was his Indianness I was drawn to. He had walked more of my road than I had.

Not knowing what to do, I told the story of the ride on the C&NW tracks with Rosaphine. I made it sound like a wild and funny story, not letting it be black as it was. I could see in his eyes he knew it was black. His eyes made me feel how black it was.

"Sorry for the way I told that," I said.

"That's the story of a lot of our people, *kola*. I'm glad you see it for what it is. Once you see, you can do something."

The waitress refreshed my cup of caffeine.

227

"I got to tell you honest," said Chup, "I heard the story about the railroad-track ride before. Told different. Rosaphine and Sallee, they are my nieces."

I gave him a look, I can't imagine what it was.

He grinned and his eyes twinkled. "It's okay. It is."

I fidgeted and fumbled. "What else do I need to say?" Then, embarrassed at my own pretense, I hurried forward. "I need a sponsor."

"I'm willing to sponsor you." Said softly and simply. "I want to sponsor Indian men who want to recover."

"How do we start?"

A sponsor is a crucial part of the AA program, especially when you're a beginner like me. You need a person who's further along in the program to guide you. And for the sponsor, going over fundamentals is a help to him.

"You work the Steps. One by one. As much time as it takes for each one."

"Big commitment."

"Only way to recovery." He blew smoke and looked into it. "You willing or not?"

I knew this was a crossroads. *Red road or black road? Lazy way or hard way? Death or life?*

"I'm willing," I said.

"Meet you next week, same time, same place."

"Okay."

We got up to leave. Emile got up too. "One thing," I said. "Week after next I won't be at the meeting."

One of his eyebrows crept up.

"I'm going on the mountain."

"Good for you, *kola*. Meetings *and* the Pipe."

What Blue Crow Saw on the Mountain

O n the thirty-third day of my sobriety I went with Emile to Pete Standing's place to go into the sweat lodge. I took a buffalo robe, which I borrowed from Emile, and the Pipe inherited from my great-grandpa.

To my surprise and pleasure, Chup Tails was there.

I gave Pete sage, pieces of cloth in the colors of the four directions, and bundles of sticks, as required. He asked me if I had been sober for at least thirty days. I said, "Thanks to the power of the Pipe, yes."

He made tobacco ties from the cloth. He smeared red paint on the stem of my Pipe, filled it with tobacco and sealed it with tallow. Then he led us into the sweat lodge, purified us, gave me instruction and advice, and prayed fervently for my success. His last instructions felt supportive and frightening at once. "Wakantanka always answers the prayers of those who come to him humbly and sincerely, asking for help. But He does not always appear to answer them right away. Sometimes a man or woman must go on the mountain over and over before he is permitted to see beyond, into the spirit world."

So, on my thirty-fourth day without a drink, in company with my supporters Pete and Emile, I headed for the mountain. My mind, heart, and spirit were absorbed with wild fantasies. I imagined having a heart attack or a stroke brought on by hunger and thirst, and dying there on the mountain, alone. I imagined being savaged by bad spirits. I imagined the worst of all, that I would sit on the mountain for four days, and nothing would happen, nothing at all—*so I will be exposed as the fraud I am.*

My people have gone to Bear Butte, on the north side of the Hills, since before the memories of the grandfathers of the oldest men. It is one of our sacred places to cry for a vision. The white people honor it too, for they have set it aside as a state park and reserve it for those of us who follow the way of the Pipe to go on the mountain.

Just to walk around Bear Butte is inspiring. Seekers usually come with tobacco ties as offerings, tobacco wrapped in small squares of cloth in the colors of the four directions, yellow, white, black, and red. These are strung in the trees, like strings of popcorn at Christmas, but unlike white people we keep foremost in our minds the sacred purpose of our ceremony. Everywhere the seeker is reminded of his many predecessors here, the many prayers sent up to the Grandfathers from this place. The very air feels pure with dedication and purpose.

Driving up this time we watched the weather—huge, dark clouds, sheets of lightning, big curtains of rain. "*Wakinyan,*" said Pete, "*washtay.*"

I sniffed involuntarily. The presence of the Thunder Beings wasn't good, not as far as I was concerned. It was scary. First, I didn't want to get dumped on. Or even snowed on, I thought—yes, it's sure possible in October. *My sacrifice is to go without food and water for four days, and to use no shelter but a robe. I don't wanna be wet and cold the whole time.*

Lightning crashed down, right where the butte must be on the horizon. Then a great fork slammed the hills to our left, KA-BAM!

Pete chuckled. "The *Wakinyan* welcome you. *Washtay!*"

There's nothing washtay *about it,* my head screamed. As a matter of fact, as we all knew too well, having a vision of thunder, lightning, and rain turns your life upside down. The way the story goes, these storms, the *Wakinyan*, are the creation of *Inyan*, Stone, the oldest of the gods. In the same way the moon is the creation of the sun, and the wind the creation of the sky. As the stone is solid and immovable, the thunderstorm is fluid, dynamic, unpredictable. Its power is so great that it must shield itself in clouds, so as not to destroy our eyes.

To dream of the lightning, thunder, or rain is so powerful it topsy-turvies your life. In the old days ... Let's just say that if you met a man with the word *lightning* in his name, or *thunder,* or *rain* or *hail,* he was carrying the power and the burden of a great dream. He was so changed, it was like his life was struck by lightning.

A Thunder Being dream ... *I am not ready.*

O how strange are we human beings. We cry to Spirit, "Oh, give me what I need—but not that, Spirit, not that."

From the upper parking lot Pete and Emile walked onto the mountain, carrying the bundles of sticks and some sage. They would prepare my place, the sacred circle where I would spend the four days. I stayed in the car and watched the weather. The lightning, thunder, and rain had stopped now, and the sky was clearing. *Good signs!*

In an hour they were back, and told me how to find the spot on a northeast buttresses near some firs. I stripped to my bathing suit (in the old days we walked in naked!), carried the robe over one arm, my moccasins folded in it. Holding my Pipe in front of me, I stepped forth bare-skinned and barefoot, and threw myself on the mercy of the Powers. As I walked, I uttered the ancient prayer of this way, "*Wakantanka onshimala ye oyate wani wachin cha!*" Great Mystery, have pity on me that my people may live!

Pete and Emile had made a circle of the tall sticks, one in the center and one at each of the four directions, each of these about ten steps from the pole. Bundles of short sticks with small bags of tobacco were tied to the tall sticks. A bed of sage had been laid by the pole, running to the east. This was where I was to lie down when I was tired, or when I slept. Here I put the buffalo robe, and I took up my Pipe, the instrument I used to ask this blessing to come to me.

My job was to Pray, to cry for a vision. I was to do this unceasingly for four days, to beg the powers to take pity on me and grant me power. I stood at the pole, took several deep breaths, which did nothing for my oh-shit feeling, and began.

Holding the Pipe with its stem pointing before me, I walked to the west, singing out the same prayer. I stepped very slowly—I may have spent an hour taking those ten strides to the west and back. When my voice grew weary, I prayed the words silently in my mind. When I wearied of those particular words, I simply focused my mind on the Great Mystery.

For a beginner this work is incredibly difficult. Concentrating, not delving into stray thoughts, is nearly impossible.

I walked crying to each of the four directions. I spent maybe an hour or two stepping toward the pole, all the while praying. When I reached the pole, I returned to the center, for the center of all things is Wakantanka, to whom we must always return. At the center pole I raised my Pipe to Father Sky and asked all the winged creatures to help me, and then pointed the stem to the Earth and asked everything that grows on Mother Earth to come to my aid.

All this time I watched for any creature that might come to me. A bird would be especially important, because they are nearest to Father Sky. But any creature might be a teacher or a messenger, even a bug. If I was granted a vision, any messenger might bring it, one I might not even recognize at the time.

The visions my people seek are not like the ones in the Bible. Moses went up the mountain and came down with Ten Commandments, clear and exact—Do this, don't do that. Saul was struck by a light on the road to Damascus and given instructions to carry the message of Christianity to the gentiles.

Our visions are not so clear-cut. Maybe an animal will appear in the ordinary way, and maybe there's a message if you're willing to listen. If a hawk flies over, that maybe means Spirit is sending messages—look and listen. A hummingbird may signify joy, and its feathers are used to make love charms. Mouse is a scrutinizer, a close-seer. Fox gives the ability to adapt, to blend in, to go unseen. So what you see on the mountain may lead you to learn from nature.

Or a vision may be a dream, waking or sleeping. You may see two-leggeds, four-leggeds, wingeds, rooteds, you may hear winds or waters or the Stone People. Whatever you see is a gift from Spirit, a showing of the way. That's why many of my people are named after an animal they saw in a dream.

Whatever you see, you must receive it not only with the eyes of your head but the single eye of your heart. This is the eye that sees inner reality, and the world of the spirit.

Understanding what you see on the mountain isn't easy, it comes slowly. You ask the counsel of the medicine man who put you on the mountain. You pray, and ask the help of Spirit to understand. You get a reminder, or make one—a feather, a claw, some beadwork—and keep it close to you and listen to what it says. Sometimes it takes a whole lifetime to understand a vision.

But no vision came to me that first day, not even an animal coming in what seemed a significant way. The wingeds stayed so far off I could not see if they were eagles, hawks, or ravens. I was afraid Raven would come to me. *Maybe I will die.*

That night I laid down, exhausted from the mental effort, and slept immediately. Though I hoped to have a portentous dream, either a waking or a sleeping dream, I blinked awake before first light and remembered no dreams at all.

I looked around and saw the Morning Star. That was good, the morning star was still easy to see. I took up my Pipe, and walked to the east, holding it in front of me. Silently I asked the Morning Star for wisdom. My task was to hold the Pipe toward the east, and Pray to the Morning Star, until the sun rose.

A Pipe weighs perhaps a pound. It seemed only moments before the weight became almost insupportable. In my mind I cried out for strength to hold the Pipe whatever time was needed.

Immediately I felt stronger. My mind told me I could not hold the Pipe until sunrise, but my arms felt surer, bearing it up. And something else happened. I began to feel something from the Pipe.

I cannot say what it was. Energy, perhaps. The essence of the Pipe. The spirit that lived in the Pipe and emerged to help those who called upon it. Something, and the words for it don't matter. I felt this something come into my arms.

I wanted to drop the Pipe. I was afraid. I glanced almost sneakily around the sky. No clouds. I felt like the Pipe was vibrating with some kind of energy—I wanted to throw it down and run.

I will not. One of the few things I will not do, no matter how scared, is to throw down my great-grandfather's Pipe.

I wondered if the energy came from my great-grandfather. *I do not even know your name!* I lifted the Pipe higher, and my arms trembled.

As suddenly as the energy came, it left. My arms relaxed. Something in me wanted to look around for my great-grandfather, but I knew he was not here in that way. I saw that the first light had put away the Morning Star. Soon the Sun would ease over the horizon far to the east, across the Great Plains.

I rejoiced. In my mind I thanked Wi, the Sun, for all his blessings upon the earth, and all living creatures.

When Wi appeared, I cried aloud, "*Pila maye,*"—thank you—and sank to the ground, arms shaking, body exhausted.

After a couple of minutes I stretched out on the bed of sage, head properly touching the pole, and pulled the robe over myself. The dawn was cold, and I was shivering. Under the robe I cradled the Pipe against my chest. And soon it began to thrum.

I do not mean a sound, but a kind of vibration, or perhaps just an emanation. Somehow, I could feel energy radiating from the Pipe.

My shivers shifted into shaking, my whole body quivering and flashing hot and cold under the robe. I began to wonder if I was getting sick. And then I began to see. Or rather I began to hear.

I heard the song again, the song I heard the month before, when I had thrown away my job and I sat in the car, stupefied and sun-dazzled. Again it was a chorus of scores or hundreds of voices, again men's, women's, and children's voices mixed together, and again without words. Part of my mind realized—sitting in the car that day, I had a first glimpse. I actually saw beyond, in a kind of hint, that day.

Maybe that helped make me so crazy I tried to throw away my life that night.

Most of my mind now began to see as well as hear, and it was something entirely different from the time in the car, not vague or fragmented—everything was unnaturally clear, sharp, and brightly colored. I saw a park of grassland, richly green and watered with myriad small creeks that flowed out of the timbered hills on all sides. Somehow everything was peaceful, imbued with harmony and serenity. Clumps of buffalo dotted the valley. Small clusters of deer, does and fawn, browsed among the groves of aspen. Wolves played near a creek, cuffing each other and tumbling playfully. Most important, people, Indian people lived in villages of tipis right among the animals. Children played with coyotes. A mountain lion and two cubs walked comfortably around a group of tipis. Everything was in harmony, as though the buffalo did not eat the grass, and the people did not eat the buffalo.

I was transported instantly, in a *swoosh* more magic than flying, from one village to another, and saw big changes. The people wore different clothes. In the first village the tipis were white canvas, and the people wore a mixture of clothes made of hides and of cloth. But in each village I flashed through, everything got older. The tipis were of buffalo hide, the clothes of deer skin. Soon cooking pots disappeared, replaced by bows and arrows, spears, and war clubs. Soon the people did not display beadwork on their clothing but quillwork, and the women did not wear small bells on the moccasins, but the dew claws of deer.

Further up, near the head of the valley, the people lived in brush huts, and wore clothing that looked inexpressibly ancient.

The strongest impression I had, though, was of infinite harmony, peace, and happiness. It was like everything was a movie about a lost world of unspeakable beauty and perfect happiness, a Shangri-La of Indian people, and joy danced in the air.

But *all* the people of all times were there.

And the song, I could hear the song, but I could not make out the words. Only the repeated phrase, as before, "The father says so, the father says so."

The valley drifted away, it faded to nothing, and I was left with the song only. I could hear the melody with aching clarity, and I could hear the moccasined feet making the only drumbeat that existed, soft, soft, and they sounded like the heart of Mother Earth beating, eternally, eternally, eternally.

What the hell? I thought.

Then suddenly I felt confused. I was aware of the buffalo robe again, hairy and itchy, and felt that my body was still a little cold beneath it. I popped my eyes open.

Then I realized. What I had seen and heard beyond was gone.

I felt a pang of yearning for the sun, for its warmth, and threw the robe off and stood up.

I saw beyond. That felt very good, though I had no idea what I had seen, or what its meaning might be.

The seeing is gone. I had ended it. Or had it evaporated on its own, like dew before the sun.

It was incredibly clear. And I knew I was awake the whole time—it wasn't like a dream at all. It was so real that for a moment I thought it was this physical world, not the spirit world.

Spirit world! Those words brought me a shiver of doubt. *Foolishness! Imagination! Ghosts and goblins and children's bogeymen!*

I brought back a memory of what I saw. True, I didn't understand it, not a bit. But it was real, absolutely real. I could not explain. I pictured myself taking my doubt, like a suspicious package that has come in the mail, and setting it aside for someone else to open, an expert, some other time.

I felt a rush, a fever of excitement. I raised the Pipe before me, began stepping slowly to the east, and raised my voice in the traditional prayer. "*Wakantanka onshimala ye oyate wani wachin cha!*" Great Mystery, have pity on me that my people may live!

All the second day, riding on the excitement of having seen something beyond, anything, I walked from the center pole to the east, then the south, then the west, then the north, holding my Pipe high and praying to Wakantanka.

I saw nothing more.

Sometime after the sun passed the midpoint, though, I got tired, sleepy, weak. My mind began to beg for food and water. I laid down on the bed of sage and rested. There I prayed for strength to endure the hunger and thirst, the heat and cold, and whatever else might come. The hot sun felt good, and I soon dozed a while.

I rose. I prayed, I lamented, I asked for a vision.

I saw nothing, not even a bird flying close enough to name.

Dark came. I laid down under the robe and closed my eyes, waiting for the vision that might come, or the dream that would bring me news from the other world.

I saw nothing. When I woke, I could not remember dreaming.

The third day I passed in Praying and asking for a vision. This day I felt indifferent to hunger and thirst. Often I lost concentration, though. My mind wandered off into the world I came from, to people I wanted to see, to tasks I had to do, to talks with friends....

Stand up and pray! You are here to seek a vision.

I already got my vision! Leave me alone!

I threw myself into a frenzy of prayer, which became genuine as I gave my energy to it.

Late in the afternoon I laid down to rest.

When I woke up, the wind was chill, and gray clouds were gathering. I stood up and forced myself back to my duty, to walk forever to the four directions and cry for Wakantanka's pity. But my enthusiasm was gone, my spirits sapped. My feet inched feebly in each direction.

This is your last night on the mountain. Pray!

Doubt came back to me. *Why am I doing this? Why am I not eating and drinking? This is ignorant, this is superstitious. Idiotic!*

My mind reminded me that I had seen beyond, but my mind also undercut that. *You imagined an Indian paradise. So what? It's just a fantasy. Go get lost in fantasy with the other old-timers, the ones waiting for the buffalo to come back.*

Around sunset the clouds got darker, they bunched up dark, like dirty gray rags all knotted together. They seemed to be piling up right on Bear Butte, for in all directions the sky was a lighter, gentler gray. The clouds looked threatening, and I thought it might snow.

I got afraid of snow and cold. I laid down on the sage and wrapped myself in the buffalo robe. The nights here were cold enough without snow.

I watched the gray clouds. Though they never blew away to the east, sometimes they seemed to squirm slowly, to twist and writhe in place. I imagined I heard the mutterings of old women in pain. I knew, though, it must be the rumble of thunder.

I stared into the clouds for maybe an hour, chill, but not yet cold. After a while the chill deepened, and I began to shiver.

In the shivering I lost track of time. Time, that big boss that runs the white world. Time, which pushes you hither and yon like dust in front of a broom. The world has never known a people so absorbed with time—your digital watches are accurate to a fraction of a second, and in a century will gain or lose less than a minute.

Here's a weirdness: Though you are persnickety about seconds and minutes—the radio station sold ads by the

second, and timed the news to come on just as the sweep
hand re-e-e-ached TWELVE!—you whites are insensitive to
the larger, grander motions of time made by the natural
world. Normally you do not know whether the tide is in or
out, the moon new or full. Though you speak of the seasons
incessantly, you are only half alive to their signs, to when
cows are calving, when ice rims the creeks, when the willows
are green and supple and when dry and brittle. And you are
not alive to the great movements of the constellations in
the sky, different in summer than winter, different in early
evening and early morning. Most of all you know nothing of
Timelessness.

I say all this with a shamed face. I have lived that way
myself, almost my whole life. Early in my life Grandpa told
me about the place where the world does not crank like a
mechanism but is at rest, the still point of the turning wheel.
He tried to make me a gift of this awareness, but I received it
in an offhand way, not understanding its value.

Somehow I stopped shivering. I dozed a little. Now, in
full dark, the clouds were harder to see, just a mottled gray-
ness above me. I drifted in and out of sleep.

Gradually I became aware that I was hearing something.

A low rumbling, or mumbling. Like rockfall, or an avalanche, heard from afar. Like the clouds rubbing against
one another in low voices. Like people moaning. Like the
basso bawl of a big wind. A low, restless sound, writhing in
the currents of air, twisting, twisting, turning, churning,
over and over and over and over moaning, groaning, howling, mumbling.

The Pipe, held on my chest, seemed to quiver faintly to
the rumbling.

I felt like I'd lived in that low chorus of sound forever. I
stirred and squirmed, my body swayed slowly. I was like grass

in a stream, and the moans made my body undulate, as the current does the green blades. The moans were the fluid I lived in, my water and my air in one. Gently, rhythmically, I waved to the liquid sounds of a low, distant misery. The Pipe and I both vibrated gently, almost imperceptibly, to the sounds.

Now I wondered for the first time if the moans were human. The road we walk on Earth is a trial, and maybe, somehow, I was hearing one of the human responses to it, maybe I was hearing our ancestors and ourselves in pain, maybe I was hearing all the human people, past, present, and future, and we were all, in a mass, in one great consent, giving voice to human suffering.

In the darkness and the shadows black silhouettes stirred in a low huddle and moaned in a chorus, and of the moaners I was one. I uttered moans, and I became moans, and my soul itself moaned, was Moan.

I felt sleet striking my face, and I opened my mouth to it, thirsty, and it was blood, it was the chilling bloodshed of eons past and eons yet to come, it has human suffering, and I did not want it, but I opened my mouth wider and wider and drank it in.

The sleet ceased, and I wormed my way deeper into the buffalo robe, cold, bloodied, heavy with the misery of thousands of generations of human beings.

We moaned. Of the millions of people writhing in misery, moaning out misery, I was one.

Perhaps there was music beneath this human expression, the universe thrumming in accompaniment to our misery, or in harmony with it, but my ears could not quite bring in the music, it eluded my hearing, tantalizing me.

One more time the moans surged, not low now, not from far away, not at all away, but here, within our mass, within us, beside me, inside me. Not moans but howls, great rendings of anger and agony. They bubbled within me like hot springs, they churned, they boiled. Tears burst forth upon my face, hot, scalding tears with no solace. I cried them out as well, and the voice of agony ripped out of me like hot lava. It tore my chest and my throat, but I could not stop it. I did not want to stop it, I wanted to roar, I wanted to rip myself....

The soundless music changed, and I felt a stirring within me, something new, a possibility....

The tears felt soft now. The voices moaned, but there was sweetness somehow in the moan, and acceptance.

On my chest the Pipe felt warm.

The world turned itself inside out. Everything was quiet. I was quiet. All around me was nothingness and around the nothingness was silence, utter silence, as in outer space, or ultimate inner space. I could not tell the quality of the silence, whether it was healing or frightening. I drifted.

Still. I am still. I can feel Earth beneath my body. I am among the people. Yet something is wrong, something is awful, something is terrifying.

I am in a landscape that seems like a huge painting that has the feeling of ceremony. It is nearly half or more abstract. Though Emile paints no abstracts, it is somehow a painting he would do, his style. The entire lower half of the painting, more than half, is white, an endless, cold, opaque white. The upper middle is thick, violent slashes of red through the white, jagged humps. Above the slashes is a black deep as raven wings spiked with big, bright, icy blue-white splotches in the shapes of stars.

For reasons utterly unknown to me, the painting is terrifying beyond terrifying.

I yelped in panic. I woke up. I sat up, grabbing the edge of the robe, and felt sleet cold on my hands. While I had been seeing beyond, in the ordinary world sleet fell. My fingers shook, and my body quivered, not from cold.

I lay back. I breathed deep. I drifted. Time passed. Yes, Time.

After a long while I looked at my hands, and sleet was under my fingernails. Now I felt the cold of South Dakota as winter approached.

I sat up in the robe in my circle on Bear Butte. Sticks marked the four directions. I pared the sleet from beneath my fingernails, then put one hand on the center pole.

I was returned to the normal world, the realm of Time.

Exhausted, I covered myself and dozed.

Later I stirred, opened my eyes, sat up. A small wind buffeted my face. The air was clear, no sleet. The clouds had unraveled themselves, and they strung toward the east. Directly overhead stars glittered.

I lay back. I had seen beyond. I shivered with excitement, and with fear. *I have seen beyond.*

What had I seen? Why did I see one vision and hear another? What did they have to do with each other? What did they mean?

This you will discover through counsel and prayer, I told myself.

But I saw beyond. *Pila maye,* I murmured. Thank you, Tunkashila, for opening the eye of my heart.

I squiggled in my blanket, searching for comfort. I murmured thank you again.

I turned my mind back into the place beyond, and felt the low moans begin to lift me. I felt afraid now, but beneath the fear was a tranquillity.

I put the moans away, got comfortable, closed my eyes, and asked for sleep.

When I woke, the Morning Star stood in the east, Venus, promising love.

I saw beyond.

Yes, but what did I see?

Today was my last day on the mountain. Some time this afternoon Emile would come and get me.

I will spend the day in rejoicing and thanksgiving.

I faced the east and lifted my Pipe high.

When the sun rose, the source of all energy on Earth, I raised my voice in a heartfelt cry. *Pila maye, Tunkashila.*

Thank you, Grandfather.

PART FIVE
TOWARD WOUNDED KNEE

WHAT DOES IT MEAN?

We crawled naked into the sweat lodge. Pete sat next to the entrance, and I sat across the door from him. I was feeling ... hell, I didn't know.

Emile wasn't here, Chup wasn't here. Pete had fed me a little. This sweat was for me to tell the medicine man what I saw on the mountain, and for him to help me understand it.

I am going to pull a veil over Pete's prayers, and my own. It's enough to say that we gave thanks that I saw beyond, and asked for help in understanding what came to me.

After the first round, while we cooled off in the air from the open door, I told Pete what I heard the second morning and saw the third night on Bear Butte, like the sound of heaven and the sight of hell.

I spoke in the Lakota language, and a miracle came to me. My tongue changed. Gone was Blue the jivey DJ. Yet the voice that emerged from my body did not belong to Joseph either, the one who went to college and came back shorn of wisdom. Nor to the young Bud. I spoke with a tongue that was new to me, or perhaps long forgotten. This was the voice intended for me by Spirit from my birth, strong, confident, reverent, centered in the sacred. Right now I was aligned with the Powers that were willing to help me.

I told what I saw beyond, almost all of it, keeping back small bits for myself alone. (Yes, I have also kept some from you.) The voice stayed with me and bore me up.

Pete heard my story with rapt attention, and I took support from the solidness, the lack of anything fanciful, in his brown eyes. He said nothing.

"Close the door!" he said, and I did. We dove once more into the dark, the steam, the heat, and our cries for pity.

This round was my turn to pray. I will not tell you my words, but I will tell you what is more important, the unfortunate voice that spoke them. The new, strong voice was suddenly, incomprehensibly, gone. I prayed in the voice of Bud, Joseph, Blue, or some mixture of them. My voice pled for understanding, but it asked from weakness. The throat the words came through belonged to the man who had spent years in disguise as the radio showman, Blue. The mind that formed those words was the good Indian, the Indian who wanted to be educated, who wanted a good job, who wanted success, who wanted to throw out the old ways and bring on the new, who wanted to be a white man. My heart was the empty heart of the Indian who sought not the old strengths but the powers of the diploma, the job, the reputation, which are no powers—for nothing others can grant or withdraw is true power. So I knew I did not yet have a grasp of my new voice, my new self. I was given only a glimpse, and tantalizingly, it disappeared.

I asked silently to find it again. I pledged to look for it with the eye of my heart. I couldn't reason toward it, but I might be able to feel my way.

That day in the low lodge I asked to see truly, to see with the *chante ishta*, to know the meaning of what I saw on Bear Butte, to discover again the voice that came to me and disappeared. But my heart was dead. *And the killer, O the killer is me.*

When Pete told me to open the door, and the steam drifted out and the lodge cooled, he looked at me for a while without a word. "I dunno," he finally said. "Maybe I can't help you."

I studied his stolid face. It told me nothing. Lips and eyebrows were expressionless, mute. This was a man who simply said what he meant.

"Maybe only you can help you."

I felt a quiver. I was not ready to walk strong on my own feet. My whole spirit was begging Pete in silence, *Help me, help me.*

"I do see one clue." My heart stirred. (What a coward I was, thinking I could live as a man only with Pete's help!) "You are not telling me something." He looked at me indifferently but softly. "You are holding something back, as you should, something for you and you only to turn over and over in your mind, to look back at. That's good. But you are holding back something else, something you need to tell me. You know what it is."

He waited.

He was mistaken. I didn't have the power that day to know clearly, from the heart (what you call intuitively), what I should tell and what I should not. But empowered by his confidence, I began to know.

Uncertain, in a tremulous voice, I started singing the song I heard in paradise. High and sweet I sang it, just as I heard it behind the faces of my people, and their ancestors, and their ancestors. In a pale and quavery voice I sang it once through, saying "hi-ye hi-yo" where I should have used words.

Then, with the power of the sweat lodge, I began again from the beginning, and this time came the day's second miracle. I sang the words of the first two lines. Where the words came from, I do not know. I did not understand them that night on the mountain, despite straining to hear them, despite yearning to hear them. Now they flowed from my mind and my tongue.

The father says so,
The father says so.

But there were more lines, and the other words were beyond my grasp, the words that bore the real meaning. And I felt an impulse to utter some shape—SOMETHING was itching deep in my throat, wanting to come forth. But I could not find that utterance. I looked at Pete ruefully, for my spirit as yet had no strength. I swam in feelings of guilt, foolishness, weakness, and mocked myself for diving into those feelings so quickly.

He nodded to himself, and nodded to himself again. He knew something, I could see, and whatever it was surprised him. "Close the door," he cried in a loud and sudden voice.

Once more into the darkness and the heat, painful and oppressive for the weak, healing for those with the strength to find healing in it. In this third round I was feeling unsure of myself. Oh yes, my heart might have been singing. Hadn't the words from my vision come to me, suddenly, vividly, miraculously? But I was quailing yet.

I suffered. Pete's arm tilted the water from the dipper onto the hot lava rocks continuously, and he prayed in a crackling roar, entreating the powers ... for whatever I needed.

I was busy suffering. My mind told me the steam falling on my shoulders would blister the skin. My lungs told me I could not breathe. My eyes spoke of darkness. I cowered. I wanted to whimper. When Pete cried "Open the door!" I wanted to dart out like a rabbit.

I forced myself to wait.

Pete sat there, his eyes half down, his face intent. I could see he was searching for something inside.

Finally he said, "Maybe I know that song a little. Maybe. I'm not sure."

He heaved a big breath in and out.

"I can't think of anyone you can ask." He nodded to himself. "You need to talk to old people who know something, who remember the old songs. Chup can give you names to start on. You need that song."

Then he did something completely un-Pete-like. He rolled his eyes with a bizarre effect, comic and scary at once, and cried, "Close the door!"

The last round was the hottest time I can remember in the sweat lodge. But my spirit felt a little stronger. I did not spend the time feeling sorry for myself. I put my mind into Pete's prayers, and added the small strength of my spirit to send them up to Tunkashila. And somehow, somehow, in the way of the sweat lodge, the suffering was sweet.

When the door was opened the last time, Pete thumped his fingers on the ground in an odd way, perhaps distracted. He beat all five fingers of his right hand on the ground at once, like drumming. All of a sudden his eyes came back to this world and time, to me. He said, "I can tell you something." He drummed his fingers on the ground. "I think you saw Big Foot's people, the dead ones." Suddenly came a faraway look, and then he was back with me. "The other people, in that good place with the ancestors, I don't know. You better find out."

Now he drummed with both palms flat on the ground, beating out a rhythm I could hardly follow, wild and mad. For a moment I thought Pete might have something of Coyote in him, the trickster.

The grin he gave me was all challenge. "Are you ready," he said, "for a big vision?" He cackled. "Were you ready? Are you ready?" Now he whooped the words. "Ready are not, here we come! Ollee ollee oxen free!"

The big man laughed, and the laughter sounded free and easy.

Now he settled down. His body stopped shaking, and his eyes grew both serious and kindly. "Don't worry," he said. "No one is ever ready. You can't be ready for this.

"But on second thought," he said with another cackle, "do worry! Yes, a big vision! Do worry! Every reason to worry! Spirit," he declared in a mock-important way, "is gonna kick your ass!"

PECKING AND HUNTING

I steered out of Pete's driveway, if you could call a two-track loop a driveway, bumped down to the highway, trundled to the crossroads, and stopped. Pulled onto the dirt. Turned the engine off, threw my arms on top of the steering wheel, plopped my head on my arms.

I didn't have any energy to go on. Don't mean being tired from the sweat, though I was. I mean my life was out of energy. Tank on empty, ergs zero, no more zippedy doodah for Blue Crow.

I *flumphed* out my breath, let my lungs sit a minute, eased air back in.

Maybe it was a hopeless task. I mean the song I sang in the lodge, and the missing lines. *Oh shit.*

Eased air back in again. "You need that song," Pete said. Know all the words. Maybe know who made it, who sang it, when, and what it was about. That was the road I needed to walk, for now. I asked for a vision, Spirit gave it to me. I didn't understand it. And it looked like the first big step was finding out about the song.

Maybe I can go on. Don't know how? That's why they call it faith.

Umm-hmm. And how was I gonna do that? Where was I gonna point the hood ornament of the Lincoln from right here on the side of the road? Just drive up and down the dirt roads of this rez, pick up hitchhikers, and hope? Drive the

Cheyenne River rez, where the Big Foot people came from? All the other seven Sioux rezzes, and the highways in between?

I didn't have the gas in my tank, in my body, or in my spirit.

I got out, opened the trunk, and got into the cooler that was acting as my grocery store. Palmed out two apples, bit into one (you shouldn't clobber the digestive system after a four-day fast). To the right Chimney Butte jutted up. To the north, out of sight in the bottoms, White River coiled its way through the Badlands, slithering northeastward, gooey with sediment and colored with the clays of the hills. In every other direction the buttes and cliffs jipped and jopped and jumped up. Since the autumn sun was setting, they caught its horizontal light. The natural whites flamed quietly, rose-colored.

My home country, the strange, haunted Badlands. Or once my home country, when I had a home. Not far from here, as rez distances go, lived Grandpa and Aunt Adeline. They would be eating in the squaw cooler about now. To go home, that's supposed to be the easiest thing, that's where you can always go. This is more true among my people than yours. But I didn't feel it, not then. I hadn't felt it for twenty years. As long as I was falling between two stools, I couldn't feel it.

Okay, Emile's, my temporary residence. But I couldn't face the thought of home-among-the-white-folks tonight. I'd been in that place, from South Dakota to Seattle, for twenty years. I didn't want to be there now.

So I thought about what I wanted right now. To be around Indian people. Thought where I could do that, be around a bunch of Indians, not just find one family in these lonely hills. I headed north to Scenic, South Dakota, and the Longhorn Saloon. Hey, if it's a sad decision to hang out with drunks, that's what my people are right now.

Ha, ha, I caught you. You think I was gonna get drunk. Actually, I was determined not to drink. Oh, I had the desire.

I'm an alcoholic, and an alcoholic always has a hole inside needs filling with booze, and he always feels the hole. But the mountain and the sweat had left me strong in myself. Times like that, the hole don't feel like much.

I liked the Longhorn for a couple of reasons. One, it had a giant sign on the roof, NO INDIANS ALLOWED. Of course, being just off the rez, no problems with the law, it was a hard-core redskin watering hole. On the same roof sign words scrawled big in Lakota said, INDIANS WELCOME HERE. Guess the owners didn't read Lakota. So it was the closest place I might find a few friends. Felt like right then I needed friends.

Who I found was Sallee Walks Straight.

She sat alone on a bar stool, looking sexy in a powder blue tank top. I hauled up next to her and her Virgin Mary.

When she finally noticed me, she said softly, "What are you doing? You tried to kill my cousin."

"I'm glad to see you," says I.

"I wouldn't sit there. You'd be letting yourself in for some adventure." Her voice was mimicking someone or something, and she showed a corner of a grin.

"I'm sober. Going to AA. Haven't had a drink since that night."

"Goody-goody for you." *Rosaphine—it was Rosaphine she was imitating.* "I think the little woman's about to get square with the big man."

At that moment an arm took a choke hold on me from behind, *oomph*ed me backward off the bar stool, and dropped me hard on the floor.

Cuss words were slapping me upside the head. Rosaphine's voice.

I could take the words but not the kick. I rolled.

Rosaphine's foot sailed into the air like a punter's. She fell backward, but from the bar stool Sallee caught her with both hands. I noticed Rosaphine's vocabulary of cussing was quite creative, combining *mother*, the *f* word, *bitch, bastard, asshole*, and other epithets in ways I hadn't heard before.

Came the kick again. I crabbed sidewise, moving good for a big man. Rosaphine's foot slammed a chair into a table and cracked the back.

Her second round of cussing descended from creativity to chaos. I heard *mother-bitching* and *son of an asshole*, among others.

People were clearing out of the way. Out of the corner of one eye I saw the barkeep heading for the corner of the bar with a baseball bat.

Rosaphine stepped closer and wound up the third kick, which was meant to score from a hundred yards.

I was pinned between chairs.

The barkeep appeared behind her, cocking the bat.

"Behind you!" I yelled.

She grinned maliciously, and I thought, *That's how our women used to look when they tortured prisoners.*

When the bat was at full cock in back of Rosaphine's head, Sallee grabbed it and held on.

Here came the roundhouse kick.

I rolled under the table.

Crash!

The heel of Rosaphine's cowboy boot caught the edge of the table.

The table teetered away from me.

Then it tottered back my way. I was crabbing out from under, belly up.

A full pitcher of beer cruised sweetly off the edge, pivoted in midair, and dumped its full load, right on my crotch.

I fell back.

Rosaphine howled.

Sallee did a cat screech. The barkeep hee-hawed. The rest of the crowd made up for Sallee with a handsome roar.

The beer was trickling through my crevices, you know where.

After forty days in the wilderness of abstinence, my cock finally gets a drink.

Rosaphine grabbed a glass in each hand off the next table and dumped them where the pitcher went.

Matter of fact, it got plastered.

The roars got louder. The barkeep was crying and choking on his own laughter. He'd dropped the bat.

"Done put that fire *out!*" declared Rosaphine. She paraded around, her fists raised in triumph.

"Rosaphine, I'm sorry," I called loudly. "What I did was dumb beyond dumb." She just kept on parading.

I stood up next to Sallee, who was covering her giggles with a hand.

"Can we talk?" says I.

She caught the bartender's eye, said, "I think we'd better go."

I've never liked baseball bats.

Outside she said, "You sure don't smell clean and sober."

I rubbed my hands flat down the front of my jeans. No way to get wetter. I looked around at the starry night. "Thirty-eight days," I said.

"Not thirty-eight days dry, that's for sure."

"I want to see you."

Something dark ran through her eyes.

"I want apologize to you," says I.

She shrugged.

"It was dumb. It was the worst day of my life. No, that's wrong, it was the best. Because it made me start climbing out."

I took a couple of breaths. Like a blast, I remembered. Fourth step: Take a serious moral inventory of myself. Eighth step: Make amends to all I've hurt, where doing so would not damage them or others. I hadn't gotten as far as these steps yet, but I knew I owed Sallee. "I deserve for you to be angry. I deserve it."

She looked into my face, probably hunting for signs of a con job. Finally she said, "Rosaphine more."

"Absolutely, amends. I don't think she's listening."

Sallee burst out with high laughter.

Rosaphine honked the horn, and Sallee held up a hand at her.

Yeah, that's what they say about the eighth step. You can make amends, but you can't control how the person responds.

"I'd like to tell you my story," I said. I realized with some surprise that I was telling the simple truth, not selling something.

"Why me?" said Sallee.

"Just do," I said.

The horn honked again. Sallee turned and hollered, "Cool it!" I was pleased to hear how the ladylike young woman had been with her sisters.

"I know things about you," she said. "Uncle Chup has your phone number on the refrigerator with the other man he sponsors. He hasn't broken your confidentiality, but I hear you guys talk long times on the phone. I know you're taking your recovery seriously. I like that."

The horn honked again, and Sallee ignored it. "I don't think there's time for a story right now. And I'm involved in something big, take a couple of months. You know about the Big Foot Memorial Rides?"

I shook my head no.

"Why don't you ask Uncle Chup?" I looked at her, wondering. "Really, do it. And we'll talk sometime."

She turned away from me, and I watched her glide to the car. Rosaphine cranked the engine and ground across the gravel. Sallee didn't look back.

THE BIG FOOT
MEMORIAL RIDERS

Maybe I heard vaguely about them, some rides honoring Big Foot's people who got killed at Wounded Knee. Emile's father, who was a full-blood, dismissed it as something the half-breeds were doing. I guess I did too.

"Sallee's made a commitment to ride this year." Chup looked at me, and I could see the questions in his eyes.

Some people consult their advisors in the confessional. I have coffee with mine at Lucky's.

"Tell me." I had a feeling beginning to rise inside. I didn't know what all it was, but it was sizable, and it was eager, maybe too eager.

Chup took a sip of his coffee, which was so unusual I wondered what to expect. Probably he was feeling like he oughta protect his niece against a drunk and depressive who had attempted suicide.

But this is what he said. "I see your heart is good." He started rolling another smoke. He could spend a lot of time at that. "Okay. 1986, some of us started doing rides to Wounded Knee, to remember. Started from Big Foot's camp, followed his route to Wounded Knee. Arrived in time to be there, where it happened, on December twenty-nine."

The day the Seventh Cavalry, Custer's old outfit, attacked a whole village of Mniconjou on the way to Pine Ridge to make peace. Killed three hundred men, women, and children, almost all unarmed.

I'd avoided that place my whole life, except the day Unchee's funeral was there.

"Four rides so far. Last one coming up this December, one hundred years since the massacre. Seven generations. Ceremonies on the big day, Wiping Away the Tears ceremony, and Feeding of the Spirits ceremony. Big doings.

"I tell you, in the winter those rides haven't been easy. Cold."

The feeling was singing in me. On the mountain I'd seen Big Foot's people, that's what Pete said. On the mountain ... but I didn't want the feelings. Something in me didn't want to hear the song.

"I need to ride," I said.

He nodded slowly, and I could see pain and doubt behind his eyes. "Only you can know." He sighed, I didn't know why. I thought he might ask me if I was wanting to be around Sallee. He sighed again. "I have a feeling about this, about hard things. Sometimes hard things, they're what we need." He eyed me while he thought on it. "Only you know." He blew smoke out. My nose was getting raw from all the smoke, and I thought how different cigarette fumes are from the smoke of the sacred Pipe.

Finally he went on. "You better go see a man, Tyler Red Crow. From Yellow Bear Canyon, works at Allen, alcoholism counselor." He scribbled something on a scrap of paper. "Here's his office phone number."

How strange. What am I—a detective? What are my clues— scraps of paper, wisps of smoke?

"Can you tell me anything else?"

He stared at his own hands for a minute. "I can tell you why I'm riding," he said. "My great-grandfather was killed at Wounded Knee." He didn't say any more for a minute. "How well you know the story?"

I shrugged. "Not much."

"Maybe you better find out," he said. "You told me you had relatives there?"

"I guess. My grandmother's family, Big Foot people. Her father was killed at Wounded Knee."

At the mention of Unchee his thick eyebrows went up. "Your grandmother's ... ?" he said in an odd voice. He took the time to finish rolling one. "That's all you know?"

I nodded.

"You're not a member of the Wounded Knee Survivors' Association?"

"Never heard of it."

He looked up into the cigarette haze. "Friend," he said, "I suggest you find out what your ancestors did at Wounded Knee, and what was done to them." His lips got hard, and I thought he was done. "I mean it," he said. "I got a feeling of bad things."

He brought his eyes back to me. "And you better go see Tyler." He got up, dropped a buck for coffee, buck for a tip, plus one fat, hand-rolled cigarette.

I felt antsy. Didn't wanna go home to Emile. Didn't want to be anywhere, really. So in a couple of hours I was back in Kyle, old stomping grounds. Old haunting grounds.

Still antsy. Didn't wanna go see Grandpa and Aunt Adeline (it was too late anyway). Didn't wanna do anything.

Too damn late for anything, I told myself.

I went and stood in front of the boarding school and looked at it. The night was dark and the building poorly lit. I reflected, Twenty-three years since I stood there for the first time with Grandpa and Unchee. That day I knew I had to go in and hated it worse than anything. Twenty-three years since the principal, Mr. King, told me everything would be fine, meaning it would be fine now that I'd decided to be a white man. Twenty-three years since this biggest lie of my life. Twenty-three years since this place, this institution intended as benevolent, had put my feet on a long and alien road.

Was it, looking back, all the way a black road? Now I was standing at a crossroads, one road more Indian, one more white. The Indian looked more like a good red road, and I was going to take it. Yet I didn't feel ready, running my mind over the years, to add them up and say the road that started here was a black, black road.

What I saw, standing there, a man not a boy, was that the building wasn't the same. Or it didn't feel the same. To the outer eye it had hardly changed. Big old brick building, tired, shabby. Maybe it was ominous-looking. For sure I could remember the demons, the men or devils who punished me, imprisoned me, who made me do exactly what they said. *Exactly what I say, and do it now.* The moment was defined by their imposing their will on me, and both of us being changed by that.

I hadn't forgotten a bit. I heard a song recently, even aired it on KKAT when I shouldn't have, that summed up my experience at the Kyle Boarding School. It's a take-off on the old Sinatra tune, "My Way." It's intended to be all about going to college, but for me it was Kyle. Called "Their Way"—can't quote it for you, can't even find it. What it says is, I went there and got along by doing things their way. I remember some of the rhymes: "They gave me grades, not in a fair way." "I learned to walk the doctrinaire way." "I learned to climb life's golden stairway—and do it their way."

A mockery, but that's what Kyle School was.

I still felt some of the old dislike of Mr. King and Mr. Banks and the truant officer. Somehow, though, standing in front of the building for the first time the demons didn't seem properly black. Somehow the building didn't glower and loom. It looked older and grimmer but not particularly haunted.

And I found that vaguely unsatisfying.

I went to the convenience store (like the two general stores but less satisfying) and was vaguely pleased to find a dreamsicle, my favorite ice cream of my teenage years. Standing outside, leaning against the storefront, I ate through the orange and savored the creamy ice cream inside. (If an apple is an Indian who's red outside and white inside, what's a dreamsicle?)

I remembered Mr. Plebus, the bootlegger, and wondered where my beaded turtle pouch went. Couldn't say I'd missed it much, emotionally, that sign of the physical connection to my mother. Maybe that was too bad, but I didn't feel the loss, not anymore.

Still, if it was in a museum and we could get a repatriation going, it would be fun to tweak the white tail.

What in hell am I gonna do now? Not Grandpa and Aunt Adeline, no, but ...

I then took thought, and something in me said, Yeah!

I got a blanket out of the trunk of the Lincoln, the Pendleton I always kept there. Then, gingerly, I got out the beaded bag that held my Pipe. I'd taken it on the mountain, and to the sweat, and hadn't been home to store it away. *Why do I want it now? What am I going to do with it?* Didn't know, felt the need.

I left the car parked at the convenience store and walked down the Allen highway in the dark. About a quarter mile down I thought I spotted the place and turned into the sagebrush. I walked no more than a hundred yards west, in the dark with no moon to see by, and honestly thought I found the spot. For sure there was no sign of the doe, not after all these years. And it's true, if sagebrush looks like a sea with no landmarks during the day, it's worse at night. But the place *felt* the same to me.

The cold shadow of the raven's wing was here.

I laid the blanket down, laid down, and folded it over me. I held the Pipe in its bag on my chest with one hand and put the other behind my head, elbow cocked, and looked up. I didn't see the stars, though. My inner eye flicked away the picture of the dead doe and brought up the ravens, six or eight of them on the doe's body, hopping and pecking, hopping and pecking.

I played the scene over and over in my mind. Suddenly one raven—Raven—flapped into the air and flew straight toward me. It hovered a foot away, and I felt like it was looking me in the eye, and its eye was …

Raven's eyes bugged out. They stood in air at the sides of his head. They grew to the size of black suns. They gleamed at me. They made little circles against the dark sky. They turned red-hot and glowed….

But I clasped the Pipe to my breast and I did not fall topsy-turvy into them. It was different.

I ran the scene back and forth in my head like a video tape. I elaborated it. I made it more horrific. But it was different, I was different. Yes, I felt the shadow again, and, yes, it was dark and cold. But not as dark. Not as cold. Not as frightening. It didn't paralyze me anymore.

Great-grandfather, what was your name?

Suddenly my outer eye brought me the stars. They nearly flashed at me, they were such a shock. I saw millions and millions of them. Here in a high country with little electric light, there were many times what you see in a city, or at the seashore. Seattle was deprived of stars, compared to this. They peopled a vast darkness, a greater darkness than I or anyone could imagine. But they were light. And in their light I could rest a little. Later the moon would rise, the light would be more, I would be able to see this earth better, much better. But for now I had the light of the infinite stars. It was not enough to bask in, but it was comforting. For my people the stars are a mirror for life on Earth, and a guide to the sacred walk.

After a while, as though to test myself, I deliberately entered the dramatic scene with the raven again. I replayed the scene a dozen times or more. I created terrifying pictures. Sometimes I frightened myself. And I thought a couple of times, *Oh, yes, this is my home, I belong here, this is my natural place, in the shadow of the raven's wing.*

My outer eye rescued me once more, which outer eyes seldom do. It brought me a shooting star. This was a brilliant one, with a long fall from the upper left center of my vision to the lower left corner. Instead of just blinking out, as they do, it seemed to pulse brighter at the last instant and then douse utterly. It felt good, that shooting star.

I stretched my outer eyes all over the sky then, watching for more, and saw a half dozen, then a dozen, a score, and then what seemed like hundreds. It must have been a night of meteor showers, but I don't read the newspapers. I watched them, and I watched the streaks of light against the infinite blackness, and in some way my heart was at ease.

I don't remember falling asleep, never intended to. I woke when the Morning Star rose, and there were no more meteors.

The sky lightened gradually, in the smallest gestures. It was pearly. Tiny clouds dotted the crests of the western hills like beads of my favorite color, Cheyenne rose. I saw the overhead sky was gentling into blue, a very, very pale blue. To the east, beyond the vast plains, the horizon grew yellow and orange. I had seen this so many times that I thought, Who cares? At that moment I blinked, and the horizon glowed in rainbow colors. I blinked again, and the rainbow disappeared, but now the sunrise had a touch of magic.

As the time approached, I got the Pipe out and loaded it with tobacco. I sat up in my blanket, arranged it around my shoulders, and turned my face to Wi, the sun. The low hills were black, and their shoulders radiated yellow-gold, like breath easing out.

Soon Father Sun made his entrance, a fiery glob. He was simple, declarative, and all-powerful. I lit the Pipe.

I rose to my feet in one movement. As I raised my arms, the blanket fell away. I held the Pipe high, then puffed and began my prayer. "I offer this smoke, my breath and my prayers, to the Powers of the East, home of the Sun, powers of beginning things, of initiation. O powers, run strong in my blood."

As tears started down my face, I turned clockwise, sunwise, Pipe held high. Then I put it to my lips, drew the smoke into my mouth, and blew it out. "O powers of the South, home of the flowing waters, source of growing things, father and mother of coming to fruition, may your waters flow in me."

I raised prayers of smoke to the other directions, to the West and the Thunderbirds and the powers of fecundity, to the North and its cleansing winds.

I prayed to Father Sun, bringer of light, to Earth, and to the seventh grandfather, the mysterious one, the center of self and of the universe.

I asked the strength of the powers in my new venture, the Big Foot Memorial Rides, the journey back to Wounded Knee, where Unchee's father and three hundred other Mniconjou died. I asked to be shown the path one step at a time. I asked for faith to follow that path one step each day, without knowing the future, or asking. And last I prayed the most difficult prayer of all for me. "Tunkashila," I cried, "bring me what I need for my growth into a good human being. Bring it whether I feel ready for it or not, whether I want it not. I declare that I want to change. I give myself to your power."

I sat in silence a while, and smoked until all the tobacco was turned to ash.

Then I said the final words of all Lakota prayers, "*Mitakuye oyasin*"—We are all one—and felt that oneness bountifully. That blessing, the deep sense of oneness with all things, a sense that seemed like the longest lost of all my blessings, brought me the deepest gratitude I can remember, and brought once more the tears.

Mitakuye oyasin.

An Experience at
Wounded Knee

The next morning, after a night in the Lincoln, I felt different. My mood (or would you call it the state of my spirit?) was up, my mind was clear, things felt simple, and I felt like doing things simply. I was pleased by the change—so many years I'd felt grumpy, out of sorts, wry, cynical, all that *stuff,* I thought that was normal. This morning I went about normal things, gassing up the car, having breakfast at the Wild Horse Cafe. I enjoyed noticing what I was doing, just being aware.

After breakfast, I thought. No, don't want to drive down to see Grandpa and Aunt Adeline. So I called Tyler Red Crow, and fifteen minutes later he pulled into the parking lot at Little Wound School and I jumped in. We shook. He was driving over to Pine Ridge today, something about his job, and invited me to ride with him.

Tyler is a tall Oglala about my age, hint of a belly, genial, articulate, a likable guy with a lot of bubbly energy, and he likes to put that energy into talking.

"I am traditional," he says right off. "I grew up, one foot in the traditional Lakota way, one in the Christian way. One *hunska* [grandpa] traditional, the other, Episcopal priest. I *chose* the Lakota way of praying."

He eyed me sideways and scooted the truck around a corner too fast. I fidgeted.

"We'll go by the massacre site, okay? I stop there to pray when I can."

I nodded and fidgeted some more.

He looked at me long, until he ran the front right tire onto the gravel—that road is a twisty one. He corrected easily and looked at me again. "I'm not easy in that place," I said. I began to get a dark feeling.

"Hey, Lakota people, we ain't gonna be easy, that place. 'Less you pray a lot there, make peace."

"Never."

"Your relatives died there?"

"Yeah." The feeling was dark and heavy both. "My grandmother's father."

He eyed me long again. His face turned sober and he studied the road hard. "You need to go," he says, fingers drumming on steering wheel. "You need to go. Well, we're going."

Then his energy burst into talking again. He hopped from subject to subject like a jackrabbit. My mind was half somewhere else—already at Wounded Knee—but I can tell you some of the things he said.

"For twenty years, me, no praying. Back from army, 1976, I renewed my Lakota spiritual life. Chose the Lakota way of praying, best thing I ever did."

I didn't feel like talking—I was dreading seeing the massacre site again. But I managed to get out some words that said, "In a way I'm the opposite. Raised traditional, pushed onto the white road, then chose it, now maybe choosing to come back to traditional."

"I'm so happy now," puts in Tyler. "I'm *rich.*"

I was quiet, thinking on Wounded Knee.

Later—"You go Christian when you went the white way?"

"No."

"I consider all Christian churches my enemies. I don't associate with them whatsoever."

Later—"Hope what's coming, strong revival of traditional life on the rez. Hope these rides bring back those values. To me, that's what they're all about."

Later—"I want the rez to be traditional. I invite Lakota who want to be modern to leave us by the year two thousand. We want to be traditional."

Later—"Chup tell you how these rides got started?"

"He told me to ask you."

"Birgil Kills Straight, Alex White Plume, Jim Garrett, coupla others." (Kills Straight and White Plume were old Pine Ridge rez names everybody knew.) We say, ourselves, "It is now seven generations since Big Foot's people died at Wounded Knee. Black Elk said the hoop would be mended and the tree would flower in the seventh generation. We need to do something to help the people heal."

Now a different feeling came, a sense of rising in my heart. It mixed peculiar with the dark feeling from before.

"We decided, wanted do something, start mending the hoop, didn't know what. So we went to Curtis Kills Ree and asked for guidance." He looked sidelong at me. "You know Curtis?"

I shook my head no.

"Medicine man, good one. Curtis, he says, 'Make a pilgrimage, repeat Big Foot's ride to Wounded Knee four times, plus a fifth ride on the hundredth anniversary of the massacre. Pilgrimages to release the spirits of those who were murdered, finally, and wipe away the tears of the people.' "

My feeling was big now, the rising, but really my heart was all up and down, like a stick tossed on the waves of the ocean.

"So we did a Makes-Vow ceremony. We promised to do that thing."

After a little bit Tyler went on. "On the day of the hundredth anniversary, perform the ceremony Releasing of the Spirits." He fixed me hard with his eyes. "You know this ceremony?"

I shook my head no again.

"It can be done once every seven generations, that's all. Release the spirits from that place."

With these heavy words we both fell silent. Though I didn't know the story well, I knew the spirits of the people who died in the valley of Wounded Creek a hundred years before were still there, still suffering. In fact, the massacre itself was still going on, on and on, time without end. Time, we Lakotas know, does not truly divide itself into past, present, and future—this is one of the great illusions. All time is happening forever in the eternal moment. And some darknesses must be … exposed to the air for healing. Darknesses like mass murder.

The truck nosed down a hill. Porcupine Butte was off to the right. "This is where it started," says Tyler. "The people fled from Cheyenne River, heading south toward the Badlands, escaping from the soldiers and heading for Pine Ridge. Right off the army got real excited—find those Indians, they're gonna join the Ghost Dancers, Badlands, big trouble. Army units ran all over the place, Cheyenne River to Pine Ridge—find Big Foot!

"But the people traveled way faster than the whites thought they could. Every place the soldiers looked for them, the people were already gone. Even with Big Foot getting sicker all the time.

"Then Big Foot, he sent some men ahead to tell the chiefs at Pine Ridge, I'm coming. I'll be at Porcupine Butte tomorrow and Pine Ridge the next day.

"The Seventh Cavalry was camped at Wounded Knee, looking for Big Foot." Tyler nodded three or four times. "That Seventh Cavalry," he repeated grimly, and shook his head bitterly.

Custer's old outfit.

"The Pine Ridge chiefs sent word back—the soldiers are looking for you around Wounded Knee, better swing to the east and avoid them. But Big Foot was so sick by that time, he decided to head straight for Pine Ridge, never mind the soldiers.

"Big Foot's people and the soldiers, they met here at Porcupine Butte, everyone got ready to fight. But the soldiers said, 'Hey, peace if you give up your firearms.' Big Foot didn't like this, afraid of trouble, but looking like bigger trouble if he didn't. So he says, 'Let the army escort the people to Wounded Knee Creek, we stay the night, talk about the weapons the next day.'

"Big Foot was really sick by this time, coughing up blood. The soldiers put him in a wagon to make the trip.

"So. Yeah. This is where it started."

We rode in silence. I can't say where Tyler's mind was. Mine was on the mountain, and the people I laid with there.

In the darkness and the shadows black silhouettes stirred in a low huddle and moaned in a chorus, and of the moaners I was one. I uttered moans, and I became moans, and my soul itself moaned, was Moan.

Pete said what I saw on the mountain was Big Foot's people at Wounded Knee, dead. My people.

The truck topped the rise and pointed down into the wide valley surrounded by low hills, the creek in the middle, the church on the hill just west of the road. I had never wanted to check out this place, to feel what was here for me. When I drove this way, I kept my eyes on the road and my foot on the gas.

Tyler pulled up in front of the big sign, WOUNDED KNEE BATTLE, turned off the engine, and went to the sign. I shambled out and stood beside him. Someone had crossed out the word *battle* and written MASSACRE.

The sign explained what happened here, but I couldn't bear to read it all.

Huge hands gripped my stomach and wrung it like a dishrag.

Tyler walked around the sign and on up the hill. I followed him. It was a short walk that was very long.

In front of the small, white Catholic church ("I consider all Christian churches my enemies," Tyler had said) stood the mass grave. It was surrounded by a low wire fence with a creaky gate. In the center was a monument listing the names of people of Big Foot's band buried there. "Hundred forty-six," said Tyler. "Not so many names on the monument. Joseph Horn Cloud had the monument put up, tribute to his father, name Horn Cloud. See here by the name, it says, 'Here the peacemaker died innocent.' "

Tyler lit a cigarette, blew out the smoke. "The total Indian people killed, like a lot of other things about the massacre, it's in dispute. Don't matter, you can't get your mind around it, can't feel it, all them people snuffed. I try to picture so many, try to feel so many wounds, so many lives put out, and I gag."

I walked to the other side of the monument, away from Tyler's gab.

How is it you white people, so eager to tell us right from wrong, kill three hundred men, women, and children here, no reason?

And why don't white people think there is evil in the world any more, think that's superstition? Hey, we Lakota, we know about Iya, the Evil One, Wind Storm, and all his bad doings. You showed us.

Tyler and I stood on opposite sides of the monument and looked. I made myself breathe in and out regular.

My eyes ran up and down the list of names. "Hired civilians brought the bodies up here," said Tyler, "dug one big hole, dumped them in, and posed for photographs standing in and around the grave."

Partway down the first column of names, I thought, I should look for the name of Unchee's mother and father here. Then it struck me. *I know nothing about them, nothing, not who they were, how many children they had, what members of the family died with them.... I don't even know their names.*

I threw my head back, sucked at the sky with my eyes, gaped my mouth open as if to scream, and Raven shot down my throat.

Knowing, I fell, and my spirit plummeted to ...

I was in a world I did not know, along a river in a canyon. The walls stood red, orange, and brown. Above, the sky was violet, and unbroken as far as I could see, ahead and to the sides, unmarked by any cloud, or even the slightest variation in color. The ground at my feet was silver-gray. In this world apparently was no vegetation of any kind, not trees, not bushes, not grass under my feet. To my left a river roiled, a great, snarling flood of yellow-orange, molten, like lava—and not flowing in the ordinary way but holding itself like a cable of twisted wire and writhing past me, downhill, the opposite of the way I needed to go.

But ... where should I go?

Black shadow.

I looked into the violet sky, which had no sun at all, though I stood in bright daylight. Suddenly from behind came a black speck, growing. Its shadow fell on me, and was chill.

Raven blasted into sight over my head, immense, and roaring like a jet. He circled to the right, wingtips spread like dark fingers, and from behind me roared over my head once more. His roar was the call of all the ravens of the world, though this Raven gave none. He began to wing-flap up the valley, and I knew that I must go. Raven was my guide.

He grew to a speck in the distance.

Black fear shot through my blood.

I shuddered all over my body, I felt my limbs shake crazily. About to put my left foot out unwillingly to take the first step on a journey, I waggled my head violently and shouted, "No!"

"Blue Crow!" cried Tyler. He rocked me by the shoulders.

I shook my head again. "No!" I forced my eyes open.

I did not snap back from the strange land, wherever or whatever it was. For a moment I was completely clear about this—I had a choice. I could stay in the strange world, extend my foot, bring it down, and begin the journey with Raven. Or I could be at Wounded Knee with Tyler.

I boomed my shoulders and trunk upright and threw my arms out to prop myself. For a moment my head swirled— my physical head, here in this world—but I refused to lie back down.

Tyler put an arm around my shoulders to help me stay up. "Blue Crow, are you okay?"

I shook my head slowly sideways, back and forth. He must have thought I was saying, No, I'm not okay—because he pressed in close behind me.

"I'm all right, I can sit up," I said, and edged away from him. "I saw something, I went somewhere. I don't know what." I stretched my body this way and that. "Guess I don't know what happened for sure. Maybe I saw something, maybe I went somewhere."

I forced myself to stand up.

Tyler eyed me hard. "Did you cross into the spirit world for a minute?"

"Maybe," I said quickly without thinking. I wasn't going to give room to that notion. "It's over now."

I want it to be over.

O strange! I am standing at the Wounded Knee mass gravesite for the first time. I have never been here, and at the same time I have always been here.

I don't want to be here. Why would I ride across the plains and Badlands for endless miles in the winter to get here?

"Let's sit in the truck," I said. Somehow it seemed protective, like the air in the truck wouldn't be the air of Wounded Knee.

While I got into the cab, Tyler came partway down the hill, found some white sage, knelt, said a prayer, and picked the sage. Back in the truck he opened the glove box, got out some shiny red ribbon, wrapped the sage, and hung it from the rear view mirror. "I asked for good things for our ride to this place," he said, "and good things for you from this place." He let that sit a minute. "That last one," he went on, "that's a hard one. Hard for you here."

Being Tyler and always in motion, he started the truck and headed south toward Pine Ridge. We rode in silence. Finally I said, "Why do you say Wounded Knee is hard stuff for me?"

He grinned big, and his eyebrows danced like Groucho Marx's. But he held in whatever was funny. "You know," he said at last, "I've seen a lot of different reactions from people about their ancestors dying at Wounded Knee. I'm a member of the Wounded Knee Survivors' Association, you know about that?"

I shook my head no.

"Maybe you want to check it out. Anyway, all the reactions I've seen, yours is real strange."

I looked at him, and he looked back.

"You said, 'My grandmother's father died at Wounded Knee.' " He looked at me and I waited. "Those were your relatives that died that day. *Your* relatives. How come you didn't say that? *My* ancestors were murdered here."

I didn't have anything to say.

"There's stuff you gotta check out, *kola*. About yourself."

Tyler did his business at the tribal office and we ate lunch at Big Bat's, the gas station–convenience store. When we finally started rolling back toward Kyle, I said, "Okay, you think I should come on the ride?"

He raised that right eyebrow at me. "I can't say, *kola*. And we don't recruit people for the rides. Curtis told us that. Don't ask nobody. The spirits will bring those that should come. The spirits will bring them."

The right front wheel of the truck hit a pothole hard. Nobody fixes rez roads.

"So tell me about the rides. Who are the leaders?"

"Our leader is the staff. Nobody's the leader, we all be common as grass." This is an important virtue to us Lakota, and hard to explain. It's important to be common, not exceptional. "We follow. The staff, it guides us.

"In the first year there were nineteen riders and one support vehicle. Each year there have been more. Whatever number comes this year, it's the right number. The spirits bring the right people. The ride's been growing each year. Arvol Looking Horse been riding with us too."

My head did a little dipsy-doo. Arvol Looking Horse was the keeper of the White Buffalo Woman Pipe. This Pipe to us is like what the Cross or the Ark of the Covenant is to you, except it's still with us, still working, a living presence. Our ways are, more than all else, our stories, our ceremonies, and the Pipe.

The Pipe Keeper still bears the original Pipe White Buffalo Woman brought. Scientific tests show that it's at least four thousand years old. Seldom is it displayed. When it is, our people cherish its appearance, and use the occasion to deepen their dedication to our ways.

For me, if the Pipe Keeper was involved, the Big Foot Memorial Rides were connected to the center of the sacred circle of Lakota life.

"This year we're expecting ... well, we don't know. It's the centennial. It'll draw some press. Media people been in touch, but just Europeans, not the American media. Pretty funny, huh? European, not American. These guys, still carrying on the fight."

He took a curve too fast, and a pothole bounced us to the outside. He corrected with a little jerk. His face, though, showed his mind was somewhere else. "Truth is, we're still carrying stuff, too."

"What do you mean?" *Hoka hey*, we lost the Indian Wars a century ago. The end was when they killed Crazy Horse, or when Sitting Bull gave up and went to live on a reservation.

Tyler was quiet a while. Finally he began, "Let me tell you a story. I saw this war movie with Gene Hackman. He tells a story about Korea. On the retreat from Choisin Reservoir, we were getting our asses kicked, and the ground, it was too frozen to bury the dead. Day after day, more dead, more trucks full of stiffs. Hackman says he dreamed about those dead for years.

"Guy asks then, 'They ever go away?'

"Hackman, he says no. Then he kind of smiles. 'Finally I made friends with them, though.'

"We gotta make friends with our dead, *kola.*"

We were passing Wounded Knee, and we both fell silent. My mind went up and stood in the mass grave. One hundred forty-six of Unchee's people there. My people.

Tyler didn't stop this time, and I was relieved. We rode on and on in silence, passed Sharps Corner and got nearly to Kyle before I broke it.

"So. What's the program for this year's ride?"

He looked quick at me. "The rides are hard, you know that? We tell people, you gonna ride, be sure you mean it. It's tough. You start, you have to go through with it, can't back out in the middle.

"We start at Cheyenne River, Big Foot's camp. We'll ride the old path." His mind wandered somewhere, maybe into the previous rides, maybe into the journey of the Big Foot people.

Before I knew we were there, he pulled up behind the Lincoln at Little Wound School, stopped, and turned off the engine.

"We get to Wounded Knee, on the hill by the church we will do the ceremonies. At the mass grave. Two reasons. Release the spirits of the people killed there a hundred years ago, and wipe away the tears of all the people. We hope we can end seven generations of grief right there. We can heal."

"And heal the riders?"

"Here's something I've learned. To heal, you have to start right where you are. Right where you hurt. So you have to know that place first."

I gave a sort of half nod, looked at Tyler's soft eyes, and received their blessing.

"Yeah," he said. "There's healing in it." His eyes were kind, and in their gaze I felt the meaning of compassion.

It was time to get out, to let Tyler go about his business, and to go about mine, whatever that was. The trouble was, I didn't know.

From my heart I gave a lurch of words. "I want to ride."

Tyler studied me. Finally he said, "Then getting ready starts today. You know in your heart what you need to do to get yourself ready. Nobody else knows."

I felt a moment of panic. *I didn't know. What should I do?*

I got out of the truck, said, "*Washtay*," and waved. Tyler headed back to his house. I stood in the dust in the town where I'd started one kind of learning so many years ago, and abandoned another.

What should I do?

Suddenly a big breath burst out, and I relaxed. I could see the first step. *Go to Grandpa and ask questions.*

I didn't know the second step, or the third step.

Hell, nothing to do but take the first one.

THE PAST BITES MY ASS

It was a warm day, Indian summer (why do you call it that?), and Aunt Adeline was cooking in the shed kitchen. I said, "*Washtay.*" Having heard my car and my steps, she just nodded at me.

Grandpa was in the old recliner a few steps away—God knows where it was scrounged. An old wool blanket covered him to the waist, his hands and forearms were under it, and his eyes were closed. Since he was turned to the west, the late-afternoon sun rested on his face, and I thought maybe there was a half smile from the pleasure of the sunlight.

This was the way I found him on most of my visits the last few years. He was ninety-one now, and had the right to doze with the sun on his face if he liked. But I didn't like it. I hated seeing him that way.

I turned toward Aunt Adeline at the wood stove. Even keeping my eyes a little down and to the side, I saw that her look was suspicious, or mean, or bitter, just like it had been for years—not welcoming for sure. *No welcome for your brother's son*, I thought—*strange*. But hey, Aunt Adeline was over forty when I was born, and even when I was a kid she was mean.

I handed her the groceries. "*Washtay,*" she said. Good. She was making a stew on the old wood-burning stove, and my contribution was welcome—not only potatoes, carrots, celery, tomatoes, and onions, but ground beef. Meat was expensive, and whatever other meat she had in the stew would be what she caught or trapped, or what someone gave her. Rabbit, probably; sand turtles, maybe. If she was lucky, deer meat. We Lakota love flesh, and we like lots of different meats in the same stew. No matter how many there are, I can taste them separately, and enjoy each one.

She broke one pound of burger straight in and set to chopping the vegetables. I saw that the corners of her mouth were turned down, like always.

I took the rest of the burger, soda pop, cheese, and ice inside to the ice box. Not being on the electric grid, Adeline and Grandpa use an ice box. For years Grandpa cut ice from the river in winter and stored it in the ice house, though it never lasted through the summer. Now Adeline probably bought dollar blocks of ice from the convenience store, when she could afford it. Since she liked cold orange pop, a block of ice was always welcome.

I carried three opened bottles of orange pop back outside. Grandpa was still dozing. I handed one to Adeline. She was starting the cowboy coffee now, which meant we'd be eating soon. I liked cowboy coffee.

"*Washtay*," Grandpa said behind me. I turned and offered my hand. "*Takoja*," he said, meaning grandson, and shook my hand spryly. He was like that—one minute looking like he was dwelling half in the spirit world, and the next minute ready to joke or gossip or play cards. These days he passed a lot of time playing solitaire, which he learned in France during World War I.

It was hard for me to get over the way he was, out of this world (seemed like) one minute and all the way alert the next, and smart as anything. Guess that's what it's like to be ninety-one years old.

I pulled a log end up to his chair while he sat back down. "I quit my job."

"*Washtay*," he says. Good. Grandpa always thought spinning tunes and splicing them together with patter was a truly silly way to make a living.

"I quit drinking."

"*Washtay*," says he. This time there was a glint in his eye, and it wasn't hard to read. His only son, the only one that lived, threw his life down the toilet of booze. Was still throwing it down.

"I went on the mountain."

"*Washtay*," says he.

"Pete Standing put me on," I said.

"*Washtay*."

I could see he understood every bit all the way.

"Supper," says Adeline.

We went inside, the sun was sinking fast. Grandpa and I sat across from each other on benches at the Formica table, the sort popular in the fifties. Adeline sat next to Grandpa, and put the corners of her mouth into sourness.

It's not our way to rush to our reason for visiting. After all, the main reason is just to be there, with your relatives. At least it should be. And eat.

After dinner, over cowboy coffee, I couldn't wait any longer. "I've never known," I said to Grandpa, "about my ancestors at Wounded Knee."

"The one that knows is me," says Adeline—kind of mouths it half soft, really.

"There's been snow, so I can tell," Grandpa says. I don't think he was shutting Adeline out or being rude to her, he just didn't hear or didn't notice. Now he set out in a high voice and a serious, respectful style. "My family is all Oglala," meaning Pine Ridge Lakota, not from Big Foot's band, which was Cheyenne River people. "But Unchee's family, they were Big Foot people."

"The one that knows is me," repeats Adeline, louder. Now her jaw was sticking out, made her look like a bulldog.

Grandpa took notice this time. "That's true," he says, "Adeline does know best about your ancestors through Unchee." And he waited politely for Adeline to take up the story.

"You never paid no attention to me," says Adeline, giving me a sideways flash. She'd been muting anger her whole life. Now she jutted her chin out again and spoke out the window to the Badlands, not to me. "I am Unchee's oldest. By her first husband, John Running. He died when I was seven, in the influenza epidemic of 1918. I barely remember him. *Atay* here, he's the one raised me. I never forget that, he's my real dad." *Atay* is our word for "father," and Adeline really did never forget it—that's why she was here taking care of Grandpa in his old age. Her old age too, for that matter.

"Don't know what you know. I had a sister, Ainie, was eight, a brother, Robert, was two. They all died of influenza, all on 'em." She stared out at something no one else could see, at least not anyone in this reality.

"Janey Running, your Unchee, she was born in 1890. Not *just* in 1890. She was born the day after the massacre." Adeline looked at me triumphantly.

My head did a loop-de-loop.

"Her mother died in childbirth. That was one killed in the massacre, though she died the next morning. Shot, lost too much blood."

She sat there and waited to see the impact of her revelation.

Though I was beginning to shake inside, I outwaited her.

"She told me this story, told lots of times. She didn't tell it to nobody else, she couldn't stand to. I was the one. 'You remember,' she said, 'someone's got to. But you keep it inside, don't gab it around.' So I didn't."

She flashed her eyes at me irritably. "Do you want to hear this story?"

The first time my voice didn't work. Then I got out, "Yes."

"Then you listen good.

"Your great-grandfather, Unchee's father …" She hesitated. It's not good to say the name of a dead person, better just to point to him with another name—your uncle, or like that.

"You don't know his name, do you? Unchee never told you." She paused to give it emphasis. "Blue Crow, he was called Blue Crow."

I'll be damned.

"Yah, yah, that's the name Unchee gave you the day you started white-man school. She told me all about it. Unchee got nothing of her mother and father's, nothing but that Pipe. Everything else lost. She save that Pipe, give it to the right one.

"You come along, she say, 'He is Blue Crow, he carries the spirit of my father.' That's why you got the name. That's why you got the Pipe. That's why you were held aside as a child, away from white people."

Her tone said, *See, you don't know everything.*

Feeling flooded up and carried her along. "I am mad about this fifty years, yes mad fifty years, still mad." Now she almost glared at me, and threw her voice hard. "My son, that Pipe, it should have gone to him. My son. I was the one my mother shared with, this burden, this strength. She save her father's Pipe, she think it bring something back, someday. My son, the one to carry that Pipe."

She stood up abruptly. "I got to do the dishes," she said. "Two men, sit living room." In other words, *Get outta here.*

I stifled my own anger, and Grandpa helped me. He took my elbow, and I steered him to his favorite living room chair, another Salvation Army-style recliner, not as threadbare as the one in the yard.

If I wasn't going to piss off Aunt Adeline, I needed to calm down. I wandered around the room, looking at the things I'd lived with the first fourteen years of my life. There were old, ceremonial things on the walls or displayed on tables—an eagle-wing fan, an eagle-bone whistle, a drum painted with a featherburst pattern, a rattle made from a buffalo scrotum. Unchee told me about that rattle once. It was used by a *yuwipi* man and had 405 stones in it, pieces of crystal and agate he gathered from ant hills. These were the talking stones, the tiny rocks that spoke spirit language during the ceremony that only he could understand. But that *yuwipi* man was not my grandfather—everything was lost but the Pipe, Aunt Adeline said.

I reached up and took the rattle off the wall. Even the bone plug that kept the stones inside was missing. I felt the old hide, then raised it and shook it in the air, empty. No sound. *What is the sound of one hand clapping?* And the rattle didn't speak to me. It struck me that this rattle was like a lot of what we have from the old days, a remnant of something that was good, but with the essential part missing, the voices of the spirits.

"Adeline," cried my grandfather in his high, weak, old man's voice, "Make us another pot of coffee."

So he intends to patch things up.

Anyway, my great-grandfather's things, they were lost. Like most of our ways. Like the old power.

Aunt Adeline brought us each a mug of coffee, hot and steaming, then joined us with another cup.

I waited. She waited. Finally I said, "Aunt Adeline, will you tell us what you know about my great-grandfather Blue Crow?"

For a while I thought she wasn't going to answer. When she did start, her voice was mild.

"He was a good man, Blue Crow, respected, and a *yuwipi* man. He had a *pte hiko*, buffalo stone. True, he was young, only twenties, but people saw, he was a *wichasha wakan*. He found a missing child. Parents were haying on a white man's ranch, child got into the mother ditch, swept away. No one saw it. Time they missed her, too late. Your great-grandfather saw with the inside eye where the body was, took people to it.

"This story, it comes from the people who raised your Unchee.

"Blue Crow, he had two children already, your great-grandfather, with his first wife. Your great-grandmother, I don't know her name, she was his second wife, Unchee was the third child.

"The day of the massacre, I don't know much about it. You could look it up in them books they got, maybe, if they ain't all lies."

She gave a harsh look, like the books in the libraries came from me.

"This is what Unchee told me. She was in her mother's belly the day of the killing. Blue Crow and the two wives, they was Ghost Dancers. Not everybody in that band was, they was divided on it, but your great-grandparents was, big ones. Regardless what anybody tells you, the Ghost Dance was a peaceful way.

"Oh, you don't want to hear all this. You ain't never cared."

"Adeline," Grandpa said gently. He was still her *atay.*

She waited. She sniffed. "I don't actual know more," she said.

"Tell him about Lucky."

She sniffed a couple of times, and I realized Aunt Adeline was teary.

"Lucky was my last-born, my baby."

She waited so long I thought she'd gotten lost, maybe in the past or maybe in her sadness or misery.

"He was smart. Everybody saw it, he was smart. I asked your Unchee to hold her father's Pipe for Lucky, until he was old enough. Right quick Unchee says no. He's smart, she says, but he don't have the spirit for this, the spirit that's right. She was sure she'd know the spirit when she saw it."

Sniff.

"The white people thought Lucky was so smart, they wanted him to go away on the railroad to school. That Carlisle. I argued against it. My husband, he was for it. Thought on it long and hard but came down for it.

"Lucky didn't even last till Christmas. Then he could have come home for vacation and I'd have kept him. He hung himself in the boys' toilet, hung himself by the neck."

She stood up, swinging her empty coffee cup in such a way I thought maybe she'd throw it. "I'm clear about this, Joseph Blue Crow, have been for a long time. You got my boy's name, you got my boy's Pipe.

"Here's what else I'm clear on. You throwed the name in the mud, with your drinking. You throwed the Pipe away, with your drinking.

"It's you deserves be dead, my boy alive."

She stomped into the kitchen, rude as a Lakota can be.

I looked at Grandpa, but he didn't look back, probably too embarrassed.

There was nothing to say.

Over the next weeks I thought a lot about Aunt Adeline's stories about Blue Crow. I don't know what I did with her accusation about me dishonoring the Pipe. I'd been a drunk for ten years, for sure. I guess maybe I put her words in a place where I didn't have to look at them. Every day I knew real clear what they said, and I held them in cold storage, until the day came when I could throw each word on the hard ground of truth and it would break.

I wasn't sober long enough for that, not yet. I didn't know when I would be, or what I had to do.

What I did was get ready for the Big Foot Memorial Ride. I don't mean ready physically, gear in order, horse rented, that sort of stuff. I mean spiritually ready. I went to a meeting every day. I talked to Chup about how to stay straight and about how to do the ride in a good way. I went to Pete's every Sunday and sweated.

I prayed, too, using the Pipe handed down to me from my great-grandfather Blue Crow. I'd never prayed that much. I asked for the ride to teach me. I asked for the ride to show me how to help the people. I asked for the ride to wipe away the people's tears. To make the sacred hoop whole again. To make the tree flower.

I prayed to the Grandfathers, I prayed to Wakantanka, and I prayed to Blue Crow. Yes, to my great-grandfather, Blue Crow. I apologized to him. *I spent my whole life running from you. All that time I am you.*

I spent my whole life running from my dead, when I should have made friends with you.

PART SIX
THE BIG FOOT
MEMORIAL RIDE

PLEASANT SUNDAY

Emile and I lurched out of the darkness and cold through the doors of the Takini School, December 22, 1990. I hate cold. I was miserable and scared. Even after two months of getting ready spiritually and emotionally, I was in a funk. Tomorrow I was going to start riding a horse six days through below-zero weather—that's in the daytime—toward a place my relatives didn't want to go and where the U.S. cavalry killed them. I was going to travel with people who were obsessed with a past that had been deadly to their forebears and still seemed to hold them paralyzed. I would be miserable the whole time, and angry at myself for coming. *Talk about a fool's errand.*

I'd never been to this schoolhouse on the Cheyenne River Reservation, and I didn't like it. It was ponderous and ugly, looked like a place of dead concrete, not of live minds. A glance at Emile told me he didn't like it either. As an artist he is a kind of Indian elf, all light and airy, not one for heavy places.

We hauled our sleeping bags and packs down the hall and across the gym floor to some bleachers. Lots of people were already nestled down here, snugged into the foot places between the seat places. I gave the world a scowl. These foot boards weren't big enough for a full-sized man, in fact none bigger than Emile. I hitched my gear higher on my back and headed for the end of the bleachers, and Emile followed without a word. I gave an audible *hmmpff!*

I looked around for reasons to be grumpy and found them. There were a lot of white people here, many of them carrying cameras and notebooks. I remembered something Tyler had said—"We decided to use the media to broadcast our message far and wide."

Beyond the bleachers was some room in a chaos of sleeping bags, packs, and horse tack. I threw my stuff on the floor, and then spotted more reasons to be grumpy. A dozen or so Japanese monks and nuns sat on their bedrolls, heads shaven, all smiling, all facing the center of the gym, and all drinking something out of identical cylinders. *What the hell are the Japs doing here?* I speculated irritably that they would all drink their tea or whatever at the same instant with the same motion, like in a store window of mechanical toys.

What are the Japanese doing here? And all the white people? I asked myself more seriously. *Isn't this our problem? Isn't the broken hoop ours to mend?*

Two tall Indians walked past us looking for a place for their sleeping bags. They looked about fifty, and the gray was beginning to show. They also looked familiar.

"Who's that?"

Emile glanced up and said, "Russell Means and Dennis Banks."

"Oh, shit." To me, if the names meant leadership—Wounded Knee II and a hundred other protests—they also meant grandstanding for cameras and microphones. *I'm here to do personal spiritual work.*

"Which is which?"

"The one with an expression like he's looking for some-one to snarl at is Means." So Banks was the one who looked like he found the world quirky and funny.

Emile arranged his blankets and sleeping bag neatly, and folded his parka for a pillow. I looked at him and thought,

Banks and Means and the media and everything else is a distraction. Keep your mind on why you're here.

A microphone man in the middle of the floor announced something, I didn't hear what. As I turned toward him, I almost bumped into Chup, who was reaching to touch my sleeve. He grinned. "Great start, freezing our asses!"

Sallee stood behind him, kind of backing away.

"Hi, good to see you."

"Hi," she answered. "I'm glad you came." She seemed, well, grave about it.

I touched my hat and tried for a devil-may-care grin. "Really glad to see you. Ride along with Emile and me."

"I'm walking," she said. "Like them." She nodded at the Japanese. "They're wonderful people. I met their leader, June San, the one standing." A woman of rimless glasses and forbidding aspect. "I'm hugely impressed that they come halfway around the world to wipe away our tears."

"There are walkers?"

She nodded. "Some of them are fasting, too. I'd be nervous about that."

"Unbelievable." It didn't come out the way I wanted it to, as awe and admiration.

Sallee turned gracefully and walked to join the Japanese. *Never will be able to suit that woman.*

"Don't try," said Chup, and I laughed at how he always read my thoughts.

Emile tugged my sleeve and pulled me toward the center of the floor. Now I understood what the announcer was saying—a ceremony called Shaking of the Hands. Easy. We were going to say hi to everybody.

Everybody meant several dozen Indian people and several dozen white Americans, Europeans, and Japanese. Tyler had talked excitedly about numbers. "Scads of people,

I bet over a hundred riders to start with, and more every day of the ride." Now I looked at them as they gathered on the gym floor, these people I would ride with for six days. Some of them would pledge to ride or walk the entire distance, in honor of the dead. Some would drive cars, haul wood and water, and do whatever else was needed. Others would come back and forth to support family members who were riding. We had, maybe, the beginning of a common purpose.

Half the time I don't know what my *purpose here is.*

The drum struck up the beat, the singing voices rose high, and we started walking. We stepped in an Indian double circle, a sort of coil of two rows of people facing each other and walking opposite directions. We shook hands and kept moving, but there was courtesy in it, an ease that allowed for human contact. I didn't focus on how many people were non-Indians, and I let my eyes speak white-man body language, lingering, making real contact with each face. The faces were open, the eyes joining with mine. We said a word or two of greetings, warm greetings, and moved on, circling, circling.

I came to the Japanese and now was struck by the imperial beauty of the woman in rimless glasses. She nodded her head to me, a kind of bow. Yes, severe, and her face seemed to reserve her beauty for a higher purpose.

I came to Banks and Means. Banks looked tickled about something, and Means seemed to convey the high seriousness of the occasion with his great dignity.

I was getting into the spirit of the thing. People had come from everywhere for a high purpose. They were here to release the spirits and wipe away the tears of seven generations. Me too. Something in my heart eased.

"*Hau, kola,*" said the next face circling. It was Tyler, grinning big at me. I shook his hand a little tentatively, remembering the day I fell down at Wounded Knee.

Right behind Tyler came a big, shaggy, Indian-looking guy, maybe sixty, with wild, bushy gray hair down his back and the friendliest face you ever saw. "Pleasant Sunday," he said, "Cherokee and Shoshone," and moved on, saying the same words to everyone. For a moment, though, he held my eye, and I thought I saw a special glint for me.

Pleasant Sunday, Cherokee and Shoshone? What the hell is that? On a Saturday?

Now the song rose higher and stronger, the fervor grew intense, and I began to feel the rhythm of the moving lines. Whether we were clumsy as individuals or not, the arcing lines glided across the floor in stately fashion, with a sexy, sinuous beauty. I began to feel myself as part of a whole of many parts, subtly interlocking, smoothly gliding in and out of one another. And our lives individually were difficult, maybe unattractive, but we created a new life together, serpentine and majestic.

I stopped seeing individual faces and introductions. I listened to the song and felt the beat of the drum throb up from the floor into my feet and through my body. I reached out and gave the beat to another human being with every handshake.

People were smiling now, and weaving a dance motion into their sideways steps, their reaching for hands, the bobs of their heads.

I laughed. *This is FUN.* Sallee and Chup approached. After shaking Sallee's hand, I twirled her gently in a full spin. She laughed. Chup made like he was tapdancing. I let out a whoop. I danced right through until …

The song ended. The announcer called for us to take our seats for the Makes-Vow Ceremony. Sitting down felt like suppressing myself.

A man I didn't recognize introduced the ceremony and said a prayer for those who would come forward and take eagle feathers from the sacred hoop. I should not write down the words of a prayer—sacred things are not to be written, not to be photographed—but here's the gist of it. He said, "When we take a feather, we vow to make the ride, the same ride Big Foot and his people made it a hundred years ago. We're honoring them. If we take this vow, we say we're going every mile. It's like a Sun Dance. No matter how hard it is, we're gonna do it. No matter how cold, no matter how much we hurt. We pledge every step, all the way to Wounded Knee. Our pledge will be fulfilled when we stand in the circle around the mass grave on Cemetery Hill. If you are willing to make this pledge, no matter what, step forward and take an eagle feather from the sacred hoop. That eagle feather, it shows you promised."

Then he begged the help of Wakantanka and the Grandfathers, to give us the strength to keep this vow.

The eight men of the drum raised sticks and started the music. The song, a strong, high, unison melody, raised to the gym roof. Men, women, and children lined up to make their vows.

In the center of the circle stood ten or twelve leaders of the ride, including Tyler and Alex White Plume. One man held the sacred hoop, draped with eagle feathers. It was Arvol Looking Horse, the keeper of the White Buffalo Woman Pipe. In each generation one person in that family is entrusted with the Pipe, the one White Buffalo Woman brought us. Though I didn't know him then, I recognized him from pictures in the Lakota *Times*. He had a solemn face, reflecting the weight of the vows being taken. One by one people plucked feathers from the hoop.

I got ready. I was going to make this vow. I'd spent two months preparing my spirit to do this, and I was going through with it. Along the way I'd gotten the willies a dozen times. I'd told myself every bad thing I could think of, I'd shaken every accusing finger I had at me. *You're going back to the blanket. You know better than this. You might as well refuse medicine and blood transfusions—you might as well dance with rattlesnakes. It's like being a fundamentalist.* I'd said all of this. Ain't it funny how, when you set your feet on a good road, thoughts come and bedevil you. Sometimes I think that's Iya, the Evil One, Wind Storm, always working at us.

Here I am. I am going to make this vow. I don't know why. When I make it, I am going to fulfill it.

The fellow of "Pleasant Sunday" stepped in behind me, and grinned in a way that seemed lit especially for me. He said, "I saw that my introduction was confusing. My name is Pleasant Sunday. I'm Cherokee-Shoshone. Call me Plez, rhymes with *rez.*"

I just looked at him queer. From the front his hair looked like a stick of broccoli, tight to the back of his head, and then a clump of curls. His face was shaven clean as an egg, but everything else was hairy, even the backs of his hands. Hair stuck out above the top button of his shirt, and tufted out of his ears. Nobody should be that hairy. I turned back to the hoop.

I feel shy about telling you the details even now. I waited, my mind on nothing but what I was promising to do. When my turn came, I took a feather. I felt Looking Horse's grave demeanor without looking at him. I kept my eyes on the hoop of the people, which I hoped to help mend. I looked at the feather which represented my task.

I walked back changed. I walked back scared. *I have a big purpose.*

I sat down on my rolled-up sleeping bag. Emile said, "For tonight, you want me to tie the feather into your hair?"

I thought, and discovered I did. "Thanks."

He got down on his knees behind me, and I felt his fingers tug my hair. He stopped. "Up? Down? Sideways? What do you want?"

I remembered Grandpa had said Crazy Horse wore his eagle feather pointed down. Grandpa's story was, that's because when the eagle angles its tail down, it's about to kill. "Down," I said. *I am going to kill the drunken, drifting, self-pitying Blue Crow, and rise a new man.*

Emile's fingers went back to work.

Pleasant Sunday, Chup, and Tyler strolled up. "Call me Plez," Plez said to Emile, "rhymes with *rez*."

I was gonna get sick of hearing that.

Tyler says to me, "This is a good man, this Pleasant Sunday. He knows things, help you maybe." And walked off.

Chup says to me, "This man, I've been wanting you to meet him. He … like Tyler said."

Pleasant Sunday grinned at me. *What is this, a conspiracy?* There was something about him like out of *Alice in Wonderland*—the Cheshire Cat?

He turned to Emile. "Want me to tie your feather in?" he says, touching the crown of Emile's head.

"Yes, thank you," said Emile, "tip up."

"I'll tie yours," says Chup to Pleasant Sunday.

So there we were, four men doing each other's hair, or having it done. I would have made a circle and tied in Chup's, but it was already tied to the button of his baseball cap. This cap was fully beaded on the brim, and the crown said in big letters, FBI, and below, "Full-Blooded Indian."

"Next is an honoring song for Sitting Bull," called the announcer.

"I'll just tie this off temporary-like," said Plez, and jumped to his feet.

Emile finished my feather in a jiffy. I'd never worn an eagle feather before. Had never been entitled to. It felt good.

The voices of the drum group seemed to me very beautiful in this song: high, heroic men's voices, giving honor to one of our great ones. A man who himself was a poet, a songwriter, a seer, a lover of the old ways, that's what I heard about him. That's why we gave him an honoring song, and stood while they sang it.

When the song ended, Plez said to me, like in the middle of a conversation, "He loved the old ways, you know, way loved them." *Lot of folks completing my thoughts around here.* "That scared the agent on his reservation, and he marked Sitting Bull down as one of them backward ones, a force for 'savage' ways. Which put him on the government's list of conservatives to be silenced. Indian policemen rode out one cold morning and murdered him on the steps of his own house. The agent didn't order the killing, but he set it up."

I stared at him. *Who is this Cherokee-Shoshone telling me my own history?* Of course, I'd just learned it myself.

Tyler pitched in. "He didn't go for the Ghost Dance, Sitting Bull, or go away from it neither. He was sitting the fence when they killed him."

A woman I didn't know, Celene Not Help Him, had started a talk about Wounded Knee, what it really was. She was the granddaughter of Dewey Beard, a man also known as Iron Hail, the best-known of the survivors of the massacre. Our stories about that fight don't always match the white-man stories, and I believe our people. Unlike the white soldiers, they didn't have anything to cover up.

I listened carefully to Celene. Though I'd read the white-man books, I wanted to hear a Lakota tell it—sounded like she'd researched it deep. She started with Wovoka, way over in Nevada. That Paiute medicine man had a vision of a better world. The Indian people's ancestors were alive again, the buffalo were back, and the white people were gone. Indians from a lot of different tribes made the journey to Mono Lake to hear Wovoka tell his vision. They took it back to their people, with the dance he told them to do, the Ghost Dance, and the Ghost Shirt he told them to wear.

From there it was the basic story of Big Foot. How Big Foot's people took off from Cheyenne River across the Badlands toward Wounded Knee. How Indians from the Pine Ridge and Rosebud Reservations were doing the Ghost Dance day and night up in the Stronghold, a far corner of the Badlands. That had the whites bad scared. But Big Foot wasn't going to them, he was headed for Pine Ridge.

The army chased all over hell and gone, looking for Big Foot, but never found him until he sent word to Pine Ridge where he was, and that he would arrive the next day. Then they intercepted him and made him camp at Wounded Knee, guarded close by the Seventh Cavalry. The idea was to take all his guns away. That was a hard, strict order.

Everybody was tense the next morning. All the men were gathered at a council, all in one place, with troops all around them. The young men didn't want to give up their rifles, good repeating Winchesters. They needed those guns to feed their families. The soldiers insisted, and were searching them, one by one. One Indian's rifle went off accidentally, straight up in the air. The soldiers had been ordered to fire at the first sound of shooting. Two troops of cavalry fired point blank into the grouped-up Indian men, and the killing was on.

But that was only the beginning, Celene Not Help Him insisted. Then the soldiers fired the fast-shooting cannons straight into the Indian village, mostly women and children. After those left alive fled the village, they tried to hide in the ravine. The soldiers shot their rifles and their Hotchkiss guns down into the ravine, slaughtering people at random, warriors, old men, women, children, everyone, not caring who.

The white people say about a hundred and fifty of Big Foot's people died. The Lakota's estimate, and they know better, is about three hundred.

When she finished, people started crawling into their sleeping bags. Emile, Plez, Chup, and I untied each other's eagle feathers. Ever helpful, Plez stitched them onto our hats for tomorrow, with needle and thread. We put the hats on top of our packs, well off the ground. You don't let an eagle feather touch the ground.

Then Plez and Chup stretched out on either side of me without a word. Plez tucked his broccoli hair to one side and lay on his back. My sponsor on one side, good—but this new guy between me and my oldest friend? Seemed odd.

After lights out, I felt restless. Soon comes this whisper. "You 'sleep?" It's Chup.

"Hell, no," I said.

"Let's go somewhere," says Plez. "I got a thermos of coffee still hot."

"You go," says Emile. He was halfway asleep already.

We went up to a far, high corner of the bleachers where no one else was. Looking down on the gym floor was eerie. People left candles on so kids could go the bathroom and such, and it looked like a big tapestry, circles of glow and caverns of darkness. I wished Emile was seeing it.

Plez handed the plastic top of the thermos around. The coffee tasted strange but good. "What's that in it?" I says.

"Sweetgrass," says Plez.

Hadn't tried that before; liked it.

Chup says, "Watch this." He sets one of those big six-volt flashlights on its base, and fixes his riding wristlet around it with the rawhide thongs he uses on his forearms. When he turns it on, a dramatic-looking cone of light shoots up into the dark depths of the rafters. In the half-light, half-shadow around it, our faces look gobliny.

Chup grinned at us. "Like that?"

"Yeah," says I.

We looked at each other conspiratorially. I felt like giggling like a kid. I slugged on the sweetgrass coffee. *Let's whisper, like kids after lights out.*

Chup says—it seemed real sudden, real abrupt—"Blue, you found anything on your great-grandfather at Wounded Knee?"

"No," says I, miffed that he would bring it up in front of a stranger.

Chup goes on, "Try Plez."

Uncomfortable silence. Three goblins fidgeting in the otherworldly light and sort of smiling at each other.

"*Kola*, what's happenin'?"

I didn't answer.

Chup looked at me expectantly.

Plez sighed. "I think I can help you. I have that sense. I got it when I first heard about you from Chup and Tyler."

"Tyler?"

"He said you went to Cemetery Hill with him, never been there, fell down unconscious, give him a scare."

I looked hard at Chup. *My friends've been gossiping about me.*

Chup says, "Your sponsor, I can't talk about some things to other people. But you came to here to get help—we all did. Get help for ourselves, give help to the people. I'll tell you, Plez is your man. I know him a long time."

I had this trembling in my throat. I was afraid it showed, afraid the skin was wobbling. I decided to stop it. "I don't know what happened that day," I said to Plez. "I kind of passed out. I saw things...." I looked up into the rafters, asking the dark reaches to help me. "It was like a dream, only brighter and stronger."

Plez chuckled, "Oh, you're a good one. That's easy to sort out, in a general way. You got a glimpse of the other side."

I waited and sort of nodded.

Plez gave me a canny look. "That happen to you before?"

I nodded bigger. "When I went on the mountain, coupla months ago."

"So you had it before, you know that's what it was. What was so different?" He grinned, "Oh, yeah, on the mountain you were looking for it."

"Yes."

"At Wounded Knee it jumped up and bit you. Scared you." He cocked an eyebrow at me.

"Yes."

"Anything you want to tell me about it?"

I waited a long time. He must have thought I wasn't gonna answer, but he never stirred. Finally I says, "I saw a guide. Raven." I looked up at his lighted face and down at my shadowed knees. "A special raven. Now I tell myself to call him Spirit Bird. Scares hell out of me, always has. I didn't go."

Plez nodded slow several times. "You know much about Spirit Bird?"

"What I see around me. He's a capital-R Raven, and ravens feed on death. And what I see in my dreams. Raven is black shadows."

He nodded slow several more times. "Yeah, you want to work on this Raven, things are there for you. Maybe I can help you a little. For sure I can point a way toward help. Meanwhile, how do I say ... ? Why are you on this pilgrimage to Wounded Knee?"

"To seek healing for myself and to wipe away the tears of the people." I was surprised at how easy it came out.

"That's good, but ... you have relatives there?"

My hands felt like drumming on my knees, and at the same time felt frozen. I looked and saw they were shaking. I knit my fingers together.

"Yeah. My great-grandfather was there, name Blue Crow. Anybody heard of him, I'd like to know. My grandmother was born the day after. That's all I know."

"Don't know anything about your great-grandfather, great-grandmother?"

"I don't know what happened. Unchee never talked about it. Would never. *Hard* would never."

"Oh, *kola,*" says Plez. Then he surprised me. "I'm so glad you came. I can help you."

I looked at the two of them. For some crazy reason a memory flashed into my mind, me sitting, legs crossed like this, with my dad and his brother, playing that silly game where you clap your knees and then clap against another's guy's hands, and clap your knees, all in a certain pattern and rhythm.

"It's true, Blue, I don' have any ancestors at Wounded Knee, being Cherokee and Shoshone, you know. But my wife, she is Mniconjou, she had relatives there. So I started with the second ride, three years ago. Between rides I been out putting together the story behind the story." He smiled. "Reading the books, going around gathering up people's stories, what's been handed down in their families, and the best way. Journeying there in spirit, seeing it for myself."

He said it so easy.

Something in my belly lurched. All those demons leapt at me with their sweet voices of reason—*See, this pilgrimage stuff is looney tunes. Back to the blanket, back to the nuthouse.* The demons had ninety-nine choruses of such stuff to sing, but I cut them off. *I saw miracles on the mountain.*

I looked up at his eyes. Even in the weird light his face was sweet and kind of simple. "So I can help you, you wanna know," he said, his voice gentle. "What happened to your relatives, what hold it has on your spirit."

"Part of me doesn't want to know."

Silence, while he thought this over.

"What was your grandmother like?"

"How would I know? She kept herself closed off. Mad. Mad inside all the time, I think. She gave me my name, didn't tell me it was my great-grandfather's. Gave me his Pipe, told me nothing about him."

"*Kola*, you need to know."

I didn't answer. My stomach felt like a pot being stirred.

"You've needed to know your whole life."

THEY RIDE

The next morning at Bridger, South Dakota, where the Big Foot people started running south, the corral was chaos. Riders tried to move gently among the horses, twitching their lariats and then floating them over the necks of their mounts. But the horses spooked, dashed from one side of the corral to another, reared and pranced. When the riders got saddled and mounted, the horses reared and crow-hopped. Lots of riders had to start again from the ground up.

Emile and I looked for a two-horse trailer with a four directions wheel painted on the side. This would be a guy from Wambli Mom knew, who had promised to rent us horses. Right away we found it and got them unloaded, a sorrel mare and a dun gelding, both young-looking. When I hauled out the saddles, I got a nice surprise. Mom apparently had saved my old saddle from Grandpa's. Since my bottom hadn't changed much in twenty years, it would still fit. I looked at the horses with a hard eye. Would they hold up for a week of riding in this cold? Word was, the high today would be ten below or the like, and no change in sight. Would we end up hoofing it and carrying our saddles over our shoulders? I checked their hooves. I checked the way they moved. They looked sound.

Emile paid the guy and reminded him to meet us at Wounded Knee on the twenty-eighth. That place was what I was trying not to think about.

Emile said gently, "May I ride the sorrel?" He went to the muzzle, held his nose to the horse's nostrils, and exchanged frosty breaths.

I mounted, noted that the dun didn't move off. The saddle felt good. I pulled on the reins and said, "Back!" and it even backed a few steps. It seemed to have a soft mouth. It might do. We would get to know each other.

We rode to the corral and tied the horses to the rail. Our gear would go ahead of us to tonight's camp in the support vehicles.

Half the riders were still trying to catch their mounts and get saddled. Among these was Pleasant Sunday. He wore a beautiful, flowing capote, made from a powder blue Hudson Bay blanket with a black stripe, but he couldn't flick his loop over the horse's head. It was a big, black, active gelding quarter horse, and the head was practically bouncing toward the clouds. Way Plez was going, he'd still be in this corral on the twenty-eighth.

I slipped into the corral, said, "Lemme?" and took the lariat from Plez. Then I got the bridle from the fence post.

Yeah, let me help you do something.

I pussyfooted the animal toward the narrow end of the corral against a building. I was moving like a cutting horse, gently but quickly, nothing wasted, nothing big, anticipating the animal's moves. It watched me. It knew.

We eyed each other. I stood so still he didn't even blink. After a while, the black seemed to sigh, and lowered his head. I walked easy to him, touched his muzzle, slipped the bit into his mouth, and put the bridle on. Never even bothered with the lariat.

Meanwhile, there was a pandemonium of whinnies, pounding hoofs, and whirring lariats all around us.

I was watching Plez without seeming to watch. He accepted the reins and said, "You got a touch with horses."

"Thanks. You ride much?"

Plez was putting on the saddle. "Naw," he says. "You know, my dad's people. Cherokees, we're more farmers and tradesmen than horsemen. Hundred fifty years ago your great-great-grandfathers were riding down the buffalo, big stuff, big adventure. Know what mine were doing? Running the general store. Planting and harvesting crops. One was editing the first newspaper among the Cherokees."

He pulled the cinch too tight. I adjusted it, and showed him how to slip three fingers behind the cinch—if you can't get them in, it's too tight.

We hopped up on the rail next to Emile. I was feeling a little better about Plez, but not about the day.

"You feeling marbinschilling?" he asked me, beaming as usual.

"Marbinschilling?"

"It's a word my grandfather taught me—means a little out of sorts."

"Cherokee word?" I asked.

"Naw, it's a word a grandpa made up for the fun of his grandkids. Well, are you marbinschilling?"

"I'm cold," I said.

I was done up in longjohns, pacs, a padded working man's zipper suit, gloves and liners, ski mask, and hooded parka. The only thing exposed was my eagle feather. I had to turn my whole body to check the corral with my eyes. It was going to be a while before we started.

"I'm gonna find us some hot coffee," said Emile, and slid off the rail.

"My grandfather taught me a lot," Plez rambled on. "Can't tell you how much. He also give me my name. I mean the first name and the family name, Sunday. Our original name was Cheatham. My grandfather, Pleasant Cheatham, was born again at a revival held in Oklahoma by Billy Sunday. Accepted Jesus, praise the Lord!" (Plez's eyes hinted at irony here, but his smile was tireless and his tone enthusiastic.) "When my dad was born, later that year, my grandfather wrote himself down on the birth certificate as Pleasant Sunday, and my dad was Orel Sunday. That's how I come to be Pleasant Sunday, the Second. That's the truth. You can see I was born to be a man of Spirit."

Now I had some ammunition. "You're Indian and a born-again?" I know plenty of those, but I was about to do a Tyler Red Crow on him—"All Christian churches are my enemies."

"Naw," says Plez, "I walk the Indian way only." He considered what he wanted to say. "And I have the gift. I see things."

"What do you mean, see things?"

"I see things of the Spirit. I see you're irritable now. Last night I saw you're afraid about this ride. You wanna know what happened to your relatives, and at the same time you don't wanna know. You feel maybe like a fool. You think maybe I can help you, but you're half-scared of that."

I looked at him in the eyes, white-man style. They were merry and his grin was easy.

"You might be wrong."

He shrugged with his eyebrows. "I have other gifts, too," he said. "Journey through time."

"You what?"

"Told you, I've been to Wounded Knee, saw the massacre."

We sat there and looked at each other for a moment. Plez kind of looked like he was laughing—not laughing at me, but laughing at everything, enjoying the world.

"That's hard for me."

"It's the shaman's way. I can go into the Spirit World. I can talk to spirits there. I can talk to our departed ancestors. Sometimes, if things are right, I can go be with our ancestors somewhere they were. Like Wounded Knee. Beyond people's stories, beyond what I read, was what the spirits showed me. Direct. I was there."

I felt a spasm, anger roiled up with nausea.

"Anybody ever call you crazy?"

"Oh yeah, that's a favorite." He was just grinning and nodding.

I jumped down from the rail, untied the reins, and switched the post with them hard, like I meant to hurt it. I was getting out of there. I glared at Plez.

"Remember, that's what *Wanagi Wacipi*, the Spirit Dance was about. People went and visited the Spirit World."

I stood there with my mouth hanging open.

"Yeah," he said, "you might be able to go back there. Some people can, some can't. When we talked last night, I thought, *This fellow has the gift.* At least I bet you could do it now, when your mind and spirit are so close to that day a hundred years ago."

I made myself turn away, looking for Emile.

Plez put a friendly hand on my shoulder. "You wanna go see what happened to your relatives there, Wounded Knee, you lemme know. We'll try."

I pretended I hadn't heard and walked out from underneath the hand.

I stomped around the corral and stood on the other side. Here the cold wind was in my face, and it hurt. I realized I was aching terrible: ears, nose, fingers, feet. *Where's Emile? Where's that hot coffee?* I stomped on, searching for my friend. My eyes were tearing from the cold, or anger, or fear that Pleasant Sunday, man of the old ways, might be telling the truth.

After way too long a time, all the horses were saddled, and we riders formed a big circle in the empty space next to the store on the highway south. We were a funny-looking crew in all our winter headgear: cowboy hats, parka hoods, knit caps, Scotch caps, baseball caps with eagle feathers jutting everywhere—up, down, sideways, and just swinging in the breeze. At powwows you see Indians wearing eagle feathers with their dance outfits. Here everyone wore one with the way we dress now. I thought it meant we were bringing our religion into this life today, and I liked that.

Later I heard there were 129 of us riders starting out. There were also a lot of walkers, including the monks and nuns. And people, more and more people, would be joining us every day, until we came to Wounded Knee.

Some of the leaders, men who had put the rides together, sat their mounts in the middle of the circle— Arvol Looking Horse, Birgil Kills Straight, Alex White Plume, Jim Garrett, Ron McNeill, men I didn't know. A medicine man prayed, and the men of the drum pounded out a rhythm. Then we kicked the horses to a trot, circled sunwise, and we were off.

Eagle feathers fluttered in the cold wind. Women trilled—a sound you don't hear much any more, exciting. In front we heard riders yelling, "*Heyupa! Heyupa!*" and we all joined in, voices raised together.

After all that standing and sitting around, the motion of the horse felt good. Being Lakota felt good too.

When we settled down to a walk, someone brushed my stirrup, and I was glad to see it was Emile, not Pleasant Sunday. Today was Sunday, two days before Christmas. "This ain't no pleasant any day," I said. Emile smiled his beautiful, delicate smile at me.

Matter of fact, it would be a long day, thirty miles to ride, and it was going to be brutal. How was my butt going to hold up for thirty miles? I hadn't ridden in years. How was I going to survive the wind and cold? This country is sagebrush plains, oceans of ridges of sagebrush, nothing to break the wind.

How was I going to pass the time?

I told Emile about what Plez said, claiming he could time-travel, saying he'd been to Wounded Knee, saying maybe he could take me there.

"I don't think it's exactly time-traveling," Emile said. "My grandmother's brother, he could journey to the Spirit World. He wouldn't tell anyone much about it. I heard he could go to the underworld and bring people back, people who had just died. He also got a language from there somehow, his own language. Songs too. Brought 'em back."

"You believe that?" Don't know why I sounded so challenging. I'd always heard *yuwipi* men could do some of that.

Emile didn't answer for a moment.

"Plez said that's what the Ghost Dance was about, talking to the departed spirits."

Emile looked at me. "Yes."

"You believe in the Ghost Dance? I mean, our ancestors thought the Ghost Shirts would turn away bullets, and it got them killed."

"I don't know what went wrong there. They got killed, that doesn't mean the whole Ghost Dance was wrong." He hesitated, then went on in his delicate voice. "I danced one. At Crow Dog's. While you were away at college."

"So you do believe in it."

"Yes. Mostly I believe in the unseen. It's there, it's real, people don't see it because they've learned not to look. I believe something else, too." He looked at me openly, seriously. "Art brings the unseen into the world. That's why I don't paint what I see, or things based on old paintings. I paint what I dream. I'm bringing the other world into this one."

What do I say now?

"Blue, you know this. You haven't been living it."

"Drunks can't live much of anything."

I stared into the wind and held my eyes open until they teared. The tears froze my ski mask to my lower lashes.

"*Kola,* he's offering you a gift, why don't you take it? I mean, try it?"

Something ran up my gullet, burning bad. I kicked my horse to a canter, wheeled around, and raced back along the margin of the road to get away, alone.

I walked the dun back along the line of riders, looking for Sallee. Not a tree in sight on the plains, and the wind slapped at me. Front to back, I didn't find her. All the way at the rear I found Tyler.

"Where's Sallee?"

"The walkers are going another way."

"Oh." He rode an old, wheezing bay mare. "Why you at the back?"

"I'm keeping an eye out, making sure nobody drops behind unnoticed, helping them as gets in trouble. We keep count, especially after dark. Last year one of the walkers fell back in the dark, spent the night out, almost died. That woman who's the leader of the monks and nuns."

I eyed his mount suspiciously.

"Friend, it's a hard time. We lost twelve horses already, lame, breathing problems, everything. We been picking them up with horse trailers. Then the riders become walkers."

I looked back along the way and saw nothing. We'd been riding up a big hogback on someone's ranch. "Where are the walkers?"

"Us riders go cross country, like Big Foot. The walkers follow the roads." Which in country like this would mean right angles along the section lines. I wouldn't see her until camp tonight. I felt a pang.

"It's gonna get worse, *kola*. When we top this hogback? Think about the wind up there."

When I hit the wind about midday, I thought some riders would die. Wi, Father Sun, was out full, giving us what he could. But Waziya, the cold giant who lives in the north, and Tate, the wind, they were stomping us. Maybe worst weather I ever saw in this country. *Is this Evil One, the Wind Storm, toying with us?*

At the top of the ridge overlooking the Cheyenne River valley, where we came from, I rode past a support vehicle parked beside the road, a blue van. The wind hit it so hard it swayed on its springs. I looked at the window-framed face of the white man in the driver's seat, and saw he looked kind. *Easier to be kind when you're next to the heater!* He rolled down the window and handed me his smoke. I dragged deep, and it felt good. "I'm Tony," he said.

"Blue." We shared the smoke. He was warm, I was cold, he was white, I am Indian, but I felt a bond with that man for that moment. It was lovely. When he stubbed out the cigarette, I rode on without a backward glance. Not that comfortable with the bond.

I swiveled in my saddle and looked at the other riders. Everybody's head was down, arms drawn to the body, trunk squeezed tight on itself. Every scarf was wrapped as high as the eyes, hats pulled down, ear flaps extended, big goggles in place over the eyes. Emile had no scarf, so his face had the color and texture of setting concrete.

The horses looked worse. Their chests and front legs were sheeted with frost. Their breaths came in gasps and snorts. Their eyes were red. Their gait was near a stagger.

316

Why, Grandfathers? We are doing a good thing. Why must we suffer so?

Maybe it wasn't the Evil One doing this, maybe the Grandfathers were testing us. We Lakota say the only thing that is truly ours in this world is our body. So when we want to make a sacrifice for Spirit, we let our bodies suffer, like in the Sun Dance.

Now the wind slapped me, and I wanted to cuss Iya, the Evil One who performs his role with malicious glee. He pissed me off.

With my knees I urged my horse down the road, off this exposed ridge. But his best pace now was a funeral march.

I rode alongside Emile so close our stirrups bumped. I wanted to reach out and squeeze him to me, intertwine arms and legs, so we could be each others' extra coats. The high today had been eight below, so people's car radios said. The wind mauled us.

Plez stood his horse in the middle of the road, waiting for us. For an old man and an inexperienced rider, he seemed to be surviving better than we were. He stuck out that thermos to me. I took it—hell, I wasn't proud. I fumbled at the cap and almost never got it off with my stiff fingers. It was sweet, hot tea with sugar and lemon. I don't drink tea, but I never tasted anything so good in my life. I passed the thermos to Emile.

"Kill it," said Plez.

We did.

"I wonder if there was weather like this, them dancing, a hundred years ago. The Indian agents, the soldiers, the government all said, 'Stop that dancing.' Big Foot answered,

'Our people will abide by our religion, and the white man has nothing to say about that.' This is one of the reasons they figured Big Foot wrong, as a troublemaker.

"You know this story? The whites, they sent an officer to Big Foot's camp and he stayed with Hump a few days. These white and red soldiers, they were friends, they fought in the campaign against Chief Joseph together. The officer, he told Hump the Ghost Dance was a bad thing. Hump was an enthusiastic Ghost Dancer, and a lot of people followed him and they danced a lot—night and day for weeks, sometimes—many of Big Foot's other people. But when this officer friend left, Hump turned against the Ghost Dance, and his followers did the same."

Plez was looking at us bright and birdlike all the time. Now he says, "Hey, you got questions, ask 'em."

He waited. I murmured clunkily, "My lips have turned to frisbees."

Plez laughed. "Big Foot, he was caught between the people who wanted to dance, who thought it was the only way of hope, and people who didn't believe in it."

"Not everybody did the Ghost Dance?"

"Okay, let's call it the Spirit Dance. Better translation, at least truer to what the dance was.

"No, not everybody. Among all the Lakota, maybe a third. Big Foot's people, maybe half. Kicking Bear, he was one that went to Nevada and talked to Wovoka, he was Mniconjou, and he preached the dance hard to his band. But by this time he was off in the Stronghold, dancing night and day.

"Anyway, the people were divided about it. Big Foot, he was always a negotiator, a compromiser, that's what he was good at. He told the dancers to buy more ammunition for their rifles, in case the soldiers tried to stop the dancing by force. And the people who didn't dance, he counseled them to be patient. That way he kept them more or less together on it."

I'd read some of this, but it hadn't stuck.

"Well, you know, on December fifteen the tribal police killed Sitting Bull. That scared some of his people and they ran off. On the eighteenth maybe two dozen of them came staggering into Big Foot's camp on the Cheyenne River. They asked for food and shelter, and of course Big Foot helped them out. They also told how Sitting Bull got killed. That scared everyone.

"Hey, you got to watch out. Indian policemen killed Sitting Bull. Indian policemen arrested Crazy Horse and held him. Just happened the bayonet that killed him was held by a white man. You got to watch your ass. They can always find one of your own to do you in."

"Shot while trying to escape," I mumbled gummily. "The traditional death of an American rebel."

Plez chuckled and went on. "The next day this officer, Sumner, he comes to camp. He suggests Big Foot throw the Sitting Bull people out—they're troublemakers. But Big Foot won't turn his back on his relatives when they're in need. Later Sumner sends a courier, says, 'Get your people ready and go to Fort Meade.' Fort Meade was maybe sixty miles west of there, up toward Deadwood. Sumner has orders from above, and the soldiers are worried about this Ghost Dancing—it may stir everything up. The army isn't saying so, but they've decided to disarm Big Foot's band."

"They just ordered hundreds of people to march around here and there? In the winter?" I was pissed.

"If you wanted your rations, you went. Matter of fact, Big Foot wasn't thinking about going to Fort Meade. His mind was on Fort Bennett, same distance downriver. That's where the people got their rations, and they were hungry. His mind was also on Pine Ridge.

"I said Big Foot was a negotiator. Well, the chiefs at Pine Ridge fell into conflict. Some of their people were out in the Stronghold with Kicking Bear and Short Bull, dancing up a storm to bring the millennium. You know about the Stronghold?"

"Yeah," says I. I figured if I moved my lips once in a while they wouldn't fracture.

"No," says Emile. The word sounded swallowed.

"The Stronghold is way in the northwest corner of the Badlands, a sort of table separated from the rest of the country by a land bridge no wider than a pickup. Hard to approach and easy to defend. The most keen Spirit Dancers, led by Kicking Bear and Short Bull, about the first of December they marched to the Stronghold. They meant to dance night and day until the millennium came, and they weren't gonna let anybody stop them."

"This is sad," says Emile. "This is hard." He also must have been looking for a reason to move his lips.

"Yeah?" says Plez, like a question.

"Hearing about people of faith, people searching for a way, people following their hearts and heading into so much trouble."

"Yeah," says Plez. He reflected for a moment. "You bet.

"Anyhow, some were dancing at the Stronghold, mostly Rosebud people. At Pine Ridge, some were dancing in their camps, some refused to have anything to do with the dance. Pretty big disagreement. The Pine Ridge chiefs, they sent word to Big Foot to come help them settle their differences. Promised him a hundred horses to do it. So Big Foot, he's thinking Fort Bennett, and he's thinking Pine Ridge, and he's not interested in Fort Meade, though he doesn't tell Sumner that.

"On the appointed day, the twenty-second, that's a hundred years ago yesterday, Big Foot doesn't show up at

Sumner's camp. So Sumner sends a local rancher, name of Red Beard, to repeat the message. Now, no one knows exactly what Red Beard said. But the impression the Mniconjou got was, You got to come to Fort Meade or the soldiers will march you in at gunpoint, and when you get there, your leaders will be arrested and put in chains and sent by train to an island in the eastern sea."

"I know that one," I said through stiff lips. Now my teeth ached every time cold air got in my mouth. "The Dry Tortugas, where the soldiers planned to send Crazy Horse if they could arrest him."

"That evening, when the scouts reported soldiers on the way, they lit out for Pine Ridge.

"Hey, that's enough of the story for now, gets us almost up to where we are. You want, I'll tell you more later."

"I want," says Emile.

"How you feeling, brother?"

Plez wasn't gonna let me get comfortable in my ignorance.

"I have a bad sense. Feel like I'm sinking into a swamp, the sticky muck and dank water of the past. I'm afraid if I go in, I'll never come out."

"Friend," says Plez, "you been in all your life. Only way you can go is out."

THE CAMP IN THE STRAW

Come dark we were still riding. Camp, they told us, would be at the place of a friendly white rancher, and it would be set up, fires burning, food ready, when we got there. Those of us without a tipi or tent could sleep in the barn. I figured I wasn't going to make it that far.

wwI couldn't remember pain like I was feeling. My joints felt raw, like my bones were mortar and pestle. Shoulders and elbows were bad, hips and knees terrible. I couldn't move my head for fear it would fall off my neck.

I wondered if it was better or worse for the walkers. A picture of the monks and nuns came to mind, banging their prayer drums, chanting, walking forever. One of them had the face of Sallee, yellow-skinned, second in line, banging her drum and chanting a language I would never understand. She wore huge glasses that kept me from seeing her eyes.

I saw Plez take off his glove and touch the eagle feather tied to the blue hood of his capote, almost caressing it. He noticed me looking at him, smiled, and said, "Soul food."

I imitated his action, felt the feather sewn to my hood in back. Through the mittens, gloves, and liners that wrapped my fingers, it seemed barely present. But I lacked faith to take off the hand wraps and try for real soul food.

Emile and I hadn't spoken in a couple hours. I was far past any place I could move my lips, or move my brain to convey words to my tongue. Sometimes Plez was riding beside us, sometimes gone, like a ghost.

Tyler rode by and told us Chup's mare had gone lame. He was one of the walkers now. However bad walking was, seemed like it couldn't be worse than this.

Dark and an hour beyond dark, on into the night we rode, the temperature plummeting, who knew how far, probably thirty below or worse.

I'm gonna die.

Plodding on, plodding on.

I don't know how long until we turned into a lane bordered by trees, and I knew this had to be the ranch. I didn't think I could ride the last few hundred yards.

Plez pointed, and I saw lights ahead in a field, headlights. I grinned, and it felt like my lips shattered, like they were water ice given a sharp rap. We rode toward the lights.

When we got a hundred yards out, Plez said, "Watch!" and pulled his horse off to the side away from camp. "Look!" Riders passed us, now silhouetted by the headlights. The passing forms were eerie. Their shadows stretched long and rippled across our chests and faces, ghostly fingers touching our hands, lips, and eyes. The strangest part was, the one thing I seemed to see on every rider—man, woman, and kid, was his eagle feather—his will, his determination, his vow.

We rode into camp last, and into the circle around the big council fire. I wanted to get off the horse, but I didn't—I was afraid of the pain of moving, and afraid I would fall.

Someone in the circle prayed, and his words seemed to fracture in the cold between us—I couldn't make out what he was saying. The drum sang a song, and the melody, punctuated by the sharp drumbeats, was eaten by the cold. *Waziya, the mean giant of the north, is hungry.*

When the song ended, I lurched off the horse. I stumbled out of the stirrup, but was caught and held up by, surprise, Sallee and Chup. I thought Sallee smiled at me in the dark, and her hands felt good. They led the way, and us three riders staggered fast toward the fire to get close. We were too cold to eat. We burned first our fronts, then our backsides at the fire, then each side again. We rubbed our hands together, moved the fingers, then rubbed our cheeks and noses, snaked our lips around. We stomped our booted feet and waggled our toes. After this workout we trundled toward the pots, where the women had made huge batches of buffalo soup and fry bread.

I sat on the ground to eat, then got up because the earth was freezing my ass. I ate, and ate some more. When feeling human rose on my horizon, I said, "Where's that barn?"

Straw can be your friend, and it was tossed thick over the floor of the hay loft. We took a place by the second-story door—the five of us seemed to accept that we were traveling companions now—and piled up straw deep. Other folks were in the stalls, in corners, everywhere. We laid our sleeping bags on this pallet, and piled straw on top of the bags. The prediction for tonight was forty below. Emile and I crawled in one side, Chup and Sallee in the other, Plez in the middle. I felt a little jealous about Sallee being next to Chup, except he was her uncle, her mother's brother. Plez tucked the straw up close to everyone's heads, like a papa. Then, of course, we were too tired and achy to sleep, and there was too much talk in the barn.

I turned and squidged and flopped. "Somebody say something," I says. The voice I really wanted to hear was Sallee's.

Plez sat up, and I could see in the moonlight he'd snugged the blue hood of his capote around his face. "Seeing as we are in a manger," says he, "I will tell jokes on the clergy. Being a man of the cloth myself, sort of, I am entitled."

Emile and I groaned and moaned instead of laughing for maybe twenty minutes, but we liked them. I will repeat my favorite.

Two nuns were driving down a street in New Orleans, the younger one at the wheel. A small demon jumped up on their windshield. The younger nun flipped on the windshield wipers and knocked him off.

But the demon jumped right back on the windshield and cast his baleful eyes upon them.

"What'll I do?" cried the younger nun.

"I filled the wiper fluid with holy water," says the older nun. "Squirt him!"

The young nun squirted the water and flicked the wipers. The demon steamed and fell off.

But he jumped right back up in their faces, hissing horribly. "What'll I do?" wailed the younger nun.

"Show him your cross!" said the older nun.

The younger nun rolled down the window, leaned her head out, and shouted, "Get off my fucking windshield!"

We laughed so loud a male voice hollered, "Pipe down over there!" Then we talked quietly.

The jokes wound down, and I never heard Sallee say anything, or even laugh. I wasn't ready to go to sleep—I liked the comradeship in the strange light. It was peekaboo light from a quarter moon coming through the cracks between the barn boards. The only face I could see was Plez's, round and glowing like a little moon. So I says to Plez, "So. Is it true that the Ghost Dance, I mean Spirit Dance, was all about trances? All about visiting ancestors in the other world?"

"Sure," said Plez.

"Guess I read that, but I didn't get it."

He was quiet. I turned my ears toward Sallee, but she seemed to be neither breathing nor stirring.

"Tell us," Emile said.

"They went into trances. It's an ultra-simple, repetitive dance, hypnotic, so it gets the mind on the edge of the other dimension. In the old days maybe a medicine man would come up when you got to the edge and wave a feather in front of your eyes, get your concentration on that, and soon you would slip into a trance. Fall down, journey, talk to your ancestors. Mooney thought it was hypnotism, but that's just because he took the secular view, didn't believe in the other dimension."

"What did they see?" says I.

"Wonderful things. The Messiah, the one the white people killed when he came before. He came back and turned everything into a glorious world. The main thing was, the ancestors were alive again. The buffalo came back, too, and there was plenty of good hunting. Everyone was happy, nobody was cold or hungry, and nobody ever got sick. Some people said there were no white people in that world."

"That's what caused the trouble?"

"Sort of, not really. What scared the whites, the Indian agents especially, was just what looked like a comeback of the old religion. They held the silly idea, which they thought was a hope, that the Indians would learn to farm, learn to read, become white men, and become Christians, in that order. The dancing meant to them that the Indians were backsliding, would remain savages, might go on the warpath again, might even take their land back. The Indian agents got really worried, and did everything they could to stop the dancing. The dancers out in the Stronghold had them most worried.

"But the dancers holding out in the Stronghold, and some others, they had an agenda. Word went around that if they danced hard enough, and prayed hard enough, the Messiah would come back, green-up of 1891. They were ready for that. They were fed up with not being able to hunt—hey, they were starving, freezing in the winter, children dying of diseases no one ever heard of before. Fed up. Bring on the millennium."

"Sounds like you're making fun of it."

"Not at all. There is another world where our ancestors are alive, and all things dwell in peace and beauty. I know that place." I waited for more words, but he didn't say them.

"How come the Messiah didn't come back and change everything?"

"Because he's already here. That beautiful world is already here. It's spiritual, not physical, so it exists in the dimension of Spirit. It doesn't happen yonder, neither at green-up or after you die. It's within you if you know how to find it. If you don't know, it's still not yonder, it's not in the hereafter."

"*Hau!*" said a whisper, and to my surprise I recognized it as Sallee's voice.

"That's where the people misunderstood Wovoka's vision. That's where the Christians misunderstood the words of Christ. It's a world of Spirit."

We were silent for a while. I felt like we were on the edge of quicksand.

Finally I asked Emile, "You saw these trances at the Ghost Dance you went to?"

"Yes."

"You thought they were real?"

"No question." He pondered a little, maybe remembered. "One woman wore the Stars and Stripes upside down, just like the old Ghost Dancers did. She went into a trance and saw Big Foot's people die at Wounded Knee again."

He said nothing more. I repeated the words to myself several times. *Saw Big Foot's people dying at Wounded Knee.*

"Hear that, my friends? She *saw* it. Blue, you wanna know what happened at Wounded Knee?"

Before he could go on, I interrupted. "No."

"Yeah, right." He grinned, and gleamed his eyes at me. "You wanna know what happened, you ain't gonna know it from me or any teacher. You got to go see for yourself." He laughed in a sweet, silly way. "Seeing is believing," he sang in a childlike voice.

"*Hau!*" whispered Sallee.

It was a long time before I fell asleep, a long time of mind drifting. What kept coming back was that painting I saw on the mountain. I wondered if I should tell Emile I'd seen a painting the way he would do it. I wondered if I should tell Plez, or anyone else, about what I saw. "Don't work on it," Pete had said. "Just let the picture come back to your mind. It will tell you what it means, you don't have to chase it. And don't talk about it without a good reason." No, I would keep this to myself.

I floated the picture again and again into in my mind, the big field of white, the jagged slashes of red, the blackness above with its icy, bluish stars.

Suddenly I am in the painting. I am in the edge, red against white, I am in the violence of the slashes.

I see around me. I feel horrendous pain. I cannot move.

I become aware of the other slashes, like a jumbled pile of pencils, and of long shapes in the whiteness below the slashes. We are a jam of logs in a river deeper and darker than any river of Earth. The water coils around us, prods, pries. The cold here is terrible, but I know, we all know, the cold is more terrible below, where the current will eventually take us. The night is black, but not as black as the depths of the waters. One by one, each log of us is growing colder, coming to the cold of the waters of death. One by one we let go, ease off, and slip downstream in silence.

With a start I came back to the world, the loft where my friends laid sleeping, and I laid remembering. I touched my face, and it was wet with salt tears.

Now I know.

The Second Day,
Christmas Eve

Over coffee in the morning I felt shy, didn't want to meet anyone's eye. I saw Plez and Sallee looking at me like they had thoughts of some kind. We went into the circle for prayers. Emile, Plez, and I stepped out sunwise with all the riders for another day's journey. Chup and Sallee headed off with the walkers. All I put my mind on was camp tonight. Camp tonight, camp tonight—at a church, we were told.

The wind eased, the temperature rose, the day was not so bad. Of course, the painting kept coming together in my mind. I'd tried to stay blank, just to ride, but my mind ...

Silence, seeing, silence, seeing, it was unbearable.

"Okay," I finally said to Plez. "You can go see the ancestors, talk to them. By choice."

"By intention," said Plez.

I took that in and nodded. "See the ancestors by intention. How?"

He beamed like a slow student was finally catching on. He and Emile smiled at each other like they were in cahoots some way.

"Hey, medicine men know how to go into the other world. We've done this for thousands and thousands of years."

"Yeah, but, I mean, how exactly?"

"I've done it a lot of ways. Dancing. Drumming. Hungering and thirsting. Praying ceaselessly. But there arc easier ways now."

"Out with it, out with it."

He grinned. "Well, normally I would beat the drum for you. But whcn we don't want to disturb other people, I use a tape."

"A *what?*"

Emile chuckled out loud.

"A cassette tape." He reached inside his big capote and fished out a Walkman. "Right here. I carry the other world on audio tape." He was really enjoying himself, and Emile was enjoying him. It was like Emile knew everything ahead of time, but he didn't.

"This Michael Harner, he's a white guy, but he's a sha-man. He learned how to go journeying. He also learned drum beats work really good, really send people into a trance. Put two different beats on opposite sides of a tape, fast and slow. Works great."

"A white guy."

"Yeah."

"On tape, nine bucks and ninety-five cents or something."

"Yeah. Cheaper than Delta. You don't get frequent flyer miles, though." He shook the Walkman. "And I'll tell you, beginners do well with this. What's best is going to a Spirit Dance. Sing and dance your way to the Spirit world. The tape is twenty minutes. For people I work with, though, I spliced it into an hour tape."

"There are still Ghost Dances."

"Yeah. At my mother's rez, the Shoshones do one. They say the dance is real old and was originally theirs."

"You guide people to the other world."

"Yes. You need a guide. Some people don't come back easy. Until they learn the way."

"You do this."

"My gift is to bring other people blessings of Spirit." There was a big difference in his tone now.

"A lot of people."

"People who have the awareness, people who have the desire."

"God," I said, "I want *not* to go. Most of me."

"You know, it's not easy. No one can do it for you, to you. You gotta concentrate, you gotta commit, you gotta be brave. You have to fly on your own wings. Hey, it's easy not to go."

I looked him in the eyes. I didn't know what to do or say.

"You hungry?" says Plez.

"My stomach's never gonna speak to me again."

"Over there," he says merrily. "I got some soul food." He motioned with his lips to one of the giant round bales of hay. (Indian people consider it rude to point with your finger.) Me, Plez, and Emile eased the horses to the downwind side.

In the lee of the bale, I says teasingly, "What we gonna do, eat eagle feathers?"

He handed me something, Emile the same. Reese's Peanut Butter Cups. "Very spiritual," he says.

I ate two packages, four cups. Ate them very slowly, relishing each bite, licked my fingers, then sucked my fingers.

Emile surprised me by speaking. "I never tasted better food in my life."

"Nice being out of the wind, ain't it?"

I nodded. After that trip I will never love Tate, Wind, again. Well, maybe if he stays away from Iya, Wind Storm.

"You know," Plez says, his voice gentle but his eyes right on me, "you better go journeying. Go to Wounded Knee in spirit. You got to know. See it. Go through it."

"I'm afraid," I said. I met his eyes. "I'm really afraid."

"There's things to be afraid of. Look, I could give you all the reasons. I'm not gonna. I'm gonna tell you to look in your heart and see what's good for you."

I nodded stupidly.

Plez asks, "You with me on this, Emile?"

"Absolutely," said my best friend.

"You got a lot of help right now," says Plez. "I don't mean me. I mean what you saw on the mountain, whatever it was. I mean your emotion around this trip. Your spirit is big now. Yeah, you're afraid, 'cause you're close to a big step. You can feel your connection to your ancestors. You sense a sweeping change in your life." He swept his arm like a clock.

"These six days you're walking in the very footsteps of your ancestors, right where they walked. At Wounded Knee you will stand where they stood. Where they died, you'll do a ceremony for healing.

"Between you and them, any day of your life, there's only a thin membrane. But normally it seems like a lot to us, like they're a long way away. Now they're close. Now they're here with us. Last night riding in the dark, especially, I could feel them.

"Let me tell you a story. My first ride was the second one, 1987. That year we had thirty-six riders. The third night, it was just like last night, riding way late into the dark. Tyler, he told me this when he finally got into camp. He and Alex White Plume, once in a while they would set up at the head of the line and count the riders as they came. Somebody might have fallen, or maybe his horse took off on him— you never know. Just making sure all thirty-six was still with them, not lost in that bad night.

"One time they counted, right away, Tyler, he noticed something was different. More of the riders looked like they were wearing hides, or real old-style clothing. Some of them were carrying staffs and lances. Blue sparks danced around the horses' hoofs. Sometimes blue lights seemed to hover around people's ears, or the tops of their heads.

"Tyler counted eighty-six riders.

"Time he was done, all the hairs on the back of his neck and head were standing up, wiggling.

"He looked across, and Alex looked as scared as Tyler. 'How many'd you count?' asked Tyler.

" 'Eighty-six,' said Alex, soft-like.

" 'Me too,' says Tyler.

"When they come into camp an hour later, there was only thirty-six riders."

Plez looked around at us one by one. His eyes were lit by an inner fire.

"Those spirits, though, they were good. They crossed over to help.

"Sometimes the membrane, it's thin, and crossing over is easy. You could do it now. I'll help you. I bet Sallee will help. Cross over, see, hear, smell, feel. Come back."

I wondered what Sallee could do.

"It's healing, I promise. It hurts, yeah. The more it hurts, the more you need it. The sharper the hurt, the greater the healing."

I looked at him. I had the willies in my knees, like I was standing on the edge of rimrock and my knees felt like I might jump.

"Maybe," I said. "Maybe." I heeled my horse toward the other riders.

When we got to the church, only a half hour after dark this time, the little building was padlocked and dark. Someone said the landowner would be glad for us to sleep in the church, but he was in the hospital, beyond asking. We ate another supper of buffalo soup and fry bread. I spent dinner looking at the empty church, the empty sky, and the empty plains and thinking how cold it was gonna be tonight, especially without shelter.

The walkers came in after us. Sallee's hands were almost frosted, and she let me rub them for a long time. Even when the ceremonies started, we sat that way. There were speeches, good ones—Alex White Plume and Arvol Looking Horse spoke. There were honoring songs. And finally there was a talking circle.

Our custom goes, the person who has the talking stick talks until he's finished. No cross-talk. That's also the way we do it in AA, which is kind of nifty. You say all you've got to say, then you pass the talking stick. Other people, they speak for themselves, they don't quarrel with you.

At this first talking circle mostly Indian people spoke. Some voiced bitterness toward whites for Wounded Knee, most expressed a desire for reconciliation. Been no whites there, maybe more anger would've come out. It's rude to talk hostile to guests.

I was listening with some attention, not a lot, and then Tyler spoke, and said words that were good for me. He says it's okay for me to set his talk down here. "I know whites who want to learn traditional Lakota ways. Releasing of the Spirits, like. A Ph.D. from Harvard, other academics in psychology, they want to. I showed them the Releasing the Spirits ceremony. They cried and cried, said they want us to teach that ceremony for all people.

"But here it is. We can't teach it *until we forgive*. I myself can't forgive, not yet, what got done to *my* ancestors at Wounded Knee. Nope, not yet. I have to heal myself before I can teach others. This ride, that's what I come here for, learn to forgive."

When it was over, the people fasting retired to their own tent. Fasting seemed an awesome sacrifice to me, more than I would ever be able to do.

I said to the group at large, "We're gonna freeze." Except for Sallee's presence, I would have added "to death."

She said, "Some people are going to the schoolhouse in Interior," a nearby town. "You want to go?"

My heart leapt up like she'd asked me to bed her. I looked at Plez, Emile, and Chup. They nodded. "Yeah," I said. "And I want you to help me go journeying to the Spirit World. Will you?"

"Of course," she said, and her eyes looked softer in my direction than I had seen them. "What do you want me to do?"

"We gotta ask Plez."

THE FIRST JOURNEY

Where do you want to go?" asked Plez. "What do you want to see? You gotta name your intention very exactly. Journeying is walking the razor's edge."

The floor of the Interior school gym was already crowded, and the whole room buzzed low with conversation. All those people made me nervous. Didn't want witnesses to my veer into ... whatever. I couldn't take my eyes off them. *They'll think I'm insane.*

I was stretched out full on my sleeping bag. Plez was sitting on one side of me, Sallee on the other. Emile and Chup were talking quietly to each other.

Where do I want to go? What do I want to see?

This is insane.

"I want to see a Spirit Dance."

"Good. How about the Stronghold? It's nearby, on that tableland we saw to the south. The dancers were there a hundred years ago today. They were the most passionate dancers, the real believers. You'll see a good one."

"Okay."

"Sallee, you willing to help?"

"Yes."

"Why?" Plez asked.

"I want to come close to that world. I want to hear whatever Blue is willing to tell about it. I want to help him with this important undertaking."

Plez nodded. He handed me the cassette player. I put the earphones on.

"Here's what you do. Take Sallee's hand. Then say your intention out loud three times. Be very specific. Then let go Sallee's hand, push the PLAY button, and close your eyes. When the drum starts, go to someplace you know that opens into the earth, a hole, a cave, a spring, something like that. Go down through that. You may see a guide. Ask it to take you to the Stronghold a hundred years ago so you can see a Spirit Dance. If you don't see a guide, just go on your own. Let your mind go with the drum beat, you'll find it pushes you right along. I've put it on the slow beat side the first time.

"Sallee will be right here the whole time. So will I. If you want to come back early, come to the hole and reach for Sallee, or just reach. She'll take your hand and bring you back. Otherwise, in twenty minutes the drum will tell you when to come back. Return to the hole where you went down, come up, and reach for Sallee. She'll take your hand.

"Any questions?"

I looked at Sallee and saw in her eyes that it was all right. I took her hand. It felt warm, comforting, human. "No questions."

"Remember, the Spirit World isn't harmful to us, it's good for us. As long as you come back, you'll be fine. Will you come back?"

"Yes."

"By the way, it's Christmas Eve. Have a good trip."

I took a deep breath, let it out, and began.

"I want to go to the Stronghold a hundred years ago and see a Spirit Dance." Big breath in, then out.

"I want to go to the Stronghold a hundred years ago and see a Spirit Dance." Big breath in, out.

"I want to go to the Stronghold a hundred years ago and see a Spirit Dance." Big breath in, out.

I let go of Sallee, pushed the PLAY button, closed my eyes, and the drum started banging in my ears.

At first I only listened. Surprising how big and restless that drum felt, like a mountain lion pacing in my mind.

Then I remembered. A place came to me, along Medicine Root Creek when I was a kid. It was an outcropping shaped like an arrowhead, facing the creek, maybe fifteen feet high and ten feet across. The altar, I called it. When I was a kid, I went to the outcropping to say my prayers. Later, when I hardly prayed any more, I sat there and watched the creek and the birds and the day. Always on the altar was a lot of coyote dung, like that trickster guy hung out there a lot, maybe howling his prayers. In the middle of the altar was a hole, maybe big enough for a ten year old to worm his way into. It squiggled, and I couldn't see the bottom. I was fascinated by the hole, and imagined it went to the center of the earth, but I was scared to crawl in.

Now I went in, used that as my entrance to the other world. At first it was hard to squeeze through, then I wiggled through fluidly, and then I fell, drifted, floated weightless through space to the … earth, if the name for it is earth.

I stood on barren ground in a place like the Badlands. I looked exactly like me, except I was wearing a breechcloth, moccasins, and nothing else. Though a hundred years ago it would have been a winter day, I had no sense of cold, or warmth, or any kind of weather. The sky was bright and cloudless, but no sun was visible.

I looked around and saw rough, broken country in every direction, white cliffs jutting out madly, a rugged, wild,

uninhabited land, like where I grew up, yet not a place I recognized. Next to my feet was something like a dry creek bed,
except that it moved. It turned, corkscrewed, and seemed to
flow away from me, leading me downstream.

Near my left hand on a boulder sat Raven. With my mind
only, I asked immediately, *Will you lead me to the Stronghold?*

Yes, said Raven without words. We could send each
other thoughts without speaking, which seemed natural
and simple.

We started, Raven flying slowly ahead of me. *This time
I'm not afraid of you.*

You've always had a thing about me, said Raven in a matter-
of-fact way.

He flew slowly, or came back and glided at my shoulder,
or hovered in the air. We didn't speak again.

Soon I recognized the big mesa on our left, the one
called Cuny Table. And beyond that, on the north, pro-
jected a much smaller mesa which I'd never seen, perhaps
a couple of miles long, a natural fortress guarded by huge
rock walls. What the history books called the Stronghold.
Where my dancers were.

Soon I started up a steep, rocky side hill toward a saddle.
I noticed that when you're a spirit, physical exertion isn't
exertion. You do it easily, no push of muscle, no heave of
breath. Quickly, I glided up to a pickup-width land bridge
between the big mesa and the little one. This was why they
chose it—so narrow it was easy to defend.

Raven settled on my left shoulder. I felt a faint shudder
inside, but let it go. I could hear Raven think, *I'm not going to
reassure this man, he's supposed to know.*

We walked onto the Stronghold openly, past two look-
outs who saw nothing. Strange, being there but not being
there in body.

Raven flapped off toward a lookout point, an outcropping above the flat-topped table. From the top I saw lodges everywhere in small circles. Horses and cattle were grazing here and there, no reason to keep them close-herded. Plenty of grass, though it was brown, and grass meant springs. *About five hundred lodges,* said Raven without words. *Plenty of cattle—they won't starve. Took the cows from the tribal herd on the way here, without paying.*

Five hundred lodges, four, five, six people to a lodge—a lot of people, more than I'd realized.

We stepped lightly down the rock, through the grazers, past the circles of lodges, and toward the dance circle. I felt exactly like myself, yet I did not seem to inhabit a body in the usual way. I wondered again how I could be perfectly comfortable in nothing but a breechcloth on a winter day. No one noticed us.

Raven said wordlessly, *They have spent the morning sweating and painting and dressing for the dance. It will begin soon.* Yet Raven did not need to say this, because I found that I knew what had been going on this morning without being here to see it, or having to ask. I knew to some extent what was in people's minds, and in their hearts.

Men and women alike showed faces painted with circles, crescents, and crosses, representing the Sun, Moon, and Morning Star. Mostly the color was red, color of Wi, the Sun.

They wore the Ghost Shirts that Wovoka called for— loose, sacklike, cotton or muslin garments ornamented with more circles, crescents, and stars, and with paintings of birds, especially Raven and Crow. The shirts bristled with feathers, mostly Eagle but also Raven, Crow, Magpie, Sage Hen, and other birds. *Raven is patron bird of the Spirit Dance?* I asked Raven without words.

Yes.

Who is Raven? I asked, looking at him. I felt a pang with the question, for the first time in my life wanting to understand my nemesis.

I saw his black eyes gleam, as in mischief. Suddenly he flew to the dance circle and lit at the top of the sapling at its center. From it hung an American flag, which puzzled me. Yet I saw that some dancers wore, over their Ghost Shirts, an upside-down American flag. I understood that the sapling was the Tree of Life, and on its summit perched my messenger of Death.

The dancers formed a circle of perhaps two hundred people, sitting. In the center stood about a dozen men and women, and I understood them to be leaders, medicine people. One was Short Bull, the Rosebud medicine man who traveled to Nevada to hear Wovoka and then taught the Dance passionately to all Lakota who would listen. He addressed the dancers.

"The day the Messiah brings the new world, I told you this day will come in two seasons. However, since the whites have interfered so much, I will advance the time from what my Father above told me." He paused dramatically—he was an effective preacher. "At the end of one moon the earth will shake and the wind will blow and we will go among our departed relations." Suddenly he declaimed like thunder. "Now for one moon we must dance the Spirit Dance with all our hearts!"

His voice ran like horses. "If the white man comes here, we must not let him interfere with the Dance. We are dancing to bring a new world! If the soldiers press close around you, pay no attention to them, continue the dance. If the soldiers surround you four deep, three of you upon whom I have put holy shirts will sing a song, which I have taught you, around them, when some of them will drop dead, then the rest will start to run, but their horses will sink into the earth; the riders will jump from their horses, but they will sink into the earth also; then you can do as you desire with them. Now you must know this, that all the soldiers and that race will be dead; there will be only Indians left living on the earth. My friends, this is straight and true."

I watched the people as Short Bull preached, and with my power as a spirit felt of their hearts. They believed truly. Their zeal for the dance was impeccable. They were willing themselves passionately toward the future utopia. Their dedication virtually transported them to the world they sought.

Another leader now prayed. Though my translation isn't word for word, he said roughly this. "Wakantanka, now we begin the dance you gave us. Our hearts are good, and we seek to do all that you ask. In return we implore you, Give us back our hunting grounds, and the animals that live upon them. O Wakantanka, transport those dancers who are sincere to the Spirit World and there let them see their ancestors."

This last sentence thrummed my heart like fingers on guitar strings—*that's what I'm doing!* Suddenly I heard consciously the drum beat, the heart of a wildcat inside me that bore me on this journey. I flung my mind back to the scene at the Stronghold.

The leader went on. "Show them the good life you are making ready for us, and then let them return to this world. O hear my cry, Wakantanka!"

Now the people stood and raised hands their hands high to the West, where the Messiah would come from. Two young women rose at the base of the Tree and held up objects, one a Pipe, the other a hoop whose significance I did not know. Following a lead voice, all lifted up the first song of the Spirit Dance.

The father says so, eyayo!
The father says so, eyayo!

My heart swayed. I recognized the melody and words from the mountain, from my seeing beyond.

The father says so,
The father says so.
*You will see your grandfather—*eyayo!
*You will see your grandfather—*eyayo!
The father says so,
The father says so.
*You will see your relatives—*eyayo!
*You will see your relatives—*eyayo!
The father says so,
The father says so.

This song began again. It was long and mesmeric, the voices light, floating on air, and the repetition seduced the mind deeper into its world. I knew that in the words *father* and *grandfather* the singers meant both the father and grandfather in blood and the father and grandfather in Spirit, the Messiah.

The song rose again. "The father says so, the father says so," lulling in its repeating of the words, of the words, its melody lifting yet infinitely gentle, infinitely drawing the heart and mind to …

Beyond the song I was hearing something.

A low rumbling, or mumbling. Like rockfall, or an avalanche, heard from afar. Like the clouds rubbing against one another in low voices. Like people moaning. A low, restless sound, writhing in the currents of air, twisting, twisting, turning, churning, over and over and over and over, moaning, groaning, howling, mumbling.

I recognized this—*the sounds of the night on Bear Butte when I saw beyond. Again I live in that low chorus of sound forever.*

The singers cycled back to the beginning—"Says the father"—for the fourth time, or sixth. The two songs waved me like a blade of grass in a stream, the first song of the Spirit Dance and the moaning, eternal moaning. The two singings were the fluid I lived in, my water and my air in one. Gently, rhythmically, I waved to the liquid sounds of a low, distant ...

Of the singers I was one, of the moaners one.

The song surged, and the moans surged, around me, inside me. Both song and moans, bubbling within me like hot springs, bursting forth upon my face, tears scalding and soothing, salt and sweet at once. I did not know why I cried.

You will see your relatives—eyayo!

You will see your relatives—eyayo!

The father says so,

The father says so.

The song cycled once more to its ever-beginning which proceeded to its never-ending. My eyes became the soft, damp earth. They gave forth the sweet trickle of a spring. My face was the mosses it ran upon, and the water was sweetness, and it was succor, and it was forgiveness.

Now I had lost the mesa and the dancers and the people who lifted their voices in song. I drifted in a world of mystery, wail, despair, promise, fate, the music of the earth.

I felt myself gather in some way, as a mist gathers itself from the thin air. I felt myself lift, airy, and I felt myself as mist, as breath, as spirit, and I felt the goodness of this way. Gently, I lifted myself from the dewy grasses and the sparkling needles of pine trees, and I rose, filling, completing myself, and I raised my eyes to the high peaks above me, peaks beautiful when wreathed in mist, and I beheld the infinite sky above and beyond things, the sky where go our breaths, our mists, our spirits, and I most gently lifted....

The drum *ratattat-tatted* hard, fast, rude, in my ear. *I don't want to go there, I want to go ...* The mountain cat cuffed me, the drum banged me down, thumped my awareness back to earth. *Will you come back?*

Yes. I promised.

With infinite reluctance I reached for Sallee's hand. Her grasp was warm and fleshly. I was glad, yet ... I was glad. I settled into my body and onto the floor of a gym in western South Dakota. After a long time I opened my eyes. The faces of Plez and Sallee gazed down at me, loving. "Welcome back," said Plez. "You looked like you were getting lost in the other world. Welcome back."

I looked into his eyes, and then into Sallee's, and held them, and said, "Thank you."

Sallee kept holding my hand. I felt ... vastly tender toward her, vastly loving, without man-woman overtones. Toward Plez too.

"Now you know," he said.

"Now I know."

"Did you like it?"

"It was ... indescribable. It was wonderful. It was incredible."

We sat for long moments. I felt no need to do or say anything.

"Maybe later you want to tell me what you saw. Good idea the first few times."

I looked into Sallee's eyes. "There are things I don't understand," I told Plez.

"You bet. Tomorrow," he said. He rolled onto his side and then slipped into his sleeping bag, stretched out on the far side of Sallee's.

She let go my hand but kept smiling at me. She tucked her sock feet into her sleeping bag, then her bluejeaned bottom, then everything up to her shoulders.

I rolled onto my side, facing her. She faced me. I looked into her eyes, which felt like another way into the new world I had discovered. I smiled at her and myself and the universe.

As I drifted off to sleep, I held my mind in the small space between our faces, and our breaths mingling in the center.

BLUE'S PAST LEANS ON HIS PRESENT

The next morning, Christmas morning, we came to Big Foot Pass, which meant the Badlands. People who haven't seen this country can't really believe it. It is torn up, humped up, eroded, washed out, gouged—everything that can make a country up and down and hard to get through has happened here. That's why they call it the Badlands.

A hundred years ago Big Foot's people had their hard travel here. Some scouts led the way down a ridge that switched between ice, snow, and slick clay. The horses hated the footing, and the sheer drops on either side. The wagons had to be lowered with ropes. It was a nasty descent, and the few hundred feet took several hours.

Now Plez, Emile, me, and all the riders lined up at the top of the pass, staring down at the same icy ridge. It looked treacherous as hell.

"After this we'll be on Indian land," said Plez. I gave him an impatient glance, but he ignored me. "No fences, no roads—we'll sleep in our own place."

I could feel Emile wanting to put a stop to this cheerful baloney, but my friend would never act rude.

"Look at that nice, flat run over to White River."

"No problem but getting down this nasty shit," I said. I wondered about this horse that I didn't really know. If he got skittish there ... On the other hand, if we stood in this cold wind any longer ...

"This was a big moment on the first ride." It was Tyler's voice, and his mount nosed up next to me. If he'd arrived, all the riders were here. "We stood looking down and couldn't figure which way to go. We were cold and we were scared. Too many choices, all of them looking like short ways to hell. Then we saw two coyotes trotting up this ridge right here. They stopped and looked at us. Riders pointed up. Two golden eagles were circling over our heads. The coyotes looked at us some more to see if we got the point, turned, and trotted down the ridge. We knew the coyotes and eagles were showing us the way. We followed and came to the bottom okay."

Ron McNeill started down, leading, and we all reined our horses after him. I didn't like the way my mount's hooves slipped around on the clay, not a bit. I kept him slowed right down and talked to him easy and kept my eyes looking for the best footing. It was over sooner than I expected, and camera crews waited at the bottom to film us. Like everyone else I hooted and whacked my horse on the rump and scooted across the flat at a run.

Bridle to bridle, I told Plez what I saw at the Stronghold. I told him about the people's zeal for the dance, about Short Bull's preaching, about my mixed feelings about having Raven as my guide.

In his eyes I saw he was pleased.

I was damn well pleased.

Then, with fumbling, I told him about how the first song of the Spirit Dance had come to me in my vision at Bear Butte this autumn, how hearing had half-transported me to that experience, how it and the song got mixed up. "The words to the song, I felt like I heard the words originally but couldn't understand them." I sang the song half-voice for him. "The words ..." I hesitated. "They're the great promise. 'You will see your relatives.' "

I looked at him with longing. "I felt like I could go into the world Wovoka saw, the perfect world, and that's what I wanted, the only thing in the universe I wanted."

He didn't say anything, but I could feel how he was toward me.

"Can we see our ancestors again?" It was a lament.

"Vision is truth. What you see, that's fact. Vision is truth. How to understand vision, how it may come to pass, that is the hard part." We rode. "Wait and it will become manifest."

"I want to go back."

He chuckled. "What a surprise!" He changed tone. "You have the gift. Know that. You have the gift. You accomplished great things for the first time."

Now I committed the sin of pride.

The horses walked, and today it was a good walk. We'd grained them well. The cold was not so painful today. I felt like a new man.

So now I said to him, "I liked having Sallee hold my hand."

"There are good things between your hearts and spirits," he said. "I want to help your relationship blossom."

Says I, "Our relationship is her thinking I'm a bum."

"Yes," said Plez, "and a drunk, but she has other thoughts too."

"How'd you know I'm a drunk?"

"I didn't, that was a guess."

At least Chup and Tyler didn't tell him that.

"Not too hard a guess. An Indian man like you, sensitive, he feels despair. He seeks to numb the despair."

We rode on a little. We tied the horses, stood in some cottonwoods along a main ditch, and had cigarettes. *Okay, I gotta speak up.*

"Numb despair, it's worse than that."

He looked at me kindly.

I told him about Delphine.

I told him all of it. How I sought her as a way out of what I am, a reservation Indian. How she was never comfortable with being what she was, black. How we never knew each other. How nobody ever knew Delphine, knew the darkness she lived in. How she put an end to it.

"I live in the shadow of her death," I said. "I call it ravenShadow."

"Raven shadow?"

"One word," I said, "small *r*, capital *s*."

He pondered that and nodded.

I corrected myself. "I have lived in the shadow of despair and death all my life."

"Yeah, you have," he said.

"More than I know."

"More than you know."

We rode in silence.

"You want to do something would be good for you?"

I started to say "maybe," as is my habit, and changed it. "Yes."

"Tell about that tonight. Tell me, Sallee, Emile, Chup. Open it to your friends. Better yet, tell the talking circle. How you live in ravenShadow."

That scared me. I couldn't say anything, and the horses' breathing banged in my ears.

"You have come on this trip to lay your burdens down," he said.

351

"Okay," I said. Which didn't make me any less afraid.

I waited for the talking stick to come around the circle to me. Damn, I'd broadcast to a hundred thousand people on the radio, but it felt hard to talk to these hundred folks, on the same pilgrimage, people of hearts like to mine. Hard to tell them about my real self, truly.

I stared into the bonfire in the center. I didn't see Christmas night, 1990, I didn't see Red Water camp, or the ride leaders, or the people in the circle, even my friends next to me. I saw a fourteen-year-old boy a few days before Christmas, 1967, in the road outside the general store, a lonely crossroads in Kyle, South Dakota.

The stick came to Sallee, on my right, and she passed it to me without a word. I grabbed that thing like I was gonna strangle it. I made myself run my eyes around the circle once.

"I'm going to tell you a story. About how I betrayed myself and my people," I began, "and how I came to live in ravenShadow."

They waited. I looked left and took strength from Emile's face. "I didn't go to school till I was fourteen. My grandparents held me out. Didn't speak English, didn't know how to use a grocery store or filling station, nothing."

I didn't have to explain to the Lakota here what that meant—held aside to be a bearer of the old ways.

"Couldn't stand school. Unbearably lonely except for you, Emile, and ... You guys know about that. Come Christmas, I was gonna go home to Grandpa and Unchee, hadn't been home since first day of school. Wanted bad to go home, didn't want to come back, knew Grandpa would make me. Christmas was, I don't know, was always a bad time anyway."

I grinned at them, knowing they were thinking how this was Christmas again, another hard one. That white-man God, he liked to send us Injuns hard ones. We were all tickled in a sad way. "Hardly any sunlight, dark by 5:30. Day before my ride home, I went outside in the last light, looking around, doing nothing, nothing to do. Walked up the road aimless-like and saw ...

"They were maybe a dozen ravens feeding on a deer carcass. Out in the sagebrush. I'd seen that all my life but never *seen* it. Walked close, so close I was nervous. First they flew off and fussed, me being there. I was fascinated. Suddenly one of them, the biggest, flew up at my face. He was different now, really big and commanding and for sure capital-*R* Raven instead of an ordinary bird. He'd somehow quick-like gotten white tips on his wings, but he wasn't a magpie—he had a raven shape. I felt like he was shouting something threatening at me. I backed off a few steps, fast, and fell backward and blacked out. I was down there a few minutes, and I can't say whether I lost consciousness before I fell or after. I think before. Something was going on down there, I was seeing things. At the same time the part of me that laid by the deer carcass was scared that the ravens were eating me. So I jostled myself and made myself come back. The ravens were still on the dead deer, hopping and pecking, hopping and pecking, fluttering, lifting, landing, pecking. I felt like something big happened."

"*Hau, hunka,*" Emile said softly.

I looked at him. Time to tell the rest, what I hadn't even told my best friend then.

"Then somehow I wanted to die. I felt it strong. I wanted to die, kill myself over Christmas vacation, go home, see Grandpa and Unchee, and before they could take me back to school, go to the country beyond the pines, where nothing hurts you. I thought about it while I walked back to town.

Freeze to death, I decided, yeah, freeze to death, supposed to be a peaceful way to go."

I looked at Emile, ashamed. "So I went and found the bootlegger. I didn't have any money. I offered to trade my beaded turtle, my birth bag, for a bottle. He took the bag and gave me a pint. A pint for my connection to my mother."

I took breath in and out. "But I never did use it to knock myself out." Suddenly I felt unbearably self-conscious, kind of grinned. "I discovered basketball that Christmas vacation." I thought back on the True Bull brothers. "Sounds dumb, but that's the way it was. Basketball, the modern form of warfare!" I looked at them, Sallee to Chup to Emile to Plez, and they were tickled. "I gave the pint away."

"It changed me, though. RavenShadow, I'd seen it, recognized it, knew it as ... Ever since, it's been my closest friend. Not best but closest."

I looked into Emile's eyes, letting him know. I looked into all their candlelit faces and into their open eyes, one by one. *This is who I am, this is what I did.* I looked back at Emile. *I'm sorry.*

"I'm telling you this story because many Indian people live in ravenShadow. One of the biggest shadows is Wounded Knee." Now I ran my eyes around the circle and saw the faces, attentive and sympathetic. "I came here to throw off that shadow, for myself, for my people."

From around the circle came a chorus of staccato cries—"*Hau!*"

"I got a place," says Plez. We trooped out of the gym after him, Sallee, Emile, Chup, and me. Tonight the Little Wound School in Kyle had opened the gym doors to us. The fasters were in tents out at Red Water camp, where Big Foot's people stayed for two nights, resting, trying to let Big Foot get better. Since we were on the Pine Ridge rez now, many riders and walkers were at their homes, spending Christmas night with their families.

He led us through some halls, outside, through some more halls, and held open the door that said CUSTODIAL OFFICE. It was a big room, with utility shelves stacked with industrial-strength cleaners. Here and there were rotary polishing machines, push brooms, mop heads and handles, buckets. Just inside the door was an aisle, and Plez had put five candles in a circle there. Plez pointed behind the door. Improbably, for no reason I could guess, a huge buffalo head, mounted, hung from the wall.

"Wasn't this room locked?" I says.

Plez twinkled at me. "You think a lock slows down a shaman? Everybody sit behind a candle," he says.

We did. "By the way," says Plez, "we should honor this school. Little Wound was not only a big chief but a Ghost Dancer who had a great vision of the Messiah."

I joked, "Should we honor the Messiah's birthday? This is it."

"I don't know," says Chup. "Santa Claus, he didn't bring us redskins any presents."

"No turkey, either," says Plez. We'd eaten buffalo soup again.

He lit the candles and flipped off the fluorescent lights. Somehow the candlelight on our faces made us seem a true circle, a wholeness of some kind. He says to me, "You want to say more?"

I'd told him I did. In the pickup on the way into Kyle from Red Water camp I thought about it, and wanted to tell the rest of it. I looked up the buffalo head and asked silently to see deeper into myself and tell the deeper truth.

"My grandmother. I was raised by my grandparents; she was closed off and sullen her whole life. Never had much to give or take with me, or any of her grandchildren, or I think probably her children. She lived in darkness. Early on, my guess is, she let Grandpa share that with her. Time I come along, she made him an outsider too. Way it looked to me.

"Secretive, hidden. She gave me her father's name, but never told me whose it was. She gave me his Pipe and didn't tell me why. She never told me a thing about herself, or about Wounded Knee. Even yet I don't know the name of her mother."

I looked into the faces of my friends. "And I never asked. My ancestors were killed at Wounded Knee—I guess they were, I don't even know that for sure—and I never cared. I turned my back on it.

"I tell you, you can turn your back on the nine-hundred-pound gorilla, but your mind is right on it.

"I been living in the shadow of Wounded Knee and pretending I didn't. I grew up with a strange, withdrawn parent because of it. I grew up with expectations I didn't understand. I grew up to a mission, I didn't know what it was. I grew up with the past weighing on me, and I pretended it wasn't there. I felt the pain but held onto the pretense, held on hard.

"I am here to change that. I'm here to know what happened. Then I'm gonna march myself out of that shadow.

"I've resisted this like hell, knowing who I came from, what they did. Now I'm gonna look at the past. Not like a historian does. I look at the past because it's biting me in the ass."

"It's very late," Sallee said. She looked excited. "Why don't we stay up very, very late?"

"I haven't done that in years," said Emile.

"Youngsters," said Chup in mock disgust.

Plez whipped some more candles out of his back pack. "You're going to get too tired to journey tonight," he said.

I nodded. I wanted to be here with my friends.

Plez lit the candles and the little flames flared. It was like the light on our faces was the bond that held us.

"Why do Indian people kill their feelings with booze?" Plez started. "Who can stand feelings like living in raven-Shadow?" It wasn't a question to be answered but a comment.

I could see Sallee deciding to speak. She spoke only occasionally, and then spent words carefully, not like a miser but like a person who knows they are valuable and sets them out one by one with attention, so that others can see their value. "My mother was a remarkable person. She was born into what you call ravenShadow. This is her story, the way she told it to me.

"Her great-great-grandmother survived Wounded Knee but lost all her family, not only her husband, parents, and children, but aunts, uncles, cousins—every adult. *Every* adult. After the massacre she stayed with a family at Pine Ridge, then married a Pine Ridge man. A lot of Wounded Knee survivors stayed at Pine Ridge, didn't go back to Cheyenne River. About six months after the massacre my mother's great-grandmother was born. Then an unbroken chain of us first children for five more generations, girl babies every one. My mother was born in 1953, the same year as you, Blue. I was born in 1970. I am the seventh generation.

"I figured it out. Though some of those women were mothers as early as fifteen, some a little later, on the average every one of them gave birth to a girl baby at sixteen. That was the way it was in the old days, probably, and that's why we say seven generations is about a hundred years.

"As far as my mom could remember, these women were drunks and led useless, shattered lives. Mostly they had busted marriages, or no marriages, and mostly they didn't live long. My mom was a single mother. Her mom was a single mother. She didn't know who her father was. Neither do I. My mother's grandmother, born in 1921, lost her husband to World War II. So there it is, a chain from 1890 to 1990 of girl children with mostly no fathers, no families, no way to have a life. Alcoholism, depression, every disease that comes from hopelessness.

"My mother was the same, seventeen years old, new kid, didn't know who the father was, drunk a lot, stoned a lot, no job, living with her mother. She spent my first year drunk and stoned, she told me this. On my first birthday she went out with her friend, Virginia Wayans, drove to White Clay, gonna meet some guys, drink.

"I was born January 20, so it was middle of winter. Virginia was getting stoned, driving. Culvert. She was going fast, did something wrong, went into a skid, went off the highway, back onto the highway, right into the abutment.

"That abutment came right through the driver's door. Virginia got mashed into my mother's seat. Mom got slammed hard into her door, but she only had cuts and bruises and a couple of teeth knocked out.

"At first they thought Virginia would be okay. Then she seemed to be getting worse in the hospital, and they figured she was bleeding internally. They didn't get it stopped. About dawn she died.

"Virginia was my mother's best friend. Had been all her life.

"Mom said she came home and promised me things were going to be different from that day, promised me though I couldn't even talk. She was probably in a daze, but that was one serious promise.

"She went to AA. She stopped drinking, she stopped using. She left me with her mom and went to college, worked her tail off, graduated in three years, studied social work. Came back and went to work for Social Services, an alcoholism counselor.

"She never fell off the wagon. She never used. She told me lots of times she had to be a warrior every day, and she was. She never got married or had any more children. She did more good on this rez than ten, twenty, a hundred people. She worked for the people. And she worked for me. She told me there was this chain that started at Wounded Knee, this misery handed down, generation to generation, maybe even getting worse and worse. And she said it was stopping with her. She was breaking the chain, she was not handing that to me. And she didn't.

"She's my hero.

"She was leaving the filling station down here last December, started to pull onto the highway, saw somebody driving too fast and stopped. That drunk lost it, came off the road and put his front end right into her. Killed instantly. That's when I went to live with Uncle Chup.

"My mother is my hero. She was born in as dark a shadow as anybody, but she didn't murk about in it. She did something about what's wrong. And she loved the idea of these Big Foot Memorial Rides. She said that was the way to wipe away the tears, heal the people. She would have ridden if she could have gotten the time off. That's why I'm here. I'm riding for her."

Sallee looked straight at me, then at my chest. "RavenShadow, that's an excuse. It's not a warrior's way. You give in or you fight. My mother fought."

We all sat silent, but Sallee had no more to say. She'd said plenty, from my point of view.

"What was your however-many-greats-grandmother's name, the one who survived Wounded Knee?"

"Walks Straight. I took her name when my mother died."

I made up my mind, inside myself, to look for that woman at the first Wounded Knee, if I got there.

WIN BLEVINS

Chup pitched in. "Hey, I agree with Sallee. I understan' it, understan' why all of us Indi'n people want to drink our- selves to death. But the reasons don' make no difference. You want to drink, that's your enemy. You deal with your enemy, every day, one day at a time." This was just what Chup said to me every time we talked. That's what a sponsor does.

Everybody waited.

"What I do," says Emile, "is paint them. Those feel- ings. I would have painted Raven threatening me, and the ravens feeding on carrion in the background, paint it like a dream, and full of terror. Some way that changes it, when I paint it."

Everybody waited. It was up to me. "What I did was, I lived in it and it lived in me." I looked at Plez. "I better tell them about Delphine."

He nodded. "These are your friends. Lay down your burdens."

So I did it. Just like I told it to Plez. I even said one thing I hadn't said before. "I haven't thought of this before, but I think, I think Delphine's blackness meant something bizarre to me. I think it connected her to Raven in my unconscious mind and in my heart. I think, when I chose to live with her, I chose to live in ravenShadow, and somehow I knew it, and I sought my own destruction. With queer satisfaction I sought my own destruction."

They looked at me with kind eyes.

I felt ashamed. I felt relieved and grateful.

Plez waited. Finally he said, "You want me to offer some words? Is this a good time?"

I thought on it. *I'm afraid you'll make my effort less, some- how.* I nodded yes anyway.

"What's hard here, what tells a story, is that you never told your best friend how Delphine died, you never told your wife, you never told your sponsor. You never told them about the feeling of ravenShadow either. So you didn't have any help. That's what alcoholics do, they bear their burdens in secrecy, then they try to drown them.

"Tonight you laid some things down. Now what you want to do, you want to use your Pipe and tell these things to Spirit and ask for help. That's what you want to do, *kola*."

I looked at them all. The candles were guttering out, the light flickering, their faces fading. I looked up. *Buffalo, help me finish what I started.*

"My Pipe. You know, that's where I went off the red road. I was fourteen, Grandpa and Unchee said, 'Go to school.' Another year or two I would have gone on the mountain. Then I would have had something to guide me, and I would have been carrying my great-grandfather's Pipe. That was where I was supposed to walk. But when I went off to school, I lost the path."

They looked at me, their faces barely lit now, darkness descending on all of us.

"I abandoned the good red road," I said, "and put my feet on the black road. That's how I dived into ravenShadow."

Sitting under that big buffalo head, Plez says, "You know that word *ravenShadow*, I like it, I like the way you spell it. But I think you need a bigger understanding. Raven, he's a trickster."

I said, "I know Raven and Crow, they're essentially the same."

"Yeah, and Magpie is their close relative too. But that's not what I mean. Raven, he's *real* tricky. He is what he is, but he's also something else, maybe even the opposite. I say he's black but he's white, too. That Spirit bird you've seen, Big Raven, he's white on the tips of his wings, you said. That's telling you something.

"Raven is the creator, did you know that? We think of him as black, the bringer of death, but he's also the one created all living things, made the crawlers, wingeds, swimmers, two-leggeds, four-leggeds, everything. But here's the trick. He creates by guile. He brings things into being by guile. I don't why, I guess 'cause it tickles his bird fancy. He creates by guile.

"So if Raven was my animal guide, my Spirit bird, I'd know everything he brought was a little off from what it looked like, maybe a lot off. Hey, Spirit is everything. Made everything, is everything. And one of his favorite things is playful."

The Second Journey

O, friends, I need this day off!" Plez stretched his arms high into the air and then snuggled back down into his sleeping bag. It felt like we'd slept half the day, and Chup's old pocket watch said we had. Sallee was sitting on her bag, tight in its storage sack. She looked perfectly dressed, hair braided, poised. I wondered how she always looked perfect with the rest of us were so disheveled. Emile was getting up, another one who always looked perfect. Chup was all spiky hair and sleepy eyes, about like me.

"How about some breakfast?" said Emile. He was the smallest and always the hungriest.

"I'll bring nuked breakfast from the convenience store," said Chup.

The folks who'd gone home for Christmas night would stay home today too, be with their families. We'd agreed to hang around the school today, the five of us—agreed not to take ourselves mentally back into the world of highways, television, and coffee shops, but to stay mentally with the pilgrimage. Which meant we were not going out to eat at the Wild Horse Cafe.

The riders were taking the day off because Big Foot's people did. They gave their chief a rest; we would give our horses and our butts a rest. Or for Sallee and the other walkers, their legs. A day of not being in the dreadful cold.

Though no day had been as bad as that first day, none had gotten above zero either. Was it Wakantanka teaching us the meaning of suffering, or Waziya, the mean giant of the north, tormenting us gleefully? Or Iya, the Evil One, acting malicious?

"I'm worried about being bored all day," I grumbled.

"Here," says Plez, "read this." He hands me an old book, *Fourteenth Annual Report of the Bureau of Ethnology, 1892–93, Part 2.* Oh, the regular title is, *The Ghost-Dance Religion and the Sioux Outbreak of 1890.* 1896, it says on the inside—a real old book. By James Mooney.

"Was Mooney white?" says I.

Plez grins. "An Irishman."

"I read all the white-man books on this I want."

"What, you think Spirit is a racist, picks out people by their red skin, points them toward the truth?"

I shrugged.

"Those other books you read, learned a lot about the massacre. This one, teach you about the Dance. About the Dance, where you're going tonight. See where I dog-eared a page? Skip everything else, start there."

"Okay, I'll read today."

"I am gonna sleep," says Plez, "then see if I can get Sallee, Chup, and Emile to play dominoes with me, fetch us all supper from somewhere."

"I'm going to sketch," says Emile.

"I'm going to sew," says Sallee.

"I'm gonna have one more day of sobriety," says Chup.

I flipped through the book. It had pictures of Ghost Shirts, a Thunderbird, and other ceremonial items of the Dance. Then I found the Ghost Dance songs, then the Sioux Ghost Dance songs. I saw the first one, "Opening Song," was

the song I heard on the mountain and in my journey yesterday. I spent the whole day lost in Ghost Dance songs.

Come dark, we feasted. "Here's to wild horses!" hollered Plez.
He'd bought fifteen meals of double burgers and fries for
the five of us at the cafe. I thought three apiece was ridiculous, but when Sallee and Emile left a burger each, Plez and I
knocked them off. Don't have many memories of feeling that
satisfied. Must be that you use a lot of calories staying alive in
below-zero cold, and we needed all the fat we could get, even
hot oil for deep frying.

Anyway, it brought my head out of my book. The songs
had inspired me for another journey.

Sallee modeled her sewing project, and it flabbergasted
us. She had cut plain, white muslin into a Dance shirt, loose
and flowing as a nightgown. And with fabric paint she had
made red suns and crosses and moons and black ravens all
over it. Her eyes gleamed. "I will wear it at the ceremony on
Saturday. In honor of our people who danced."

"Under twenty pounds of warm clothes," said Chup.

While we picked at the leftover fries, Plez beat Chup at
dominoes for what seemed like the hundredth time.

"Enough to drive a man to drink," said Chup with a grin.

"Blue," said Plez to me, "you ready to go journeying?"

I'd been longing to go all day. "Yes."

"Let's use the janitor's room again. Buffalo power! Sallee,
you'll stay with him?"

"Yes."

Stretched out under the buffalo head, I declared
my intention aloud three times. "I wish to return to the
Stronghold and see the rest of the Spirit Dance."

The drum banged at me. I hurried to the altar, and dived down the hole like it was easy.

As I floated out of the tunnel this time, I recognized the Badlands, and Cuny Table. Raven hovered in the air. He did not carry me to the Dance on his back but guided me as I myself flew at his wing to the dance ground, where the rite was in progress.

I looked around. Nothing seemed changed—same medicine people, same watchers, same dancers in the same circle. Some were on the ground inside the circle, making their journeys or being attended to. I accepted calmly the ease with which I had traveled to a time a hundred years past.

I knew that the first song had just ended, and the refrain words, "The Father says so, the Father says so," sang themselves in my head. The dancers were at a pause.

A lead voice sent up the second song. The dancers grasped hands and began the slow shuffle step to the left, sunwise, and immediately lifted their voices in the song. Like the first, it was voices alone, unaccompanied by drum, and I realized that I had heard no other Indian songs without drum. The words were,

My son, let me grasp your hand,
My son, let me grasp your hand,
Says the father,
Says the father.
You will live,
You will live,
Says the father,
Says the father.
I bring you a Pipe,

I bring you a Pipe,
Says the father,
Says the father.
By this Pipe you will live,
By this Pipe you will live,
Says the father,
Says the father.

During this song another woman began to fall into a trance, an old woman with a kind-looking face. I stepped close behind and danced with her. First she showed difficulty stepping sideways. Then she began to tremble, and her movements got stiff and awkward. I danced behind her to my own eternal music. A medicine man hurried to her and began to wave an eagle feather in front of her eyes with one hand and a white scarf with the other, and looked at her piercingly. I looked away from the feather and scarf, up at the sky, and thanked Wakantanka for all. She staggered toward the center, I followed. The dancers closed the circle behind her. Her eyes glazed, she fell to the ground, and started making motions almost like convulsions. Everyone left her alone now, gave her room to make her journey to see her ancestors. I sat beside her, as a companion. I did not let myself look into her mind, or go on her journey.

Incredible. Incredible how much I know of things that did not exist for me only two days ago.

I made no effort to think, to use the thinking part of my mind to make ideas about her journey or mine. I did not let her shakes disturb me. Though I felt no convulsions, perhaps my body, back in the other world next to Sallee, looked the way this woman's did. I simply sat there, thinking my spirit might make her feel less alone.

Other people began to fall into trances, journeys to see their relatives of the near or distant past. The dancers closed the circle behind them, the singers lifted one song after another, repeating each many times, the ceremony circled on and circled on around us, those who traveled the circle of time dancing around those who visited the still center point of eternity.

The old woman came back to consciousness from her journey. Someone threw a blanket over her shoulders. She sat by the Tree of Life for a while, and then rejoined the singing dancers.

I added my spirit to the Dance, and that seemed good.

I will not set down all the songs for you, nor do I remember how many they sang, or what all the words were. I don't know how many people went into trances, though at times there seemed to be a score or two on the ground. I sat in the circle of the Dance for long hours, far into the night, and for me the time could as well have been moments or infinities. I let my spirit mingle with the spirit of the words lifted to Wakantanka, felt the hearts of the people devoted to the spirit of the Spirit Dance.

I have almost nothing more to say about it. I joined the ceremony my people believed in, I saw them commit their spirits to it, I saw them give their lives to it, and I knew that it was good.

I knew that back in the other world, the normal world, I could wonder whether it was good. I could wonder whether the Dance itself had led my ancestors to Wounded Knee and to their deaths, or if not, what forces had led them. I could wonder how so much good could come to so much evil. In this world I was comfortable with the ceremony.

When the Dance ended, they feasted. But I, a spirit, needed no feast. I felt ready to go back to the world.

Wondering where Raven was, I realized he was perched on my shoulder, and had been all along. He said without words, *The same way Raven can be Creator of all things and the bringer of Death.*

I accepted that peaceably.

I saw myself gliding upward toward the hole in the bottom of the altar, swam into it, and like a diver broaching the surface from a deep dive, came to consciousness in the ordinary world.

I opened my eyes.

I reached for Sallee's hand, and she took mine.

In calm I sat up and looked into her eyes. She poured me some coffee from Plez's thermos, and I took it gratefully.

THE THIRD JOURNEY

The morning of Thursday, December 27, I felt like I'd forgotten something. We were riding and walking to Wounded Knee *physically*. We couldn't float through a hole in the Earth, we had to do it one step at a time in bitter, bitter cold. Like Big Foot's people did it a hundred years ago, only colder.

A British guy by the name of Ian gave us a ride to Red Water Creek in his van. This guy, he came all the way across the big water for this pilgrimage, and he'd taken a role of helping more than journeying. He stayed and cleaned up camps after we left them, drove behind the riders and picked up anyone who had trouble, got to camp early and built fires and helped put up tipis—he was really making a servant of himself. I admired him.

Tyler came and stuck his head in through the window Ian was rolling down. "The horses got away," he said. "Somebody left a corral gate open. Maybe two dozen gone, who knows? Take a while to get started."

Didn't affect Sallee or Chup, who jumped out and strode straight over to the other walkers. The fasters had broken their fasts yesterday, feasted in fact, and I noticed they looked better, their faces not so pinched and gaunt.

Ian left the motor of the van running and hustled out to do whatever work was in store for him. I was glad to stay by the heater, and I know Emile and Plez felt the same. Because

Waziya, the mean giant of the North, and Iya, Wind Storm, were throwing cold at us in big winds, storm winds—hell, typhoons.

About midmorning, finally, we formed a circle, prayed, and headed out behind Ron McNeill, who carried the staff. Now there were nearly two hundred riders. In this weather we stuck together pretty well, the staff leading and Tyler and Percy White Plume, Alex's brother, bringing up the rear and herding stragglers. Up a rutted path toward the crest of a hill we rode, and then followed the crests that cupped Red Water Creek. Wi, Father Sun, was bright, but Waziya's wind had the upper hand today. It felt like he was slapping us. When we hit the blacktop and turned toward Kyle, the country was all flat to the north and west. That meant the wind began to howl for sure. I screwed everything tight around my head, bandannas, scarves, collars, and parka top, but they couldn't keep the wind out, or the snow it whipped up and threw in my face, sharp and cutting. I squinched my eyes as near closed as I dared and retreated into a private world.

In another hour, or one small eternity, I decided I had to have one big breath, freezing or not. I cracked my defenses, heaved air in, and cast my sight out and about. Riders were almost invisible in the ground blizzard, like shadows against the white, flat-blowing snow. The breath I took pained in a way I'd never imagined air could hurt human lungs. Retying the bandanna, I found it crusted hard with ice from my own exhalations.

The water tower at Kyle stuck up on the horizon. Kyle, Kyle, Kyle, it was all around me on this trip. I'd spent two nights in the school already, and would spend tonight there. I was about to eat lunch there. After the years in boarding school, I still hated Kyle.

Now, though, I set my eyes on that water tower and tried to draw myself toward it, like it was a giant magnet.

Lunch, lunch, lunch, I kept saying. That tower didn't get a bit closer, and for a while I swear it was farther.

Ten miles, three hours.

When we dismounted, I started to speak to Emile. My jaw made a loud cracking noise right in front of my ear, and that was the only sound that came out. I didn't dare try to speak again.

Buffalo soup yet one more time. And an hour in the cafeteria, in the warmth.

While we were eating, the walkers came in. They'd started before us, walked a longer route because they stuck to the roads, and finished after us in those terrible winds. The way Sallee looked scared me—her clothes were caked with ice, her steps wobbly as a drunk's, her eyes red, her fingers frosted. I put my arm around her and guided her to our table, then stood in line and got soup for her and Chup.

That was an afternoon of mystery and magic. Thank godamercy, the wind eased off. Riders opened the bundles around their faces enough to actually smoke. People talked. The afternoon was comfortable—ridiculous word!—compared to the morning. Which was a damn good thing, because we had sixteen more miles to go to Red Owl Springs, where the Big Foot people camped the last night before they met the soldiers. There were jokes about us making the same mileage as the guy who ran the first marathon in Greece a couple of thousand years ago. Someone said he dropped dead when he got there, but Plez said he was a soldier and made the run to bring home news of a great victory for the Athenians over somebody. Lots of us thought we might get a great victory and drop dead, both.

The mystery was the unpleasant kind, a guy who kept leapfrogging us in a nice new pickup. He would cruise past nice and slow, stop up ahead, and watch us ride by. He was an Anglo, not much hair on his head but plenty on his lip. As we passed, he fussed with something in his lap.

Said Plez, "FBI don't mean Full-Blooded Indian."

"What?"

"Oh, I imagine we are watched, our movements duly noted, and the records thereof preserved in the vaults of the Hoover Building in Washington, D.C."

"You're paranoid." I didn't feel as sure as I sounded.

He lit up. "Hell, yes, and that don't prove no one's after me." He chuckled. "Shee-it, I been on every list they got for forty years. They was keeping files on me when Russell Means was in diapers. Boy, I can smell them agents, and I know all their mean tricks."

"You checked out your file under the Freedom of Information Act?"

"They wouldn't send it, on account of the federal treasury couldn't hack the trucking costs."

He was enjoying himself now.

We said no more about it. The guy in the new pickup kept cruising by, doing something in his lap as we passed one by one, and cruising by again.

I saw this old movie, *Harvey*. In it Jimmy Stewart had an imaginary friend, Harvey the Rabbit, who was essential to his life. The FBI has imaginary enemies, essential to its life.

The magic came at the end of the day's ride, the last strides of the marathoners to Red Owl Springs. For once we made good time, because the afternoon wasn't harsh. When we topped the hill above the campsite, Wi the sun was about to touch the horizon. Support people like Ian moved around the camp, fires were lighted, tipis erected. The staff bearer stopped, and slowly all two hundred riders filed to the top of the hill. We sat our horses stirrup to stirrup for moment. I looked up and down the long file of the riders,

WIN BLEVINS

the display of eagle feathers, and thought of the commitment represented here. With the sun fading, we each were
tall shadows, like the feathers floating up from our heads,
so that the hill itself seemed to wear a vast war bonnet of
human beings devoted to a single cause, wiping away the
tears of our people. In the last light of Father Wi, Emile and
I looked into each other's eyes, and Wi made our skins red-
der even than they were.

This was the last camp where the Big Foot people were
free. The next night, at Wounded Knee, they were under
heavy military guard.

I felt the moment instead of seeing it. The staff bearer
started down the hill. One by one the riders walked behind
him in perfect silence, in perfect order. It was like we all
heard the same muffled drum, and marched to it in a rhythm
we all sensed as one, an army of spiritual warriors. Maybe the
drum was our hearts, beating right together for this one time.

The women below, making the food, saw us and raised
the high trills, the old-time greeting women gave to their
men returning from battle. Men ran out of tipis and banged
drums. The last of the sunlight rested gentle on us, a blessing, and the wind stilled.

I looked at my brothers, my fellow riders, and knew
inside what it is to be part of a people. Holding the reins, my
left hand shook so much I put it on the saddle horn. Tears
streaked down Emile's face. Togetherness …

Brothers, we come to more together than alone.

And we are all related. *Mitakuye oyasin.*

That evening, after the council fire, riders and walkers
and support people littered the floor of the gym at Little
Wound School in their sleeping bags. Russell Means came
around and announced that there would be an AIM meeting in ten minutes in the lunch room.

Rez talk about Means, Banks, Wounded Knee II, and all the rest of it, you couldn't get away from it during the seventies for and against. But I missed the rebellion at Wounded Knee, just went to school every day. Partly it was because Grandpa and Unchee disapproved, thought it was a bunch of outsiders stirring things up. Mostly it was because February and March 1973 were the climax of the basketball season, I was a star, and counting coups on the other schools had me hot. So I didn't know anything about Means and Banks and AIM, not personally. That's why I went with Sallee and Emile to the meeting. Why didn't Chup and Plez go? Because Russell Means is a guy Indians like or they don't, strong both ways.

Understand, most rez people don't think of him as one of us. Maybe he was born at Pine Ridge, but he grew up somewhere in California. He doesn't speak Lakota, and he has no damned idea of Lakota courtesy. I was going to the meeting to behold an oddity, not hear a comrade.

Means started off with the sort of speech that turns a lot of traditional Pine Ridge people off—belligerent, defiant, in-your-face. I hope you have seen by now that we aren't like that. Still, what he talked about was okay. The governor of South Dakota, George Mickelson, had christened 1990, which was the anniversary of Wounded Knee, the Year of Reconciliation in South Dakota. Means ripped into that as a contemptible fraud, and then ripped a lot of other things that need ripping.

I just observed. One of my observations was that a lot of the white riders and walkers and media people were here, and most of the Indians were out in the gym.

Dennis Banks, though, is hard not to like. His approach is sly. He tells a story, lays in a joke, and slips up on an idea like, We gotta get the Black Hills back. They belong to the

Lakota people by treaty. They were taken illegally. No, hell no, we can't accept payment for them. We want the land.

Yeah, yeah, he's an Ojibway, and they're enemy. That name "Sioux" you call us by, instead of "Lakota," *Sioux* is the Ojibway word for *enemy*. Still, he's lived at Pine Ridge a while now, and I like Dennis Banks.

The meeting? AIM? I left shrugging my shoulders. I came on this ride to see, to understand, to accept, and to heal. Not to rattle political sabres.

"What's your intention tonight?" asked Plez.

We were back in the custodial room at the Kyle School. Plez and Sallee sat on each side of me, Sallee holding my hand. This place was my Cape Canaveral launch pad.

I said, "I want to return to the Stronghold and hear some dancers tell what they saw in the Spirit World." I uttered the same words twice more, Plez punched the tab on the tape recorder, and the drum whanged me on my way.

To the altar, down the hole, tumbling out the other side. This time I didn't see Raven. I did float to the ground right in the Stronghold.

It was morning. People were eating and just starting to get ready to dance. I wandered around, tipi to tipi, watching mothers feed their children, their men, and themselves, watching dancers begin to paint their faces and make their minds and bodies ready for the trip to the other world.

I had nothing to do but wait until the ceremony started. I knew from Plez and the books that sometimes people who crossed over and returned testified about what they had seen. I studied faces. Some I remembered from the center of the Dance space, some from the circle of dancers, some not at all. I noticed that some spirit travelers marked their journey by adopting new emblems for the Dance, different feathers, or feathers worn in a certain way, what they'd seen one of their ancestors do.

I felt a pang. Right now I wasn't looking for my own ancestors. At Wounded Knee—just tomorrow night—I would.

After a while the dancers assembled and the medicine people prepared to start the ceremony. One of the leaders thanked the spirits for answering our prayers and helping some of us to the other world. Then he invited dancers of the previous day to tell everyone what they saw when they crossed over. I will set down for you what three of them said.

"I saw a great eagle come," said one man, "a messenger from Tunkashila. He flew directly to me, and I understood that he would take me to see Wakantanka himself. I reached out my hand to him, and somehow ... he disappeared. He disappeared, and I could not find him again."

Then a man named Two Bulls, a man of medicine, told what he saw. He mounted a ladder of clouds and passed through the sky to the spirit land. There Wakantanka greeted him, and showed him wonderful things. He saw the lodges of kindred and friends long dead. He saw infinite prairies of wild grass, and infinite herds of buffalo grazing on them. For three days he watched the people live happily in the old way, cooking buffalo meat and eating plenty.

Then Wakantanka took him into a big tipi filled with the spirits of the departed.

Suddenly the village was enveloped in fog, and Two Bulls could see nothing. When the fog lifted, the village was gone. A man covered with short hair all over his body, and of evil appearance, came up and spoke to Wakantanka. "I demand you give half the people in the world to me."

"No!" Wakantanka answered, and answered no again and again to the evil man's repeated demands, until finally

Wakantanka compromised. "All Indian people will be mine," he said to the evil man, "and all white men will be yours."

Wakantanka then declared his intentions to Two Bulls. He would cover the Earth with new soil five times as deep as the height of a man, and thus bury all white people. Then He would cover the new Earth with grasses and running water, and make all oceans around it impassable.

With these promises Wakantanka sent Two Bulls back to the ordinary world.

A man named Big Lodge had crossed over and spoken to his ancestors.

"As I fell into the trance, I was carried away by a great and grand eagle. We flew over a big hill and saw a village like in the old times, tipis made of buffalo hides, and bows and arrows in use. The people had nothing of the white man's making in this beautiful country, and no whites were permitted to live there. Fertile fields and great forests stretched in every direction, and their beauty brought me joy.

"I was taken into the presence of the Messiah. His countenance was beautiful. I wept, for he bore scars on his hands and feet, where the whites once nailed him cruelly to a cross. In his side was also a scar, but he covered this with a mantle of beautiful feathers.

"He spoke to me. 'My child, I am glad to see you. Do you want to see your relatives and children who are dead?'

"When I answered yes, the Messiah called my friends. They rode toward us on the finest horses I ever saw, dressed in splendid garments, and looking very happy. Recognizing even the playmates of my childhood, I rushed to embrace them, tears of joy on my cheeks.

"We went together to another village to see Wakantanka. He had women bring us a meal of meats, wild fruits, and pemmican. We smoked a Pipe ornamented beautifully with feathers and porcupine quills. We went together into a big valley where thousands of buffalo, deer, and elk were feeding. As we talked, Wakantanka said that Earth is now worn out, and that Indians need a new dwelling place where we won't be bothered by the whites. So he instructed me to return to the people bearing this message: 'Be faithful in the Dance and pay no attention to the whites. Soon I will come to help you. If the spiritual leaders make dance shirts and Pray over them, they will protect the wearers. If the whites shoot bullets at dancers wearing these shirts, the bullets will fall to the ground harmlessly, and the shooter will drop dead.' "

I felt a twist of anguish at this part of the vision.

"He also said He has prepared a hole in the ground full of fire and steaming water for all white men and those who don't believe in the Dance.

"When he had spoken these words, he commanded me to return to Earth."

With this command to Big Lodge, I felt a pleasant, gentle tug inviting me back to my normal world. With perfect confidence I reached out and said, "Sallee." She took my hand.

I opened my eyes. The custodial room was dark. A match struck, and Plez's fingers set a candle next to our clasped hands. I looked into Sallee's face, and Plez's face next to it. They were smiling at me.

"I saw it," I said.

"God is good, God is great," said Plez. I chuckled at his Muslim tease.

"That trip seemed short."

"Journeys exist outside of Time. You got what you asked for?"

I nodded yes. "I'm getting tired. Tomorrow night …"

Plez hee-hawed. "Tomorrow night you might run out of energy. Tomorrow night you will see …"

He stopped and didn't go on.

Tomorrow night we would be at Wounded Knee.

"I want to tell you, both of you, what I saw." I laid out Big Lodge's vision for them, every word. I could hardly believe how surefooted my recall was. Whatever I saw on a journey, it was completely clear when I came back. "The part about the shirts that turn away bullets, that bothers me," I said, and looked pleadingly at Plez.

"I told you, brother. Visions are truth. Know that. Understanding them, that's another thing. Sometimes knowing what comes to you from the Spirit world and what comes from the evil in your own heart, that can be tricky. First place, remember that bulletproof shirts, they weren't part of Wovoka's vision. You Lakota added that. Second place, there *is* a place the soldiers couldn't hurt anybody, can't hurt us, and you get there by the Dance. It's the spirit world. Maybe they misunderstood what their visions were bringing 'em.

"You know, us Shoshones, the Dance started with us. Wovoka's vision was all peace with the white men. But the Lakota, they began to say things like, 'If the soldiers shoot at us, they will all fall dead.'

"You might be upset about the fires the whites were supposed to fall into, too," he went on. "I think that comes from the hatred in the Lakota hearts. They had a harder time than most any tribe, they were starving bad, they hated the whites. Wovoka's vision, though, it wasn't hatred. The old-time Shoshones, they say the Lakota brought Wounded Knee on themselves by corrupting Wovoka's vision with hatred."

I threw hostility at him with my eyes.

"I don't say it's true. But them old-time Shoshones, some of them think so."

"Anyhow, the parts the Lakota added, those we gotta doubt. At that time it didn't come from good hearts."

I felt exhausted. "I need to sleep," I said. "I'm worried about tomorrow night."

"Oh, save your energy, brother. You're gonna rock and roll." And he cackled. "You're gonna rock right into the thick of it!"

TO WOUNDED KNEE

W e started out on the morning of Friday, December 28, with a prayer, and a reminder that this day's ride was dedicated to the spirits of the people buried at Wounded Knee. Each day of this climactic ride was dedicated—the first to the children and orphans, the second to the elderly, the third to the sick (the ill in any way—physically, emotionally, spiritually), the fourth to the imprisoned, the fifth to the women, today to the spirits of the people buried at Wounded Knee, and tomorrow to wiping away the tears of the people.

A couple of people spoke. "The spirits have been with us all this way," one said. "They'll be with us today when we ride into Wounded Knee."

Others said there would be TV cameras and print reporters at Wounded Knee when we rode in. "Look proud."

"Let the elders and young people see we have hope in our hearts," someone said.

"It will be hard. Remember that you're honoring Big Foot's people with suffering of your own."

It looked like a day for suffering. The sky was mottled with dirty-looking clouds. KILI, the little rez radio station at Porcupine, said it was thirty below, with no prospects for warming up during the day.

Emile, Plez, and I walked the horses with grim determination. We simply endured the two-hour ride to the little village of Porcupine. There they gave us coffee, we warmed up inside, and we listened to a man tell about his experience at Wounded Knee II.

My mind was back a hundred years, on what happened to our ancestors—my ancestors—near here, before the village existed. Big Foot's people ran into four troops of the Seventh Cavalry of the United States Army. The Mniconjou tied up the tails of their horses for war and rode them back and forth to get them into their second wind. The troops formed a skirmish line and unlimbered the Hotchkiss revolving cannons.

Big Foot intervened. He ordered the wagon where he laid, coughing and spitting up blood, to be rolled forward with a white flag. He and the cavalry commander shook hands. On the advice of a breed interpreter, the commander agreed to forego disarming the Indians until a time when everyone was calmer. The Lakota agreed to go to the basin of Wounded Knee Creek four miles away and camp with the bluecoats. From there ...

At Porcupine we got word that the temperature outside was fifty below. We started the four last miles to Wounded Knee like a funeral cortege.

As we rode out of town, I couldn't help but wonder, *What would it be like to work for KILI?* FM, no power. Hardly any money for programming, so local stuff, music the jocks like, interspersed with public service announcements, interviews, and programs about issues. And next to no money to pay the staff. It made me shudder even worse.

Along the road Indian people sat in their cars and trucks and watched us pass. Some rolled down the windows, even in the awful cold. Some made small salutes. Most simply looked at us with solemn, honoring faces.

Somehow the riders and their mounts survived to the crest of the hill above the wide, shallow bowl that is the basin of Wounded Knee Creek. I stopped my horse and ran my eyes from horizon to horizon, east, south, west. Emile reined up beside me. I looked for his face but his expression was concealed behind the thick wraps, kerchiefs, scarves, and the hood of his parka drawn into a tight arc around what must have been his nose and eyes. Behind us I heard a voice, low and muffled but not a whisper, Plez's deep voice. "Behold the sun," he said formally. "Wi is not a fiery ball today but a solid disc, pale, like a worn-out coin. Across his face blow clouds driven by the North wind, and in them the Spirit eye sees truth, truth of a hundred horseback shapes of fantastic warriors, the men of a hundred years ago marching south, their heads bristling with eagle feathers, honors earned in war. Among them are women dragging travois, driving wagons, the women who have always been the strength of the Lakota nation. And children, the seed of seven generations to come.

"Wi appears weak today, as the hoop of the people was that day weak, frayed, ready to break. Today, by joining with the spirits and coming to Wounded Knee, by the ceremonial Feeding of the Spirits tomorrow, by the ceremonial Wiping Away the Tears, we make the hoop of the people strong again.

"The seventh generation is here, my friends. We ride to Wounded Knee bearing hope in its name."

In Plez's words we found the inspiration to urge the horses downhill toward the church, yet a couple of miles away, and the gravesite.

Ahead we heard shouts. "Walkers! You walkers! *Heyupa! Heyupa! Heyupa! Heyupa!*"

Riders were passing the walkers. Some walkers lifted their fists in salutes. Others shook hands with passing riders. Emile, Plez, and I kicked our horses to a trot. *We have*

been separated from the walkers when we should have been together!
Crowded to the left side of the road, the first walkers we came
to held their hands up toward us, rigid. I slowed my horse
to a walk, leaned left in the saddle, and as I passed, touched
each extended hand with my own stiff fingers, like playing
a glissando on the piano. Emile and Plez did the same. Now
I saw the line was swelled with children, with walkers who
joined in only today, even with veterans in wheelchairs. I
touched every hand. Soon I came to Sallee and Chup, reaching up eagerly, and last, at the front, to the monks and nuns.
As we touched, the Japanese never stopped their chanting,
harmony and rhythm for the melody of our hands.

*I have separated myself from the people I should have weaved
my being into.*

Suddenly, at the end of six days of effort, we arrived.

*I have made my pilgrimage to Wounded Knee. Thank you,
Grandfathers.*

Emile and I looked at each other. My eyes were too cold
to tear. My body was too cold to permit much emotion.

At the foot of Cemetery Hill the leaders turned us into a
single great circle. Boys came around with bags of tobacco,
and every rider took a pinch and held his over his head with
his left hand. A harsh wind rose. A medicine man prayed
aloud, but the words were carried away with the spumes of
blowing snow. Finally he cried loudly, "*Mitakuye oyasin!*" We
all flung the tobacco into the wind, which swept it away to
the uttermost ends of the Earth. *To Earth.*

Emotion tried to lift me, but I was too heavy. With huge
relief, I dismounted. The man who rented us the horses
appeared, and Emile and I handed him the reins. "Hear the
riders are gonna make a circle at the gravesite tomorrow
morning."

We nodded yes.

"You wanna join 'em? Be part of it?"

Emile and I looked at each other. We'd spent all we could afford on the horses.

"No charge," he said. "I'm staying over for the ceremony."

"Thank you," I said, and meant it.

"See you here in the morning."

The wind whipped and lashed at us. *Let's get out of here.*

I turned to my friend. *Is it really over? Have I really done it? Have we done it together?* In a shaky voice I said to Emile, "*Mitakuye oyasin.*"

Then I turned my back to the wind.

"The buffalo is resurrected!" cried Chup. In other words, it was buffalo soup again. Everybody was gathered into the high school in Manderson.

We ate while people made speeches. We were all speeched out—tribal president, congressman, hell, we didn't care. I went through the soup line three times.

Finally, while that Indian congressman was rambling on, I scooched next to Sallee and took her hand. She didn't resist, but hers felt kind of dead. We looked each other in the eyes. She knew what I was telling her. Finally, she squeezed back, and we watched the ceremony that was starting.

It was a feather ceremony for the very youngest Big Foot Memorial Rider, an eight year old named Joshua Moon Guerro. Alex White Plume gave the eagle feather. Arvol Looking Horse himself, the Pipe Keeper, prayed over it. One of the original nineteen riders tied the feather into Joshua's hair.

Suddenly a drum I couldn't see hammered wildly, and twenty-five chosen riders started circling Joshua, coming to him from three different directions. Each rider danced ceremonially to Joshua three times, and touched his hair each time.

I never saw a kid look so proud.

Said Plez, "That there's the seventh generation."

"Where you gonna sleep? Where you gonna do your journey?"

We shrugged. "The gym floor, I guess."

"Tradition!" sang Emile, to the tune of the song from *Fiddler on the Roof.*

"I know the caretaker for the church," said Plez. "I already asked him."

I pictured Sacred Heart Catholic Church, silhouetted on the brow of Cemetery Hill.

"Special to be there," said Plez, "right there. Right where it happened."

I nodded.

The five of us trooped to Plez's king-cab truck.

I said to Plez, "Plug me in." He grinned and rolled his eyes and dug into his pack for the cassette player and tape.

We were in the basement of the little church, Plez, Sallee, Emile, Chup, and I. In the basement, in a meeting room, not in the church proper, where the altar was. The Spirit Dance brought me all the Messiah I needed.

He handed me the equipment, and I put the headset on. "Sallee will be right next to you," he said, "the whole time."

I gave him a look of gratitude. Strange journey—earphones, wisps of wire, a box I didn't understand and a skinny strip of brown tape—all these were my road into a world I'd never known.

I laid back on my sleeping bag. "Say your intention," said Plez. "Say it out loud three times."

I murmured to myself, "I want to go to this night a hundred years ago, with my people. I want to see them come to Wounded Knee. I want to see everything that happened that night. I want to feel everything that happened to the people, and especially to my relatives."

I considered what else I should say. Maybe I should ask to come back. That seemed cheap somehow. My people didn't come back, most of them. Their bodies ended up strewn all over this valley, and beyond. Snow covered them the next night. Not for several days did a burial detail move the corpses up the little hill and stack them in the mass grave.

I repeated the words. "I want to go to this night a hundred years ago, with my people. I want to see them come to Wounded Knee. I want to see everything that happened that night. I want to feel everything that happened to the people, and especially to my relatives."

I pondered. I'd said enough, and to hell with the rest. I would take my chances. Once more I said the words.

I hit PLAY. The drum started its fast beat. I went to the hole in the altar and began the descent. A bluebird flittered around my head on the way down, unnaturally bright, and then I fell past it, and fell and fell and came to …

The sun was setting as the people walked, rode, and rolled down the road from Porcupine Butte into the valley of Wounded Knee Creek. The shallow bowl looked like a place that counted for a little something. The post office and store run by Mousseau huddled near the bridge over the creek. There one feeder road slanted off to the northwest, and a quarter mile down, another road headed the same direction. Beyond the bridge the main road ran north and south, the way the creek ran.

The people moved slowly, and their bodies showed their hearts and minds. They were exhausted from six days of desperate travel. They were hungry. They were cold. They were angry at the soldier chief's demand that they give up their guns. They were angry at being treated like prisoners. They were afraid, under the guns of all these soldiers. They didn't trust any soldiers, and this bunch, the outfit of Yellow Hair Custer, least of all.

The interpreters barked the soldier chief's order to go on past the store, past the straight, tidy lines of cavalry tents, and make camp. Most people went, tired and uncaring. A few ignored the soldiers and went into Mousseau's store to buy small items they needed, coffee, sugar, candles.

Where the church stood in the modern world, a knoll overlooked both camps. I walked up for an overview and saw a cabin crouched there. I wondered whose it was. It looked empty. East of the hill the soldiers' tents were set up in their white-man ruler lines. The village was assembling south of the hill, more than a hundred long steps from the soldiers, just this side of a ravine and spread on both sides of a spur road.

Looking at the ravine and knowing, it made my guts clench, and I refused to look that way again.

In the last of the light I could see the village rising, tents and tipis in the shape of a fat crescent moon. In the women's movements erecting their homes, pounding down stakes, unloading wagons, in the way the men staked the horses, I could feel their fear, their fatigue, and a curdle of anger. The ponies felt it too—they stomped and whickered nervously. The dogs slunk around.

Then I noticed the effect of journeying again, more real than real—even in the darkness of a moonless night I could see, like in those weird night shots you see in the movies, everything looking dark but clear at the same time. Strangely, like everything in a spirit journey, it felt natural, normal to see in the dark.

A darkness inside me hinted it might be better to be blind.

Something odd—the soldiers pitched a tent for Big Foot at the edge of the soldier camp. I saw them carry the sick chief in, and then a big wood stove, and chunks of firewood that must have come by wagon. Though Big Foot was on their enemies list, for tonight they meant to keep him alive. He had promised to give them what they wanted, the weapons. And when you give a man a licking, you want him to feel it.

Suddenly I saw horses coming up toward me, pulling two of the Hotchkiss guns. I felt uneasy and moved halfway down the hill toward the villages. The soldiers arranged the gun muzzles so they pointed over my head and straight at my people's lodges.

Pictures of tomorrow's mayhem began to whirl in my mind. But I told myself, *Let it come tomorrow. I will feel more than I want to then.*

I slipped down into the village, uneasy that I could walk this ground untouchable, when so many of my people were about to …

You are here in spirit only. See, hear, feel, and bring back what is good for you, and good for the people.

At the edge of the village I saw the soldiers establishing watch posts circling the people all the way around. An officer ordered a corporal to have patrols march between the posts constantly, back and forth. "No one gets out of this camp tonight," he commanded.

I decided to wander through the village looking for women who were big with child, who appeared to be in the ninth or tenth moon. (You call the time of gestation nine months. We call it ten moons.) How would I find Blue Crow? How many big-bellied women would there be? Would I feel a special connection? *Surely my heart will tell me when I near my own great-grandfather, my own great-grandmother.*

If I saw them, knew who they were, I would have to be with them tomorrow, I would have to go through whatever they did. Maybe this would heal the hole in my heart. More likely, watching them die would give me a wound I would carry back to my own life, and I would live forever in ravenShadow.

By now people had eaten what food they had, and were sitting around shivering, waiting, enduring, maybe wanting their lives to end, surely wanting this kind of life to end.

I walked and saw no women who were obviously pregnant. Suddenly I had a thought. I wanted to look in on the Horn Cloud family, more properly Horned Cloud. I had read about them in the book, and felt curious about them. Horn Cloud was a leader, a headman next to Big Foot. Horn Cloud scoffed at the Spirit Dance, and the family kept themselves apart from it. But the young Horn Cloud men and the fighting tomorrow ... I had read their deeds.

I felt in a whirlwind about the dance. One breath of me wanted to believe in the good Big Lodge saw, in the vision of a world that was a more beautiful way to live. Another breath of me could not reconcile the vision of beauty with the way Big Foot's people died in an orgy of bloodletting. But doubting the Spirit Dance, that felt like doubting the Lakota way, Lakota life itself. It felt like doubting my own journey, my presence here.

The whirlwind ripped at me.

Where was the Horn Cloud tipi?

I heard the clink of shod hooves on stone. I looked out to the east and saw cavalrymen far beyond the road, circling toward the soldier tents. Lots of troops. No one else took note, no one else could see so far in the darkness. *More troops.* Darkness expanded in me, like ink clouding water.

When I wandered near the Horn Cloud tipi, I knew them, and slipped into the tipi to watch and listen. Behind the center fire sat Horn Cloud himself, a sober man of maybe fifty, with the gravity and solidity of a leader. I reached out to his spirit, and it felt leaden, burdened by leading the people at a terrible time. His wife, who looked endlessly cheerful, was doing something domestic with a younger woman at the back of the tipi on a pallet of blankets—then I saw they were trying tiny moccasins on the feet of a small boy. Wet Feet, I remembered from one of the books, son of Dewey and Wears Eagle. Three young men talked somberly among themselves. The handsome older one must be Dewey. There was another grown son, Daniel, three teenage boys, Joseph, William, and Sherman, and a teenage girl, Pretty Enemy. Dewey, whose name was properly Iron Hail, kept sneaking looks over his shoulder at Wears Eagle and Wet Feet. His face went serious when he looked at his brothers, playful when he turned toward his wife and son.

I wondered why she was called Wears Eagle, which seemed a name of honor. Why did she and Iron Hail have traditional names, the four younger brothers white names? It was as though the two were blessed with the old medicine, the four shorn of it.

Wears Eagle started tossing the baby in the air, and Iron Hail could stand it no longer. He excused himself and went to his wife. They rocked tiny Wet Feet back and forth, wiggled his hands and legs, then tossed him lightly from mother to father and back, all the while chanting something. I slipped closer to hear, wondering if it was a song Unchee cooed to me decades later.

The words were a heavily accented version of, "Rockabye baby, in the tree top, when the wind blows the cradle will rock."

I almost hooted. How did they learn that song? Joseph spoke English, but he was the only one in the family. What white mother, or sister or child, taught them that nursery tune? When, why, under what friendly circumstances?

Then I wanted to squirm under my laughter. *The cradle will fall.*

Senior Horn Cloud paid no attention to anyone, saw and heard nothing, sat with the look of a man who is looking inside, and hates what he sees. His wife set a speckled enamel cup of hot coffee in front of him, but Horn Cloud took no notice.

Suddenly the scene seemed unreal. *It's pretense. You all know what's coming. Unconsciously, you know what's coming.*

At the same time this family moment was real. What would happen tomorrow, that was unreal, that was not human life....

I cannot bear it.

I rushed out of the tipi and into the darkness. Which Horn Clouds would live, which die? Except for Iron Hail, I didn't remember from the books. Three-quarters of the people in this camp would die tomorrow morning, many killed horribly. To look into a face and wonder ... *My insides are like glass being ground to bits.*

This is living in ravenShadow, for Horn Cloud and for me.

Suddenly voices. Our language. From the other side of the ravine. "Greetings, my relatives. Greetings, my relatives. Don't answer, keep quiet." A very young man's voice—I could hear it perfectly. Three or four Mniconjou men, looking about strangely, walked closer to the ravine, trying to act nonchalant. The sentries eyed them hard, and they pretended to be doing nothing.

The call came again, a different voice, an older man's. "We are Oglala, scouts."

A third voice, reedy. "My wife is Mniconjou, Sky's Bird, daughter of Black-Winged Hawk."

"Hey, my relatives," said the oldest voice, "we want to tell you, the whites have brought in lots more soldiers, four more troops."

Pause.

The reedy voice: "Two more cannons, too."

The young voice: "They have doubled their manpower and their gunpower."

Now the reedy voice. "They don't want you to know, so they didn't use the road, they snuck around to the east."

"Hey-hey," cried the older man, "be careful, this is not a time for trouble. Be real careful."

Silence. After a while one of the listeners said "Thank you" in Lakota, and the listeners strolled back into the village.

Now I saw, through the darkness, men bivouacking beyond the ravine, Oglala men, the army scouts. But they hadn't forgotten their blood, and the Mniconjou would take heart from that.

I wandered across the ravine, and noticed again that in spirit journeying there are no physical obstacles, really. If the traveler wants to cross a ravine, he goes somehow without the specifically physical acts of finding footholds to get down, and hoisting his weight up the other side. He glides.

I walked to the scouts' bivouac. About thirty men clumped around small fires, coffee cups in hands. Horses were staked everywhere. Bedrolls made dark shadows on the cold ground. Quiet conversations in our language came to my ears, talk of families, horses, weapons, births, marriages, deaths, nothing of consequence to me now. I studied the faces. They were ordinary faces, with the expressions of men during slack time on a job. I looked for signs of dissolution, drunkenness, or evil, eyes from which the spirit had fled, leaving emptiness. But I didn't see that. I saw ordinary men.

How can you fight on the soldiers' side?

I had talked to Plez about this, and knew part of the answer, perhaps as much as reason could know. Many honorable Lakota men walked this path. Little Big Man, the great friend of Crazy Horse. George Sword, captain of the Pine Ridge police. Being a scout or policeman was putting your feet on the new road, the white road. Though you loved the old ways, it might be an act of courage to throw yourself fiercely into the new. You would be following one of the traditions of your people, taking the path of a warrior. And the U.S. government, the real power in everyone's life now, would give you a horse, a rifle, and a monthly salary.

Perhaps these men made the right choice, no one can say. But the path led them to terrible conflicts and woeful deeds. When Little Big Man was taking Crazy Horse to jail, the warrior went for his knife. Little Big Man grabbed his arms, and in that grip Crazy Horse received the bayonet wound that pierced his kidneys and ended his life.

Just two weeks ago forty-three Indian policemen rode to Sitting Bull's cabin to enforce the white man's law on the venerable chief, and killed him.

Tomorrow the soldier leaders would hold these scouts apart from the fighting, not trusting them to kill people of their own blood.

I wonder how Little Big Man lived with himself. I wonder if he drank himself to death.

At that moment I saw a figure come out of the ravine, a dark shadow against the sagebrush. I watched. Without asking my heart who it was, I felt this was someone important to me. *My great-grandmother?*

The figure took shape in the darkness, and it was a woman, small and round. She placed her feet surely on the black earth, and moved her body with the grace of a dancer.

How had she slipped through the guard? She must have been very good at walking silently and using shadows.

Even now she minced along and was somehow hard to see. Her voice sounded, but I didn't hear the words. Scouts at a campfire started and looked around at her. I moved close.

"Sister," one of the scouts said, a term of respect.

She moved closer to the fire, and now I saw she was young but had a face of knowledge beyond her years, and the burden of knowledge. "Do you have medicine?" she asked. "White-man medicine for taking the fire out of wounds?" The voice had a tang, but I couldn't place it.

One of the older men said, "Is someone hurt, sister?"

"Many people will be hurt tomorrow," she answered. She had the soberness of prescience.

"The soldiers want no trouble, sister," said the older man.

"There will be no trouble," said a younger one.

Impatience flicked through her eyes.

"Do you have medicine?" *Still the tang—what is that?* Suddenly I recognized it and chuckled. Rosaphine's reedy voice. This woman had Rosaphine's voice—not her blocky body but the voice. And I knew. *This is Sallee's many-greats-grandmother.*

"The white-man doctor is here," said the youngest of the men, of noble face. He rose. "I will take you to him."

"I am Walks Straight," she said. "Thank you."

They went off into the darkness, Walks Straight padding her weight lightly behind the young scout.

They found the army surgeon at another campfire, treating a wound on a scout, perhaps an infection. I watched without listening. At first the white man's face spoke irritation. Then Walks Straight spoke briefly, and the surgeon listened with an open face. He finished up the wound he was treating. Then he sat down with Walks Straight and demonstrated to her the use of some bandages and what looked like poultices.

At last she walked back toward the village with a small bundle. She didn't bother to conceal herself from the guard coming back, and didn't stop at their shouts.

I will have good news for Sallee.

I followed the ravine to the Agency Road and walked along the road to the cavalry camp. Other soldiers were bivouacked here and there, in for a cold night, and one of the longest of the year. But the main camp was Sibley tents arranged neat as lines in an architect's drawing.

The soldiers were mostly in their blankets now. They'd eaten, they had no stoves, it was hard to keep warm. They huddled and talked, or stared into the darkness, alone, waiting. I was struck by how young they looked. The Mniconjou were all ages. The Oglala scouts were mature men. So were the cavalry officers. But the enlisted men were kids—twenty, eighteen, even sixteen. In some of the tents they spoke languages I didn't recognize, I guess European languages. I felt of their hearts, and found them even more scared than they looked. Though their ears didn't understand much English, their noses smelled trouble.

I remembered from the book that a lot of them had been in the army a month or less, and were city kids who could barely stay on a horse. In several of the tents were readers, keeping their minds occupied by lantern light. One was reading a Deadwood newspaper that was folded and refolded. I couldn't tell whether it was a story about the so-called Ghost Dance uprising over here. Was the young man becoming an actor in a drama staged by a newspaper reporter who blew things up to captivate and titillate readers? Another was reading a catalogue of horse gear. A third was reading a novel in German by the romancer Karl May, who sold millions of books about cowboys, cavalry, and wild red Indians, but never crossed the ocean to this continent.

I could feel what a lot of those kids were feeling. They were sleeping right next to savages. These people had unfathomable ways, obscure motives, alien hearts. They walked old, wicked, pre-Christian paths, and maybe they had some of the dark and ancient power too. They were half human. Savage ways and savage hearts.

It's okay—out of curiosity—to go west and see savages. Unspeakable to be killed by them. Not with civilization waiting, and a life....

First you fear, then you fight.

In one big tent some officers were having a fine time. When Colonel Forsyth led the additional four troops of the Seventh Cavalry out of the agency that afternoon, they were coming to finish the mission, to triumph and celebrate. The renegade Big Foot had been caught, and would surrender his weapons on the morrow. These officers thought they had a right to a victory and a right to whoop it up. Five of them had fought at the Little Big Horn, and even after fourteen years, it rankled deep and bitter. So they opened a keg and started the celebration early. I didn't have to listen long. Everyone knows old war stories, colorfully retold, when you hear them.

I walked across the space between the white and red camps, something over a hundred yards. This was where the soldiers would try to search each warrior for weapons tomorrow morning, this was where ... I shivered and hurried forward.

Immediately I saw a young woman coming from a tipi, and knew her. "Oh, bother!" she said back into the lodge.

She had a beautiful, round face. She was plump, and seemed to like that. Her eyes were merry. In one hand she carried a coffeepot. She was huge with child. She looked straight at me.

Unchee's mother, my great-grandmother.

I could not imagine why I had not seen her before. But Spirit shows us things in its own time.

Now her expression changed, and settled on a head-wagging, let's-do-it spirit. It wasn't me she was seeing, but a young sentry behind me. She'd picked out her man. She walked toward him—*sashayed* would be the word, even for a woman as pregnant as she was—but it wasn't flirtatious, just sassy. He was a very young recruit, red of hair, pale of skin, and uncomfortable. She hid the coffeepot under her blanket.

She smiled at him and started to slip by.

"Sorry, ma'am," he said, and stepped in front of her.

She gave him a questioning look, one eyebrow teasing.

"No one leaves camp," he said. The soldier got a frustrated expression on his face. He couldn't tell his orders to someone who didn't speak English.

She shrugged theatrically and tried to skitter around him. Her feet were quick, and she was graceful, even heavy as she was.

He stepped in front of her again. "Sorry, ma'am," he said. "No go. No go." At least the sentry had the decency to be embarrassed by the orders he was enforcing, or by his own baby talk.

This time she danced clean around him, but the sentry reached out and grabbed her arm.

"Hey," she exclaimed, and gave him a dirty look.

He dropped the arm sheepishly. Now she was standing outside the circle of sentries, glaring at him, one hand on her hip.

"Anybody help?" cried the soldier. "I don't speak Indian."

"I'll help you," said my great-grandmother in accented English, and with great delight in herself. "I gotta pee. The baby's gotta pee." She opened the blanket, put her free hand on her big belly. "And we are gonna pee."

She huffed, turned, and marched off. "In private," she called back.

The soldier flushed and turned back to the circle, acting like he didn't know she was out behind him. Sentries on each side of him grinned, but he paid no attention.

I looked inside the lodge she came from. Behind the center fire sat a tall, husky man in his early thirties with a bony face. I studied the big shoulders and the small ass. *Hello, Blue Crow.* He was cleaning a Winchester repeating rifle.

Another woman, also his wife, was singing the children to sleep, two of them, her own children, I remembered. This woman was my great-grandmother's older sister. Lots of times, among our people, a younger woman married her older sister's husband.

"Blue Crow," the woman said, "they're going to take that rifle tomorrow."

He looked up at her, and I saw my own face. I shivered a little. "No," he said softly. "We can't eat grass, Corn Woman." He said it with a light, teasing spirit.

And you're not even young enough to be a hothead.

Even feeling the tension in this lodge, I moved closer and sat down by the fire. I wanted to be with this family, my family. I wanted to talk with them, eat with them, drink coffee with them. I wanted to touch them.

None of that would happen.

At that moment my great-grandmother ducked her big belly through the tipi entrance and held out the coffeepot heavy with water. "Elk Medicine," said Corn Woman, shaking her head, "how did you manage that?"

Elk Medicine. I thrilled at the name. *I know my great-grand-mother's name.*

She rolled her eyes and answered, clearly practicing her English, "Hey, I'd have them white people in my pocket, if I had any pockets."

Blue Crow laughed, and Corn Woman looked mystified.

I laughed, too, for I suddenly thought of the meaning of Elk Medicine's name. Elk Medicine was the power of love, the power to attract the object of your affections overwhelm-ingly. Maybe my great-grandmother was a terrific lover. She had that certain look.

She waggled her big belly. "Come to white men, I get whatever I want, and I don't give nothin'!"

They all laughed again. Blue Crow's face lit up when he laughed—white teeth, merry eyes, and a deep chuckle, like a bullfrog in a well. It was a wonderful, life-embracing sound.

A swirl of emotions rocked me, like violent nausea.

I can't bear it. I can't bear to see you alive today, knowing.

I jumped up and rushed out the door. The anger gurgled up in me now, like small water spat from a geyser, such as might precede an eruption. I knew the deep, fiery wells I'd had all my life. *I will not erupt. Not when I am present only as a spirit.*

Raven sat on one of the ear-flap poles. *Hello, my friend.* He sat on my shoulder, and the calm he gave me felt good.

We walked through the Mniconjou camp. I simply looked at people. *Help me think of something else,* I asked. For instance, which of these people invested their faith and their lives in the Spirit Dance? I knew the faith, the hope, had grown big among these people. Their kinsman Kicking Bear inspired them.

Since Hump defected a couple of weeks ago, Big Foot seemed to hesitate between belief and doubt. The people were divided now.

Of those who were still wholly believers one was Yellow Bird, a medicine man. My heart rose. *Take me to him*, I asked Raven.

Immediately I stood before a man of indeterminate age sitting in front of his lodge, smoking his Pipe. Behind him the door was fastened with pegs, and I saw that no one was inside. Surely he had a family, but I couldn't tell. He sat near the cooking fire, and seemed to be staring into it. I looked at the coals, as though to see whatever world Yellow Bird saw in their glow, their dark edges and yellow-hot centers. I saw nothing but flames and coals.

I studied his face. It was set hard and impassive. Aside from brushing the smoke from the Pipe over himself from time to time, he made no movements at all. I could not read the expression on his face. It was alien, it was blank. I tried to see his heart. Often during a journey, people's feelings and spirits are as clear to me as their facial features. But Yellow Bird's heart was closed like stone.

All I knew was what the book said—Yellow Bird believed passionately in the vision of Wovoka, that the ancestors would return and the buffalo would come back. He knew powerfully that the white people would be wiped away. And he was sure beyond sure that the soldiers' bullets could not harm anyone wearing a dance shirt.

Out of faith in you young men will die tomorrow. Or out of the desperation that seduces them to vest their faith in you.

Because of them, other men will die.
Women and children will die.
The nation will die.

My mind whirled with it. I wanted to walk with my relatives as they perished or lived. To walk with Blue Crow, who gave me his very body. To walk with Elk Medicine, my own great-grandmother, as she bore my grandmother, Unchee, in her womb. To walk with four hundred of my people as most died and some lived. My arms goosebumped. My legs trembled.

Will I pass through to resurrection and come at last—O! at last!—from ravenShadow into the sunlight?

I couldn't envision that—it knocked my imagination for a loop. What I could picture was wanting to die with them. Would Blue Crow sit in council until the shooting started? Would he wear a dance shirt? Would he then work the lever action of his precious Winchester, firing at the soldiers? My spirit would scream to leap in front of a bullet thrown back at him.

Would Elk Medicine be in the village when the Hotchkiss crews started the deadly shelling? I wanted to throw myself over the very muzzle of the cannons. Yet I would be futile as the dance shirts. *The murderous metal will pass harmless through me and devastate the warm flesh behind, flesh of my flesh, blood of my blood.* It would devastate the vision offered by the Spirit Dance, and devastate a people's hope for a future. It would break the hoop of the people. It would blight the flowering tree.

Thus I would be led deeper into ravenShadow, there to abide forever.

Pain spasmed through me. I felt the shells blasting through my body, not touching me, yet working unspeakable agony. I fell to the ground, writhing. I gagged. I thought I would vomit, and I knew the vomit would choke me.

Panic struck at my heart.

Barely able to think, I reached out my right hand into some other world.

Sallee took it.

And she held it.

Plez clicked off the drum tape.

I opened my eyes and looked into Sallee's, then Plez's. They smiled. In the solace of Sallee's grasp I returned to the normal world.

Plez said, "Welcome back."

I squeezed his hand. "I got scared."

He waited to see if I would explain. I couldn't.

Finally he repeated. "Welcome back to this world."

"Thanks," I said gratefully.

I couldn't speak. A little of me wanted to tell him everything I'd seen, the horror and the pathos, and the elusive beauty of it all. But I couldn't speak yet. Besides, most of me wanted to hold it in my heart, like a precious liquid in the innermost vessel of my being, not to be disturbed, only to be held and cherished, still motionless—*hold it now, hold it on your return journey back to the spirit world.*

I looked around. The hour was late, the basement light and shadow from a single guttering candle. Lumps represented Emile and Chup in their sleeping bags. The other pilgrims of Sitanka Wokiksuye were at the school or at home in their beds. We kept this small vigil alone.

"Plez," I said, "what's normal about the normal world?'

He cackled. "Time to sleep," he said.

That startled me. I looked at him, jumpy. Then I knew. "I want to go back now," I said.

"Now?" He checked out my eyes. "You sure?"

"Yes," I said. I didn't real comfortable, but I knew it was time. "I'm sure. I want to see it all before the ceremony tomorrow."

He looked at me like a buyer checking a horse's teeth. "Okay. This may be a big trip."

"I'm ready."

"Just stick your hand out and we'll help you come back."

"I'm ready."

He chuckled, and, uncanny, it seemed the chuckle of Blue Crow, my great-grandfather, from the deep well of the past.

PART SEVEN
DEATH AND RESURRECTION

THE STORM

First came the tape hiss, then the drum beat filled my mind.

I traveled sideways through a big tunnel, or a huge version of whatever you call one of those ducts that goes from a clothes dryer to the outside world. (Yes, Spirit does have a sense of humor.)

I floated like a leaf into the dark valley of Wounded Knee. *Let it be the last time.* I felt wildly afraid and oddly calm at once. No, this doesn't make sense, but feelings don't. The day had not begun, for I could see the Morning Star in the east. The Morning Star is actually the planet Venus, visible just before dawn. Therefore, the way your mythology tells it, the universe sends this planet love even before it sends light, which I find wonderful.

Freezing air filled the valley before that dawn, and it felt to me like evil. I told you how, in our ancient stories, evil came into the world. Passion had been cast out by her companion, Earth. Stone became entranced with Passion, and ignored his companion Thundercloud for her. From this illicit union was born Iya, the Evil One, whose other name is Wind Storm, and he delighted in tormenting both men and the gods.

I knew the Evil One was playing on these grounds today. If you prefer to substitute Satan from your stories, I have no objection.

407

I meandered through the village in the predawn light. A few people were awake, edgy. Most slept restlessly. There were reasons such as the mind knows. They went to bed expecting a hard day. The soldiers would demand the guns. The older warriors probably would cooperate. The younger warriors would refuse. They'd paid plenty of money for their weapons, especially those Winchester repeating rifles, which were better than the single-shot Springfields the soldiers carried. The Indian men needed those rifles to feed their families over the winter. They might need them against the soldiers. And their hot, youthful blood needed them.

There were also reasons the mind does not know: for instance, the despair of a people who, in their own eyes, have fallen from the favor of the gods—people who have lost the good way to live, people who have lost harmony with the Earth and with each other, and are descending into confusion, anger, and bitterness. Add to this the presence of Evil One, hoping as always to inspire human beings to deeds that are ridiculous and shameful.

Now more and more people were stirring, and their spirits arose dark. I slipped like the gentle morning breeze into their tipis and stood among them as they rolled over in their blankets—warriors, leaders, elders, mothers and grandmothers, children. I wanted to feel their despair, and I did. It was stronger than a smell, louder than the language of faces. It was more tangible than the cold air settled in the valley bottom. It was like dark water seeping into the hearts of the Mniconjou, drowning their spirits. Though the sun would soon be up, the people could not rise from their blackness.

I went to the lodge of Blue Crow, my forefather. The family was stirring. Elk Medicine's words prodded the children gently. I could not bear to go inside.

Fifty years before this day in 1890, within the memory of some people here, my people the Lakota were the most powerful tribe on the plains. The buffalo provided our food, our lodging, our way of life. Our men were strong and virile, feared by their enemies, cherished by their families. Our leaders were wise. Our women were fertile, our children happy. Even the white man was a boon to us. He was so few, and he gave us things we wanted, like guns, in exchange for buffalo robes. It was a fine bargain, for we possessed robes in abundance and more than abundance—the buffalo were as many as the very grasses.

Thirty years later some of us were put on a reservation for the first time, forbidden to follow the buffalo and hunt, forced to eat the skimpy rations handed out by the Indian agents, just enough to keep the bellies growling.

In 1881, when Sitting Bull surrendered to the soldiers, every last one of us was on a reservation, and the buffalo were gone from Earth.

The white historians speak of how that made us poor. They show all the things we got from the buffalo. We used the hides for our tipis, for blankets, and for clothing. We used the meat for food, the sinew for bowstrings, the skin of the neck for shields, the bladder for a bag, the hair for ropes. We used the bones for tools, the horns for dippers and cups, the ribs for sleigh runners, the teeth for necklaces, the spinal bones for dice, even the dung for firewood. Yes, we used every bit of the animal—*pte*, buffalo, was our general store.

But the loss of all these things was not the biggest loss. Not at all. Thinking so is another sign of how the white man is limited to understanding in material terms.

The buffalo came to us as a gift from the Powers, because the people lived in a way that honored the Powers, and the Powers were pleased with them. This is what one of our leaders, Bad Wound, said about it. "The buffalo were given to the Lakotas by Inyan (Stone). They came from the Earth. Their tipi is the Earth. They know all the ceremonies. They dance in their tipi. Where round depressions are on the prairies are where the buffalo danced.

"The spirit of the buffalo stays with the skull until the horns drop off. If the horns are put on the skull, the spirit returns to it. The Earth eats the horns and when they are eaten, the spirit goes to the buffalo tipi in the Earth. The way to the buffalo tipi is far in the west.

"Tatanka—the buffalo god—is like a buffalo bull. He is like a spirit. He is *wakan*."

When the buffalo disappeared, the people were confused. Had we offended the gods? Did we allow our spirits to wander from the right way? The way of the Pipe, the Sun Dance, the Vision Quest, and our other ceremonies? Was our way of life at an end?

This did not mean primarily our physical way of life. Our alliance with the Powers, with Earth, Sky, Stone, and Sun—was all this gone wrong?

And so, as a people, must we perish?

That was the awful fate in the minds of the Mniconjou people that dawn by Wounded Knee Creek. That was the reason for their black despair.

And it was true meaning of the Spirit Dance, and why the dance was so important to us. Wovoka envisioned utopia returned. If the people performed this dance faithfully, the buffalo would come back. The spirits of our departed ancestors would come back. And all would live together in harmony on an Earth that was renewed. In harmony with Earth, with each other, with the great Powers Stone, Sky, Earth, and Sun, and with the Mystery, Wakantanka.

It's not primarily that our material life would be restored, but that the world would be right spiritually.

People without Spirit try to hold life in their desperate hands, but the precious liquid dribbles between their fingers.

Now half the people had given up on the Spirit Dance. The other half clung to it desperately. They wanted to believe in Wovoka's utopia. They wanted to believe in the parts Kicking Bear and Short Bull added to Wovoka's vision, that the dance shirt would protect them against bullets, and white people would soon disappear. To live without belief was to condemn yourself to the death which is worse than death, life without Spirit.

Walking through the village, despair, purposelessness, emptiness washing over my head, I could feel the consequences. All the people feared they were truly doomed. They saw no prospects except for a life with their blood and their spirit draining away every day. They feared that their children would find no red road to walk, and so would get lost in the white man's firewater, as my father did, and I did. They feared they and their children would become husks, bodies without Spirit.

All this has come to pass.

That day some of them grasped with the desperation of the doomed. They would take the last chance, test the dance shirts against the lead in the soldiers' rifles and the Hotchkiss muzzles. If the shirts failed, Wovoka's vision was false. Then they were willing die—they preferred to die. And they would go like gods. Apocalypse.

Wandering through the camp in the last of the darkness, I avoided Blue Crow's lodge, for it was too much to bear. In another lodge headmen were meeting, talking in muted tones. They conferred without their leader, Big Foot, who was in the big wall tent at the edge of the soldier camp, perhaps to be closer to the doctor. I noticed that Horn Cloud was among these councillors. During the time I watched, he listened and did not speak. I did not try to hear what they were saying, for I knew all too well.

In another lodge the medicine man Yellow Bird was painting himself by the light of the center fire. The dark humps on the edges of the lodge were probably members of his family, still sleeping. He rubbed blue paint all over his body, leaving big spots bare. I watched while he covered himself head to toe. He painted slowly, deliberately, with the concentration that attends an important act. Then he filled in the bare spots with yellow paint, so that his body became one large blue background with yellow dots the size of silver dollars. I did not know what the paint meant, but I thought of what it would suggest to the soldiers' minds. *Alien. Primitive. Crazy. Let us rush our civilization forward, away from this black magic; let us hurry to a future of reason and progress. On the way, let us squash these dark fiends.*

I went close to Yellow Bird's face and looked into the eyes of the most intense devotee, among these Mniconjou, of the Spirit Dance. I saw blankness, deadness, like the stone eyes of a statue.

I wandered. I went to the Horn Cloud tipi. Now Horn Cloud the elder had roused his family and was speaking to them as husband, father, head of household. This is what he said.

"I will give you advice. They say it is peace but I am sure there is going to be fighting today. I have been in war all my life, and I know when my heart is growing bitter that there is going to be a fight. I have come to tell you—all my sons—what I want you to do. If one or two Indians go to start trouble first, I don't want you to go with them. If the white people start trouble first, then you can do what you want to—you can die among your own relations in defending them. All you, my dear sons, stand together, and if you die at once among your relations defending them, I will be satisfied. Try to die in front of your relations, the old folks and the little ones, and I will be satisfied if you die trying to help them. Don't get excited. When one or two under the government laws start trouble, they are arrested and taken into court and put in jail, but I don't want any of you to get into such trouble. Stand back until all the whites assail us, and then defend our people. I have come to tell you this as advice before the trouble begins. I want to you heed my warnings."

My heart plunged down, like it was tied to a boulder and flung off a cliff, and an ocean of sadness waited below. Pictures of the carnage to come danced across the screen of my mind like mocking demons. By an intense effort of will I banished these pictures. *To live through the dying when the time comes, that will be more than enough, more than I can bear.*

I went out of the tipi. For some reason I wanted to find the spot in the village that was the very center, an equal distance from the furthest tipis in the great half-moon. When I decided where that point was, I sat down and held my head in my hands. The hidden sun was dispelling the darkness now, bringing a day that was like a thousand million other turns of the Earth around the fiery star. Yet today would change many lives forever. It would kill my ancestors. It would maim, emotionally, the woman who raised me. It would cast my life into ravenShadow. It would cast my people into ravenShadow.

I grieved so dry and bitter I couldn't cry.

I was brought back to that moment, dawn of December 29, 1890, by a bugle blowing reveille.

Soon a crier walked through the camp calling, "Come to council! Come to council!"

With these words began the march to death.

Trembling, at the same time resolute, I stood near Colonel Forsyth as he watched the Big Foot men file into the space in front of Big Foot's tent, just toward the village from the soldier camp. Forsyth looked the way Americans like their military heroes to look: a lion's mane of hair, jutting chin, piercing eyes. He saw his duty clear this morning. His instruction was to disarm Big Foot's people. Forsyth knew this Big Foot was a slippery character. He was on the list of troublemakers compiled by the Indian agents. After promising to come in to Fort Meade, he fooled Sumner on the Cheyenne River and escaped into the Badlands. Yesterday Lieutenant Whitside had been talked out of taking the weapons immediately by one of the half-breed interpreters, Shangreau. But General Brooke's orders were clear. Disarm Big Foot's band. Take care to prevent the escape of any.

Unstated was, "Sumner may have damaged his career with leniency. Whitside was soft yesterday. We need a man who can enforce the will of the U.S. Army on the Sioux." Forsyth made up his mind to be the man to accomplish the primary objective of this military mission—confiscate those guns.

He remembered the rest of General Brooke's orders— "If they fight, destroy them."

I watched the Mniconjou men sit in a big, rough semicircle facing the officers. Horn Cloud was there in the front row, sitting with other headmen. At the west end of the semicircle sat many of the young men, including Horn Cloud's sons Daniel, Joseph, Sherman, and William, with Horn Cloud's oldest son Iron Hail, and his friend White Lance. Blue Crow sat behind the young Horn Cloud men, powerful-looking, somber-faced.

Yellow Bird, blue with big yellow dots from head to toe, sat first in one place, then in another, moving restlessly. Everyone in council except Yellow Bird, both red and white, was bundled thickly against the cold. Yellow Bird wore only a breechcloth, leggings, and headdress.

Yes, medicine man, you look mythic and magical to the Indians. Unfortunately, you look devilish to the whites. O Iya, I see your handiwork here.

During the long talk some men in the half circle came and went, back and forth to the village, as they pleased. The older men looked wary to me, the young men combative. Maybe it's important that most of the older men had earned their war honors, but the younger men were without opportunities, so far.

I sat in front of Big Foot's tent where I could hear the soldiers speak and see the faces of the Indians.

Standing at the front of the half circle with some of his officers and interpreters, Colonel Forsyth gave quiet orders for the deployment of his forces, eight troops of cavalry, 470 officers and men. Plus the thirty Oglala scouts, who were stationed well back, south of the ravine, not to be trusted in case of fighting. Plus the four Hotchkiss guns and their crews on the hill overlooking the camps. Forsyth put two troops, K and B, hard by the council circle, on the western and southern flanks, at the ready. About a third of the A and I Troops were positioned on the north side of the council, about a hundred yards off. The other troops were put further back, but all within a long rifle shot, and instructed to be ready in case of trouble. Forsyth's standing order was, "At the first sound of gunfire, all units fire."

Finally the colonel addressed the men of the Big Foot band. He spoke pleasantly. They must give up their weapons, he said—the Great White Father in Washington required that. They would be compensated for the cost. When the weapons were handed over, the army would provide an escort for the long trip home. They were safe in the hands of their old friends the soldiers, he said. The time of starvation and other trouble was now happily at an end.

To this some Indians responded, "*Washtay!*"—good! But I saw a lot of stiff, stony faces, especially among the young men. Blue Crow kept his face impassive. The Horn Cloud brothers said nothing.

Now the conflict was not just weapons—Forsyth had said the army was going to escort them home. But the Mniconjou wanted to go to Pine Ridge. Many were looking forward to seeing relatives. More important, there was Big Foot's promise to help mediate the disagreements among the Oglala, and his payment of a hundred horses. Forsyth seemed devious, talking friendly and slipping in that they wouldn't be allowed to go see their own relatives.

The Indians talked among themselves about Forsyth's demands. Before long they said they wanted to send two men to confer with Big Foot. The soldiers said okay, and Horn Cloud and another leader went into the wall tent where the chief was lying, followed by the half-breed interpreter Shangreau.

Big Foot was bleeding from the nose now, and looked weak and desperately sick. The two headmen told him what Forsyth had proposed and asked his counsel. "Give them the old guns," Big Foot said. "Keep the good ones." Shangreau put in, "You better give up the guns. You can always buy new guns, but if you lose a man, you can't replace him."

Big Foot only repeated, "Give up the old guns, keep the good ones."

The two headmen went back to the council. Shangreau spoke to an officer, but I didn't hear what he said.

Forsyth now had twenty Indians counted off and ordered them to go to the village and bring back all the weapons they could find. I followed them among the lodges. Some women, I noticed, were loading the wagons for the rest of the journey to Pine Ridge. Children were running and playing among the tipis. Clearly the people were not planning to start trouble, nor really expecting any. The men took a long time, and wandered back one by one, bearing armloads of weapons. I saw that someone had brought Big Foot out now. He was propped up in front of his tent, facing his people. Most of his headmen had moved behind him.

These guns, maybe sixty, were put in two piles, one at each end of the circle, and Forsyth inspected them. I followed him to look. They were old, battered, half-useless guns, not the fine new Winchesters brandished at Porcupine Butte yesterday. Forsyth stiffened and walked like a marionette to the other pile, which told the same story.

His voice sharpened as he spoke to one of the interpreters, Philip Wells. "You tell Big Foot that yesterday at the time of surrender his Indians were well armed, and that I am sure he is deceiving me."

The warriors who searched the tipis repeated to Big Foot that these were all the weapons they could find. Almost too softly to be heard, Big Foot told the interpreter the same.

Bristling, Forsyth consulted with Lieutenant Whitside.

The tension was electric enough almost to warm the freezing, early morning air. The troops were pressed so close to the Indians, they were almost in their faces. The Indians feigned calm, but no one was calm. White and red were like two male dogs, sniffing each other, the spinal hairs on each critter rising, tails stiffening, the fight nearing.

I watched Big Foot. He knew there were more guns, and many were those good Winchesters. If they weren't in the village, they were right here, on the men in the council, under their blankets. Maybe, another time, this conciliator, this politician could have negotiated successfully. He could have said to Wells, "Let's sit and be calm and have some coffee and a smoke and talk about this." Meanwhile the older men could have soothed the feelings of the younger. But today Big Foot was feeble.

I looked at Forsyth. Even whispering to Whitside, he was agitated, his speech almost violent. He had become a man impelled to do more than complete a mission. He had to make a point. He was in a contest of wills, and he would show the savages, by God.

When Forsyth turned back to the assembly, he spoke fateful words. "Since you won't bring the weapons yourselves, I will detail a squad of soldiers to search the village."

The Indian men rumbled and grumbled. Big Foot appealed for them to keep calm.

In fact Forsyth detailed two groups of soldiers. I didn't follow them to the village, but I heard one of the officers, Captain Wallace, admonish his soldiers to be courteous. They disappeared toward the village and were gone a long time.

In the circle the strangeness began. I saw the officers of K and B Troops, the ones almost on top of the council, talk quietly one at a time to some soldiers, who were standing maybe four, five, or six feet apart. Then the individual soldier, at will, would raise his Springfield, aim it at the head of a nearby Indian, grin devilishly, and click the hammer on an empty chamber.

Indians twisted and dived out of the way. They shouted at their tormentors. Others cried, "Take courage! Take courage!"

About this time, at the west end of the circle, Yellow Bird began to pray aloud. He lifted his arms to the sky and in the voice of supplication asked the Grandfathers to take pity on the people and come to their aid.

Hammers clicked on empty chambers. Soldiers laughed mockingly, and sneered.

Indians writhed, and cursed the soldiers. Someone cried loudly, "We are not children to be talked to like this! We are a people in this world!"

Yellow Bird started dancing, a shuffle step, back and forth, back and forth. His praying elevated to singing, high and shrill, picturing now the divine intervention he sought.

Forsyth demanded of Philip Wells, "What is that man saying?"

Wells turned toward Yellow Bird.

"What's he saying?" repeated Forsyth.

Wells brushed him off with a hand. "I'll let you know anything you should know."

Forsyth barked "All right!" at Wells and walked away.

The Indians were talking angrily now, and gesticulating. Blue Crow pulled his blankets over his head and left only one eye showing, and many young men did the same. That's our traditional way of warning, "I'm getting pissed off!"

Now Yellow Bird dived deeper into his invocation. He danced in a circle around all the assembled Indians, twisting and muttering. He scooped up handfuls of dust and cast them in a circle, over the soldiers' heads and the heads of his own people. White and red men alike were transfixed by his gesticulations.

"Ha! Ha! Ha! Ha!" Yellow Bird cried. "Take courage!" he shouted at the young men at his end of the circle. "There are lots of soldiers about us and they have lots of bullets, but they cannot harm you. Their bullets will not go toward you, but will pass over the prairie. If they do go toward you, they will not penetrate you. As you just saw me throw up the dust and it floated away, so will the soldiers' bullets float away harmlessly over the prairie."

"*Hau!*" shouted Blue Crow vigorously, and other the young men cried "*Hau!*" Around the edges of their blankets their dance shirts showed. I saw that my great-grandfather was wearing a dance shirt. The young Horn Cloud men wore none—they had no protection from the bullets.

Yellow Bird kept circling, kept dancing, kept hurling words at the young men.

I looked at the faces of the soldiers of B Troop, those stationed nearest Yellow Bird. They were seeing their nightmares come to life. Here were a hundred savages, probably hiding repeating rifles under their blankets, getting more angry and hostile by the moment. And they were egged on by a crazy primitive, a mad, half-naked figure in blue paint, performing a grotesque and demented dance to his dark gods.

Now Forsyth called to Wells, "You'd better get out of there. It's starting to look dangerous."

"In a minute, Colonel." Wells spoke quietly to one of the older men, Big Foot's brother. From the body language I gathered Wells asked the man to help quiet the young warriors, and was refused.

Now I heard an uproar from the village. I put myself at the Blue Crow lodge and took a look. A soldier was trying to frisk Elk Medicine. Then I saw—it was the pale sentry from last night. He kept grabbing the edge of the blanket she was wearing and trying to open it up. She slapped his hand and snapped in Lakota, "Keep your hands off me."

Well across the village, Wallace was walking around talking soothingly to everyone, chucking children under the chin, and the like.

Now Elk Medicine switched to English. "I said, Keep your goddamn hands off—"

Her blanket came off in both the sentry's hands. He stood there looking dumb, holding the scarlet blanket. Nothing was under it except my great-grandmother, looking very cross. Her belly filled out her deerskin dress far too well for her to be concealing any rifle.

She slapped the sentry full in the face.

A passing corporal of middle age said in an Irish accent, "You undress 'em, lad, you should look for sweeter things than that."

Elk Medicine ripped her blanket out of the sentry's hands. Then she held back the tipi flap and said, "You wanna search our beds? The only gun in there will be yours. Our men got better weapons to take to bed."

The corporal cackled.

The sentry stepped awkwardly into the tipi.

Other women were having their persons and their belongings pawed, and they resented it. The soldiers were frisking the old men, too.

Wallace barked at a couple of soldiers, "Remember courtesy!"

I went back to the council ground, and beheld something bizarre. A big strapping Indian was stalking Wells, every step. His blood rising, Wells turned to face the man. The Indian tried to slip behind him. Wells faced him. The Indian tried again. Now Wells planted his rifle butt, clapped his hands on the muzzle, and pivoted toward the Indian, glaring, whatever direction the Indian went.

Blue Crow gave the strapping man a look and a negative shake of the head. The man stood to one side.

Captain Wallace, back from the village, slipped over to Joseph Horn Cloud, who spoke English. He said softly, "Joseph, you better go over to the women and tell them to let the wagons go and saddle up their horses and be ready to skip. There's going to be trouble."

Joseph gave Wallace a startled look, turned, and padded swiftly toward the tipis. The men of K troop stopped him—Forsyth had ordered an end to men coming and going from the council. But Wallace nodded to the troopers and they let Joseph through. He hurried into the village.

Wells came to Forsyth and said about Yellow Bird, "That man is making mischief."

Yellow Bird was dancing all the way around the circle, throwing dust in the air. The colonel and interpreter walked over to the medicine man and ordered him to sit down. Big Foot's brother answered, "He'll sit down when he finishes the circle."

Forsyth and Wells backed off reluctantly.

When he completed the circle, Yellow Bird sat down.

Suddenly a whine stopped. It was like I'd been hearing it unconsciously and it had risen gradually in intensity. Now came an eerie quiet.

The two details returned from the village, and I saw the weapons they bore were a joke. Yes, they'd found a few decent guns. But mostly it was kitchen knives, hatchets for chopping kindling, bows and arrows, and the like. Though the faces of the Mniconjou were stony, the eyes of Blue Crow and some other young men danced with mocking laughter.

Now Forsyth fumed. He paced back and forth. Finally he said to Wells, "Tell them each man must submit to inspection. I don't want to have to search them by force. Ask them to come forward to here individually, man by man, take off their blankets, and put any weapons on the ground."

Wells told them, and added his own harshness to Forsyth's words. Part Santee Sioux and part white, Wells felt superior to full-bloods. His voice, his whole manner spoke his arrogance.

Still, some of the older men greeted his words with, "*Hau!*"

About twenty older men walked to the front, near Big Foot's tent. One by one they dropped their blankets. No weapons were revealed.

Wells repeated Forsyth's order and the young men, sullen and grumbling, lined up for the check. Blue Crow was well back in the line, and I couldn't read his expression—his Winchester had to be under his blanket. Horn Cloud's sons, except for Joseph, stood in the middle, looking miserable.

Yellow Bird started throwing his words at the young men again. "Take courage! Be ready for what is coming! The soldiers' bullets will not penetrate us." Now he pulled his dance shirt over his naked torso. He glared his defiance and strutted his invincibility at the young warriors.

On the first three young men the soldiers found two rifles, one a Winchester, and a bunch of ammunition. They took the rifles and dumped the cartridges into a sergeant's hat.

Yellow Bird began to scoop up dust and let it drift between his fingers to the ground.

The lieutenant in command of K Troop said in a low, controlled voice to his soldiers, "Be ready. There is going to be trouble."

The men of K Troop were more than ready. Their bodies were twisted like wire with tension, their nerves screaming. Fear and rage built in them like lightning in black clouds.

A young Indian named Black Coyote stood up now and jumped around holding his rifle with two hands above his head. Black Coyote was deaf. He yelled in Lakota, "This is *my* gun. I paid a lot of money. Nobody's going to get this gun without paying for it. Nobody." He repeated these words over and over, gyrating about like a crazy man.

Blue Crow and several others in the circle talked among themselves and then got up and went toward Black Coyote. He was a wild young man, a bad influence, and he hadn't been able to hear any of the talk. They intended to calm him down and explain to him in sign language why men were giving up their guns.

Before the Indians got to Black Coyote, some soldiers slipped up behind the deaf man, grabbed him, and tried to wrest the rifle out of his hands. Black Coyote fought.

Just at this moment Yellow Bird grabbed a handful of dust and flung it in the air.

The rifle tilted, muzzle to the sky.

Somehow it went off.

The shot echoed through the valley of Wounded Knee Creek.

I saw knowledge on Blue Crow's face. On the faces of the Horn Cloud sons. On the face of every man in the circle.

At point-blank range red eye looked into white eye, white into red.

The Indians hesitated. The soldiers hesitated.

The invitation to horror was recognized. It was accepted. It was welcomed.

One eternal moment ticked past.

Apocalypse came as the rage of Thunderstorm against Wind Storm.

A half dozen young Indians threw off their blankets and brought up their rifles.

The soldiers of K Troop fired a volley into the mass of Indians on the council ground. Then their lieutenant drew his revolver and screamed, "Fire! Fire on them!"

The men of Troop B, also hard against the Indian men in council, fired.

Indian men with and without dance shirts fell, or stood to shoot again.

Divine and demonic forces came screaming onto the field. In ancient enmity Wind Storm and Thunderstorm howled and raged. The cosmic energies crashed and boomed, and the merely human was destroyed. I could almost hear the mocking laugh of Iya.

Instantly dust, smoke, and din half-blinded and half-deafened everyone. Soldier and warrior shot it out at close quarters through the murk and haze. When Indians missed, some of the shots ripped through the village. Women, children, old men, dogs, and horses burst into an uproar.

Wild shots from the soldiers ripped across the council ground and hit other soldiers.

Big Foot was propped up on one elbow. Immediately an officer and an enlisted man shot him in the upper chest, as though fulfilling an assignment. His daughter, who was standing by the sick man's tent, dashed forward to her father. The same officer shot her between the shoulder blades.

The headmen sitting behind Big Foot took one of the first blasts from the Springfields. Bodies flew in wild directions, fell in agonized postures. Among those never to get up was Horn Cloud.

Captain Wallace ran to his station at the rear of K Troop. As he got there, a bullet knocked the top of his head off.

Colonel Forsyth ran to the top of the knoll, perhaps to get a better view, perhaps to be near the cannons.

With Indian and white so mixed up, hand to hand, the Hotchkiss guns could not fire.

I went to Blue Crow. He was kneeling, working his Winchester quickly and beautifully, shooting soldiers.

The strapping Indian who stalked Philip Wells now pulled a well-honed knife, raised it above his head with both hands, and drove it at the interpreter's face. Wells fell to one knee and blocked the knife with his rifle. His eyes grew with horror—the sharp point missed his forehead but slashed downward and sliced his nose nearly off.

The Indian drove the knife downward again. On his back, Wells once more blocked it with his rifle. When the Indian pulled the blade back, Wells smashed him in the head with the muzzle.

While the Indian was stunned, Wells jumped up and shot him in the side. A corporal ran up and finished the warrior with a shot in the back. Instantly the corporal fell to a shot from a soldier across the council ground.

Drenched in his own blood, mad with pain, in shock, Wells ran for the trader's wagon. On the way he grabbed his nose, hanging by a thin bridge of skin, and tried to tear it off.

"My God, man," cried an officer, "don't do that! That can be saved!"

On the council ground, Wind Storm and Thunderstorm wrought pandemonium.

Seeing his father fall and Big Foot killed, Iron Hail charged the soldiers of B Troop. The swirl of smoke and dust attacked everyone's eyes, ears, noses. Dewey could see little but the shiny brass buttons of the soldiers' uniforms, and hurried toward those. A rifle went off next to his ear, deafening him. Iron Hail grabbed the rifle and twisted it away from the soldier. Then he thrust his knife into the man's chest. The soldier clutched Iron Hail by the throat, and the Mniconjou drove his knife home, near the heart. The soldier crumpled. Iron Hail stabbed the man in the kidneys over and over, and over and over, until he stopped moving.

Seizing the soldier's rifle, Iron Hail sprinted between the tipis toward the ravine. The village was a chaos of the screaming, the dying, and the dead. He was hit by a bullet in the arm, and as he leapt into the ravine, another struck him in the groin. Stunned, he looked back. Soldiers were rushing the ravine. He fired, reloaded, and fired several times.

The rifle fragmented in his hands. Realizing it had been hit by a bullet, he threw it away and hauled himself painfully to the bottom of the ravine.

On the council ground the magazines of those Indians left fighting were empty. Some red men dashed to the east, toward the creek. Troop G was a hundred yards off, firing. Most red men ran crazily toward the village. On the way they grappled one-on-one with soldiers. When they could, they seized weapons and fled.

In the council area now sprawled more than twenty of their fellows, dead, wearing dance shirts or not, indiscriminantly. Ringing these bodies lay more than thirty dead and wounded soldiers.

O, those Winchester repeating rifles!

I saw Blue Crow, miraculously unhurt, bolt through the K Troop line, within reach of two soldiers, and sprint toward the village. *He is going to get Elk Medicine and run ... to the ravine?*

I wanted to cheer and vomit at the same time.

In the pandemonium on the council ground, the surrounding units did not shoot, the Hotchkiss crews did not fire, for fearing of hitting their comrades. They waited helpless, their fury mounting.

When the Indians fled in all directions, a dam holding back the guns of the other troops and Hotchkiss crews broke. Their fire raged down like lightning.

From the northwest end of the village the pony herd stampeded northwest, along a road. A group of women and children piled onto wagons and followed the ponies, right across the front of Troop E. Seeing that they were not combatants, the officers yelled for the men to hold their fire against the people, but to knock down the ponies.

The Hotchkiss guns took aim on the village. Each Hotchkiss could be fired fifty times a minute, and each shell flung shrapnel in every direction.

Blue Crow and other warriors dashed around the village, crying to their families to break for the ravine. Most Indians there were women, children, and old men, running frantically in every direction.

Elk Medicine trotted toward the ravine, herding the children with her hands and her voice. She kept looking back toward where Corn Woman lay....

Scurrying around the village, Blue Crow was stopped by a pile of rags, half-familiar, a tattered ... body. Face down. Slowly now, gently, he turned the face to one side and looked at the profile of his wife, the mother of his children. He started to turn the body over, so he could see her fully one more time. He put his hands on her ribs. He drew them back in horror, and knew that body would not turn.

Elk Medicine pushed the children toward the ravine and sprinted back toward the village. *I cannot lose sister and husband both.*

Blue Crow jumped up screaming at the Hotchkiss crews. He flung wild shots at the batteries on the hill. He emptied his Winchester at them, and then hurled the most awful words he could think of.

Elk Medicine reached for her husband, screaming sense at him.

At that moment a Hotchkiss shell hit him square in the belly. It made a hole gaping wide enough for me to put my arm through.

My great-grandfather stood there for a long moment, and then slowly, stiffly, limb by limb, tottered to the ground.

Elk Medicine wailed her way to the ravine.

I felt like my skin was aflame.

I stood there in the village, bereft. Shells blew holes in the earth around me, and in my heart. They tossed human beings—what were once human beings—in the air and let them *clomp* to the ground. They tore the tipis to shreds. They knocked tripods and cook pots and medicine bags helter-skelter. They ripped flesh until bodies became odds and ends, scattered strangely, absurd remains of the games of evil gods.

Then the batteries turned their attention to clumps of people running away.

Having survived the hell on the council ground—somehow—Yellow Bird now got into a tipi on the edge of the silent village. Troops K and B, still in their positions, stood nearby. The medicine man slit the canvas and, one by one, took potshots at soldiers.

Some saw where the fire was coming from. "I'll get the son of a bitch out of there," yelled one private of K Troop, and ran at the tipi waving a knife. Yellow Bird shot him in the stomach.

"My God, he has shot me. I am killed, I am killed." The private staggered back toward his outfit and fell, dead.

The soldier's comrades raked the tipi with rifle fire. From the hill two Hotchkiss shells made direct hits on the lodge.

Still Yellow Bird lived. *Their bullets will not penetrate you.* His sight searched out targets. His rage blazed out the barrel.

Outside I saw angry troopers push a bale of hay against the tipi on the medicine man's blind side. They lit it. Soon flame crackled up the canvas to where the lodgepoles jutted out. Black smoke smothered the lodge. I watched for Yellow Bird to come bursting out, into a hail of lead. He did not come. He chose to stay inside. *The medicine of your dance shirt does not protect you against suffocation, or burning.*

I did not need my spirit sight to know what happened to Yellow Bird within.

Now, suddenly, the whirlwind seemed to slow. Up to that moment the clash had been immense, titanic, worthy of elemental Powers. But here came a small lull, a slacking. Most Indians alive had made it to the half-shelter of the ravine, though some were in the creek or had fled elsewhere. Occasional shots came from the ravine, but nothing forceful.

With what mental strength I had left, I hurled a message at the mind of the officers. *Pull your soldiers back, out of rifle range. Send an interpreter to talk to the Indians. You can end this horror.*

But Iya was rampant on this ground, and his malice is lava that boils, bubbles, and erupts prodigiously.

He delighted in the white people's four centuries of fear and hatred of Indians. Perhaps it was he who taught them to use "Indian fighter" as a term of honor. It was he who kept the acrid bitterness of the defeat at the Little Big Horn alive in the hearts of the officers here today. It was he who taught whites, from the beginning, to give their stories of Indians a dark and demonic face.

Iya needed to give no help to the rage of these Indian people. They had seen their relatives killed, their children shot, their homes blown to bits. Worst of all, they had seen their dream of a future, their beautiful picture of an ideal world returned, smashed to smithereens.

They were unspeakably sorrowful, unspeakably angry. One warrior said later that if he had eaten a soldier at this particular moment, it would not have satisfied his rage.

Therefore the evil god Wind Storm now ruled the killing ground: The batteries of artillery aimed their shells at the ravine.

Here huddled most of the survivors—warriors, old men, women, and children crouched in fear. The shells sent them scurrying.

Some ran along the ravine in both directions. Others bunched under an overhang, where the ravine made a sharp turn.

One big bunch burst out of the ravine and ran south, away from the fighting and toward the road to Pine Ridge. But this put them in front of the guns of C and D Troops. Stationed on the far side of the ravine, these soldiers had fallen back away from the shells, driving the Oglala scouts further from the action. When the officers saw the people run out of the ravine—Indian men, women, and children mixed up—they yelled, "Commence firing!"

One officer wrote later that the soldiers "fired rapidly, but it seemed only a few seconds till there was not a living thing before us; warriors, squaws, children, ponies, dogs—for they were all mixed together—went down before that unaimed fire. I believe over thirty bodies were found on our front."

Meanwhile some of the scouts dropped into the ravine and started carrying surviving relatives to safety on the hilltops.

Wears Eagle despaired of finding Iron Hail, or anyone else in the family. Near the rim of the ravine she frantically dug a small hole in the earth. She intended to put Wet Feet in it.

Elk Medicine crouched beneath the north rim, and pulled the two remaining children to her. Her sister dead, her husband dead. Her eyes were vacant with death.

In a few minutes a Hotchkiss shell exploded on the floor of the ravine below them, and shrapnel ate the air in every direction.

The two children died in her arms. Elk Medicine felt a stabbing pain in the groin.

She held the children. She held them long past the time she knew they weren't breathing.

She was far beyond thinking. Yet something within her, perhaps an instinct, perhaps the pulse of a person-to-be, reminded her. *Save the child within.*

She lurched to her feet, and the pain stabbed her. She grabbed her thigh near her elk medicine, near where the unborn child would emerge, must emerge.

She did not scream. She did not make a sound. She stood there. After a long time she thought to staunch the bleeding with her skirt. Then she staggered down the ravine, she didn't know why or where.

Iron Hail limped along the ravine with his two wounds, calling, "Wears Eagle! Wears Eagle!" He heard no answer. In the din no ears could have heard an answer.

I looked for his wife and saw her. She was still there under the rim, where she'd been digging a place for Wet Feet. Below her right eyelid was a crusty red hole. The little boy, a few weeks old, nursed at his dead mother's breast.

"Wears Eagle! Wears Eagle!" cried Iron Hail, wandering on.

Now soldiers ran to both rims and fired down directly at whatever appeared to stir—man, woman, child, or play doll.

An old man shoved a rifle at Iron Hail. With two others he climbed the south rim and charged some soldiers. His comrades fell, and Iron Hail was driven back.

He stumbled down the ravine in a chaos of flying bullets, dust, smoke, and the screams of the wounded.

In the haze he suddenly saw a woman's figure staggering, about to fall but still on her feet. Suddenly he realized, *Mother!*

He ran to her. She was bleeding, walking like a drunk, swinging a pistol wildly. She said to her son, "Pass by me. I am going to fall down now."

Suddenly bullets from both rims racked her body, and she fell dead.

Both mother and father dead!

He crawled, limped, and staggered on down the ravine, dazed, stunned, maddened. He cried, "Take courage! Take courage!"

Suddenly appeared in the murk his brother William, collapsed up on the bank next to his friend White Lance. Both were shot. William tried to speak but couldn't. He bled from a wound in the chest.

Iron Hail and White Lance helped William to the bottom of the ravine, and he wheezed, "Shake hands with me, I am dizzy now."

"Take courage!" cried Iron Hail. "Our father told us it is better that all of us should die together than we should die separately at different times!"

William clumped hard to the ground and sat, his eyes glazed.

Now the fire came thick as hail from the sky of Wind Storm and Thunderstorm.

Surely the word *terrible* was invented for this moment and the ones that followed.

Iron Hail dragged William to the overhang, which gave the best remaining protection. He and others crawled to the top and shot.

A corporal in one of the batteries saw that the overhang was the source of what little return fire still came. "Roll this gun!" he ordered his fellows. "Get 'er down there!"

The batterymen rolled the Hotchkiss downhill. A captain hollered for them to come back, but the corporal ignored him. They fired at the edge of the overhang.

Still return fire came.

"Get closer!" yelled the corporal. The men pushed the gun nearly to the ravine. A lieutenant ran down the hill yelling at them, but a bullet stopped him.

The gunners fired again.

Still fire came. Indian bullets tore the batterymen's clothing. Their bullets bored holes in the gun's big wheels. One shot knocked a live shell out of the corporal's hand. Somehow the shell did not explode.

"Closer!" bellowed the corporal.

Crying "Remember Custer!" and "Remember the Little Big Horn!" the gunners pushed the cannon point-blank to the edge of the ravine.

At the rate of nearly one round a second, they shelled the ravine and the overhang itself.

When other artillerymen yelled for them to come back, they hollered, "Someone bring us a cool gun!"

They pummeled the overhang with their shells.

It collapsed on the Indians.

Men, women, and children squirted in every direction. Their last shelter was gone. Bullets and Hotchkiss shells hailed on them.

A bullet shrieked past Iron Hail's head and whacked into a woman's back. Her face brightened, she laughed out loud, sagged to her knees, and died.

I saw other incidents of horror, so many that even today I cannot bear to write them down.

Now, in this storm of gunfire, these dying people sent up their sacred death songs. The sound was wild, barbarous, heroic. Each song was grief and acceptance in one.

All together the voices rose to the Powers as one great wail. It was as though a thousand great bells rang out at once, and every leaf of every tree shrieked, and the rocks of the mountains themselves cried out in anguish.

The anguish was not only for themselves and their dying relatives, but for a people, and that people's way of living, and their dream.

I wept, and wept, and wept.

As the songs rose stronger and stronger, my eyes dried. I entered the realm of sorrow that is beyond weeping.

Iron Hail was one of those few Mniconjou who survived the horror at the overhang. He scrambled out of the ravine, by luck hitting a spot that had no soldiers. Blind with pain, he staggered across flat ground.

And thus came Joseph, his brother, a ghostly figure materializing impossibly in the haze of dust and smoke. Earlier, when Captain Wallace told Joseph to warn the women and children and get away, Joseph went to the village, and delivered that warning. While he was gone, the fighting erupted. Now, returned to help his family, he boosted Iron Hail onto a horse and led him away.

Deliverance often appears as miracle.

In the ravine, only faint stirrings of life.

The rank smell on the wind was death.

About that time, far too late, a thought struck the half-blood Philip Wells. *More people, red and white, might survive this awful day.* He walked to the edge of the ravine, his nose still swinging on a bridge of skin, and called in Lakota, "All of you who are still alive, get up and come on over! You will not be molested or shot anymore!"

One by one they emerged, walking and crawling. As they approached the soldiers, many still cast their death songs into the winter air. Some soldiers walked forward to help the afflicted.

Then Wells walked to the council ground, strewn with red and white bodies. He called out, "These white people came to save you, and you have brought death on yourselves. Still the white people are merciful to save the wounded enemy when he is harmless, so if some of you are alive, raise your heads. I am a man of your own blood who is talking to you."

Perhaps a dozen figures began to struggle up from the ground.

From the west edge of the ravine came a burst of gunfire from E Troop. These soldiers had not heard the call for truce.

Colonel Forsyth, the officer in command, stalked down off the Hotchkiss gun hill, through the wreckage of the village, past mutilated bodies, through carnage, to the ravine. When he shouted his order, the screech in his voice gave him away. "Stop it!" he yelled. "For God's sake! Stop shooting at them!"

But the soldiers stopped only slowly. Here and there shots split the air; other flesh was savaged. People hidden in a clump of brush were shot down like dogs. Another group at the head of the ravine came out only after several Oglala scouts talked to them for half an hour, and the soldiers backed off completely.

An Indian woman was found three miles away, shot in the back.

On and on went the slaughter, away from the central area. Most of the Mniconjou fighting men had died on the council ground or in the ravine, trying to defend their relations, a warrior's death. Now few but women, children, and old men were left alive. The troopers tracked fleeing Indians across the plain, into brush, into ditches, over hilltops. There they took aim at cold, stunned, terrified people and slaughtered them. Skulls were hammered with rifle butts, stomachs slashed with sabers, dead bodies riddled with bullets. The butchery went on for hours, into the afternoon.

The energies of killing, once aroused fully, subside slowly.

I avoided looking into the hearts of the soldiers. I knew what was there, and it made me ashamed to be a human being.

A fleeing woman tried to protect two children not her own. A mounted trooper caught her and shot the two children out of her arms. Then he reloaded and shot the woman. While she pretended to be dead, he lifted her skirt with his saber, looked, and rode on.

Again: A woman sat rocking a baby. A soldier tore it from her arms and shot it. The woman leaped for the baby. The soldier clubbed her in the back of the head with his pistol, put his boot on her throat, and shot her four times.

I moved back to the village, to where the community once was, where the people once made a circle of life. Fires still smoldered. Bodies were flung everywhere, as by a malicious god-giant. They lay on their backs, on their faces, and in great piles. They were hacked, contorted, mangled. Their mouths opened to the sky, arms and legs fixed in excruciating gestures of protest. Dead mothers held the corpses of infants. Old men and women reached forth, their hands as empty as their eyes. The smell of burned flesh twisted my guts.

Later Sidney Bird, one of our elders, said, "The hearts of the white men who executed the deed were full of evil. What else would compel them to behave so outrageously?"

Yes, evil.

Iya, the ancient Evil One, Wind Storm—he blew the evil in their hearts from embers to conflagration.

Which does not balm my grief.

Which did not ease my hatred.

All my relations.

Those words felt like gall to me. Yes, all creatures are my relations—all two-leggeds, four-leggeds, wingeds, swimmers, crawlers, and the rooted, all sentient beings, even the flowing waters and the stones and the star people. But that day I could not bear to say it, not about white people.

I hated them. I hated you.

⚜ ⚜ ⚜

WIN BLEVINS

I flailed for Sallee's hand. Plez clasped mine in one of his and snapped the tape player off with the other.

Up through the tunnel in the altar I came. I gasped my way into this world like a fish flopping onto the bank.

His face looked grave. "Are you okay?"

I breathed. Then I whispered, "I'm in a rage."

Sallee sat up in her sleeping bag, rubbing her eyes.

Plez took that in for a moment. "Tell us," he said.

I kept my eyes closed tight and hard against the evils of the world and there in the darkness, in the nether regions of the small Catholic church that could absolve nothing, I told Plez and Sallee what I saw on these grounds a hundred years ago. So as not to wake Emile and Chup, and so as not to agitate myself, I murmured low. The words alone, half-whispered, were dreadful enough.

"You must go back again!" he said softly.

"No!" I cried.

"Better for you," he said.

He reached out his hand. I put mine up to block it. His eyes smiled at me. He clicked the cassette player on.

A SEARCH FOR MIRACLES

I floated into a sky, perfectly clear, perfectly blue. An empty sky far, far away, cleansed by interstellar winds.

I'm lost. I've never seen this place.

Desperately I looked around for Raven. I had not seen him, he had not been beside me for a long time.

At that moment Raven filled the sky. He was huge, he made a mountain look petite, he dominated the sky and took up maybe half the range of my vision. He appeared as Thunderbird often does, breast to the front, wings opened to the side, head turned to the left beak and eye seen in profile.

He was black. Blacker than tar, blacker than pitch, blacker than black-black—he was a vibrant, pulsating, eternal black.

A thrill of darkness ran through me.

Raven turned white. Utterly white. Glistening, gleaming white, whiter than the snows of unclimbed Himalayas, vaster, softer, more radiant, more inviting.

Nothing changed but his color.

And in a blink there was nothing but the sky.

I floated lightly to the ground in the valley of the Mniconjou dead. A few flakes of snow drifted light and feathery beside me. The night was dark, the clouds low and threatening.

Earlier tonight, the night of the killing, new snow fell heavily, and froze everything in place, as though preserving it for posterity.

I was shocked that no one was there to bury the bodies. Then I remembered what the books said. The contract for burying was given to civilians. They didn't come for five days because they were haggling over the price per corpse. When at last the detail showed up, they dug a mass grave on the Hotchkiss cannon's knoll, thereafter known as Cemetery Hill, and interred 146 bodies: eighty-four men and boys, forty-four women, and eighteen children.

Many more Mniconjou dragged themselves away from Wounded Knee and died elsewhere. The bodies of others were taken away by their relatives. My people believe that as many as three hundred perished in the massacre.

Suddenly I felt revolted by myself. I knew I was floating to avoid being on the Earth, truly seeing the death spread before me, smelling it, knowing it. Immediately I forced myself to the council ground.

The scene of carnage looked like a field where men have been felling dead trees; bodies like logs scattered everywhere, with bare limbs sticking up at grotesque angles. Big Foot sat half-reclining, his trunk sticking above the white snow.

No, don't punish yourself. It was no use to look at one after another of these contorted bodies and grimacing faces, to wallow in horror. But I didn't know what I did want, why I had come.

I wandered. I stumbled through the ruined village. I stood at the edge of the ravine. The merciful snow spared me the details of the vast tapestry of death woven by Iya, Demon, and other gods who bring evil to Earth. I could feel the abyss, and it was in the pit of my stomach.

I wandered to the ravine. I had last seen Elk Medicine staggering down the ravine to the east. I eased into the ravine and followed her. The scores of bodies near the overhang, I had no need to check these—she'd been further along. Through the dark I walked. I felt glad that I was a spirit, and could move among these bodies, this rampaging death, without touching them, without corporeal intimacy. And I felt ashamed of that feeling.

I wandered. When I saw human-shaped lumps, I made sure the clothing was not Elk Medicine's. I avoided faces.

I wandered through the vasty night, not knowing where I was going or why. Any sign of her passage would have been covered by the snow. I checked every body I saw. I listened for the cry of a baby, the cry that would be my grandmother, Unchee, Janey Running. I felt like a man rummaging for treasure in a garbage dump.

In the morning the carrion feeders would be here, the ravens, the vultures, the eagles.

I heard Raven call across a great distance. First I thought, *You were not with me today, you did not guide me through the horror.*

Raven was away, was somewhere else, and did not reply. But quietly and clearly, without words, he said, *You will not find Elk Medicine there.*

I knew where Raven was and what I would find. I climbed out of the ravine and strode back to the village. It was a charred forest of lodge poles holding up nothing, half-fallen, or splintered on the ground. In the devastation I could not remember where the body would be. I looked around the village, getting oriented in the dark. I felt a sharp fear—*I will never be able to find Blue Crow.*

Raven called without words, *Over here.*

I saw his black shape perched on the shards of a wagon, wheels splayed from a fractured axle.

When I stepped behind the wagon, I saw myself.

I caught myself in the mistake, and shuddered.

I saw Blue Crow.

I wondered how, in my spirit form, I could get the snow off his face. I had a thought. I blew gently, and the snow swirled away. His countenance did not look serene, or angry, or surprised. It had no expression, was simply blank.

I looked at his chest, near the spot I did not want to see ever again. He wore a plain deerskin shirt, having thrown his blanket off somewhere. His Winchester, loose in his grip, propped itself against one hip. Someone would steal it tomorrow.

I looked at his features, which were mine. At his shoulders and chest, which were mine. I wanted to hold him. *Thank you.* My heart flowed with love for him, where it has often been dry for myself. *Thank you for being born of woman. Thank you for bringing your spirit into flesh and bearing its afflictions. Thank you for loving your children. Thank you for giving me life.*

A memory came to me, and it jolted. Way back in Seattle, Delphine, Daniel, and Li Ming took me to a movie I didn't want to see, called *Virgin Spring*. It was a story set in medieval Europe, about the virgin daughter of a local squire. She rides her horse some miles toward the church, bearing an offering. But some goatherds, ruffians, rape her and kill her. When her father discovers the deed, he takes revenge on the herders. Then he rides out to find his daughter's body. She's laying there in her white dress, with her pale face framed beautifully by her golden hair. He lifts her bloodied head, and a miracle springs forth. Water gushes from the place it laid. Miracle and the promise of redemption.

I knelt by Blue Crow's head. I pictured the father in the movie lifting the mortal skull and opening the way for the miraculous waters to gush forth.

As a spirit I had no hands to lift Blue Crow.

Besides, I knew there were no miracles, no redemption. Not here, not yet. Not for Wounded Knee.

This time I grabbed for Sallee like a man surfacing desperately from deep water.

She clasped my arm, and Plez clicked off the recorder.

"What did you see?" he asked softly.

I told them about Blue Crow, everything.

He said to me seriously, "Black Elk said the hoop will be broken and the tree will not flower until the seventh generation. The seventh generation. That's now. The time for miracles is now."

My faith in miracles felt shaken.

Finally I said, "I don't know what happened to Elk Medicine."

He pondered and hmmmed. "That can wait. For now, get some sleep. We have ceremonies to perform in the morning, and miracles to work."

SITANKA WOKIKSUYE

They woke us up before dawn in the church basement, the women. Upstairs, there was a mass to celebrate. Down here, there was coffee to make, Styrofoam cups and packets of white sugar and nondairy creamer to set out, packages of donuts to put on the tables in their plastic bags. The women were quiet, and I think they were surprised to see us, though they didn't let their faces show it, out of politeness.

Plez sat up and looked around cheerfully. "Room service!" he exclaimed.

Chup made grumbling noises from the depths of his sleeping bag.

I sat up next to Sallee and met her eyes. "Today is the day!" I said. I felt ... everything on the color wheel of feeling.

Sallee walked up the stairs and saw that mass was being conducted in the sanctuary behind us. I wanted no part of that, even if most of the worshipers were Lakota. *I don't associate with Christian churches whatsoever.*

We stepped outside, and I gasped. The cold felt like a whack in the face. Somehow I'd thought, when the ride was over ... We scurried right back in. Later Ian got the Porcupine radio station, KILI, in his truck and said they were reporting the high today would be thirty below.

The five of us consumed coffee and donuts like we'd ridden twenty miles in that weather. We went outside. We jumped back in and ate more coffee and donuts. Finally, somewhere after ten, we had to face it.

Emile, Plez, and I headed out. As I walked around the fenced gravesite, I couldn't help looking down at where the village stood, and seeing what the gunners saw as they sighted. The distance was incredibly short, maybe forty steps to the nearest tipis, and the elevation of about twenty-five feet gave every advantage. I shuddered.

We found our man with the trailered horses below the hill, right where the cavalry pitched their tents a hundred years ago. In a few moments we were bridled, saddled, and ready.

"Where is everybody?" said Plez irritably. We'd had two hundred or so riders. Less than half were here now.

"Pisser," I said.

"Maybe they're up there on foot," said Emile. "Not torturing the horses any more."

The leaders angled slowly up the hill behind the staff, which had led us all the way, and the rest of us filed behind them. As we came, Bill Horn Cloud gave an invocation over a bullhorn.

When we topped the hill, the harsh wind strengthened. What skin it struck hurt instantly, hurt sharply. We made a complete circle around the gravesite clockwise (sunwise). I was snuffling, I was gasping every time a breath hit my lungs. *It's going to kill me.*

In anguish I let a tear go. It felt cold, and I reached up to brush it away. It was already ice.

When the riders were in place, the Feeding of the Spirits ceremony began. Four spiritual leaders stood facing the monument. One lifted a Pipe while praying. I could hear his voice but couldn't understand the words. Just staying in the saddle seemed hard.

Finally the man with the Pipe signaled, and we rode back down the hill. I tumbled out of the saddle and let the man from Wambli have the horse. One thing I knew—that horse would never let me near him again.

I felt like tearing the flesh off my face to stop it from hurting. Emile and Plez were a step ahead of me getting into the pickup that hauled the trailer. The cab was actually half-warm.

Each of us rubbed his face, unable to speak.

In a few minutes we ran for the warmth of the church and the comfort of hot coffee.

On the way Plez spotted something and led us through the gate to the monument. At its foot, below the names of some of my people who died here a century ago today, laid oranges, bananas, fry bread, apples, pemmican, and tobacco. I beheld these offerings to the spirits of my ancestors. "Be well," I murmured. Then I fled into the church.

The coffee and donut folks were making a hubbub of talk about one subject. Russell Means had turned George Mickelson, the governor of South Dakota, away from the ceremony.

We got the story in pieces. Some said Mickelson had been invited, was even invited to speak later in the day. Others put in that he was making a gesture, this being his Year of Reconciliation (which most Indian people thought was a joke). Mickelson had arrived in an unmarked car, and walked up toward the gravesite alone. Means and some other AIM guys stepped in front of the governor, and Means said, "You aren't welcome here." The governor trudged back to his car.

Most Lakotas in the room were incensed at Means's behavior. "He had no right!" "He ain't from here anyway." "Who the hell does he think he is?" "Don't even speak Indian." "This was a healing ceremony for everybody, people of all colors." The controversy carried over into the newspapers the next week.

Myself, I didn't want to talk about Russell Means, or the governor, or anything else. I felt overwhelmingly sleepy. My sleep had been spotty all week, and now I was incredibly drowsy. Tonight's big ceremony, Wiping Away the Tears, was set for the gym at Little Wound School. "How about the custodial room again?" I asked Plez. "I gotta sleep."

He grinned. "You got a journey to make."

THE QUEST FOR UNCHEE

I slept in the back of Plez's king cab on the way to Kyle, and by the time we got there, I was keen to go journeying. One idea throbbed in my mind. *I have to find Unchee, I have to find Unchee.*

We hurried to the custodial room. I wrapped myself in a blanket and laid down below the buffalo head, Sallee next to me. At Plez's urging I stated my intention three times. "I seek to find my great-grandmother and my grandmother near Wounded Knee a hundred years ago today, and to know what happened to them."

Plez reached out, the cassette player clicked. The drum *pong*ed again, and again and again.

Holding fear cold in my throat, I descended once more.

I floated toward the killing ground, tumbling slow somersaults on the way. I landed feather-light and saw that I was standing on the edge of the ravine. I was east of most of the fighting, and carefully did not look in that direction. When I last saw her, Elk Medicine was stumbling along this ravine further to the east, toward where Sun lives, bearing in her belly the infant Janey Running, my Unchee. My great-grandmother was darting everywhere and nowhere, crazed by pain, stunned by terror. Half by luck, she staggered away from the fighting, not back into the fray.

Some distance away, a man in uniform walked toward her, but they could not see each other. By my gift I knew his story. This man, Benjamin Running Hawk, broke ranks with his detachment of scouts five minutes before. He ran east to escape the shelling, which was far too close. There, out of sight of the commanding officer, Lieutenant Taylor, he got off his horse, slipped to the edge of the ravine, and looked around. Running Hawk hesitated, trying to understand where he was and what on earth he was doing. In the ravine was pandemonium—Hotchkiss shells exploding, cavalrymen shooting—all hell was busting loose down there.

Running Hawk hesitated. He was beyond the firefight, well to the east, out of danger.

Lakota men, women, and children were dying in that ravine.

Running Hawk was wearing the blue coat of the enemy. How could he go in and help? His own people might shoot him!

Benjamin Running Hawk clambered down into the ravine and walked toward the shooting. He called in Lakota, "I am Oglala, I come to help! I am Oglala, I come to help!"

Two or three Mniconjou women wandered by him, one at a time, looking dazed but not hurt. Running Hawk plunged on toward the fighting. The dust rose harsh in his nose, the smoke acrid. Then came a woman who looked stunned. She was staggering, zigzagging. Below the knee one leg, a foot, and its moccasin were drenched in blood.

Ben Running Hawk took Elk Medicine's hand.

She shrieked and tried to run away.

Running Hawk grabbed her by the shoulders.

She fell to the ground, screaming, kicking, beating her hands in the air, weeping. He didn't understand her words—they were in English.

He addressed her respectfully in Lakota, "Sister, I come to help you."

Her hands slowed and her feet grew still.

"Sister, I come to help you."

Maybe it was the language that soothed her, for now her breathing eased. When she spoke, it was in Lakota. She said, "I'm having a baby."

In a few minutes Running Hawk had Elk Medicine out of the ravine and on the back of his horse.

A half mile away from the fighting, toward Pine Ridge, he stopped to bandage her wound. He was embarrassed, this good man, because of where the wound was. He told her what he was going to do. "You have lost too much blood already," he said.

"Save my child, please," said Elk Medicine, "my first-born."

When Benjamin Running Hawk lifted the skirt and moved the leg, the bright blood started flowing again. He knew the danger, so he did what was necessary. He tore his uniform shirt and bound the wound tightly. Then, as fast he could, yet gently, he spent all afternoon carrying my great-grandmother home to a cabin near Pine Ridge, to the help of his own wife and daughter. On the way she told him her story, and she asked him to take her husband's body off the battleground and bury it, and save his Pipe for the unborn child.

I recognized the name Running Hawk, but had never met the family. I wondered if Unchee's name, Janey Running, was a shortening of Running Hawk. I made a mental note to go to them after the ceremony, yes, a hundred years later, and to bear them gifts in thanks for their ancestor's courage and kindness. Except for Benjamin Running Hawk, I would have died at Wounded Knee, too.

Lakota women know how to bring children into the world. The old way was to form a tall X out of stout sticks. Before this

X the woman would squat. When the pains came, she would cling to the bars and push the newborn downward. It was a better way, I believe, than bearing a child in bed, especially a hospital bed.

But Elk Medicine didn't have the strength even to squat. When her husband brought the woman in, Mouse thought she would die any moment. Mouse and her oldest daughter got the wounded Mniconjou into bed and spooned some broth into her.

"What happened?" Beatrice asked her father. Beatrice had been away to boarding school and had some training as a nurse.

Benjamin said slowly, "Everybody went crazy at Wounded Knee Creek, by the store, and started shooting each other." He kept his head down. "Everybody shot each other." He raised his face to his wife, and she saw it was running with tears.

Beatrice made a shushing noise and concentrated on tending the wound. What her father said was already more than she wanted to know.

She looked at the pallid figure on the bed with a nurse's eye.

I looked at my great-grandmother with admiration. *You have come this far to accomplish one thing, I know that.*

Through the evening dark Mouse and Beatrice coached the mother-to-be: "Push! Push! You must help!"

Usually Elk Medicine made a good effort, but she was weakening, fading toward the other side.

Elk Medicine, thank you for your woman's courage.

The labor went on all night. The child struggled toward life. The mother struggled to keep her hold on life a little longer, enough longer.

Finally, in the last of the darkness before dawn, Beatrice said, "It's no good. We have to cut the child out."

Mouse gave a little shriek. "We'll kill the mother!"

"The mother is dying! If we don't act, they'll both die!"

Beatrice got a butcher knife from the wood stove.

"Let's heat the blade!" whimpered Mouse nervously. This much she had learned from her daughter.

Beatrice gave her mother a menacing look. She pulled Elk Medicine's skirt up above her waist. For an instant she stared at the distended belly. Then, firmly, as she had watched surgeons do, she cut.

I could not bear to watch.

After an infinity, after bloodletting and grunting and struggles of hands inside my great-grandmother's belly, Beatrice lifted up a small burden in hands that were as bloody as any at Wounded Knee.

My grandmother, Janey Running.

Mouse took the child to the bucket to wash her off.

Beatrice checked Elk Medicine's eyes.

Then the nurse sent up the ancient wail, my people's mourning for the dead.

I stood at attention, raised my eyes to Wakantanka, and sang inside myself, *Elk Medicine, thank you for your warrior spirit.*

My heart tried to look at once at the dead past and the living future. It split in two. It gushed tears and blood.

I heaved in great racking sobs, and my own heaves blew my heart and soul into …

I don't know where I am.

Suddenly, I felt panic. *I am lost between the spirit world and the world of time.*

Lost!

I flailed wildly for helping hands.

They grabbed me, each hand.

"Blue, come back. Blue, come back." It was Plez's voice.

Slowly the ordinary world assembled itself through my sense of touch. I felt Plez and Sallee's hands. I felt the cold air on my face. I felt the solid floor beneath my butt and back. I pictured what I would see when I opened my eyes. Then I let the lids come up gently.

I looked from Plez to Sallee to Plez to Sallee. His face was grave. Hers was tender, inviting.

"We are alive," I said.

SIGN-OFF

A couple of days after the last ceremony, I drove up to Red Scaffold to see Plez. He had a little farm, didn't grow a thing, said he just liked to watch the rocks bask in the sun. It was a pleasant winter day, so we spent the afternoon walking the fences and ditches of his farm.

"Help me," I asked him. "I've seen the spirit world. That's where I want to be."

Plez looked at me with kind of a twinkle. "That's good," he said. "You don't ever want to lose what you saw, the world beyond, and how close it is to us, and how it's part of our lives."

He turned and walked backward in a smooth glide, placing his feet blind like he knew every inch of the bumpy ground. "You remember, though, what you said when you came out of that last journey? 'We're alive'? Being alive means you have a life *here* to live. However much you journey in the spirit world, your life, it walks across a certain time and place on this earth. You got things to do, got to make a life. That's what you're here for."

He turned back around, and walking forward flung his arms wide at the sky. "What to do? Ain't that the question? It's different for every man. Emile, easy for him, paint-paint-paint. Maybe he has a little romance sometimes, good, but really, just paint.

"You? Hmmm? I say, maybe find a woman and make a way of living satisfies the heart. I say, maybe learn to make a living without letting that run things. Maybe make a home and fill it with children. Take care of your family, especially the old ones, make sure they got what they need. Hang with your friends. Act like a neighbor to your neighbors, you know, feed the dogs when they're gone. Look out for the people in your community. Root for your high school basketball team.

"I tell you this, I tell you this. The eye of your heart knows, it does. That's enough. The eye of your heart knows."

We walked in silence for a moment. I mumbled, "Seems flat, compared to the spirit world."

He turned those shiny buck teeth on me. "You walk the earth, you look at the stars, you fall flat on your face. You look at this earth. Take care of your life here. You want to know my advice? Set your attention here. Then you come back, I'll help you see the other world, I will."

So we made a deal for me to drive over the next Sunday, spend the day journeying.

He flipped around and did his trick of gliding backward again. "Remember, for this stuff you gotta stay sober. Got to. Then you get to see it all, feel it, live it."

Now Plez strutted out a preacher's style. "Life is a gift of the gods. It can be traversed as a black road, full of difficulty and strife, or it can be walked as a red road, in harmony with blood family, with community, family, and with big family—Earth, Sun, Moon, Sky, Winds, and Waters." I reflected again that it's funny how we call the bad road black. Road that turned out bad for us was white.

Now he put a little dance into his glide. "It doesn't come at us, though, like something grand. It comes, maybe it's a kid crawling into your lap with a book. Maybe it's a friend calling with, 'Let's go fishing.' It's your woman chuckling

455

in bed when you pleasure each other. It's making pitcher of lemonade on a hot, dusty day and draining that sucker down-down-down."

He looked at me and wrapped it up with, "So, Joseph Blue Crow, you got a lot to take of. And sometimes you come here and learn. You got the gift. You got something to contribute. Just get your feet on that red road first."

So I set out to take care of things.

I went first off to find the Running Hawk family outside of Pine Ridge. They confirmed it—the family name got bobbed off to Running for a while, but they'd reclaimed the old form. I took them a big sack of groceries, and I sat in the kitchen two straight afternoons and listened to what they knew about my Unchee. Actually, I taped it—I have some good equipment—and the way it turned out, that was a good story.

Beatrice, the nurse, kept the baby. She'd been married but had no children, and lost her husband. She took Unchee for her own.

The trader came and took the child and gave her to one of the officers from Wounded Knee. That officer wanted to give "that unfortunate offspring of the battlefield a better chance in life."

Beatrice snuck over to the wet nurse's home, stole the kid, and went out into the Badlands where they wouldn't find her. She raised Janey Running by herself.

The Running Hawks didn't know a whole lot more than that, 'cause they didn't see Beatrice much any more. Janey Running, they knew she ran off with a rodeo rider as a kid herself, made some kids with him, lost him to the influenza, married her near neighbor, my grandpa, had some more kids.

I felt deeply grateful for the story, and plenty glad I had it on tape.

I thought about it, and it told me some things. No mother, no real family because she was hiding out there in the Badlands—Unchee came to be a loner honestly. Lived in ravenShadow, and the shadow was cast by her parents' death in the massacre.

On the weekend I drove to Oglala, walked unannounced into the house, hugged Sallee Walks Straight, and cooked steaks for her and Chup. Late that night, sitting on the front stoop in below-zero cold, I asked her to be my wife. We've been married for about a year now. Sallee's seven months along.

How to make a living and sure not let it run things, hey, that's been harder. Sallee is painting, and she got some pieces in a juried show in Rapid last summer. But her sales about pay for her art supplies. My unemployment and severance pay, they've been supporting us.

After I taped the story of Beatrice Running Hawk and Unchee, I went and taped Grandpa and Adeline. I taped Chup's wife. I taped some members of the Crazy Horse family, and descendants of Black Elk. Their stories, I got them down, griefs, triumph, prides, everything. I am a good interviewer. Sometimes I can get the shames, too. Sometimes I can get a lot of the truth.

I have looked at these truths myself. I know there's a price, and there's a reward.

Right along I've made myself go to meetings. As of the day I'm writing this, I have 472 days of sobriety. I still take them one day at a time, and I always will.

After a while it struck me that those stories I was taping, they're valuable to the people. If people knew the stories, what has happened to their families and friends and neighbors, they would see more. They would see how we're all the same. *Mitakuye oyasin.* They would see we can learn from each other, teach each other, help each other. So I ate my pride, went over to KILI, the tiny, insignificant radio station on our rez, and asked for a show. *Stories of the People*, it's called, on the air every Thursday, two in the afternoon, one hour.

I have good response to that show. KILI wants me to work there full time. A publisher in fancy New York City, he says he's interested in bringing the stories on the tapes out in book form. I said audio form. Guess we'll end up doing both.

That's *after* he publishes this book.

I'd like to do another show, too. *The Old Ways*. Interview spiritual leaders, people who've kept alive the old ceremonies, Sun dance, Yuwipi, sweat lodge, vision quest, all those. Get them to tell about it. Let others know. Mostly people need to know it's still here, it's still working.

Some traditional people will object. "Our sacred ways aren't to be recorded, book, photo, tape, anything."

I'll just tell them, "Times change. We know things, hey, save the world. We open them to everybody, make human life on this earth, make it better."

Maybe I can make a living doing this taping work. It's healing. That's what I want to do, heal my people, heal myself.

For a while I'd get down every week or two and bemoan my fate. "Oh, hell," I'd tell Sallee, "maybe I've set my feet on the red road now, but look at all the years I wasted. Why didn't I follow the path of the Grandfathers from day one?"

She would say, 'What matters is what you do today, the path you walk today. It's the only day you have."

I think that's true. But after a while I started thinking something else. Those twenty years weren't wasted. School. College. Seattle. Radio. Probably I didn't have to pair with Delphine on her slide into blackness. Probably I didn't have to spend that many years doing AM in Rapid City. For sure I didn't have to drink as much as I did. But the years weren't wasted. I have strengths now to bring, strengths I wouldn't. I know things. I might even be bold and say it right out. I know how to bring the white man's knowledge of *things* and use that to broadcast our knowledge of the heart, and of the spirit.

Maybe I wasn't far from the path my grandfathers intended all along, maybe not.

I believe writing this book has been part of the path. It's been my big work the last year and more, writing the pages you're reading, telling my truth.

That publisher in New York City, he says he'll print my words and put them in people's hands.

Healing. I mean these words to be one of the ways I do healing.

I send them now to you, every human being of you, don't matter man, woman, red, white, old, young, and I invite you to partake of whatever healing is here for you.

One nation of us has been a people defeated in war, crushed in spirit, a terrible fate.

Another nation of us has been a people who destroyed other human beings and the way of living they loved for no good reason, also a terrible fate.

One nation of us has been slaves, another masters of slaves. One nation of us has been conquered, another conquerors, all conditions that yearn for healing.

Take here whatever will help, my friends.

Mitakuye oyasin.

Author's Note

Though this is a work of fiction, the two worlds in which it exists, 1890 and 1990, are drawn with great care to tell both fact and truth. One of my primary goals is to draw an honest picture of the Ghost Dance and the Wounded Knee Massacre a century ago; another is to offer to the world the remarkable acts of devotion made by the Big Foot Memorial Riders, which began in 1986, came to a high point on the centennial of the massacre, and continue today.

Joseph Blue Crow, Sallee, Plez, Chup, Unchee, and the rest of Blue's family and friends are children of my imagination; however, they are based on Indian people I know, and I believe they are true to the reality of contemporary Indians.

In the part of the book set a century ago, the depiction of the Ghost Dance, white and Indian attitudes at the time, the journey to Wounded Knee, the interaction of the Indians and soldiers, the massacre and its aftermath—all this is intended seriously, and I believe it to be scrupulously historical. Except for Blue and his ancestors, everything is actual—the Ghost Dance songs are real ones; the teachings of Wovoka, the preachments of Short Bull, the visions of Ghost Dancers, the statements of Indians about the dance, the living circumstances of the Lakota in 1890—all this comes from the record. Big Foot, Yellow Bird, the Horn Cloud family, senior Horn Cloud's advice to his sons on the morning of the fighting, Black Coyote, the circumstances around the first shot fired, the awful slaughter that followed, the acts of Iron Hail and other combatants on both sides—none of this is invented Colonel Forsyth and the other officers named, and their interpreters, are shown as the record shows them, doing what they did and saying what they said.

I hope Americans of all colors find it appalling.

My portrayal of the Big Foot Memorial Riders is also intended seriously. Alex White Plume, Jim Garrett, Birgil Kills Straight, Ron McNeill, Curtis Kills Ree, Percy White Plume, Arvol Looking Horse, June San and the other Japanese nuns and monks, Celene Not Help Him, Dennis Banks, Russell Means, Joshua Moon Guerro—these are real people, and I have sought to be faithful to what they actually did and said. The rides exist on film, in books, and in works of journalism. I talked to some of the principals, and traveled to Wounded Knee to witness the centennial ceremonies. Conger Beasley, Jr.'s *We Are a People in This World* is a remarkable documentation of the rides, and I recommend it as the best starting point for any serious student. To me the Big Foot Memorial Rides show what heights human beings can reach when we seek the guidance of Spirit and act from love for self, family, and people.

In recreating the events of 1890 I have relied on sources that are well known, especially the Ricker interviews and Robert Utley's *Last Days of the Sioux Nation* (using the facts but not the underlying attitudes). I have also sought the knowledge and oral traditions of living Lakota people. The old records alone are at best facts deprived of their meaning, their living truth.

In 1975 I set out to write at least two ambitious books about the lives and ways of the Lakota people. The path has led me to become myself a carrier of the Pipe, habitue of the sweat lodge, seeker of visions, and traveler in the spirit world.

The journey brought me to the heart of whatever under-standing I have of Indian people. The fruits of the journey I can offer to the world are this volume and my biographical novel about Crazy Horse, *Stone Song.*

Now, looking back on the enterprise begun in innocence and hope so many years ago, I see that its real gifts were per-sonal, spiritual, and they are many as the infinite stars. From my deepest heart I thank the Grandfathers for them.

Mitakuye oyasin,

Win Blevins

Bluff, Utah, February 18, 1999

ACKNOWLEDGMENTS

Perhaps five years ago I was talking excitedly on the phone with my friend Jane Candia Coleman, a fine writer, about two books I was pondering about Wounded Knee, one set at the time of the massacre, a sequel at the time of the great Wiping Away the Tears ceremony a century later. In a blessed blunder I spoke of them as though they were one book, with a single character somehow participating in both events. Immediately I said, "Whoops! I'm sorry—slip of the tongue."

Jane answered, "I don't think so."

I felt a sort of burst inside, as when a gas oven ignites. Reason leapt up and objected—How could someone be at events a hundred years apart? Imagination answered, *Via the magical and mystical.* In that moment this book was conceived. Thank you, Jane.

I have incurred innumerable other debts along the way, some to people I talked with back in the mid 1970s, when I first turned my mind toward writing about Wounded Knee. Some people in this large group I've forgotten, for which I apologize.

Important among my conversational companions about Lakota people and Wounded Knee have been Larry Gneiting, Richard Wheeler, Lenore Carroll, Linda Hasselstrom, Bobby Bridger, Dale Wasserman, Martha Stearn, Page Lambert, and the people mentioned below.

I owe particular thanks to Los Angeles teacher Sandra Porter, who helped with research in the early years; novelist Terry Johnston, who made the trip to the centennial ceremonies at Wounded Knee with me, and was a fine sounding board; Marilee Gordon of Jackson, Wyoming, who gave me shelter when I needed it; Michael Moffitt of the Seattle Public Library, who gave me information about the world the character Delphine grew up in; fellow writer Martha Ture, who helped me with the political aspects of Delphine; Monica Drapeau of Martin, South Dakota, who offered bed, board, and valued friendship; Jim Cross of Yellow Bear Canyon, Pine Ridge Reservation, who invited me into his sweat lodge at a crucial time; Kay Roo of Bozeman, Montana, who explained the workings of radio stations to me; to Alex White Plume and Jim Garrett, originators of the Big Foot Memorial Rides, who made generous gifts of information and understanding.

My special brainstorming companions during the writing were my son Adam Blevins, Jenna Caplette, and Madam Mishy.

Meredith read the manuscript with a fine eye for good storytelling, and has been my loving companion every day.

My editor, Dale Walker, made an amazing contribution to the first page.

Two other men, one Lakota and one Anglo, were generous enough to read the manuscript and give me the benefit of their special knowledge.

Conger Beasley, Jr. walked on the centennial Big Foot Memorial Ride in 1990 and transformed his experience and research into a grand book, *We Are a People in This World.* He kindly read my manuscript and gave me valuable corrections and suggestions.

Joseph Marshall, author of *Soldiers Falling into Camp, Winter of the Holy Iron,* and other books, is uniquely enabled to comment on this manuscript. He himself has lived a life much like my principal character Joseph Blue Crow, raised away from white ways, not even speaking English, yet later college-educated, finally a citizen of two worlds but deeply Lakota. Joe's expertise on Lakota language, customs, worldview, and on the history of Wounded Knee is formidable. I could not have written this book without him. Thank you, Joe.

As always, I owe a special debt to my longtime mentor and friend Clyde Hall. A Shoshone taught in Lakota ways, Two Spirit, vessel of medicine, Clyde has been a fountainhead of information and wisdom. He also took me by the hand and introduced me to the great gifts of the vision quest and spirit journey.

Enormous thanks to my companions in the Naraya Dance, especially Clyde Hall, Charles Lawrence, and Ann Roberts, who have offered love.

My heartfelt gratitude to Phil Heron, who introduced me to the Harner method of journeying. And to Larsen Medicine Horse and Tyler Medicine Horse, men of medicine and guides.